MASKS and SHADOWS

STEPHANIE BURGIS

MASKS
and
SHADOWS

an imprint of Prometheus Books
Amherst, NY

Published 2016 by Pyr®, an imprint of Prometheus Books

Cover illustration and design by Nicole Sommer-Lecht
Cover image © iStock photos

This is a work of fiction. Characters, organizations, products, locales, and events portrayed in this novel either are products of the author's imagination or are used fictitiously.

Inquiries should be addressed to
Pyr
59 John Glenn Drive
Amherst, New York 14228
VOICE: 716-691-0133
FAX: 716-691-0137
WWW.PYRSF.COM

20 19 18 17 16   5 4 3 2 1

Library of Congress Cataloging-in-Publication Data Pending

ISBN 978-1-63388-132-7 (paperback)
ISBN 978-1-63388-133-4 (ebook)

Printed in the United States of America

For my parents, with love and thanks for taking me to that very first opera performance, all those years ago.

ACT ONE

Chapter One

1779

"Did I tell you Niko's invited a castrato to stay?"

"What?" Charlotte von Steinbeck nearly spilled hot chocolate all across her silken sheets. She tightened her grip on the ridiculously fragile, overpoweringly expensive cup, and sighed. Her sister had done it on purpose, she was certain.

Sunlight streamed in through the open windows of Charlotte's guest bedroom, sparking off the gilded leaves that edged every blue-and-white surface and turning her sister Sophie's unpowdered blonde hair into an utterly incongruous halo.

"Oh, I suppose we ought to call him a *musico*, to be polite. But you know what they really are." Sophie's eyes glinted with mischief over her own raised cup. She sat on the edge of Charlotte's bed, pressed against Charlotte's knees with easy familiarity despite the many years they'd spent apart. "I've heard this one's slept with half the grand ladies in St. Petersburg. Half the gentlemen, too, according to some gossip."

"How—? No, never mind. I don't want to know." Charlotte set down her cup carefully on her bedside table.

Sophie had been teasing her all through the past week, ever since Charlotte had arrived at Eszterháza. She had to learn to hide her chagrin, or she'd be tarred as the naïve country mouse forever. When had her younger sister grown so sophisticated?

Still, Charlotte couldn't help giving in to curiosity, even if it did allow Sophie to lord it over her even more.

"I thought that was illegal now," Charlotte said. "Doctors aren't allowed to perform the operation, are they?"

"You've lived in Saxony for too long, Lotte." Sophie took a long, lux-urious sip of chocolate, sending the lace-trimmed silk sleeve of her neg-ligée sliding down her fair arm. "Oh, they aren't allowed to *say* that's why they're doing it. But in Italy, they have all sorts of marvelous excuses. 'Bitten by a swan' . . . 'fell off a horse' . . ." She paused, raising her eye-brows innocently. "Aren't you thirsty anymore?"

"Not really." Charlotte topped up her cup anyway, with hot cream from the silver vase that stood on the little tray her maid had brought her. She needed sustenance to keep up with Sophie nowadays.

Not for the first time, she wondered whether it had really been a good idea to accept her sister's invitation. The offer had seemed so appealing when it had arrived in a gilded letter, overflowing with scented ink and kind words. After twelve long years apart, she would finally be with Sophie again—and in a refuge far from Saxony, her overbearing step-children, and the chilliness of her new widowhood; a home, equally appealingly, that was far enough from her calculating, manipulative parents in Vienna that she might escape their new marital schemes for a year or two while she rested and regained her confidence.

Best of all, it was the palace of the greatest magnate in Hungary, and therefore an eminently respectable option.

From the moment she'd first arrived, it had been made abundantly clear to Charlotte that she'd been wrong about that last point.

"Ah, well." Sophie abandoned the teasing with a shrug. "We should have beautiful, beautiful music at any rate. Signor Morelli is rated very highly. Niko's kapellmeister is positively bouncing with joy at the news."

"Herr Haydn?" Charlotte brightened. "Have you actually spoken to him? The concerts have been heavenly! I've played his sonatas so many times, I would love to meet him. If he ever has time . . ."

"He's only a musician, Lotte. If you want to meet him, then Niko will command him to attend you." Sophie rolled her eyes. "Honestly, the way you talk . . . it's a good thing you aren't in Vienna with *Maman*. You'd be eaten by the wolves there."

"Or by Maman," Charlotte murmured into her cup.

For a moment, their laughter mingled. It couldn't last, though. The memory of their mother only brought the specter of her disapproval into the room. Charlotte couldn't meet her sister's eyes.

The one name that Sophie had never mentioned since Charlotte's arrival was the single name Charlotte had most expected to hear. Charlotte's own husband had been too ill for her to make the long trip to Vienna for Sophie's wedding to Friedrich von Höllner, three and a half years earlier. Charlotte had read reams of description from her mother, though, who had been more than contented with the match and eager to pass on all the details of their new in-laws' social standing. Charlotte had received even more letters when Sophie was invited to live at Eszterháza as a lady-in-waiting to the Princess Esterházy while Friedrich took up an honorary post with the Prince.

Charlotte had never imagined, in her weeks of jolting coach travel across half the empire, that she would arrive at Eszterháza to find her brother-in-law mysteriously absent and her younger sister publicly ensconced as Prince Nikolaus Esterházy's acknowledged mistress.

"New visitors should liven things up, anyway." Sophie yawned delicately and rose to her feet in a flutter of lace. "I must be off, Lotte. Dinner is in only three hours, and my maid hasn't even started on my hair yet." She narrowed her eyes at her sister. "And as for yours . . ."

"I'm sure I'll find something to occupy my time." Charlotte matched her sister's stare evenly.

Charlotte might indeed be a widow, crossed into her thirties and living on her sister's lover's hospitality . . . but Sophie was in error if she thought her older sister could be bullied into complete submission.

"Of course," Sophie murmured. "Perhaps you can practice your music."

"Perhaps." Charlotte took another deep sip of chocolate as she watched her sister waft out of the room. She could almost feel the weight of soft draperies lifting off her.

The end of her marriage, despite all its attendant grim misery, had felt as if it might signal her awakening at last from the long and clouded dream that her life had somehow become. Even now, Charlotte often felt herself only half-awake, as if some indefinable essence had disappeared, or wasted away from lack of use, and she no longer knew how to regain it.

Still, she knew enough to see that she'd never find her own way again if she allowed herself to become only her sister's latest toy. This palace could far too easily become a gilded prison.

And now a castrato was coming to stay . . .

Charlotte shook her head ruefully as she set down the chocolate and rang for her maid.

Eszterháza was anything but what she had expected.

"This is wild country indeed." The English traveler, Edmund Guernsey, lifted a scented handkerchief to his nose and leaned away from the carriage window with a shudder. "I wonder that you gentlemen would brave such dismal surroundings for pleasure. The smell alone is torture!"

Carlo Morelli, the most famous castrato in Europe, looked out his own window at the clusters of straw huts that dotted the harsh brown landscape. In the distance, high walls surrounded Eszterháza Palace, home of the wealthiest nobleman in Hungary. The contrast was . . . instructive, to say the least.

Only two nights ago, in Vienna, an idealistic young poet had ranted at Carlo for an hour about the wonders of the shining new Enlightenment that would soon make all of Europe a paradise. That news had plainly not yet reached the Esterházys' serfs. The men and women who worked outside looked like skeletons, digging hopelessly for roots in the dry, arid ground, their thin frames bent by the wind that swept across the plains. Carlo had never seen such wretched poverty, even in the village where he'd grown up. Yet it was only the smell of the pigs' filth that bothered Guernsey?

Across from both of them, Ignaz von Born let out a short laugh that twisted his thin, ascetic features. "You'll find Eszterháza rather different from the rest of the Hungarian plains, my friend. It is quite the Versailles of our empire . . . apart from the Empress's own Schönbrunn palace, of course."

"Every prince has his own Versailles nowadays," Carlo said quietly. "I've sung in most of them."

"And better, I'm sure." Guernsey leaned forward eagerly. "You've sung for the Sublime Porte in Constantinople, have you not?"

Carlo leaned back slightly, keeping his fixed smile. "And the tsarina in St. Petersburg."

"A happier choice." Von Born fixed Carlo with his glittering gaze. "Our co-regent, Emperor Joseph, is none too happy with the Turks, these days."

"Really?" Carlo said. "I thought he'd be happier than ever, now that they've displayed such weakness before the Russian armies. The gossip in St. Petersburg was that he and the tsarina together might well carve up a new Ottoman Empire for themselves . . . if only they can create an expedient political excuse to do it."

"You're in Habsburg lands now, my friend." Von Born wrapped his bony hands around the elegant, ornamental walking stick that he held even while sitting in the carriage—an odd affectation for a man who seemed otherwise uninterested in fashion. "I would judge your words well."

"Yet I am no Habsburg citizen, and music knows no borders." Carlo met his gaze and felt, more than saw, the flinch that ran through both men at the high, sweet tone of his voice.

A freak. It was how most saw him. Every bone in von Born's aristocratic body probably felt the twinge of repulsion, yet his face retained its normal hauteur. Guernsey, on the other hand . . . Carlo had met his type too often to be surprised any more. That sort of man couldn't hide the fascination that matched the repulsion. Left to his own devices, he would probably ask to see if there was still a scar left from the operation, all those years ago.

Carlo thought back to the scarecrow farmers toiling outside. Better to be a freak, and fêted by kings, than to lead that life. If his parents hadn't listened to their village organist and taken the risk, he might well be dead by now of starvation or any one of the creeping diseases that ran amok in poor farming communities. Who would want the ability to bring more children into such circumstances?

He met von Born's gaze full-on and smiled gently. Von Born might be an aristocrat, but Carlo's voice had carried him into greater palaces than the old man's noble birth ever could.

Von Born coughed and looked away. "Is this your first visit to Eszter-háza, Signor Morelli?"

"It is."

"You'll find it a wonderland of culture after this dreary countryside." He raised his walking stick to gesture at the massive building taking shape before them. "Operas and concerts beyond compare, and one of the finest art collections in the world."

"And are you here on business or pleasure, Herr von Born?" Carlo asked gently.

Von Born stiffened. "I beg your pardon?"

"Our friend Mr. Guernsey is writing his book of travels, are you not, sir?"

Beside Carlo, the little man twitched. "It has been my dream for a long time to surpass Dr. Burney's memoirs. He wrote well about music, but he could not understand the cultures."

"Indeed."

Carlo kept his lips firm with an effort. Guernsey—if that was indeed his name—must have worked long and hard on his English accent. It was exceedingly rare to find a German native who could mimic it so well. Carlo, though, had spent a year in London, singing at Kew Palace and at the Haymarket Theater. He would swear on his kingly salary there that this little man had never set foot in England in his life.

King Frederick of Prussia had spies already scattered throughout most of Europe. Had the Esterházys attracted his rapacious attention now, as well?

"So." Carlo inclined his head politely to the aristocrat across from him. "We have all, I'm sure, heard stories of your amazing feats of alchemy, sir. I only wondered whether your trip was purely for pleasure, or if you were planning a—shall we say, professional retreat?"

Von Born's lips thinned. "The philosophical quest is a matter of passion, sir, not 'business' . . . much like the pursuit of great music, I would imagine."

"Of course," Carlo murmured. He noted to himself, however, as the carriage slowed, that von Born had refrained from answering his question.

The title of "alchemist" covered a multitude of sins, in Carlo's experience. Von Born presented himself as a natural philosopher and student of minerology, and in earlier life had become famous for his scientific experiments . . . yet his fingers, now wrapped around his ever-present walking stick, no longer displayed the tell-tale stains of laboratory work.

Perhaps his passions were leading him in other directions, nowadays.

"We've arrived!" Guernsey nearly bounced in his seat. "Eszterháza itself!"

Marble pillars soared high into the air around them. Uniformed servants pulled open a wrought-iron gate to reveal the palace itself, opening before them. Eszterháza's golden body and front wings formed three sides of a giant square, enclosing a front courtyard filled with rippling fountains, a wide reflecting pool, and classical statues that gazed coolly down at the approaching carriage. Carlo leaned back in his seat and smiled as the golden walls of the palace closed around them.

The most notorious alchemist in Europe and a probable Prussian spy rode in the carriage with him.

This might well be an interesting visit, after all.

Inside the walls of Eszterháza, at the end of a corridor through which only the most trusted servants were allowed, a plume of dirty gray smoke escaped under the crack of a closed door. It rose up into the air, twisting and contorting until it formed a snake-like, coiled mass. Deep within its roiling center, eyes opened and flashed red.

Its gaze fixed on the end of the corridor and the opening that led to the rooms beyond. Uncoiling, it flowed forward in a smooth, predatory glide.

Inside the room, a deep voice began to chant. The words rolled out, following the smoke down the corridor. It twisted and turned, fighting their grip.

The voice hardened. The smoke lurched gracelessly backward, still struggling. It clung for one last moment to the ornately carved beveling around the bottom of the wooden door. The voice rapped out a single word.

With a hiss of anger, the smoke released the door and disappeared into the room.

Chapter Two

The central kitchen of Eszterháza boiled over with activity. Black smoke billowed out of the open ovens, choking the air. Anna squeezed her way through the mass of shoving bodies and noise, fighting to keep her tray steady in her arms. Unbidden, a song rose up through her chest, a reaction to her panic. She forced it down with a gulp. Singing here, in public—that was the last thing she needed! She'd been teased enough for it back in Saxony, where at least everyone knew her and understood what she was like.

"Watch where you're going!" A big footman slammed straight into her shoulder, sending her reeling.

She scrambled to right her slipping tray. Her feet skidded on the floor. The empty silver vase teetered on the edge of the tray.

"Here." Another maidservant grabbed her arm, steadying her. Anna jerked the tray upright, just in time.

The footman who'd slammed into her strode ahead and out the great doors, still balancing his two trays perfectly.

"Ass." The other maid shook her head. "Don't worry about György. He's like that with all the visitors." She stepped back. "You're all right now?"

Anna had to think through the woman's thick Hungarian accent before she could answer. Anna couldn't tell, yet, what the minor variations in the Esterházy livery signified. Was this woman a housemaid, part of the cleaning staff, perhaps? Or another personal maid, like herself? "I'm fine, thank you." She managed a weak smile, feeling her heartbeat flutter against her chest. She would not humiliate herself and her mistress. She would *not*.

The other woman's eyes narrowed. "Are you new to service?"

"No!" Anna flushed, tightening her grip on the tray. "I've been a maid for six years—since I was ten! But I only arrived here last week. I've never seen so many people before." She ducked her head, avoiding the other woman's gaze. "I worked for a baron in Saxony, in the countryside. There were only thirty of us working there."

And I knew them all... She swallowed down homesickness, as sudden and sharp as glass in her chest. It had been her own decision to follow her mistress after Baron von Steinbeck's death, rather than stay on and work for the new baron's wife. It had sounded like such an exciting adventure...

"You'll grow used to it soon." The other woman smiled. "I'm Erzebet. You can always find me if you have any questions." She began to turn away, but stopped. "Oh, and you shouldn't have any more trouble from György—as soon as I tell him you're from the middle of nowhere, not Vienna, he'll leave you alone."

"Doesn't he care for Vienna?"

"Care for it?" Erzebet snorted. "He's jealous to the teeth of anyone who actually lives there. Our prince only visits for four months a year, so we're trapped out here the rest of the time." She rolled her eyes. "It's not as bad here as György makes out, though; don't worry."

She disappeared into the bustling crowd. Anna pushed her way through, gritting her teeth, until she could finally deposit her mistress's breakfast dishes. The clock began to toll as she set down the trays. Only two hours until the ladies went down to dinner, and she hadn't even laid out her mistress's clothing yet!

Tears blurred her vision as she plunged back into the dimly lit servants' corridor. Barely two feet wide and hidden within the thick walls of Eszterháza, the corridor ran along the edges of the nobility's halls and salons, offering discreet entrance to rooms filled with beauties and oddities. Late at night, when the nobles were finally abed, Anna had walked through those rooms, barely daring to breathe as she gazed at Chinese figurines, exotic fans, textured paintings made entirely from crushed seashells, and sculptures that gazed with impassive eyes across the marbled floors. Now, she raced through the stifling passageway, past the doors that led to the Silk Room, the Cedar Room, the Greek. There was no time to run the whole circuitous route behind the walls that would take her, unobserved, from here all the way to the servants' staircase. She emerged, head down in her rush, into the corner of the Blue Salon—

—And slammed straight into a gentleman's brocaded chest.

"Oh, no!" She leapt back and sank down into a deep curtsey. "I'm so sorry, sir! Oh, please forgive me!"

Prince Nikolaus had his own executioner, they said, and his own dungeons—and—

"Don't worry, lass!" Warm hands pulled her up. "I'm no great gentleman to offend, only another servant like yourself."

Anna let her gaze rise up from the floor. He wore a gorgeous brocaded red coat—but, yes, now she saw it: on his apple-green waistcoat, expensive though the cloth might be, the Esterházy insignia was clearly embroidered.

Gray eyes twinkled at her from a pockmarked, gnome-like face. "You see? Not so frightening."

"I am sorry, Herr—"

"Haydn, my dear. His Serene Highness's humble kapellmeister. On my way back from an excellently productive meeting. And you?"

"Annamaria Dommayer, sir, personal maid to Baroness von Steinbeck." Anna backed away. "But I am late, so—"

"On your way, my dear, on your way." He strode off toward the next room, whistling an unfamiliar melody. It sounded bright and jaunty, like a child's skipping tune.

Anna hurried the rest of the way, keeping her eyes warily fixed ahead of her and slipping as quickly as possible back into the safety of the servants' passageway. Inside her chest, though, excitement bubbled up.

Herr Haydn—her mistress's favorite composer! The man whom she was so anxious to meet—and Anna had spoken to him herself!

A song pressed against her chest, pushing to be let out.

Not now, she told herself. *But later!*

The stage of Prince Nikolaus Esterházy's opera theater was filled with singers, but only anxious, muffled whispers sounded from any of their throats today. Franz Pichler, second tenor in the Eszterháza opera troupe, leaned against the back of a painted wooden throne from last night's performance, kept his own mouth firmly closed, and refrained from joining in any of the closely huddled, gossiping groups.

"Excellent news!" The stage door burst open, and the kapellmeister strode inside, cutting off all the whispers at an instant. "A worthy opportunity! A chance to shine! Not only is the most famous musico in Europe on his way to our palace at this very moment, my friends, but the Emperor's own nephew comes to visit us in only nine days! We are called upon to create a new opera for his arrival, to amaze him and send news of our glory back to the capital. We . . . we . . ." The kapellmeister ran out of breath, blinking at the unexpected lack of response.

Franz watched Herr Haydn take in the scattering of averted faces among the gathered singers. He stifled a snort at the look of bewilderment on the kapellmeister's face. It shouldn't be amusing. It certainly wouldn't be amusing, if anyone found out his role in this adventure.

Whipping, imprisonment, expulsion . . .

No. Franz had been an actor and singer since he was ten years old. He could play the part of an innocent in his sleep.

Marianna and Antonicek were safe and far from here, free to seek their own happiness at last. He'd played the part of a hero as well as a loyal friend in aiding their escape.

And oh, what a sweet moment of vengeance for Franz to savor . . .

"But what's amiss?" the kapellmeister asked.

Franz cleared his throat, recalling himself to his role. "Madame Delacroix," he said succinctly. He jerked his head at the figure of Monsieur Delacroix, the theatrical director, who stood, wigless, his white hair disordered, glowering into the empty air. "And our leading tenor. Gone."

"Gone?" Herr Haydn sagged, his face wrinkling. Only in moments such as this, when Haydn's masterful energy deserted him, did the kapellmeister suddenly appear small and aged. "When? Where?"

"Eaten by the bloody wolves, I *hope*." Delacroix whirled around and slammed his gloved fist into the pillar at the side of the stage. "I taught that bitch everything!"

Their leading alto singer coughed gently. "Not *quite* everything, perhaps," Madame Zelinowsky murmured, just loud enough to be heard by all. "Apparently our young Herr Antonicek still had a few new tricks to teach her."

"You—!"

The kapellmeister leapt forward to pull Delacroix back. "Patience, my dear sir! Patience. Does anyone know when the two eloped?"

"Who knows? Sometime in the middle of the night." Franz kept his voice light and uninflected. So far, no one had seemed openly suspicious, but he'd noticed Madame Zelinowsky watching him a few times with an amused glint in her green, cat-like eyes. She played the humorous maternal roles in their company's productions, but her own wit was as finely honed as a nobleman's sword—and at least as biting. Franz looked away from her as he continued. "No one realized they were really gone until nearly an hour ago."

Herr Haydn frowned. "Even you, Monsieur Delacroix? You never noticed when she left?"

Delacroix ground his teeth audibly. "I am a . . . sound sleeper, sir."

A drunken fool, more like. Franz stared down at his hands to hide the contempt in his eyes. Delacroix had drunk away half the singers' earnings in the past several months. Oh, he'd behaved with admirable decorum in the first year after Prince Nikolaus had hired the troupe, but once they'd settled in, he'd fallen back into his old ways. Franz had been a fool to trust Delacroix's promises and sign the contract of employment. He should have trusted in the power of his own singing voice and dared to try his luck in Pressburg or Prague—or even, with truly wild hope, in Vienna itself. Instead of wasting away in the middle of nowhere, he could have been a star in the Habsburgs' Burgtheater by now. But once the contract had been signed . . .

A nervous tremor twinged in his gut. Within the million and a half acres of Esterházy land, the Prince wielded absolute authority. Once contracted into his service, no servant could leave of his own accord or disobey the Prince in any manner. Within his vast lands, the Prince could choose what punishment he desired for any infraction, from public whippings to executions, with no voice raised against him.

"But you must surely have more ideas for us, Herr Pichler," Madame Zelinowsky purred. "You and Herr Antonicek have kept so close lately. All that whispering in corners . . ." Her cat eyes narrowed. "Are you certain he gave you no clues at all?"

"All we ever discussed was our lack of pay," Franz said evenly. "Perhaps he required the funds for their flight, but if so he never mentioned it to me."

"How dare you goad me, sirrah, at a time such as this?" Delacroix puffed himself up, cheeks reddening. "There is no call to air such petty complaints in front of the kapellmeister! Have you no respect for the injury to my honor?"

Madame Zelinowsky snorted softly. Franz couldn't help meeting her gaze for a moment of mutual appreciation.

"His Highness will be most seriously displeased." Herr Haydn's dark complexion had paled to a sickly green. "He will certainly take it as a personal insult."

"It is an insult to me!" Delacroix snarled. "I will petition His Highness for redress. He must send riders after them at once! He—"

"I'm certain that he shall." The kapellmeister reached beneath his wig to scratch his head. He sighed. "It was a terribly rash act, I'm afraid. His Highness's soldiers will find them by nightfall, and then . . ."

"Punishment," Delacroix gritted. "For them and any who abetted them."

The kapellmeister looked at him with open distaste. "I've no doubt of it. Come, we must alert His Highness now, before he goes to dinner. And . . ." His gaze passed over the group of actors. "Herr Pichler, if you please? His Highness will want to hear your account of Herr Antonicek's conversations in the past few days."

"Certainly." Franz pasted a smile onto his face. He was, after all, experienced at handling stage fright. "I am always happy to serve His Highness in any way."

He stood up, avoiding Madame Zelinowsky's knowing eyes, and followed the two men out the door.

Friedrich von Höllner, honorary lieutenant of the Esterházy Grenadier Guards, and even-less-than-honorary husband of Sophie von Höllner, woke with a throbbing headache to the sound of his own name.

"Uhh!" His tongue felt too thick to speak. He levered his head up off his folded arms, off the table—God, he was still in the Fertöd tavern, nearly five miles from Eszterháza. Where were all the others?

Bloody Easterners. They splashed down gallons of the local firewater as if it were milk. Impossible not to at least try to keep up without looking a fool—but their heads must be as hard as the oak table that propped him up.

They'd probably all cracked jokes about soft city Westerners as they'd tromped out at dawn in their great heavy boots, on to their next adventure.

"Lieutenant von Höllner?"

Friedrich swiveled around. The cramped muscles in his neck screamed protest.

"A letter, sir." The servant who held it out looked unfamiliar. Friedrich blinked twice and took in the courier's uniform. "From the capital, sir."

"Um . . ."

Friedrich fumbled for coins, but the courier shook his head. The insignia on his uniform looked oddly familiar. Where had Friedrich seen it before?

Friedrich accepted the letter and dismissed the mystery. He let the envelope drop onto the table as the courier backed out of the room.

"There you are!" Anton Esterházy breezed into the room, brushing past the retreating courier. "Might have known it, you dog. Do you have any idea what time it is?"

"Almost time for breakfast?" Friedrich ran his hand over his face and found it greasy with stubble. Anton, of course, looked perfectly groomed. "Why didn't you wake me up last night before you left?"

"You think I didn't try?" Anton buffeted his shoulder, grinning. "City boy . . ."

"Bloody barbarian." Friedrich grinned back, even though the effort hurt his head.

"Ah, I've been out shooting all morning. We'll have a feast in the barracks tonight. It's a beautiful day. You should be outside hunting!"

"I know, I know." Friedrich pulled himself up, away from the table, feeling his mood brighten. No duties but hunting and gaming and drinking . . . Ah, that bargain he'd made with the Prince had been worth it, after all. "Tell me all about what you've been doing. Skinned six more wolves today? Bedded ten more peasants?"

"Bastard." Anton started to lead him away, then stopped. "You've forgotten something."

"Oh, that." The letter. From Vienna. Friedrich's stomach twisted.

Bloody creditors. They were supposed to send all his bills to Prince Nikolaus. That had been the *agreement*.

"Aren't you going to read it?"

Friedrich twisted his lip into a smile. "Why not?"

Sophie would throw a fit if he had to interrupt the Prince in public to hand over the bill. He could almost hear her complaints already. How much he had *embarrassed* her. The *humiliation* of her husband's appearance in public. Why couldn't Friedrich just take the Prince's money *quietly*, and stay out of his and Sophie's way, as he'd *agreed*?

It was hard to remember, nowadays, how lucky he'd felt as he'd stood with her at the altar of the *Michaelerkirche* in Vienna, swearing to honor and protect her, and meaning it with all his heart.

God, he'd been stupid.

Friedrich ripped open the dark red seal of the envelope, as Prince Nikolaus's cousin watched with blatant curiosity.

It wasn't a bill.

Brother Friedrich. The black ink spiked across the page in unfamiliar writing. Friedrich's stomach dropped.

Brother Friedrich. It brings me the greatest delight to inform you that your time for action has come at last. You have been granted an invaluable part to play in our great quest, based on the oaths and sureties you gave us last December.

"Friedrich?" Anton stared as Friedrich sank back onto the bench. "Is everything all right?"

"Fine," Friedrich said blankly. "Only . . ."

Last December? His thoughts whirled. *Last December . . .*

Prince Nikolaus and his court always spent the months from mid-November until the beginning of March in Vienna. Not as long a season as any of the other noble families spent in the capital, but still, thank God for it. Four months of civilization, drinking, gaming . . .

Oh, God. Friedrich let out a moan, ignoring Anton.

It had happened in a tavern. He remembered it now. He had made a new friend. He'd been dizzy with the excitement of the capital, the crowds . . . His friend—what the hell was his name? Had Friedrich known it even then?—kept buying him drink after drink, asking him more and more questions about his life. His position at Prince Nikolaus's court. Even, after a certain number of drinks, the embarrassing, unusual cause for that position . . .

Friedrich squeezed his eyes shut against the glare of sunlight through the window. The memories played against his closed eyelids.

They'd gone to another tavern; he remembered that much. And then a third and a fourth, and, finally, down a long and twisting alleyway, with the sound of a string quartet leaking out of a nearby building. Down a trapdoor. Down slippery steps.

He'd been so drunk. So stupidly drunk. He'd convinced himself it was a wonderful game, a perfectly safe adventure.

"Friedrich!" Anton shook his shoulder. "Wake up, man!"

"I'm awake," Friedrich muttered. He opened his eyes to finish the letter.

One of the great ones of our order will be arriving at Eszterháza soon, where he will reveal himself to you by secret signs. Your time is at hand.

Friedrich wouldn't even recognize any of the men he'd met if he ever saw them again. They'd all been wearing dark robes. In the guttering candlelight, their faces had looked like black voids beneath their hoods.

And some of the men there—some of them, he could have sworn—
No. Friedrich swallowed down the taste of bile. He'd been drunk. Too drunk to know what he was swearing to. Too drunk to tell between men and . . . and . . .

"You look like you've seen a ghost," Anton said. "What the devil does that letter say?"

"Nothing." Friedrich crumpled it into a ball in his fist. "It's nothing."

"But—"

"Forget it." Friedrich pushed himself up from the table, avoiding the Prince's cousin's eyes. No use trying for help there. Nausea clenched his stomach as he felt his wonderful, comfortable life dissolve around him.

Chapter Three

"Aha." Charlotte swept down the corridor, sighing with relief. Just one more turn—

Or not. She stood in an unfamiliar corridor, ready to scream with frustration.

How indescribably vexatious. How *stupid*, to lose herself on her way to dinner after nearly a week of living in this palace!

Of course, on every other day, Sophie had collected her and led her down safely. She'd offered to do so again today, but no, Charlotte had been determined to prove her independence. And she truly did remember, even now, how to find the salon where the courtiers would gather in four more hours to drink their pre-concert wine . . . but after following what seemed miles of twisting passageways, the location of the Sala Terrena itself was as great a mystery as ever.

She slumped. If her black skirts hadn't billowed out to such an absurd width, to match the latest Viennese fashions, she would have leaned against the painted wall and let her hair powder be damned.

After all her wandering, she didn't even know the way back to her own room.

She laughed softly, to keep herself from crying. This wasn't how she had envisioned her widowhood. Free at last from the dark, hushed confinement of her married home and nursing duties—and she couldn't even find her own way to dinner. Perhaps she should let her parents marry her off to another seventy-year-old baron, without even trying to resist this time. Perhaps she really couldn't manage her own life.

Stop it. She jerked her spine upright.

A flash of movement at the end of the corridor caught her eye.

"Oh, please!" She hurried forward, cursing her precariously high heels. "I beg your pardon, but can you tell me how to find the Sala Terrena?"

The tall figure stopped and turned, revealing an unfamiliar, older woman's face. The hauteur that stiffened her features revealed her status as a great lady, just as much as did the three maidservants scurrying in her wake. "Pardon me?"

"I'm afraid I've lost my way." Charlotte sighed and sketched the tiniest of curtseys. "I've been here nearly a week already, so my forgetfulness is really deplorable."

The woman's stern features softened into the hint of a smile. "I made the same mistake myself often enough, when this palace was first built. It is truly a labyrinth." She inclined her head briefly. "I don't believe I've met you before."

When it was first built . . . A sinking sensation formed in the pit of Charlotte's stomach. "Baroness Charlotte von Steinbeck." *Please, oh please, don't let it be* . . .

"Princess Esterházy." The Princess's face stilled. "Baroness von . . . Steinbeck, did you say?"

"I did. Your Highness."

"Then you must be Sophie von Höllner's sister."

"Yes, Your Highness." Charlotte sank into the full curtsey reserved for royalty this time, grateful for the opportunity to turn her gaze to the floor, away from the Princess's face.

Silence stretched taut between them. Heat suffused Charlotte's cheeks. She stared down at the wooden floorboards, counting her heartbeats. Damn Sophie, for putting her in this situation. Damn herself, for accepting it and never even considering the Princess until now.

"Well," the Princess said. Her voice was colorless. "I have been remiss in not welcoming you sooner."

"Oh, no—Your Highness—"

"The Sala Terrena is one floor down. If you take the next right turn, you can follow the second staircase." The Princess gave a wintry smile. "I would show you the way myself, but I prefer to eat alone, in my own rooms, nowadays."

"Oh." Charlotte swallowed. "I . . . thank you, Your Highness. And thank you for your hospitality. It has been most welcome."

"No need to thank me, Baroness. As I'm certain you're aware, the hospitality is my husband's. In this palace, nothing belongs to me."

The Princess's full skirts swished stiffly as she walked away, followed by the line of maids. Charlotte waited until the last echo of their footsteps had faded before she lifted herself from her curtsey.

All of her muscles trembled from their cramped position . . . and more.

Had Charlotte really dared feel sorry for herself, earlier? In the Princess's cold, clear gaze she had felt flayed open before a deeper and more bitter pain than she had ever known or dreamed of as the young wife of Baron Ernst Michael von Steinbeck.

Biting down hard on her lower lip, Charlotte hurried down the corridor, toward the staircase.

"There you are at last!" Sophie fluttered away from the crowd to seize Charlotte's arm. "What in heaven's name kept you so long? You must meet our new guests. Niko is late, unfortunately, so our dinner is delayed—oh, there's been a great scandal in the musicians' quarters!"

"Scandal?" Charlotte echoed faintly, as Sophie tugged her through the glittering mass of courtiers. Half-familiar faces flashed past her, scowling or open in laughter. Through the crowd, she caught glimpses of the several fountains that splashed merrily in the room, filled with marble dragons, swans, and storks. Frescoed figures stood high on the green inlay of the white walls, gazing down coolly at the assembled company, while allegorical scenes rose high above them on the painted ceiling.

"It's too shocking for words. The two romantic leads of the opera company—Herr Antonicek and Madame Delacroix—have actually eloped, in the middle of the night! They were breaking their contracts with Niko, of course, and worse yet, Madame Delacroix is married to the head of the company. Niko strictly forbids immorality among the servants, of course, so they have *twice* insulted him. He is in a towering rage." Sophie dragged Charlotte to a stop, smiling brilliantly. "And here are our illustrious guests! May I present my older sister, Baroness von Steinbeck?"

Head still whirling, Charlotte inclined her chin. The tall, spare man before her leaned on an ebony walking stick, but he took her hand in a dry, firm grip.

"Charmed." His lips brushed across her knuckles like crackling paper.

"Lotte, this is Herr von Born, the famous alchemist."

Von Born's face tightened around his smile. "Natural philosopher, please, madam." He transferred both hands to the head of his walking stick.

"Of course." Sophie brushed aside the correction. She shot Charlotte a look of pure mischief as she gestured past her. "And here is the illustrious Signor Morelli, whom I know you've been simply longing to meet!"

Charlotte gritted her teeth and sank into a slight curtsey as she turned, only as excuse to hide her eyes for a moment. "Signor."

"Baroness." A pale, strong hand took hers. As she looked up, soft, warm lips pressed lightly against her knuckles.

She had to restrain an impolite gasp. Signor Morelli was not as she'd expected. Not at all. Rather than being a flabby, womanly figure, he stood taller than any man in the room, with a broad, powerful chest. His curling black hair shone, free of powder, in its queue, a vivid mark against the sea of powdered silver heads that surrounded him.

Yet the lines of his—her? *its?*—face were disturbingly feminine, matching the unnervingly high, pure voice. It was not a man's voice—yet not, quite, that of a woman, either. Discomfort crawled through Charlotte's stomach. The curve of those smooth, soft, cheeks, untouched by hair—the full lips—

"Madam?" the castrato asked, lips twitching in amusement.

Charlotte blushed fiercely and withdrew her hand. She prayed that the powder on her face would hide her discomposure. She had stood staring at him for much, much too long.

"I look forward to hearing you sing, signor."

His dark eyes narrowed. "Ah, but I've been invited as a guest, not as a performer."

"Ah ... of course." Charlotte moistened her lips, conscious of Sophie's brimming amusement. "Pray forgive me, signor. I never meant to imply—"

"—But perhaps His Highness will do me the honor of allowing me to sing for my own pleasure one evening." He smiled, eyes glittering.

"That would be lovely for all of us," Charlotte murmured. It was all she could do not to pick up her skirts and flee the condescending amusement in his high, unnatural voice. She shot a discreetly imploring look at her sister.

"Perhaps Lotte can play accompaniment for you, signor," Sophie said brightly. "I vow, she devotes half her life to her clavichord. I know she would be delighted to assist you."

Charlotte swallowed venomous thoughts and stretched her lips into a deprecatory smile. "My skills are so poor—"

"Nonsense, Lotte." Sophie turned to the others. "Why, our old music master always called it a great pity she was born to too high an estate to pursue the vocation professionally."

Signor Morelli tilted his head. "There are some very great ladies in Paris and in Dresden who hold salons as venues for their own marvelous performances."

"I'm afraid my own talents would never merit such a display," Charlotte murmured, through clenched teeth. "Monsieur Lemartre was only being flattering, to please our mother, I believe."

"A wise servant indeed."

Signor Morelli's long eyelashes flicked down to cover his eyes for an instant, but they could not shield the dry tone of his voice. It sparked a hot flare of irritation in Charlotte's chest.

"I would be honored to offer up my skills as accompanist, though, should they prove useful to you." She met his eyes, raising her own eyebrows slightly in challenge.

His own eyes widened. "I am honored . . . Baroness."

"And what of you, Herr von Born?" Sophie fluttered her curling eyelashes at the silent figure and grinned impishly. "You must tell us all about your alchemical adventures! I am all agog. Niko—that is, His Serene Highness—has very nearly promised me that you will summon up a ghost or two for our entertainment while you are here. Please, sir, you must oblige me in this!"

He coughed into one fist. "I am afraid I pursue a line of enquiry far too tedious for feminine interest, madam. I study minerology—"

"The quest for the Philosopher's Stone?" Charlotte asked. "My late husband took a great interest in that subject."

Ernst had never believed in it—quite—or so he'd claimed, but he had often asked Charlotte to read tracts and letters to him about it, on evenings when the pain of his rheumatism was not too great to allow him to think clearly. She had penned his vast correspondence on it, too, after his fingers lost their own control.

"Was your husband a philosopher, then?"

"Only an enthusiast and a patron. I believe you knew him, actually—his name was Ernst von Steinbeck, but he wrote his letters under the name Ernst Stein."

There are few enough realms in which men may be equals, Ernst had told her, his voice gently regretful, when she had questioned him about that choice. *In the realm of natural philosophy, at least, I don't require any man's reverence for my birth.*

"Ah." Von Born's eyes widened briefly. "I did know him very slightly, then. We exchanged one or two letters on the subject of natural philosophy. A fine mind. If I'd known his true identity . . . Never mind. I am sorry to hear of his death."

"Indeed." Charlotte blinked back a sudden pang. After the long years of progressively worsening pain, Ernst's passing had come as nothing but a bitter relief, to himself and to everyone who had cared for him. Still . . .

She was glad not to be left in their estate in Saxony, surrounded by painful daily reminders. Stale and impersonal though their marriage had been in many ways, Ernst had at least treated her with a consistent kindness and generosity that had been notably lacking in her parents' household.

She forced a smile, dismissing the useless sorrow. "I often heard him speak your name with admiration, sir." She did not mention the qualifier Ernst had added in his later years—that it was a pity such a brilliant man had grown distracted from his scientific work by political maneuverings.

And yet . . .

Dropping her voice to a discreet half-whisper, Charlotte asked, "And your other philosophical quests, sir? I know my husband read the articles in your magazine quite regularly."

Von Born relaxed into a smile, lowering his own voice. "The *Journal für Freimaurer*, yes. I have been entrusted with its editorship. We publish articles of scientific and philosophical interest to all well-educated men, with the aim of spreading Enlightenment through the German-speaking world in our own small fashion. Our subscribers include many right-thinking statesmen and scholars."

Signor Morelli raised his eyebrows. "And these statesmen do not take issue with the source?" His voice remained clear and carrying as he said, "It's not every royal who supports the Freemasons' endeavors."

Von Born shrugged. "Why should they not? Any reasonably Enlightened man must support the measures that Emperor Joseph has begun to introduce through our realm since his ascent to co-regentship. We support all of them in our pages, as a patriotic function. The relaxation of censorship, the improvement of our universities . . ."

Signor Morelli's voice was whisper-soft. "The taxation of the nobles and reduction of their powers over the peasantry?"

Von Born smiled tightly, and closed his hands more tightly around the head of his walking stick. "The Emperor is still young, signor. Not all of these policies will continue unchecked."

"But what of my phantasms?" Sophie pouted. "I have been so eagerly awaiting them!"

"My apologies, madam. You would desire a different type of scholar for that amusement." Von Born's thin lips twisted. "I'm sure Count Radamowsky, for one, would be happy to oblige."

"Radamowsky . . ." Sophie knitted her brow. "I don't think . . ."

"Does he really claim to conjure ghosts?" Charlotte asked.

Signor Morelli shrugged. "A man may claim all sorts of powers, may he not? And in a darkened room . . ."

Herr von Born shifted uncomfortably. "Count Radamowsky follows Sir Isaac Newton's interest in the aether, Baroness—the idea, in short, of an ethereal medium hovering between the material and immaterial worlds, just outside the limits of our vision."

"So there may be ghosts surrounding us all the time, without our seeing them?" Sophie shuddered, eyes shining. "How perfectly horrid!"

Signor Morelli looked bored. "They may pull our hair all they will, so long as they stay quiet about it."

Charlotte tapped one finger against her skirts. "But this ethereal medium of Count Radamowsky's—you say it hovers between the two worlds. Could it, then, like a veil, be moved aside at will?"

"Precisely." Von Born nodded. "He claims the power to summon the spirits that hover on the edge of that veil, like a piece of gauze separating one room from the next, each invisible to each other."

Signor Morelli raised his eyebrows. "Are we to understand, then, that you believe his claims, Herr von Born?"

Von Born scowled. "I hardly consider our interests to coincide, signor. Radamowsky is a radical, wild for popular interest and notoriety . . . not a scientist."

"But are all of his claims therefore false?" Charlotte asked.

"Perhaps you may attend one of his salons in Vienna some day and decide the matter for yourself, Baroness."

"I certainly will, even if Lotte doesn't," said Sophie. "He sounds absolutely fascinating!"

Von Born snorted. "Fascinating, perhaps, but improvident. His creditors are rumored to be snapping at his heels, and the Emperor and Empress have refused to fund his further researches."

"Well . . ." Sophie shrugged and looked away, sighing.

Charlotte suppressed a smile. Of course, her younger sister would ever lose interest when the mention of economy entered a conversation. In moments like this, Charlotte could believe that very little had changed since their nursery days.

Sophie's eyes widened as she looked across the room. "Why, here is Niko at last! Now he may greet you properly." She lowered her voice, and added to the two gentlemen, "I was only just telling Lotte about the scandal among the actors that held him. Of course, we are trying to keep it very quiet . . ."

"Of course," Signor Morelli murmured. "One wouldn't want any gossip to begin."

Herr von Born smiled grimly down at his walking stick. "What else can one expect from that class of people?"

"I suppose you have the right of it there," Sophie agreed. "But it is a great pity that they did not think how they might reflect upon the honor of their employers. They have a duty to behave decently when they are in royal employ!"

Charlotte accidentally met Signor Morelli's gaze for a moment as her sister's royal lover strode across the room to meet them.

The shadow of the Princess seemed to interpose itself among their company.

"I prefer to take meals alone, in my own rooms, nowadays."

"A pity, indeed," Charlotte murmured, and looked away.

Chapter Four

About one thing, at any rate, Carlo was forced to admit that Von Born had been correct. The food at Eszterháza was worlds better than the slop they'd eaten in the Hungarian inns along the road. Carlo saw Edmund Guernsey, far down the end of the table, tearing into his meat with enthusiasm. Carlo contented himself with a more restrained approach and finished his glass of wine with a final, appreciative sip.

Prince Nikolaus had been leaning over to listen smilingly to the animated whispers of his mistress, but his nod sent a footman hurrying to refill Carlo's glass.

"I hope you are enjoying your meal, Signor Morelli?" The Prince straightened, patting Frau von Höllner's hand. "I'm afraid our modest fare can hardly stand comparison against some of the rich feasts you must have known in Versailles and Constantinople."

Nothing about this meal, or this palace, could lay the faintest claim to modesty, from the grossly overflowing serving platters to the great diamond studs on Prince Nikolaus's waistcoat . . . but Carlo had not risen so high by acting the honest fool.

"On the contrary, Your Highness. I am all admiration."

"You must see the view from the balcony, this afternoon." Prince Nikolaus's wolflike grin broke out fiercely from the intensity of his face. "You might not believe it to see Eszterháza now, signor, but twenty years ago this land was naught but marshland, with a scattering of peasant huts. The grimmest sort of no man's land."

Still holding his wine glass, Carlo turned in his cushioned seat to glance out the row of tall, arched windows that lined one wall of the dining room from floor to ceiling, each window separated from the others by deep gold inlay. Through the glass, warm sunlight beamed down on a classically designed green parkland as peaceful and elegant as any Grecian idyll.

"It must have been a mighty endeavor indeed, to create this fairyland from nothing." Carlo sipped at his wine, letting the flavors linger on his tongue.

"It was, by God. I had to drain the marsh, bring in builders and architects from every country in Europe . . . and the construction is not yet finished, either."

"Oh, no," Frau von Höllner chirped. "Niko has promised me a Temple of Diana!"

Carlo bit down on his tongue and restrained himself from asking whether she felt any special affinity with that chaste virgin goddess.

"I've still seen only a few of the temples and pavilions," Baroness von Steinbeck said softly, from Carlo's other side. "They are marvelously impressive."

Do they stand where the peasant huts did, before? Carlo wondered. *And what happened to their tenants?*

Carlo stifled a sigh and reined in his wandering thoughts. Perhaps these morbid musings were a symptom of his growing age. When he was younger, this would have felt like a glorious mischief: he, Carlo Morelli, Francesco Morelli's sixth son, was feasting with princes! They asked for *his* approval! Could anything be more grandly absurd?

Now, the banter and the self-conscious grandeur of it all left a bitter taste on his tongue. When Prince Nikolaus had needed funds to build the vast Temple of Esterházy that this palace represented, how high had he forced the rents from the peasants legally bound to his land? How many families had lost their homes?

Perhaps some of those families had youngest sons who loved to sing, as well. But how many of them would ever have the chance?

"Signor Morelli, you are very silent." The Prince's keen eyes fixed on him. "Is anything the matter?"

"Not at all, Your Highness. I'm only contemplating the beauty of your fine park." Carlo smiled and tilted his head toward the great windows and the expanse of manicured green lawn that they revealed, dotted with statues, fountains, and hedges. "I must reward myself with a walk through it soon. A visit with the classical gods would do me good."

Carlo excused himself at the earliest opportunity and retreated to his private chambers. His valet had traveled a half-day ahead of him from the last inn they'd stopped at and had laid out all of his belongings before discreetly disappearing. Carlo shrugged off his coat with a sigh of relief. Lord, but he was tired. Too tired to play the courtier any more this afternoon. Too tired to convince himself that it was worthwhile.

Luckily, a singer always had the excuse of practice to act as his savior in such situations. Not even the Prince Esterházy could take offence at his distinguished guest's desire to spend the afternoon in rehearsal of his voice. Not when the obligatory, "voluntary" recitals were sure to be expected, nearly every evening, after dinner . . .

It was a complicated dance, this life of wandering virtuosity, of honor, glory, riches and veiled contempt. Carlo knew the steps and had become a master at them early in his life. They had paid for his parents to live out their old age in a luxury no one in their tiny village could have previously imagined possible. His two surviving older brothers owned a flourishing apothecary in Naples, bought outright with Carlo's grand salary.

Lately, though, the moments of true enjoyment had dwindled into a soul-leeching tedium. He thought of Baroness von Steinbeck's offer to accompany his recital—pushed on, none-too-subtly, by that feather-headed sister of hers—and snorted. God save him from lady amateurs. Between thirty minutes of practice, twice a week, and the earnest applause of their music-masters, they all convinced themselves soon enough of their great musical souls.

Souls . . . Now he had become maudlin indeed, if he would spend his afternoon on philosophical quests. Leave those to von Born! Carlo opened the windows to let in fresh air and cleared his throat to begin his vocal exercises.

An unexpected sound cut him off before he could begin.

Beyond his room, floating through the walls of the other third-floor chambers as well as the open window, a glorious soprano voice pealed out, deliciously full of latent power—but, as was immediately clear, untrained. No music master had ever influenced this singer.

It took Carlo a flummoxed moment to understand why he couldn't make out the words; it was one of Herr Haydn's most popular Italian songs, but the Italian itself was utter gibberish—memorized by ear, perhaps? And by someone who could not possibly speak the language. She sang with musical feeling, but she clearly had no idea of what any of the mangled words might mean.

Carlo closed the window slowly, shaking his head, while a reluctant smile pulled at his lips. The sound of the singing continued, muffled only slightly. Only the nobility and their most honored guests stayed in this wing of the palace—yet no noblewoman would be so unfamiliar with Italian, nor sing with such a blatant lack of formal training. And as for the noblewomen he had met here . . . Frau von Höllner's speaking voice was like the bright cheeping of a canary. Carlo could swear she'd never be able to produce a tone so full and rich as this. Nor could he imagine such high, ringing peals arising from Baroness von Steinbeck's husky contralto voice.

It was a mystery, and an amusing one, to shake him out of his dreary mood. However, he certainly wouldn't be able to focus on his own practice while the mysterious soprano continued to magnificently mangle more operatic arias nearby.

He chose to take it as a sign, though, that it was time to fulfill one of his more pleasant obligations.

It was time to seek out the musicians.

The opera house stood behind the main body of the palace, facing the marionette theater and the military barracks across the wide expanse of green that led to the elaborate gardens, labyrinth and—no doubt—carefully designed "wilderness" beyond. Outer stairs led up to a curving balcony in the center of the opera house's ornate façade, where a man might stand, looking out across the grounds, between acts. Attached to the great three-story building was a smaller, rounded structure—the right size for a ballroom, perhaps? Its rounded shape was smooth and externally plain, unlike the opera house itself, which was so gilded with external decoration, it looked to Carlo like an elaborate, tiered cake.

Prince Nikolaus's pride and joy, indeed, and no more tasteful than its founder. Still, Carlo had sung in worse.

As Carlo walked along the shell-lined path toward it, enjoying the afternoon sunshine, a hatless, white-haired old gentleman burst outside, clutching a note in his hand. With a muttered, "Ha!" the old man sprinted past Carlo, not even bothering to nod his head in courtesy.

Carlo's lips twitched. An actor, obviously. Ah, but they were a relief after the arduously refined airs of the aristocracy.

He found the opera house empty, but raised voices led him through to the door to the ballroom.

An argument composed of some six or eight people broke off as he stepped into the grand room. Carlo smiled blandly and glanced around, looking for the man described by many as the greatest composer living, and the prime jewel in Prince Nikolaus Esterházy's collection.

"Ah, Signor Morelli!" The man who'd been mediating at the center of the argument burst through the ring of discontented faces and flung out his arms in welcome. "It must be you! Joseph Haydn at your humble service, signor."

"And I at yours, Kapellmeister." Carlo took the hands held out to him with real warmth. Haydn's pockmarked skin and great hook nose might be enough to keep him off any operatic stage; but Carlo found the sparkling intelligence and good humor in the composer's face deeply appealing. "I am indeed honored to meet you at last. I've brought you greetings from many of your friends across Europe."

"I—" The kapellmeister broke off to look around the circle of watching faces, all changed from chagrin to open curiosity. "Signor, I must introduce to you our distinguished singing troupe, or part of it, at any rate. Madame Zelinowsky, who plays all maternal roles—"

"—and who is most honored to meet you, signor," Madame Zelinowsky murmured. She sank into a curtsey and shot him a glance up through her eyelashes that looked far more seductive than maternal.

"—Frau Kettner, who plays the second ladies in comedies and tragedies; Herr Schwarzwald, the pedants and sober servants; Fräulein Schwarzwald, the young, sentimental *ingénues*; Herr Partl, the first tender fathers
and sedate parts; Herr Pichler, the second sentimental lovers and young
servants."

Carlo tipped his hat to the company. "Impressive indeed. But—are
you not missing a few important roles, Kapellmeister?"

Madame Zelinowsky let out a low chuckle. "Indeed, signor. How
could we function without our grand old men in tragedies? Our impulsive or funny, disgruntled old men in comedies? Our lazy servants, our
comic peasants . . ." She paused and looked sidelong at young Herr
Pichler. ". . . Our leading lovers, in all pieces?"

"I saw an impulsive older gentleman darting out as I walked in,"
Carlo said. "Does he play that role in your troupe?"

The singers stiffened and exchanged glances in a moment of awkward
silence. Carlo thought young Herr Pichler had changed color; even more
intriguingly, Madame Zelinowsky kept her own eyes fixed on the young
man's face, while a slight smile played across her full lips.

The kapellmeister coughed. "Impulsive indeed. The description you
give, signor, matches that of the theatrical director of the company, Monsieur Delacroix, who does indeed play the roles of old men in both comedies and tragedies."

"And in real life . . . ?" Madame Zelinowsky murmured.

"We are all rather disordered at the moment, I fear," the kapellmeister said. His smile looked strained. "It will all come out well in
the end, though, I am certain. Come, let me show you around our opera
house. It's only through this door."

Once they had exited the ballroom, Haydn slumped and came to a
halt, taking out a large handkerchief to mop his brow. "My apologies,
signor. We have had a rather . . . unfortunate incident this morning."

"I believe I heard something of it mentioned at dinner. An elopement
among the singers?"

"Indeed. Our leading lady, Madame Delacroix, is perhaps eighteen
years old against her husband's white-haired age and his"—he paused—

"not inconsiderable temper. Meantime, she and our leading tenor, Herr Antonicek, have of course been much thrown together . . ."

"Not entirely incomprehensible, then," Carlo said drily.

Haydn sighed. "Not at all, but disastrous nonetheless. His Serene Highness is . . . most strict, in his views upon the behavior of his servants. Had they only waited a year, until their contract had run out . . ." He shrugged his shoulders unhappily. "I would have certainly advised His Highness not to renew it—Monsieur Delacroix's management is atrocious, if I may confide that to you, signor—but then, I suppose they could not have known that they'd be free so soon."

"I see. And the punishment they'll receive?"

"Heaven knows. For Herr Antonicek—a severe whipping with the bastinado and imprisonment, I am certain. Beyond that, I would anticipate his banishment from all Esterházy lands while Madame Delacroix remains in residence."

"And for the lady?"

Herr Haydn's expression was bleak. "Her apology to the Prince, I expect, and forced return to her husband. Which, considering the public humiliation he has felt, and the extent of his current thirst for blood, will be more than punishment enough, I am quite certain." He sighed and replaced the handkerchief in the embroidered outer pocket of his frock coat. "Ah, it makes my head hurt. And all of it so needless . . ." He began to walk forward, shaking his head.

Carlo paced beside him thoughtfully. "And you, sir? Do you wish your own contract renewed?"

Haydn blinked. "I? Why, my contract was only recently renegotiated, signor, and under far more favorable terms than ever before. If you can believe it, I may even offer my own works for publication at last, to share them with the world in the form that I choose—and to make a pretty penny from them, too!" He gave Carlo a mischievous grin. "I cannot tell you, signor, how it once burned to save all my copies for my prince's sole use while scoundrels sold unauthorized versions abroad— but now that that's finally sorted, I've been approached by a publisher in Vienna, who has promised to design beautiful editions of my music to sell throughout the empire. What more joy could a humble kapellmeister ask for?"

Carlo reached into the inner pocket of his own coat and drew out the collection of letters he'd couriered. "Along with affectionate greetings to you, sir, I've also brought commissions from the empress of all Russia, among others. The tsarina is most eager for a new opera from your pen."

"In St. Petersburg?" Haydn sagged back on his heels. "Ah, signor, I am truly honored, but I could not possibly accept. My contract states explicitly that I may only compose new works for the honor of the Prince, and he is most concerned that I keep to that promise."

"But your publications—"

"Will be graciously allowed by His Highness after first performances here—and I fear the older operas I have written for this court would not do in another setting. I know my prince's taste too well, and it influences all that I write." He twisted his lips into a rueful grin. "I do not think that the tsarina would appreciate such a string of tedious long arias as Prince Nikolaus dotes upon."

"Long, perhaps, but beautiful, too. I have seen those unauthorized editions, remember." Carlo frowned. "You do understand, sir, how your reputation has spread? Even in distant England, I heard talk of you and your talents. Were you ever to leave the Prince's service—"

"Aye, and for what?" The kapellmeister laughed. "You must have been speaking to my young friend Mozart. If we ever met in person, perhaps I might shake more sense into him. The last missive he sent me from Salzburg fairly scorched my hands, it was so full of fiery ambitions for an independent life, wild and free of his archbishop's service . . . and with no promise of salary or security whatsoever. I hope my reply cooled his head somewhat." Still smiling, he shook his head. "No, no, signor. It is well and good for a great artist such as yourself to stand on your own talents and travel the world, but I do very well here as I am. I have a fine employer with a true ear for music, who genuinely appreciates my work. And my own salary is . . . not inconsiderable for an honored servant, shall we say?" He lowered one eyelid in a roguish wink.

And yet you will remain only a servant here, forevermore. But Carlo did not speak his thoughts. Instead, he handed over the collection of letters. "Your mail, sir. One of the letters is indeed from young Mozart."

"Ah, he is a good lad. 'Papa Haydn,' he calls me, you know. A tribute to my poor graying hairs." Haydn grinned and slipped the collection into his pocket. "I'll enjoy these later, at my leisure. A fine reward for haggling with these temperamental singers all day! By now I should have led a full rehearsal of my orchestra and had an hour for my own composition, too."

"A pity indeed."

"Well, never mind, eh? Come, signor, you shall not escape a view of the opera house, for it is a joy to me."

Carlo followed the kapellmeister in his tour, and roused himself to comment appreciatively on the sound qualities of the auditorium, the unusual depth of the angled stage, the fine detail of the carvings around it, and the positioning of the orchestra's benches. He even felt a mild amusement as he noted the correlation between the red and green of Haydn's uniform and the deep red and apple-green shades that dominated all the opera house's decorations, from the great velvet hangings to the plush seats in the auditorium. Someone—perhaps even the Prince himself—had an innate sense of order, or at least efficiency.

All the while, though, he felt himself abstracted, and hoped the man beside him could not see it. It was well indeed to enjoy one's position in life, and to feel that one's talents were appreciated. Yet for such a mind and talent to be confined to this petty princedom, far from the lights of cosmopolitan culture . . .

"Do you never miss Vienna?" he asked at last, after admiring the scenery and the mechanical effects that had been designed for the latest operatic performance.

Haydn's eyes widened. "Oh, Vienna . . . my dear sir, how could I not? The hours I have spent in conversation there, enjoying the finest musical salons and listening to the most exquisite performances—but no, sir, you shall not catch me out! I'm quite happy where I am, more particularly as I hie off to the capital with my Prince every year for a glorious four months." He laughed, wagging a monitory finger up at Carlo. "Not everyone is a virtuoso, signor. Someday you, too, may come to appreciate the joys of a settled and comfortable life."

"Perhaps." Carlo smiled ruefully and tipped his head in submission. It had been foolish indeed to imagine that one of the finest musical minds in Europe might be too slow to catch his far-from-subtle direction. "Perhaps I shall try it myself one day after all, and report to you upon my success."

"I hope you may. Indeed—"

A crash sounded in the ballroom. Voices rose in shock and dismay. Haydn broke off, paling.

"I beg your pardon, signor!"

He flew across the stage toward the door, the skirts of his red frock coat sailing out behind him. Carlo followed quickly.

Three soldiers had entered the ballroom, wearing full Esterházy regalia. The first raised a warrant marked with the Prince's seal and started toward the frozen cluster of singers.

"Franz Pichler, second tenor of His Highness's company?"

"I am Herr Haydn, the kapellmeister." The little man seemed to rise in height as he advanced upon the soldiers. "May I help you, sirs?"

The theatrical director burst inside, following after the soldiers. "There! There he is!" His knobbled finger shook as he pointed across the room at Herr Pichler.

The young man's face looked pale but composed as he stepped forward. "Of what am I accused, sirs? I've done no wrong."

"Witnessed! You were witnessed in the act!" Spittle flew from Monsieur Delacroix's lips. "You aided their escape, you worm! You probably designed it yourself. You—you blackguard! You devil! You—"

"What proof is there, monsieur?" Haydn demanded. "Who was this witness?"

"I received a note." Monsieur Delacroix slipped it from an inner pocket and waved it threateningly at the young singer. "You took horses from the stable. You were seen!"

Haydn interposed himself between Herr Pichler and Delacroix. "But who wrote the note?"

"That, Herr Haydn, is none of your concern. The Prince is satisfied, and that must be enough for all of us." Monsieur Delacroix shoved a tall soldier forward. "Arrest him! You have your orders!"

"My apologies, Kapellmeister." The lieutenant sighed and held out his warrant. "The Prince's orders are clear."

The other two soldiers marched forward and took hold of Pichler's arms, their expressions stony.

Panic showed at last on the second tenor's face. "There must be some mistake," said Herr Pichler. "I never—I swear—!"

"And what exactly is your word worth, sirrah?" Monsieur Delacroix spat upon his feet. The other singers drew back in horrified silence as the old man sneered up at him. "Aye, you'll have your due now. The bastinado awaits your bare back."

The soldiers marched him out silently, ignoring the young man's babbling protests. Monsieur Delacroix followed, beaming with triumphant glee. Nausea twisted Carlo's stomach as he watched them go.

"Is it likely that they're correct?" he asked the kapellmeister, once the door had closed behind them.

"Likely?" Haydn shrugged, his expression sorrowful. Behind him, one of the younger women had begun to weep quietly. Madame Zelinowsky stared down at her clenched fingers. "Perhaps, perhaps not. But they'll catch Herr Antonicek and Madame Delacroix by tonight, signor. That, at least, is certain."

Chapter Five

"*S*even . . . Eight . . ."

Franz wept, spread-eagled on the public whipping block, and saw only fire in his vision.

". . . Nine . . ."

The bastinado crashed down again, hard wood-and-steel rod against bruised and bleeding skin. The bones of his back would surely never stand such assault. They would shatter and leave him broken, useless.

". . . Ten . . ."

Bloody useless *waste*. Him. Antonicek and Madame Delacroix. Everything.

He'd thought he'd pay Delacroix back, strike for justice. Have a laugh at the old sot's expense. *Useless*.

". . . Eleven . . ."

Flame arced down his back as new skin broke open. Franz screamed, uncaring of Delacroix salivating over his pain, that filthy bastard, or Herr Rahier, the Prince's administrator, watching coldly to see that every stroke of the bastinado landed on target.

No good, no good, no good . . . Franz had tried everything, but no pleas, no amount of desperation, could ever have been enough to change the Prince's mind. Cold as aristocratic ice, ordering this torture.

Franz broken, Antonicek and Madame Delacroix dragged back to suffer more, and bloody Delacroix soaking the whole mess up . . .

". . . Twelve!"

The heavy bastinado smashed down one last time, and something cracked in Franz's back.

He convulsed, spitting and crying. In the red haze, he barely noticed strong hands removing the straps from around his wrists, throwing a shirt across his mangled back, and finally carrying him across the courtyard.

He'd meant to spit at Delacroix's feet as he passed. But he couldn't even open his eyes against the pain.

They deposited him in a cold, dark room. He crumpled onto the floor when they let go of his arms. Voices spoke, but Franz couldn't make out the words. Only the closing of the barred door sounded clearly through his haze. He was alone.

Shivers racked his body until at last, mercifully, he lost consciousness.

When he awoke, a candle stub flickered at the far end of the room, next to a bowl of water and another filled with bread.

"Naught but bread and water for one week's imprisonment," the Prince had pronounced, with that Godalmighty aristocratic chill.

Franz began to laugh, although it hurt his throat.

That bread might as well be on the far side of the world, for all the use it was to him. What good would any finer food do him? For he could surely neither drag his burning body across the floor to take it, nor swallow any food without vomiting it back up again.

Laughing, he laid his face down on the cold stone floor and fell willingly back into sleep.

When he woke again, he blinked against the total darkness. The candlelight was gone, yet he could feel the presence of another person in the room.

He hurt too much to feel any fear. What more could be done to him?

"Franz Pichler," a man's voice said coolly, beside his ear. "You'll need water. Your jailers say you haven't drunk yet."

Franz couldn't answer. His throat was too dry. But when he felt the rim of the water bowl at his lips, he managed to tilt his head back and suck down the cool, stale water. If his eyes hadn't burned dry, he would have wept again, in gratitude.

"Now," the voice said, once Franz had finished. "You're to be kept here for a seven-night, I hear—which time you'll need to heal yourself. But in the meantime, I want to give you something to think about. You are no friend, I think, to your director, Monsieur Delacroix?"

Franz snorted, painfully.

"I thought not. Nor, dare I say, to our esteemed local despot, the Prince?"

Franz swallowed. If this was a trick . . .

No. Prince Nikolaus Esterházy ruled with a grimly paternal certainty. He would punish, aye, and care nothing for his victim's agony, but then he'd consider the debt discharged. Not for him the creeping paranoia that would send spies into the darkness of his own prison cells.

So Franz licked his dry lips with his swollen tongue and told the truth to the voice in the dark.

"Never."

"Ah," said the voice. Franz could almost hear its smile. "In that case, I have a proposition to lay before you . . ."

Violins twined around each other, rising, pleading. Flutes seconded them below, adding soft voices to the plea. The cellos and basses pushed the harmony achingly wide, until Charlotte's whole body vibrated with the need for release. They were about to resolve—they must resolve—

But no, for each seeming resolution revealed itself to be only another twisting turn in a string of modulations, stretching the tension tighter and tighter yet. The sweet voice of the horns drove forward a tone that turned more dissonant with every beat until—

Pain stabbed up through Charlotte's fingers, wrapped so tightly around each other that the knuckles had gone white. She released them with a gasp and returned her attention to the orchestra just in time. Herr Haydn's violin bow swept high to lead the rest in a final, sweeping downbeat of resolution so sweet and right that it brought tears to Charlotte's eyes.

She clapped enthusiastically, ignoring the lingering remnants of pain in her fingers. Herr Haydn led the orchestra in a bow to the Prince, in the center of the music room. Charlotte flushed in pleasure as his bow took in her seat, only three chairs distant from the Prince. This glorious music was worth anything. *Everything.*

"Take care, Baroness," Signor Morelli murmured. "I fear you may be losing your seat."

It was true; she teetered at the edge of her chair. She righted herself, relieved to see no mockery after all in the castrato's dark eyes.

She smiled at him, this time without the tightening in her chest that she'd felt before him earlier in the evening. "Herr Haydn's music is marvelous, is it not?"

Sophie and the Prince were murmuring together already, while the Prince's niece chimed in with a sardonic tone that brought them all to easy laughter. In the sudden din of conversation, Charlotte found herself unexpectedly grateful to be seated by the one other person who might feel all that she did.

"I'd never seen such concerts in my life before I came here," she said.

Signor Morelli's eyebrows rose. "Not even in Vienna?"

"Oh, our parents are not at all musical, I'm afraid. And of course I moved to Saxony upon my marriage, many years ago."

She fixed her eyes back on the orchestra, hungrily observing the preparations for the violin concerto that would follow. The marble walls of the music room were ornamented with rich gilding, at what must have been a fabulous expense, and the musicians took visible care as they shifted their chairs for the new configuration.

"I've heard that even in Saxony, fine concerts do occasionally occur."

Charlotte laughed. "Not in the depths of rural society, signor, I assure you." *Though I cannot imagine you ever finding that out for yourself.* The idea of the sophisticated castrato, in his fashionable, expensive Parisian clothing, wandering the grass-covered roads of her husband's estate and attracting the wide-eyed amazement of Ernst's stuffy neighbors, was an absurdity that appealed to her strongly. She curbed her smile with an effort, and returned her focus to the conversation. "But I have been playing Herr Haydn's keyboard sonatas for years. I've even read through the arias from his operas, although I've not the voice for them."

"No?" His eyes lit with sudden interest at that, and he leaned forward slightly. "You are a . . . soprano, Baroness?"

"Hardly. An alto, if you please, signor, and a remarkably poor one."

She dared a flash of humor and met his eyes as she added, "Even my music master never flattered me on *that* score!"

"Indeed." The interest flickered and faded, and he leaned back. His high, unearthly voice was cool again. "Apparently, not all of our fellow guests are such music lovers as yourself, madam. Neither of my traveling companions seems to be in attendance now, although I saw both here at the start of this concert."

"So they've abandoned their posts? How shameful of them." Charlotte kept her voice light with an effort. Foolish and beyond foolish to feel hurt. Music opened her too wide and vulnerable for the easy parryings and dishonesty of courtly conversation. For a moment, she had believed it to have opened him, too.

"It is a remarkably fine performance, especially as it was arranged and rehearsed at only the last moment." The castrato leaned back to wait for a pause in the Prince's conversation. "Have you had any news of the two, ah, fugitives, Your Highness?"

The sudden sound of hard rain on the windows covered his words so that he had to repeat them. Once made clear, Prince Nikolaus's frown resolved into a stern nod.

"No word yet, signor, but have no fear. My men will bring them in before the night is out." His fierce eyes narrowed, focusing into the empty air. "I have no doubt of it."

Thunder rolled outside, in the distance. Inside the warm room, Charlotte shivered and wrapped her fingers around the bare skin of her forearms.

It would be a black, cold night to be afraid and in flight. She would not wish it on anyone.

The sound of thunder mingled with the deep-voiced chanting. It rolled down the long corridor, rattling the porcelain vases.

Through the open window, rain and darkness spattered into the palace of Eszterháza, but still the chanting did not stop.

"Now listen carefully, Franz Pichler," the voice said. "I represent an important and powerful fellowship of men. In Eszterháza, this prince may fancy himself supreme, but in the wider world, we could crush him at will. And if we are pleased with your service, we can raise you to great heights."

Franz began to shiver again, only partly from the cold. "What . . . what heights?"

"Have you never dreamed of making a career in the capital? Free from the provinces forever?"

Franz's voice came out as a scratchy, incredulous whisper. "The Burgtheater?"

"The Burgtheater in Vienna is yours for the taking, should you desire it. Lead roles, comic roles, a directorship . . . Certain members of our group are admirably placed to instate you in whichsoever role you fancy."

"And the Prince?"

"The Prince will be helpless to lift a finger when we remove you from Eszterháza. But." The voice tightened, shifting into aristocratic accents. "*But.* We are powerful friends, Herr Pichler, but we are even more powerful enemies. Should you try to regain the Prince's favor by bringing him the tale of this meeting, for instance . . ."

"No," Franz said. "I won't. I swear!"

"Indeed," the voice said, "you will not. You know that I found you here, in the Prince's own prisons, and passed all of his guards to come to you. There is nowhere in the world that you could hide where I or another member of my fellowship would not find you. Do you understand?"

"I understand." Franz swallowed. "What do I need to do?"

"Nothing, for the moment, but rest and heal yourself. It would be wise for you not to express your resentment of the Prince. But once you are free again . . ."

Something dry crackled as it was passed into his hand. A slip of paper. "Let no one find this. When your jailers light your candle once more, you'll see that it is our mark. After you are released, you will receive your first instructions, and you will know them to be true by recognizing that mark."

Cloth whispered across the floor. Soft footsteps stepped away from Franz.

"Do we have an understanding, Herr Pichler?"

"Yes," Franz whispered. He clutched the paper in his hand. "Yes!"

The barred door opened and then firmly closed, leaving Franz alone in the darkness.

Smoke slipped in through the open window, pooled on the ground, and slid slowly back along the corridor, toward the sound of the chanting. It paused a moment outside the doorway, then, sluggishly, gathered itself and trickled, little by little, underneath the door.

A moment later, the chanting came to a final halt, leaving the air ringing with its absence. A deep-voiced chuckle of satisfaction sounded within the room.

On the wooden floorboards of the corridor, where the smoke had passed, spots of blood mingled with the raindrops from the open window.

"Your Highness!"

Rain-soaked soldiers burst into the music room, interrupting the violin concerto. Charlotte started in her seat and turned to stare, caught between irritation and curiosity.

"Your Highness." The lieutenant dropped to one knee before the Prince, while his fellows bowed deeply behind him. Water dripped from his uniform, landing perilously close to the Prince's bejeweled shoes.

"Well, lieutenant?" Prince Nikolaus's eyes hardened. "How do you explain this intrusion?"

"I apologize, Your Highness. But we saw—you need to know—"

The lieutenant gasped for breath. Charlotte saw mud spattered across his uniform breeches. He'd been riding, then, and hard, to bring back his news.

"Well?" Prince Nikolaus leaned forward, his eyebrows drawing together. "What do you have to tell me?"

"We found the singers, Your Highness, as you commanded. That is, we think . . . The horses certainly came from your stables."

"And the couple themselves?"

"I . . . I'm not sure, Your Highness."

"Well? What did they have to say for themselves? Bring them in here—we'll all recognize them."

"I'm afraid we can't do that, Your Highness. The horses were unharmed, but the couple—the bodies—"

Charlotte drew in a breath. Against her will, she glanced at the orchestra. The instruments had been laid aside as the kapellmeister and all the musicians listened intently. To her and to the rest of the court, the singers were only names and faces, masked each night behind a different role. To the musicians, they were flesh-and-blood people, and colleagues, as well.

"The bodies had been disfigured, Your Highness. As if they'd been ripped apart and . . ."

"And?" the Prince prompted. His face was pale and stern.

". . . And sucked dry," the lieutenant finished weakly.

Charlotte closed her eyes and leaned back in her chair. She did not care to hear any more music tonight, after all.

Chapter Six

"I know what it was that killed them." György leaned across the house officers' table in the servants' hall, fixing Anna and Erzebet and two other listening maids in his gaze. "It was old Ordog."

"Or-*what?*" Anna asked.

"Ordog?" Erzebet snorted. "Don't be ridiculous."

"I'm not. It all makes sense. This demon comes in a thunderstorm, tears his victims into twenty pieces"—he ticked off the points on his fingers—"and at the end"—he lowered his voice to a thrilling whisper—"he *drinks all their blood*!"

Anna grabbed hold of the bench beneath her to keep herself still.

"No one believes in demons anymore," Erzebet said.

"No one? My grandfather says—"

"Yes, yes, my grandmother told me stories by the fire, too, all about her cousins and her uncles and all the horrors they had seen, but none of those stories were true." Erzebet patted Anna's shoulder without taking her eyes off the footman. "We're not little children anymore, to be frightened by hearth tales."

I'm not a child, Anna thought bleakly. *But I am frightened.*

The howling of the storm outside sounded even in this inner room. If there had been windows, would she have glimpsed faces peering in from the darkness? Mouths with long, yellow teeth that dripped blood?

"You're frightening Anna," Erzebet said. "Look, she's as white as a ghost!"

"I am not," Anna said. But her voice cracked as she spoke. Humiliating tears stung her eyes. She blinked them back. "What does an Ordog look like?"

"Nothing," Erzebet said quickly. "Because he doesn't exist!"

György ignored her. "Great and dark, with flaming eyes. You'll know he's coming after you when you smell the stink of swamp mud in the air. Then you'll hear hoofbeats following close behind you, though you'll see no one when you turn to look."

"But . . ." Anna took a deep breath. "How can you protect yourself?"

"Against old Ordog?" György gave a shout of laughter.

"György," Erzebet said, through gritted teeth.

"Oh, all right." He sighed. "You don't need to worry about anything, little Anna. This palace is strong, and we're under the Prince's protection here. No monsters can get in. It's only the villains, the traitors and the fugitives running around in thunderstorms at night that run the risk of meeting Ordog. Satisfied?" he added, glaring at Erzebet.

"Nearly. Anna, what did your mistress say about all this?"

"My mistress?" Anna blinked. "What would she have to do with any of it?"

"She was sitting with the Prince when the soldiers came, wasn't she? I heard there was a real commotion. Ladies fainting—"

"Oh, not the Baroness. She wouldn't do that." Anna paused. "But perhaps . . . perhaps her sister might."

"That von Höllner woman? I could well believe it." Erzebet rolled her eyes. "But didn't the Baroness tell you anything?"

"Only that the evening had ended badly. She hardly ever gossips, though."

"Oh well. We'll find out soon enough what really happened. Try not to worry—you know, it was probably only wolves."

"Wolves?" Anna repeated. Her voice rose up to a squeak. "*Wolves?*"

The other maids burst into giggles.

Erzebet sighed. "Anna . . ."

György smirked. "*Wolves?*" he mimicked, falsetto.

The other maids nearly exploded with mirth.

Red-faced, Anna pushed herself up from the table and hurried away, ignoring the sound of Erzebet calling her name.

"Ha!" Anton crowed, as his ball sank smoothly into the table's pocket. "My advantage at last, you dog! Get me a drink."

"Get yourself one." Friedrich leaned over the table, pretending to study the position of the balls. The din of the other officers' voices filled the smoky room. Behind him, one man's voice rose above the rest, laying a bet on what had killed the two actors.

"Ten *gulden* it was bandits!"

"Bandits?" Anton looked up. "What the hell are you thinking, Lautzner? Bandits don't drain their victims of blood!"

"Then what do you think it was?" Lautzner retorted. He looked around for support from his friends. "A *wampyr*? Old Ordog?"

"A ghost?" one of his friends supplied, waving his beer stein. He snorted with laughter at his own wit and raised the stein for a hearty swig.

"It wasn't a ghost," Friedrich muttered.

"What was that?" Lautzner's friend lowered his stein, frowning.

"Nothing."

"You have a problem with what I said, von Höllner?"

"No," Friedrich said, frowning back. "I just said, it wasn't a ghost." He attempted a careless shrug. "All right?"

Anton stepped up beside him, laying down his cue stick. "Of course it wasn't. We aren't peasants here, to believe in that nonsense, are we?" He stared down Lautzner's friend. "Are we?"

"Never said we were," the man muttered. "If that's what he meant . . ."

Anton smiled and stepped back. "It was probably just a pair of hungry wolves. Perfectly straightforward."

"Wolves? In the summer months?" Lautzner shook his head. "That's a mad idea. They only attack men when they're starving and desperate. This time of year they've got hares . . . mice . . . sheep . . ." He grinned. "And anyway, who ever heard of a wolf who drank blood?"

Friedrich swiveled back to the table as the argument developed. He could feel his own heartbeat pounding in his ears.

It wasn't a ghost.

Black robes formed again in his mind, settling silently into place.

Men playing at silly dress-up games, he would have said, and laughed, had anyone described the scene to him. But in the guttering candlelight, it hadn't been amusing. And some of those hoods hadn't surrounded faces; he'd been certain of that. Only black, empty voids had shown beneath—voids a man could be sucked into, screaming, as he lost his sanity. And some of those foot-covering robes hadn't bothered to touch the ground . . .

No. He lashed out with his cue stick, wildly off-target, and sent balls spinning across the table. He'd been drunk. *End of story.*

But he'd received their letter scant hours before this attack. Could it really be coincidence? Or was it sheer, bloody-minded Fate come home to crush him for all the stupid decisions he'd made in the past, like—oh, yes, so especially like—following a new friend down that slippery trap-door passageway in Vienna, all those months ago . . .

God. What if tonight had been aimed at him? They would have known he'd find out, known that he'd be frightened. What if it was a warning? A threat of what would happen if he didn't follow their damned orders?

"Not likely, my lad."

It took Friedrich a paralyzed moment to realize that Anton was talking about his last move. Anton gazed at the scattered balls on the table and shook his head, smirking.

"You're never going to win against me playing that way. I'm afraid you're going to lose our wager tonight, von Höllner."

"Just trying to throw you off your guard." Friedrich wiped a hand across his forehead and tried to grin back.

"A feeble attempt." Anton tossed down another stein of beer and picked up his cue stick. "I'm going to really enjoy my winnings this time."

"We'll see about that."

For once, though, Friedrich couldn't make himself enjoy the thrill of the wager. Thirty *gulden* from Prince Nikolaus's purse, passing through Friedrich, straight back to Anton Esterházy, the Prince's cousin . . . What did it matter, in the larger scale of things? Not much, compared to the threat of gory murder.

"I think that letter's still throwing you off," Anton said, as he aimed his cue stick. He raised his voice to carry through the room. "Von Höllner got a love letter from Vienna today, fellows . . ."

Hoots of derision and laughter filled the air. Friedrich sighed.

"Esterházy . . ."

"Made him go as white as chalk, it did." Anton swept another two balls into a pocket with one tap of the cue stick, then looked up and grinned. "I think he's got a secret family tucked away in the big city, eh, Friedrich? Was the little woman writing to tell you she'd had another set of twins?"

"Come on, now . . ." Friedrich began.

"Good for you, von Höllner!" Lautzner roared. He slammed another beer stein into Friedrich's hand and forcibly poured it down Friedrich's throat. "Tell us all about her! What's she like in bed?"

Ten minutes later, Friedrich's head was spinning happily, and he was at the center of a boisterous circle, all trying out-do each other's tales of conquests. He slammed down yet another beer stein and scooped up a new one, shouting to make himself heard above the others.

"Just wait until I tell you—!"

As the circle of faces turned to him expectantly, Friedrich's throat closed up. Tucked into the handle of the new stein was a sealed note, addressed to him. He recognized the seal.

"Well?" Anton demanded. "*Well*, damn it? What?"

"Nothing," Friedrich mumbled. "Never mind. I don't remember." He swallowed down bile. "I think . . . I have to go now."

"Bloody girlish Westerner." Anton frowned. "Hell, you actually don't look good. Shall I come with you and help?"

"No," Friedrich said. "No." He slipped the note out of the cup handle and backed away. "I need . . . I think I'd better be alone."

He walked out of the room, weaving slightly, while catcalls followed after him.

Anna whirled from one grand, high-ceilinged room to the next. In the daytime, the nobility walked these floors, and she'd never dare show her face where she hadn't a specific task to complete, even if she'd had the time for aimless wandering. Now they were all asleep in the central wing of the palace, and she was free, although she'd pay dearly in exhaustion later.

Her tears had slowed after the first few minutes. She still hated György—hated the other maids who'd laughed with him—hated . . .

She chewed her bottom lip, fighting down the misery.

More than any of the rest, she hated herself, for turning into a laughingstock just as she'd finally begun to make a few friends here.

A song welled up in her chest, crying to be released, to soothe her. But even now, well after midnight, it wasn't safe for her to sing in an open space. If one of the other servants heard, she'd never earn back any respect.

She forced herself to keep walking, despite the throbbing headache that had begun at the back of her skull. Another half an hour and she'd be able to sleep, too tired to worry about what other people thought of her, what her nightmares might be, or even about the bloodsucking demons that lurked outside the castle walls.

She turned down a narrow side corridor and then shrank back. A gust of cold wind swept drops of rain onto her arms and face. Who would have opened a window in this weather?

She took a few hesitant steps into the corridor, wincing at the cold, damp air. Perhaps she ought to close the window herself. There were expensive-looking porcelain vases standing on pedestals nearby, being spattered by the rain.

On her third step, she looked down and saw blood on the floorboards. Blood and an open window.

A silent scream swallowed up the back of her throat. Dizziness enveloped her. She leapt sideways, reaching out to the inner wall for balance—and heard a man's deep voice murmuring in the room on the other side. He spoke too quietly for her to make out any words but with a tone of compulsion that drew her closer despite herself, straining to hear more.

A hissing, whooshing sound answered the man. And then the voice rose in anger—

Soft footsteps sounded in the distance. Anna gasped and jerked back from the wall as if stung. The voices cut off. A listening silence replaced them.

A cold wind blew at Anna's back as she picked up her skirts and fled back to her own room and safety.

A minute later, a small figure in plain, unfashionable English attire appeared at the end of the corridor. It was the man known to his traveling companions as Edmund Guernsey, the nervous little English tourist.

Guernsey's face was cold and set. His eyes darted back and forth as he walked down the corridor. When he thought he heard a whisper of sound, he paused and listened intently at the wall.

But the voices had silenced before he'd arrived, and the rain had washed the bloodstains from the floor.

Guernsey walked down the corridor, shook his head, and moved softly on, through the darkened byways of the palace.

Friedrich shivered in the cold rain. His eyes were finally starting to adjust to the blackness after ten minutes of standing outside, and his head, unfortunately, was clearing rapidly. He'd much preferred intoxication.

His chilly fingers twitched convulsively, flipping the note over and over again in his hand. It consisted of only one line, in a tidy black script: *Meet me outside the opera house*, followed by the usual mark. Whoever had written it, he'd been an arrogant enough bastard to take for granted that his order would be followed, without even bothering to give a time for the damned appointment. If Friedrich had to wait another hour or two before the devil showed up, the other officers would all see him standing like a fool as they tromped back to the barracks, across the grass. Of course, by then he would have already turned into a bloody icicle, so perhaps he wouldn't even care.

The hell with it. Friedrich turned to leave—

—And froze as he heard the telltale crunch of heeled shoes against the shell-lined path in front of him.

"Lieutenant Friedrich von Höllner." A dark figure moved through the shadows, so voluminously greatcoated that he could have been either a fat man or a skeleton. "Brother Friedrich."

"Ah . . ." Friedrich crumpled the note in his clenched hand as the dark figure came to a halt five feet away. The rain was finally easing, but that was no help after all. A black, beaked carnival mask covered the whole of the man's face, which was doubly shaded under the voluminous hat that hid his hair. The sight should have been grotesque—even ridiculous—but in the black stillness of the night, with even the rain disappearing into an eerie silence . . . it wasn't. Instead, it brought back far too vivid memories of cloaks and darkness, memories Friedrich had been fighting all day.

He swallowed hard as they rose up once more. "About that—that night—you know, I wasn't thinking very clearly. Not at all."

"No?" The dark head cocked in polite curiosity.

Panic crawled through the bottom of Friedrich's stomach. "So what I mean to say is . . . is, I'm sorry to give you extra trouble, but—"

"Oh, you haven't given us any trouble, Brother Friedrich. Not at all. In fact, you've made our task much, much easier."

"Um." Friedrich took a gasping breath. *Don't think about those singers, don't even let him hear you thinking . . .* "I just think—I think you'd better leave me out of your plans, though, really." He smiled weakly and stepped back, slipping the crumpled note inside his coat. "I wouldn't be any good at them anyway. I'm not the right sort."

"No? Then what sort are you, *Brother* Friedrich?" The black shape slipped closer. "Are you the sort who takes sacred oaths only to break them? Or are you the sort who sells his wife's virtue for an easy fortune?"

Friedrich gasped. "I didn't—that was Sophie's idea! She and the Prince—"

"The sort who gambles away so much of his own family fortune that he cannot afford to turn down such an offer when it arrives?" The shape continued its inexorable advance. "The sort who gets drunk and gabbles all of Eszterháza's most private secrets to a stranger? The sort whose home and income are entirely dependent on our silence, forever?"

"Stop it!" Friedrich stumbled backward. "I am a von Höllner. I am—"

"A sot and a fool and a sworn member of our fellowship, as your own signature attests." The figure withdrew a sheet of paper from the folds of his greatcoat. "Did you never think to read what you were signing that night, Brother Friedrich? This letter gives away none of the secrets of our Brotherhood, yet it commits you to the downfall of the Empress and Emperor and the nobility itself, and it purposes you to the special destruction of Prince Nikolaus's power."

"But—!" Only the vaguest, floating memories rose to his grasping memory—someone holding out a paper for him to sign as he'd swayed . . . He must have passed out only moments later, the heat and the drink and the shock bearing him down into darkness. His head had been spinning so badly by then, he couldn't have read anything to save his life. Still . . . "That's madness! Why would I ever want anything like that?"

"The punishment for treason is execution, Brother Friedrich, after a prolonged torture session to ascertain the extent of your crimes. Do you really want to stake your life on your ability to persuade Prince Nikolaus and the Empress herself of your innocence? Against the evidence of your own signature?"

Friedrich stared at the paper. If he leapt forward—if he could only wrestle it away—

"This is not the original letter, of course." The figure tossed the paper onto the ground, where the breeze caught it and carried it away. "It's but a copy, to remind you of your obligations. The true, signed letter is in our archives, in Vienna. It will be mailed to the Empress within the week, unless I send word that you've agreed to stand by your oaths."

Friedrich scrambled forward, chasing down the paper as the breeze tossed it further and further away from the path. When he finally caught it, it was damp from the rain-soaked grass.

"You may read it at your leisure." There was a damnable hint of laughter in the other man's voice. "But I would advise destroying it, and quickly. Not an amusing discovery for any of your military comrades to make."

Friedrich couldn't make out any of the words in the dark when he pulled the paper open. But his sinking gut already knew what his decision had to be.

"What do you want me to do?"

"Take an interest in the Prince's opera company, for a start."

"What?" Friedrich snorted, caught off guard. "I hate opera. Anyway, I'd never be allowed at the performances. Sophie—"

"Not the *performances*, Brother Friedrich. The company itself. I'll expect you to start attending daily rehearsals."

"But—"

"Introduce yourself to the actors. Pretend an interest in one of the actresses, if you like." The figure shrugged. "However you do it, make certain that all of them know who you are and grow accustomed to your presence."

"And?" Friedrich said. "What then?"

"That, you do not yet need to know." The figure turned. "Good night, Brother Friedrich. You will hear from me again."

He moved away, merging into the darkness. But at the final moment, Friedrich mustered up his courage.

"Wait!" he called. "Wait. You have to tell me . . . Those singers who were killed tonight—was that you?"

"I?" The figure stilled. "Why, I was here at the palace. I never touched them."

"But was your bloody fellowship behind it? *Damn* you!" Friedrich balled his shaking hands into fists, crumpling the devil's contract. "Did you do it to frighten me? I need to know!"

The figure regarded him for a long moment, before it broke into dry, discomfiting laughter.

"That, I'm afraid, I am not going to tell you, Brother Friedrich. You'll have to learn to live with the uncertainty."

Still laughing softly, he turned and faded into the shadows.

Chapter Seven

Charlotte woke to sunlight streaming through the windows and a headache tugging at her brows. She lay with her eyes closed, fighting against the pull of the sun.

She'd spent half the night trapped in nightmares, galloping through pounding rain to escape a terrifying danger close behind. She felt as if she hadn't slept at all.

"Anna?" Charlotte's voice came out as a rasp. She heard her maid's soft movements whisper to a halt, across the room. "Why have you opened the curtains?"

"Your pardon, Baroness." Charlotte pulled her eyes open in time to see her maid drop a quick curtsey. "It's nearly eleven o'clock, and your sister usually arrives at twelve. I thought you might want time to prepare."

"Sophie . . ." Charlotte pulled herself up onto her elbows, grimacing. "You were quite right, Anna. Thank you." She took a deep breath to clear out her sleep-fogged brain, then shrugged on the lace-trimmed *manteau de lit* that Anna held out for her. "I could do with a hot chocolate, if you've brought any today."

As the hot, creamy mixture sank down her throat, Charlotte gazed out the window and fought the urge to pull the covers back up over her head. She could already imagine every word that would be uttered in the course of her sister's visit—Sophie's delighted horror in the gruesome news and her determination to shock Charlotte even further.

She couldn't bear it. Not after last night and the horrors of her dreams. They had felt so miserably real, down to the cold rain that had drenched her windswept hair. She had to touch her hair, dry and stiffly set beneath its protective netting, to remind herself that the attack had not, after all, happened to her. But it had, to two other people not very far away, and they must have been at least as terrified.

She couldn't lie here in this beautiful room, in this fairy tale palace, and listen to gleeful gossip about a horrific double murder.

Charlotte swung her legs out of bed and abandoned her breakfast. "Anna? I'll get fully dressed now, if you please."

"Madam?" Anna looked up from Charlotte's dressing table, where she had been laying out Charlotte's *negligée du matin* for receiving visitors. "But Frau von Höllner—"

"I'm afraid she'll simply have to miss me. I'm going to—to—" Charlotte searched for inspiration. "I'm going to pay a call on Herr Haydn." *Yes.* She wouldn't follow Sophie's advice and summon him like a recalcitrant errand boy; no, she'd treat him with the respect his genius deserved. She'd tell him—

"I believe he's in rehearsal now, madam."

"Oh. Well, rehearsals are open to the public, are they not?" Open, at least, to the Prince's circle.

"Yes, madam."

Anna hurried to bring layers of undergarments and a black silk sack-back gown enlivened by new lavender ribbons—Sophie's gift upon the turn of the third month of Charlotte's widowhood. Charlotte's lips twitched as she looked down at the ribbons. At last, a flash of color. She would have to try to measure up to it.

Her maid's face looked pale and tired as she arranged the padded panniers around Charlotte's hips. More than tired . . . worried. Afraid?

As Charlotte raised her arms for the stays to be laced around her waist, she asked, "Is something the matter, Anna?"

"No, Baroness." Anna ducked her head over the fastenings.

"Are you certain?" Charlotte frowned down at her. The girl was very young. Could it be simple homesickness? "How are you settling in here with the other servants? Are they treating you well?"

"Oh . . ." Anna shrugged, still not looking up.

"If they aren't, only tell me and I'll take care of it. I'm sure my sister would have a word with the steward to set it right."

"Nothing needs to be done, madam." Anna straightened and smiled unconvincingly. "I'm truly fine."

"Hmm." Charlotte watched Anna gather up the pins and fresh powder to tidy her hair. She could swear the girl was blinking back tears. But how could she force a confidence? "If anything unpleasant did ever happen to you, I would wish you to tell me. The way you are treated is a reflection on my honor, you know."

"Yes, madam." Anna moved behind Charlotte to apply powder to her hair. The maid's voice came out muffled from the pins in her mouth. "I only . . . I don't like this palace."

"Don't you?" Only long training kept Charlotte from craning her neck back in surprise. "I thought you loved it, when we arrived. Don't you still find it beautiful?"

Only silence met her question.

Charlotte sighed. "Well, we won't stay here forever. Probably only a year."

Once Charlotte's hair was freshly powdered, her boned stomacher firmly in place, and her petticoats and overskirt arranged over all her padding until they billowed out around her on each side, Anna finally spoke again, aiming her words at the floor.

"What shall I tell Frau von Höllner when she arrives, madam?"

"Tell her . . ." Looking at the girl's red-eyed misery, Charlotte had a flash of inspiration. "I know! We shan't tell her anything at all. Anna, how would you like to come along with me to listen to Herr Haydn's rehearsal?"

"Really?" Anna's face lit up. "But—"

"Why not? There are some great ladies who go nowhere without their maids." Charlotte thought of the Princess, and her smile twisted. "Do come, Anna. I know how much you love music. You can forget about your other duties for a while. I'm already dressed for dinner anyway."

The delight on her maid's face lifted Charlotte's spirits for the first time that morning.

Hurrying down the corridor away from Sophie's chambers felt like a guilty pleasure. *Escape.*

I'll make up for it later, Charlotte promised herself. *Truly*.

But once they stepped outside, there was no room for any sensation but pleasure. Soldiers in bright blue, red, and white uniforms performed their morning changing of the guard on the wide expanse of lawn between the palace and the opera house, accompanied by a band playing one of Herr Haydn's military airs. Warm sunlight bathed Charlotte's face and neck, and a light breeze carried the jaunty tune, along with the scent of freshly cut grass. In this blue-skied day, it was hard to believe in any horrors.

She opened the front door of the opera house—and nearly walked into Signor Morelli.

"Baroness." His eyes widened. He sketched a bow, his eyes flickering beyond her to Anna's nervous face. "An unexpected pleasure."

"Signor." Charlotte curtseyed, keeping her smile with an effort. After a night away, his high, alien voice vibrated through her chest with a disquieting intensity. "Are you here to observe today's rehearsal?"

"In a way. And yourself?"

"I hoped to meet Herr Haydn."

"He is much occupied at present, with three of his singers gone and the company in mourning."

"Three?" Charlotte kept her voice even, despite the heat in her cheeks. He thought her insensitive to have come today, an arrogant noblewoman who thought of no one's needs but her own. And was she? She had never paused to wonder whether Herr Haydn would be in a mood for hospitality. "I thought only two singers had been killed."

"Two indeed, Baroness. But a third was discovered to have been their accomplice, and he is held in the Eszterháza prisons for a week. Thus, two tenors and a leading soprano, gone." His shrug was eloquent. He turned away, reaching for the inner door. "Your servant, Baroness."

Charlotte felt Anna's pleading gaze on her back. She lifted her chin. "I'll accompany you still, signor, to present my condolences to Herr Haydn."

He stopped. "Madam, your concern does you much credit, but I hardly think—"

The door swung open.

"Ha!" The kapellmeister grinned infectiously as he looked from one to the other. "Signor, I hoped I'd recognized your ringing tones. Madam . . ." He bowed beautifully.

"Herr Haydn." Charlotte sank into a deep, respectful curtsey. She heard Anna's skirts rustling behind her. "I am honored, sir."

Signor Morelli began, "May I present the Baroness—"

"—Von Steinbeck, yes, I know, my dear sir." Herr Haydn lifted Charlotte's hands to his lips. "I'm entirely charmed to meet you, Baroness."

"But . . ." She rose, smiling hesitantly. "However did you know my name?"

"I should like to say that I know everyone in this palace, dear lady, but in truth . . ." His eyes twinkled as he looked past her. "I must confess, I knew you through your maid."

"Anna?" Charlotte turned to find Anna pink-cheeked, with a secret smile playing about her lips. "You never mentioned that you had met Herr Haydn."

"I did mean to tell you, Baroness, but—"

"A mere passing acquaintance," the kapellmeister said, "but a charming one indeed." He smiled at Charlotte. "And what brings you here today, Baroness?"

Charlotte felt Morelli's eyes on her. "I confess, sir, I had not considered your unhappy circumstances. I came in hopes of meeting you, and of hearing more of your glorious music. But Signor Morelli has already informed that today was ill-chosen for a visit, so—"

"Nonsense! Our illustrious friend was only trying to cosset me. I can assure you, signor, that my nerves are quite as tough as rock, and not nearly so liable to shatter. Come in, do. And signor, do not you lag behind!"

He ushered them onto the wooden stage. A group of singers filled the center, engaged in heated discussion, while orchestral musicians sat before the raised stage on long benches, tuning their instruments. Charlotte hesitated at the edge of the stage, and the kapellmeister pointed into the audience.

"There, madam, you may take your pick of seat. I'm afraid we may be embroiled in a rather tedious conversation for some little while, but with such a guest, I'm sure His Highness would wish me to order up refreshments—and afterward, I promise you more music. The first rehearsal of scenes from my new opera!"

"Really!" Charlotte traded a speaking look with her maid and chose a seat in the center of the auditorium. Anna arranged Charlotte's full skirts carefully around her chair and then sat down behind her, fairly vibrating with excitement.

There, Charlotte thought, and aimed the thought at the back of Signor Morelli's head. This opportunity had been well worth suffering a bit of condescension and nerves—and oh, so infinitely preferable to an hour of prickling gossip!

Onstage, the kapellmeister, Morelli, and the singers were talking animatedly but too quietly for Charlotte to make out from her seat. Instead, she concentrated on the wisps of fragmented tunes played by the various instrumentalists, who seemed to be reading new music from their stands. It was as impossible as it was irresistible to try to imagine how all the varied fragments could possibly be linked together into a unified whole. Caught up in the competing strands of music, Charlotte could have sat happily for hours. She hadn't even noticed Signor Morelli leave the stage until he took the seat beside her.

"Baroness." He nodded. "You're not finding this long wait too tedious?"

"Hardly." She blinked at him. "How could I, in such an ambience?"

"An excellent question."

He leaned back in his seat, crossing his legs. The dark blue satin of his breeches contrasted with the shining white of the silk stockings that enclosed his muscled calves. Charlotte blinked and quickly averted her gaze. For all that his face and voice were so disconcertingly effeminate, the rest of him . . .

No. She cut off the thoroughly inappropriate chain of thoughts with a blink, more startled than guilty. She hadn't even had such thoughts to quash for years—not since the very beginning of her marriage. Why were they returning now?

It was the incongruity of him that tugged at her, compelling her attention. That was all.

When she looked up, she found the castrato watching her quizzically. "Is this the first rehearsal you've ever attended, madam?"

"It is," she admitted.

For a man who could look so cold and forbidding, he positively radiated heat. Charlotte imagined that she could feel it tingling even through the foot of space that separated the arms of their chairs. Perhaps it arose from the intensity of his focus. Even as he spoke casually to her, she could see his eyes darting around the stage and his brow furrowed with concentration.

She wished, suddenly, that she could hear him sing. Such intensity, physically leashed . . .

She fixed her eyes on the stage and took a deep breath to dispel the discomfiting mixture of sensations in her chest. There was discomfort there, truly, but also something . . . something she could not quite name.

"What will they do about the missing singers?" she asked.

He shrugged. "We shall see. The head of the company has written to singers across the empire, inviting them to take over the abandoned positions—but in high summer most competent singers have posts of their own, and Herr Haydn doubts they'll find three on such short notice. This opera is planned for the second day of the Archduke's visit, only nine days from today, so the matter is in a fair way to become a crisis."

"Of course." She sighed. *The royal visit.* Prince Nikolaus had reminded the assembled company nearly ten times yesterday of the great honor that awaited them, and Sophie was full of plans for new festivities. Charlotte could not muster an equal enthusiasm. Her own plan for a quiet retreat here had surely been ill-conceived. "I wish them luck."

At a word from Herr Haydn, the instruments fell silent. Charlotte leaned forward in her seat as the actors spread out across the stage. A footman approached her, murmuring something, but she waved him away. *Not now.*

The music began.

Waves, sweeping up onto a rocky beach; a storm thundering overhead; afterward, the return of birds, chattering their relief in the fresh sunlight. All these Charlotte could *hear*, as plainly as she also *knew* them to be merely violins, percussion, and flutes, playing before her. And then the singing began.

Behind her, she heard Anna begin to sing along softly, following the lines of the duet. It should have been a trio—Charlotte could hear the moments of absence in the music, waiting to be filled—but still, the voices and the orchestra melted together into beauty.

Anna's voice followed along, mirroring the soprano. Charlotte glanced back and saw her maid so enraptured she seemed barely aware of the lovely sounds coming out of her own mouth. Charlotte turned back to the stage, hiding a smile. Anna's voice had always been a delight to her back in Saxony, caroling freely throughout the house whenever the girl forgot to control it—and hearing it now was like the promise of sunshine, signaling the happy return of Anna's usual good temper.

Charlotte would not disturb her maid's enjoyment, unless Signor Morelli—

Even as she thought it, he swiveled around to stare at Anna. Anna blinked and snapped her mouth shut.

"Was that you, singing?" he demanded.

Anna's face reddened, her shoulders hunching together.

"Your pardon, signor, but she meant no disrespect." Charlotte leaned between them, aiming a reassuring smile at her maid. "It did no harm, after all. I'm certain they couldn't hear her from the stage."

"That wasn't my concern." He narrowed his eyes. "Fräulein—Anna, is that your name? Were you singing in the palace yesterday afternoon?"

"Signor—"

His upheld hand cut Charlotte off. "Well?"

Anna's lips trembled. "Yes, signor," she whispered. "I'm truly sorry. I thought everyone was still at dinner, else I'd never have—"

"Herr Haydn!" Morelli leapt to his feet and waved for the kapellmeister's attention.

The music cut off abruptly. Musicians and singers alike turned to stare at the audience.

"Yes, signor?" The kapellmeister walked to the edge of the stage, still holding a sheaf of music. "Was there a problem in the balance?"

"Not at all. But I have found your replacement soprano."

Anna gasped. Charlotte stared. Only Herr Haydn did not appear surprised.

"So, little Anna is the one you heard yesterday, eh? Well, well." He smiled and held out his hand. "Come up here, child."

"May I, Baroness?"

"I suppose . . ." Charlotte shrugged, bewildered, and watched Morelli escort Anna up onto the stage.

The other singers whispered among themselves, watching Anna with blatant curiosity.

"Do you enjoy singing, child?" the kapellmeister asked, once Anna stood before him.

"More . . . more than anything, sir."

"Signor Morelli has told me he heard a marvelously strong soprano voice singing yesterday afternoon in the palace. Was that you?"

"I . . . yes, sir."

"It was," Morelli confirmed, standing behind her. "Strong and clear, though untrained."

"With such a recommendation, and in our current circumstances, you appear before us as a veritable gift from Heaven, my dear. A gift, I hope, for both of us. How would you like to train your voice and learn to be a professional singer?" He looked across to Charlotte, who still sat, now alone, in the audience. "With the Baroness's permission, of course."

"I . . ." Charlotte took a breath and looked up at Anna's shining, awe-struck face.

"I'm certain Prince Nikolaus would be happy to supply a replace-ment maid, in exchange for the addition to his opera company," said Signor Morelli.

Charlotte tightened her lips. "Thank you, signor, I am persuaded that you are correct. However, that was not what worried me." She stood and swept up the stairs to the stage, ignoring the interested gazes of the assembled company as she fixed her eyes on Anna's face. "Anna, what do *you* want? Truly?" She added, in a fierce whisper, "I do not wish you constrained by contract in a palace that you hate!"

She fancied that she felt Morelli's disapproving gaze on her. *Let him disapprove.* Two actors had died, trying to escape their contracts, only last night. She would not have Anna follow them.

Herr Haydn frowned. "We could perhaps wait upon the contract until after this performance, with the Prince's permission, and call it a trial for all of us."

"And afterward?"

"If all went well . . ." He shrugged. "His Highness would not be pleased for a singer trained here to go directly to the palace of one of his rivals in power and prestige. Thus, he might well offer a very tempting salary for her to remain."

Charlotte kept her eyes on her maid. "Anna? It is your decision to make."

Anna bit her lip. Her gaze moved from Charlotte to Herr Haydn and Signor Morelli. "Please, Baroness. I do thank you, but—to be a singer! For my living!"

"Very well." Charlotte smiled as well as she could, despite the increasing tightness in her chest. "I wish you the very best," she said. "And remember, you will always have my protection, whenever you should need it."

"Now then, young Anna." Herr Haydn took Anna's arm and drew her away. "Let me introduce you to the rest of our little company."

Charlotte retreated down the steps to the audience, holding her head high, even as pain knotted its way through her.

Anna had been the last link to her old life, and now she was left unrooted. That night, a stranger would undress her and remove the pins and ribbons from her hair. There would be no familiar smile or friendly presence in the room when she woke the next morning.

But how could she not be pleased by such a miraculous turn of events? Here was a one in a thousand chance indeed for a girl from Anna's background to raise herself. Why, if Anna was successful, what great fortunes might not await her? And oh, what glorious music would surround her . . .

Confess it now and be done with it, Charlotte thought wearily. *You are envious of your own maid. And what does that say of yourself, Frau Baroness?*

She sank back into her seat and clasped her hands together loosely on her lap, fighting the urge toward an unladylike slump. She felt drained of enthusiasm. Rest and solitude, those were all she wanted now . . . but for Anna's sake, as well as her own pride, she should stay a little longer yet.

"Baroness?" Signor Morelli stood looking down at her with an unreadable expression. "That was well done of you."

Charlotte sighed, too tired to search for any hidden bite in his words. "My sister tells me there are at least one thousand servants in Eszterháza. I could hardly begrudge Anna her opportunity, merely for my own personal whim."

"No," he said, "but many would." He paused. "I shall probably sing for the company tomorrow evening. Would you be ready to accompany me on such short notice?"

Charlotte felt a spark of life reignite in her chest, responding to the test behind his words. A *challenge*. She met his measuring gaze. "Of course," she said coolly. "If you'll send the keyboard parts to my chambers, I'll begin practicing the music this afternoon after dinner."

"Excellent. The cues are marked clearly in the parts. If you wish to simplify the accompaniment, for your ease—"

"That won't be necessary." Charlotte set her teeth together with a snap.

"I'm pleased to hear it." His half-bow was interrupted by the sound of a door opening behind Charlotte and then loudly crashing closed. "Sir?" Morelli asked quellingly, as a young officer sauntered past them.

The officer stopped, and seemed to notice them for the first time. "Oh! Beg pardon for interrupting. I was hoping to watch the opera rehearsal. I expect I'm probably late." He smiled nervously and smoothed down his unpowdered blond hair in its queue. Belatedly, he bowed to Charlotte. "At your service, madam. Lieutenant Friedrich von Höllner, of His Highness's Grenadier Guards."

Charlotte blinked. For a moment, she couldn't speak.

"Madam?" Lieutenant von Höllner remained fixed in mid-bow, his smile wavering.

"Pardon me, lieutenant." Charlotte forced a smile, aware of Morelli's watchful gaze. "I am the Baroness von Steinbeck, and I believe that you must be my brother-in-law."

He blinked. His fair skin flushed. "You don't mean . . . you're not Sophie's . . ."

"Sophie's older sister." Charlotte hesitated, searching for words. "I was most sorry not to be able to attend your wedding, lieutenant. I'm afraid my husband's health . . ."

"Not at all," he mumbled. "Actually, I think I remember Sophie saying something about that . . ."

At any moment, he would start backing away from her. Charlotte fought down a hysterical giggle. He was eyeing her like a dangerous snake. What on earth had Sophie told him of her? Or—did he fear she would tattle to Sophie of some imagined slight?

"I should not intrude upon this family reunion," Signor Morelli murmured. "If you'll excuse me, Baroness . . ."

The door opened again behind them. "Aha!" Sophie sailed into the room, beaming. "So there you are at last, Lotte! I've been looking everywhere for—"

Her face froze into a mask as Lieutenant von Höllner straightened, fiddling with the buttons on his waistcoat. He smiled weakly.

"Hallo, Sophie."

"What on *earth*—?"

"I was just making my brother-in-law's acquaintance, Sophie." Charlotte smiled desperately as she rose to her feet. "It is a fine day out, is it not? The weather—"

"What in heaven's name are you doing here? Meeting my sister? How *dare* you—?"

"No, no! I never imagined I would find her here!" He darted an anguished look at Charlotte. "Not that it wasn't a pleasure, Baroness, but—"

"Sophie, it really was the most accidental—"

"You don't even like opera! What other reason could you possibly have for coming here today?"

"I—ah . . ." He backed away, eyes darting back and forth. "Er—that is—"

"Yes?" Morelli breathed, too softly for the others to hear.

Charlotte wanted to slap him, yet she had to stifle a laugh.

"Interested in actresses?" the lieutenant offered, his eyes wide and desperate.

A woman's throaty laugh sounded onstage.

"Oh!" Sophie whirled around and swept away.

Charlotte looked from one man to another. Signor Morelli's eyes were filled with devilish mirth. Lieutenant von Höllner looked as if he might shoot himself only to escape.

"Lotte?" Sophie called from the door. Her voice trembled, but whether with rage or tears, Charlotte couldn't even hazard a guess.

"Lieutenant . . . Signor . . ." Charlotte gave them both a distracted half-curtsey, and fled.

Chapter Eight

Carlo kept his smile until the door of the opera house fell closed behind him. Then it soured, as quickly as had his mood.

Truly, he had lost his position in the dance. How else could one explain the fact that he had somehow spent the entire morning with musicians, rather than with the nobility who had invited him? There was no faster or more effective way of losing his equality in their eyes than to voluntarily associate himself with their subordinates. Only think of Herr Haydn, famed throughout Europe, sitting here complacently following all of the Prince's whimsical commands, accepting his lack of freedom as a natural state . . .

Carlo realized he was grinding his teeth. He widened his jaw with an effort and strode down the path toward the palace and his real duties.

Tomorrow morning he'd not give in to sneaking temptation and slide off to enjoy himself in lower company. No, he'd make it clear to the Prince and everyone else that he was a figure to be reckoned with, every bit as much as the titled gentlemen who lounged about the over-decorated rooms of this overblown monstrosity of a palace.

Let the musicians sort themselves out.

Late that evening, after the mandatory string quartet performance had ended and Prince Nikolaus had retired with his mistress to his own chambers, the man known as Edmund Guernsey slipped through the servants' door that was concealed within the largest landscape painting in the grand library. Hidden within the palace walls, he walked swiftly down the narrow, windowless servants' corridor, his pace shifting from the hesitant scuttle he'd adopted for public use to quick, confident strides.

He'd written already to his master, giving judgment on the Prince. No use wasting money there in vain attempts to sway Nikolaus from the Habsburg cause. The man's loyalty was as unswerving as his arrogance. Guernsey had lost interest in that path from the moment the method of the singers' deaths had been announced.

A far greater reward was waiting to be won.

Guernsey paused a moment to listen at the wall. *Silence.* He pressed the panel.

The servants' door swung open into Sophie von Höllner's private apartments, and Guernsey stepped inside.

At noon the next day, an invited party gathered outside Eszterháza's south entrance, where Prince Nikolaus's touring carriage awaited them.

"This carriage was designed and built specifically for tours of Eszterháza's grounds," Prince Nikolaus said, as a footman helped Frau von Höllner up the lowered steps. "I hope you gentlemen will find it admirably suited for an afternoon's tour."

"I'm certain we shall." Carlo gazed pensively at the eight horses gathered before the carriage and the miniature chimney that poked out the top, and forced himself to refrain from sarcasm.

Of all the grandiosities he'd seen at Eszterháza, this carriage was perhaps most flamboyant of all. Built almost as a wooden house on wheels, it could carry at least twelve passengers in comfort. Was it any smaller, he wondered, than the whole of Herr Haydn's apartments?

"I am overwhelmed, Your Highness!" Edmund Guernsey breathed. "In all my travels, I've seen nothing like it!"

Indeed, he looked near-pop-eyed with awe. Carlo had to restrain himself from offering the little man a word or two of advice on his acting skills. Surely, even His Highness's pride could not fail to see through such blatant shamming. But Prince Nikolaus barely spared a glance for the *faux*-tourist.

"Signor?" Ignaz von Born nodded for Carlo to step ahead of him into the carriage, once the Prince's niece and her companion had been settled next to Frau von Höllner.

Carlo took one of the chairs at the great table inside, seated in front of the empty fireplace and across from a large looking glass. He smoothed out his expression and looked away from it quickly. Von Born smiled blandly as he stepped inside—without, Carlo noticed, bothering to make use of his ever-present walking stick.

The carriage rolled smoothly down the paths of the formal garden. Alleys radiated out around them, lending glimpses of statues, fountains, and artificial waterfalls in abundance. Prince Nikolaus provided a running commentary on the history of each construction, while Frau von Höllner provided giggling side-notes and the Prince's niece whispered with her companion. Guernsey interjected wonder and awe at a high pitch. Carlo found himself missing the presence of Baroness von Steinbeck, who had been his neighbor at the dinner table the previous afternoon and again at the string quartet performance that evening. It would have been a relief to hear some quiet notes of sense amidst the gabble.

The carriage rolled to a stop half an hour later in front of a raised, square building in Chinese style, covered with mirrors that caught and dazzlingly reflected the bright afternoon sunlight. A marble figure crouched atop the curving roof, holding an umbrella high over his pointed hat. Servants waited outside the building with blankets already spread out across the grass and special seats for the ladies in their billowing skirts.

"The Bagatelle," Prince Nikolaus said, smiling. "We'll picnic here today."

"This *was* called the Chinese Pleasure House, you know," Frau von Höllner confided to the carriage at large, "but when the Empress came to visit some years ago, she was monstrous impressed by it. *She* said she'd seen nothing like it before, and she asked what it was called, but *Niko* told her it was a mere trifle, only—"

"—Naught but a bagatelle," the Prince finished for her. A satisfied smile played around his lips as he gazed out the window at the many mirrors glittering in the sunlight.

"Quite the bagatelle," Carlo said blandly. "How long did it take to have it built, Your Highness?"

"Over a year." The Prince shrugged, still smiling. "But well worth the wait, I think."

"Marvelous indeed," von Born murmured.

"The Empress and the Emperor have nothing so impressive at Schönbrunn," Frau von Höllner said happily, as servants helped her out of the carriage.

"Nor such opera, I hear," Guernsey added. "Did not the Empress herself say, whenever she wanted to hear good opera, she came to Eszterháza?"

"She did indeed." The Prince stepped out of the carriage and turned to Carlo. "But we should ask you about that, signor. My kapellmeister tells me that you've lent him invaluable assistance. What think you of our little opera company?"

Carlo stiffened inwardly. "I've been more an audience than an assistant, Your Highness, but an admiring audience, truly. You have a talented company indeed." He stepped onto the soft grass, holding his smile and the Prince's gaze with his chin raised and his shoulders relaxed. Servants bustled around them, pouring wine and laying out savories. "At every court in Europe, I've heard praise of Herr Haydn. Eszterháza is fortunate in its musical director."

"Mm. Hiring him was one sound decision made by my older brother."

"I loved the Turkish music in his opera last year," Frau von Höllner said brightly. "I vow, I hummed it for a week afterward." She paused, and her eyes lit up. "Niko, I have it! You must hold a masked ball here, outside the Bagatelle. Herr Haydn can compose more Turkish music for it, and we can have fireworks, and—"

"This Saturday might suit," Prince Nikolaus said thoughtfully. "What say you gentlemen? Do you fancy a masked ball?"

Von Born smiled stiffly. "A delightful conceit."

"Of course it is," said Frau von Höllner. "Niko, you can be a magnificent and frightening Pasha, and I shall dress as a Turkish harem lady. It will be most romantic." She dimpled up at her lover, who smiled back indulgently.

Baroness von Steinbeck would have blushed at that, Carlo thought—then cursed himself. What did it matter to him what she thought of her sister's behavior? But he could vividly imagine the strain on her pale, fine features. What did she really look like, beneath all those courtly layers of powder? She had surprisingly full lips for such a delicate face, and light brown eyes that could match either dark or blonde hair, as he'd swear her younger sister's hair must be.

When the footman had brought her ladylike refreshments to while away the rehearsal the previous morning, she'd not even noticed, so absorbed had she been in the music. There was true flame inside her, hidden behind her exterior reserve.

"Signor Morelli?" The Prince turned to him. "What think you of the idea?"

"Why, I am always pleased to mask," Carlo said smoothly. "What finer pleasure is there?"

And what better practice for courtly life? Even if there was passion behind Baroness von Steinbeck's own mask, it had naught to do with him, Carlo Morelli, famous virtuoso freak. He bit off the chain of speculation with a poisonous jab. Throughout his career in various courts across Europe, he'd found castrati to be valued as the safest lovers for any noblewoman with a taste for spice and adventure. The Baroness, however, was clearly not a woman who dabbled in flirtation or easy affairs of the heart. Nor had he missed the jolt of shock his voice had given her when they'd met; after marrying young to a rural Protestant landowner, who could fault her for regarding him with outright repulsion?

At any rate, she was back at the palace practicing his accompaniments now. If she played tonight with only the superficial flexibility of any other amateur lady keyboardist, her appeal would vanish at once; if not . . .

He sighed and directed his attention back to the conversation around him. There was no purpose to indulging in flights of fancy.

"So," he asked Edmund Guernsey, smiling. "What will you disguise yourself as, sir? And how does your book progress?"

Charlotte's new maid was small and quiet, with nervous eyes and quick, deft hands. Charlotte was grateful for the girl's silence that evening as she prepared for dinner. She could not have borne empty chatter. All of her concentration was focused on keeping the music of Signor Morelli's accompaniment locked safe within her chest.

It had taken her until three o'clock before she'd felt remotely secure about every part. Now, sitting before her ornate looking glass, all she could see were the chord progressions playing out before her.

She sat through dinner eating mechanically and nodding to the conversation at what she hoped were the right intervals. Again and again, she felt Signor Morelli's dark eyes watching her. Sophie chattered about plans for an upcoming masked ball. Prince Nikolaus thanked Charlotte for the gift of her maid to his opera company. She smiled and murmured something polite. Servants slipped between them to remove the empty plates.

Signor Morelli rose to his feet. Jewels sparkled on his waistcoat tonight, although Charlotte hadn't noticed them until that moment. His eerily high voice silenced the whole table as he spoke to Prince Nikolaus.

"If Your Highness would be so gracious as to allow it, I would be honored to sing to your company tonight."

The Prince's smile was the satisfied grin of a wolf, lips pulled back and eyes gleaming. "The honor is entirely ours, signor."

"Baroness?"

Charlotte nodded and stood up, keeping her expression fixed in a semblance of serenity. She hoped that no one could see her fingers trembling as she preceded Signor Morelli into the next room. As soon as she was safely seated at the clavichord, she hid her traitorous hands in her skirts. Nobles filed into the room, chatting and laughing and darting bright, curious looks at both her and Morelli. Chinese drawings covered the papered walls, framed by scented wood from India. Morelli himself, more exotic than any of the room's rich decorations, stood with one hand resting lightly against the painted nymphs and cupids on the cover of the keyboard, his smooth, feminine face as impassive and remote as a statue.

Charlotte's breath stuttered in her chest.

Stupid, she told herself, flexing her fingers. She'd performed so many times throughout her life, first for her parents' guests and then for her husband's. She'd learned so young to hide her emotions, to subdue her desires beneath those of her family, her husband, her guests. In the long, slow trudge of Ernst's dying, she had sometimes forgotten that she even had any passions or desires to suppress.

Yet in these past few days . . .

She sighed. This was no time for maudlin self-reflection, and she was no romantic *philosophe* in a Parisian salon. Yet in the challenge of Signor Morelli's offer, in the effort of practicing her parts and immersing herself in the music to an extent she hadn't allowed herself in years, she'd felt a part of her spirit stir and begin to wake for the first time in over a decade.

She had never felt so nervous, nor so irrationally certain that so much rested on a single performance, until now.

The Prince seated himself with a flourish in the center of the room. At his nod, two footmen closed the doors, shutting them in. The room fell silent. Signor Morelli met Charlotte's eyes and nodded infinitesimally.

Her hands moved, with a feeling of finality. They rippled through the first arpeggio, formed the leading chord; she watched them as if from a distance. *Too late to turn back.*

And then his voice emerged, and she suddenly had to concentrate after all, had to fight to give her hands and her music the attention they deserved. It took every ounce of willpower in her body to focus on playing the right notes and supporting his dynamics, instead of dropping her hands away from the keyboard to soak in his voice with gape-struck awe.

She'd found his high voice unnerving, and nearly inhuman. But when he sang, his voice was no longer even close to human. It was angelic. It *soared.* It shone against tones no human could possibly hit, and it rang straight through her chest. She forced down tears as she played beside him. She forced her fingers to keep moving.

By the middle of the second piece, her hands were no longer merely following the motions of the music. They were playing, playing with all her might, to try to match him. The listening silence of the room wrapped around the twin instruments of clavichord and heavenly, unnerving, melting voice. No one could exist outside that iridescent bubble. Between each song, applause sounded in the distance. Charlotte barely heard it. She was only waiting for Morelli's nod, to begin the next piece.

At last, his voice peaked high and soft, and faded gradually, lingeringly. Charlotte's fingers breathed faint chords against the keyboard. She met his eyes, waiting, watching for confirmation.

Their two tones vanished at exactly the same moment. Pearl-like silence enveloped the room. Then applause crashed down upon them.

Morelli nodded at Charlotte once, his eyes still wide and dilated, as though he'd been staring into too bright a light. Perhaps he had, Charlotte thought dizzily. Such beauty—how could one man bring forth such unearthly beauty, and not be changed by it each time?

Then he turned to bow, and she realized that the recital was at an end. There was no more music to play.

Charlotte closed her eyes and smoothed out her face, as shivers of reaction rippled through her.

"Lotte!" Sophie was beside her, shaking her shoulder. "Lotte, that was brilliant. Why didn't you stand up and bow too, you ninny?"

Charlotte opened her eyes. The Prince stood between her and Signor Morelli, holding out a pouch that rattled with the heavy clink of gold coins. Noblemen and women swarmed around the two men, all of them waiting for the castrato's attention.

"Lotte?" Sophie asked. "Lotte? Are you listening to me?"

Signor Morelli accepted the pouch with a bow and slipped it into his pocket. The Prince clapped him on the back and turned away. The castrato's gaze met Charlotte's. His face was pale and cold. His eyes . . .

His lips were moving. "Well done," he was saying to her. "Well done."

Then, with a stiff nod, he turned away, until he faced the glowing noblewomen behind him. They seized one arm each and laughed up at him, their bright voices cooing across the room.

Sophie was chirping at her side, her fingers clinging onto Charlotte's shoulder. "Lotte? What's wrong?"

"I have to leave," Charlotte whispered. "I'm sorry, Sophie. I have to . . ."

She stood up awkwardly, abruptly, and swept through the crowd, holding her head high all the way back to her room to keep back the tears that were only waiting to stream down her face and swallow her.

Edmund Guernsey ruffled quickly through the papers on Prince Nikolaus's desk, keeping half his attention on the sounds of the corridor outside. The castrato's recital had begun almost forty minutes ago. Hard to tell how long an evening's concert might last, much less how long it might hold any royal's attention. Prince Nikolaus had a reputation for musical taste, but still . . .

Architectural plans covered the massive desk. More monuments, more rooms to be added to the palace, more grandeur to be added on all sides. Nothing that aided Guernsey in his quest, any more than the masses of jewelry and other trinkets he'd found in Sophie von Höllner's rooms the night before. Piled on the desk, Guernsey found letters from architects and artists; the letter from the Archduke announcing his coming visit; more letters from the Prince's three sons, asking for money . . .

When Guernsey found another sketch in the pile, he barely glanced at it, expecting only another planned structure. But the Latin inscription in the center caught his attention.

It was not a building, but a seal. A newly designed seal—and he recognized the Prince's own strong hand in its design.

Guernsey blinked down at the sketch, caught by curiosity.

Prince Nikolaus expected Empress Maria Theresia and her son to honor him beyond measure, with a new order of knighthood designed himself. What on earth could he think to offer them, to match such wild and unlikely hopes?

Quick footsteps approached in the corridor outside. Guernsey slipped the pile of papers back into place and dived for the servants' door hidden in the gilded walnut paneling. He ducked into the dark corridor and closed the hidden door behind him, just in time. He heard the study door open and close. Footsteps moved toward the desk, and he heard the chair pulled into place.

Guernsey stepped away with a sigh of relief—and heard footsteps coming toward him down the narrow corridor. A servant on his way to bring the Prince refreshments in his study, perhaps. If Guernsey was caught . . .

He flattened himself against the wall. His vision narrowed to a thin line as his heartbeat sped up. Silently, he reached into the inner pocket of his frock coat and withdrew a slim knife.

What he would do with the body . . .

A door clicked open and shut further down the corridor. The sound of footsteps disappeared.

Guernsey let out his held breath and slipped the knife back into his pocket. He was safe.

He hurried back down the long corridor, certainty lightening his steps.

Whatever Prince Nikolaus had found that he hoped would bring him such glory, Guernsey, too, would discover. And when he did it would be King Frederick of Prussia who was the recipient, and Guernsey who would take all the reward for it.

In the depths of night, Franz woke with his face pressed against cold stone. The door to his cell was swinging open.

He pushed himself up to his knees, grimacing at the pain. "Yes?" He peered through the darkness, reaching for the piece of paper tucked inside his filthy shirt. "Is it—?"

"Pichler." Light from a taper illuminated the pinched face of Herr Rahier, the Prince's administrator, looking down at him with distaste. "I bring you better news than you deserve."

"Oh?" Franz squinted against the light and held back the curses that clawed their way up his chest.

Rahier had stood directly by Franz as he was beaten. His face had shown only calm satisfaction when the first screams were torn from Franz's throat.

"It seems that the requirements of the opera company must take precedence over the demands of justice." Rahier's nostrils flared, as though he'd smelled something unpleasant. "His Serene Highness, in his great mercy, has decided to pardon you from the rest of your allotted sentence and allow you to return directly to your work."

"His Highness's mercy is infinite indeed." Franz smiled tightly.

"Well?" Rahier stared down at him. "What more do you wait upon, Herr Pichler? You may rise."

Franz gritted his teeth. He pushed against the cold floor to lever himself up. Flames arced up his back. The thin scabs over his lacerations strained against the movement and ripped open. Franz bit back a moan. He had to pause, kneeling, to catch his breath against the pain. Rahier's satisfaction seemed to ripple through the air around him. *Damn the bastard to Hell and back.*

Once Franz was finally standing, shivering with reaction and propped up against the wall of the cell for support, Rahier sighed and turned away.

"You are free to return to your quarters, Herr Pichler. I hope this unfortunate experience may have taught you some caution and respect for the rules of this estate."

"Rest assured, Herr Rahier, it has entirely transformed my perspective." Franz smiled, thin-lipped, and limped away from the Prince's administrator, out of the dark, cold cell.

The fresh night air bathed his face like cool water when he left the building. The estate of Eszterháza lay spread around him in the glow of the moonlight, beautiful and serene. The palace was a great, dark shape on his left. Still water glimmered in the fountains before him.

He touched his shirt and felt the reassuring crinkle of paper inside. He'd devoured the image that morning as soon as light illuminated his cell, memorizing every arc of ink. *Flame shooting up from a beaker, flanked by two black birds.* It was the symbol of his coming freedom.

He'd spent all day thinking it through. The first thing he would do for himself, before anything else, was to find out who had sent Monsieur Delacroix the note that had implicated him. Then, when he received his first directions from his mysterious new employer, he would follow them to the very letter. And finally . . .

His hand clenched around the hidden paper.

Prince Nikolaus and that sot Delacroix would be humiliated beyond compare.

He turned to take one last look back at the prison, where his life had changed.

Rahier stood watching him, arms crossed. No surprises there. But behind the administrator . . . just behind him, thick gray smoke trickled around the corner of the building. But there was no smell of fire, no flicker of flame, nor—

Franz's chest squeezed tight. For an instant, he could have sworn that he saw two malevolent red eyes flash open within the smoke and glare straight at him.

Rahier turned, following Franz's stare. His gaze passed over the smoke without interest. He shrugged and turned back to frown at Franz.

Franz shivered. No wonder his imagination was conjuring apparitions, after nearly two days of hell. Now that he was standing still, the agony in his bleeding back had returned in full measure. He turned and limped away, toward the palace and the musicians' quarters beyond.

ACT TWO

Chapter Nine

All through Sunday night, Anna dreamed of disasters. She dreamed that her voice broke in front of Herr Haydn. She dreamed that she was running to attend her first rehearsal, but when she arrived she found the opera stage empty. Then the Baroness appeared and looked at her with dismay and pity. *"No, Anna, you were never chosen. Why would anyone want to hear you sing?"*

She dreamed of a sliding, slippery noise behind her, hot breath on the back of her neck, and bloodstains spattering onto the floor beside her feet.

She woke at first light, as always. Her cot felt different. She sat up, and her whole body thrilled with recognition.

It hadn't been her imagination, after all. She sat in a room—a whole room!—of her own, with a window that looked out onto the grass. She'd moved from the servants' wing of the palace to the musicians' quarters, in a building of their own. She was a singer now and a maidservant no more. Beside that miracle, any memories of blood and imagined danger faded to the unreality of a wild and unlikely dream. She'd never even hoped to be so lucky as this!

The musicians ate breakfast in their own house at eight, at a meal prepared by their own cook. Sitting in the dining hall, Anna watched the yawns of the others with wonder. How could they be tired, when they'd slept so late? She ate by herself, brimming with excitement. On Saturday, after her introduction to the company, Herr Haydn had sent her to the Prince's administrator, Herr Rahier, and the formalities had taken nearly all day. She had moved into the music house on Sunday morning, but the singers had not rehearsed that day. This was to be her first working morning. She could barely eat for excitement.

When it was time to leave for the rehearsal, though, all of her dreams rose up again to haunt her. She walked slowly, letting the other singers pass her. Every one of their glances felt like a brand against her skin. Who was she, to claim to be one of them?

She froze just before the stage door, unable to move. She still had time. She could turn around and run to the Baroness, beg to be taken back . . .

But a handsome, angry-looking man walked up behind her, and she had to step through the door and onto the stage, if only to let him through.

The rest of the company was already assembled. Herr Haydn was missing, but the intimidating theatrical director, Monsieur Delacroix, stood haranguing two actors at the far side of the stage. They all turned to stare as the door fell closed behind Anna and the stranger.

Heavy wooden and metal stage machinery hung thirty feet above Anna's head, concealed from the audience by deep red and gold curtains. Herr Haydn had shown it to her on Saturday, and explained how, properly operated, it would carry actors high into the air, like gods ascending. If it fell on Anna, though, it would crush her.

Under the stares of the other actors, she suddenly desperately wished that it might.

"Well, well," Madame Zelinowsky purred. "So the prodigal returns."

"I . . ." Anna began.

The stranger stepped past her. Something was dreadfully wrong with his back; he held it at a sharp angle, like an unbalanced marionette puppet.

"And a good morning to you all." He half-bowed, stiffly. "Thank you kindly for your welcome."

Monsieur Delacroix's cheeks flamed red as he stepped forward. "Seven days! *Seven* days, the sentence was, and not—"

"His Serene Highness displayed ineffable mercy in allowing me to leave after only two days," said the stranger. Anna wished she could see his face, rather than the back of his smooth queue of powdered hair. His voice gave none of his emotions away. "A pity, I agree, but it cannot be helped. What piece do we rehearse today?"

Delacroix's eyes looked ready to pop. "You are insufferable! If you think, sirrah, that I will allow you—"

The opposite door burst open. Herr Haydn strode in, rubbing his hands together. "Good, good, everyone is here. Herr Pichler, we are all so very pleased to have you back."

"Thank you, Kapellmeister." There was no veiled mockery in Herr Pichler's voice now. "I know it must have been your intercession that—"

"Shush!" Herr Haydn's gaze darted to Delacroix and back. "Nonsense, my boy. This company is in sad need of you. You've heard the tragic news?"

"No . . ." Pichler's head turned. His searching gaze passed over Anna without interest.

"I'm afraid Madame Delacroix and Herr Antonicek will not be returning to us. They were"—the kapellmeister paused—"set upon by brigands, three nights hence."

Madame Zelinowsky tsk'd softly. "Brigands, Herr Kapellmeister? The evidence—"

"—Is inconclusive, dear lady, as we know. Regardless, it is a melancholy loss to all of us." Herr Haydn turned back to Pichler's rigid figure. "I am so sorry, Herr Pichler, to spring such distressing news upon you. Still, you see now how welcome your return truly is. You have been promoted to first tenor, and Frau Kettner to leading lady."

"And the other parts?" Pichler's voice sounded hoarse.

"Herr Hofner shall double as second tenor along with his usual roles, for the moment. As for a second soprano . . ." He gestured. "Anna, my dear? Let me introduce you to Franz Pichler, a most highly valued member of our company. Herr Pichler, may I present Fräulein Dommayer? Discovering her lovely voice was a most fortunate stroke of luck for all of us."

Anna smiled uncomfortably and bobbed a curtsey, ducking her head. One of the other women snickered. Were actresses not meant to curtsey? Herr Pichler's eyes were clear and cold, lost in his own inner thoughts. His nod to her was the slightest fraction of a movement.

"Now, then." The kapellmeister drew in the assembled company with his smile. "Everyone still has their parts from Saturday, yes? My new opera proceeds apace, but in the meantime, His Highness has requested a special performance tomorrow of an old comedy favorite, to lighten the mood of his guests. Of course, most of you already know this little piece by Signor Piccini . . ."

He began to pass out parts, chatting casually with each singer as he assigned the roles. Anna's chest tightened as he walked closer. She wanted to turn and run. Her feet had turned into lead.

"And our little Anna! You, my dear, shall play Carolina, the romantic younger sister. The role should be perfect for your voice, so . . ." He stopped, the music still held in midair between them. "My dear, this music is for you. Why don't you take it?"

Anna half-whispered her words. "I cannot read it, sir."

"Cannot *read*—" He caught himself in mid-sentence and lowered his voice. "Cannot read music?" he finished in a murmur.

Too late, Anna thought. Now every eye was fixed avidly upon her.

"I can read and write German," she said stiffly. "The Baroness taught me years ago. But I never learned to read musical notes."

"No? No, of course not. I should have considered." The kapellmeister chewed at his bottom lip. "It is a problem, there is no doubt of that."

Anna lowered her gaze. Whispers filled her ears, along with the sounds of stifled laughter. The skirt of her dress—her new apple-green and red dress, issued yesterday from the housekeeping office to mark her change in status—seemed as distant as the moon from her blurring vision. "Shall I leave?"

"What?"

"I said, shall I leave, sir?" She lifted her chin and met his gaze. "I can tell the Baroness that you don't require my services after all."

"My dear girl, don't be absurd!" The kapellmeister gave a hearty laugh that rang only slightly false. "We certainly won't let that one little hiccup prevent us from making use of you. No, no, no. For now . . . for now, we'll simply have to make do. You can learn music by ear, that's clear enough. So before each of your pieces, I'll play you the tune, and you may sing it after me until you know it."

In front of everyone? Anna thought. But she only nodded. She didn't trust herself to speak, under so many derisive stares.

"This afternoon, and every afternoon, I'll give you an hour or two of tutoring. In the meantime—Herr Pichler?"

The actor started, interrupted from some private reverie. "Sir?"

"How fares your back, my boy? I daresay you could do with sitting down, eh?"

Herr Pichler's cheeks reddened. "Aye, sir. But it will not prevent me singing."

"No, no, of course not. But could we prevail upon you to give Fräulein Dommayer a bit of musical assistance? She is in desperate need of a quick lesson or two in reading written music."

"Oh." The young man's eyes flickered with momentary curiosity as he glanced at Anna. "I suppose so, sir."

"Excellent. Then why don't you and she go sit together back-stage. You'll find paper and pens over there . . ." Herr Haydn waved vaguely and smiled as he turned away. "I'll call you in when your voices are needed."

Anna curtseyed to Herr Haydn and walked backstage, face burning. As the door fell closed behind her, she heard laughter burst out from the entire company.

Herr Haydn's voice rose in entreaty and command to silence them. Anna tightened her hands into fists. She would not run away, nor weep in front of them. She would not disgrace herself or the Baroness's faith in her.

Herr Pichler walked through the door after her, holding a sheaf of manuscript paper, a quill pen, and a bottle of ink. His gaze was shuttered and impossible to read as he pulled out a chair from the wall and sat down.

Anna set out her own chair and folded her hands on her lap. She looked at him expectantly.

Through the thin wall, she heard a soprano and a bass voice begin to sing, imitating each other's parts comically. She needed no understanding of Italian to know that they were trading insults.

Herr Pichler cleared his throat. "What the kapellmeister told me . . . about Herr Antonicek and Madame Delacroix . . ."

Anna blinked. "Yes?"

He sat forward but did not meet her eyes. "Why did Madame Zelinowsky disagree with him? Why did she say it had not been brigands?"

Anna saw again the scattering of bloodstains on the wooden floor.
"Old Ordog tears his victims into twenty pieces, and then . . ."
Her throat tightened as she felt, again, the scream that had built up
in her chest. And then the voices behind the door . . .

"I can't!"

"Pardon?" Herr Pichler stared at her.

Anna swallowed. "I mean . . . I cannot tell you that. Because I don't
know." She wouldn't think about such horrors. Couldn't, else she'd lose
the courage she needed to carry her through today and through her new
life. She couldn't have fled Eszterháza anyway, not when the Baroness
planned to stay a full year. What was the purpose in tormenting herself
needlessly?

"Forgive me," she said to Herr Pichler. "Perhaps you should ask
Madame Zelinowsky herself what she meant."

"Perhaps I shall." He frowned at her. "Why can't you read music?
Who taught you to sing and neglected that aspect?"

"No one. I was a lady's maid until yesterday." She glared at him.
"How did you injure your back?"

"I was flogged by the Prince's orders, two days ago." He glared back
at her.

Through the walls, the duet built to a climax and then closed, with
a smattering of laughter and applause. *Perhaps we're next*, Anna thought.
Her stomach clenched.

"We might as well begin," Herr Pichler said, as the applause came to
an end. "For all the good that it may do us."

They were called in half an hour later. By then, Anna's head was whirling
with incomprehension and panic. She could almost see how the system
functioned—almost—but still the black dots refused to sort themselves
into melodies before her eyes. She felt sick with frustration as she walked
back onto the stage. The other singers dropped back, leaving her alone
in the center, underneath the extravagantly frescoed, rounded ceiling.

For all the depth of the wooden stage, it felt tiny—and she smaller yet—facing out into the grand auditorium with all its marble pillars, tiers, and galleries.

A door opened offstage, and an officer of the Prince's bodyguard sidled in, smiling sheepishly. Anna recognized him from the day before—Frau von Höllner's husband. She bit her lip in vexation as he settled into a seat in the back of the audience. She did not, not, *not* want an audience for this first attempt!

"Ah, Anna. Now listen carefully, my dear." Herr Haydn smiled up at her from his seat at the harpsichord beneath the stage and turned the pages of his score with a flourish. "In this song, your character, Carolina, is telling her older sister all about the romantic stranger she's glimpsed from her window—without, of course, having any idea that the stranger is in fact her sister's secret lover! Let us begin."

Anna listened as hard as she could, while she felt the others watching her. She held the music in her memory, she sang it back—

"No, no, *no*, Anna, no! What you're singing is gibberish, child—those aren't even real words!"

"I don't speak Italian," Anna said flatly. She hid her clenched fists in her skirts.

Behind her, she heard a woman's clear whisper: "Is anyone surprised by that?"

"Let us begin again." The kapellmeister gave a strained smile and played the opening chords. "Listening to the *words*, this time . . ."

The next hour-and-a-half was sheer torture. Every infinitesimal sound mattered, according to Herr Haydn—every incomprehensible syllable had to be correct—and the amusement of the other singers grew with every tiny misstep. From Anna's aria, they moved on to a duet with the leading lady, Frau Kettner, who tittered at every mistake Anna made. Then Madame Zelinowsky joined them for a trio.

By the end of it all, Anna was drenched in sweat. Her head felt as if it were filled with buzzing insects. So much to remember—so impossibly many syllables to hold straight—and all for tomorrow night's performance . . .

"We'll have Herr Pichler and Frau Kettner together, now," Herr Haydn said.

Anna staggered off to the side of the stage, where her legs gave way. She sat down in a heap, uncaring of what the others might think.

Madame Zelinowsky sat down beside her, smoothing down her own skirts carefully. "You aren't doing so badly, you know."

Anna snorted. She didn't look up.

"No, I really am serious. Of course it is clear—it's *very* clear indeed—that you've never acted before, nor heard Italian spoken. But what of it? We were all beginners, once."

"But you can read music," Anna muttered.

"Now, yes. And you will, too. You do have a lovely voice."

"Thank you." Anna looked up at the older woman and attempted a smile. "You do, too," she offered.

"I? No, dear, I don't. There are actresses who sing and singers who act. I am very much the former—and you, I suspect, will always be the latter. It matters very little, in terms of success, so long as you do one or the other well. And of course . . ." Madame Zelinowsky smiled slowly and tilted her head toward the audience. "You can advance your own career very easily, with only the most minimal of acting skills."

"How do you mean?"

"Didn't you hear that boy yesterday, arguing with his wife? 'Interested in actresses,' he said."

"But—"

"Oh, I'm not suggesting him for you, my dear. But you're young, you're reasonably pretty, and I'm only offering you a word or two of friendly advice. Should you desire a secure and fortunate future, you might keep an eye out for young noblemen such as him, but with rather more disposable income and influence. Who knows?" Madame Zelinowsky tilted her head closer. "The Archduke is arriving here in just six days, and I hear he won't be bringing his wife. Should he take a fancy to you . . ."

Anna's throat was dry. "I'm only here to sing, madam."

"Of course you are, dear. But it's never a bad idea to have supplementary plans for your career, is it?" Madame Zelinowsky stood up, uncoiling herself. "Ah, I'm not as young as you are. My muscles do ache when I sit too long."

"Madame Zelinowsky?" Anna looked up at the other woman's satisfied smile. "Why did you tell me such things?"

"Why, I'm only trying to be helpful, dear. We ladies should always help one another succeed, don't you think?" Her smile widened. "Oh, look. Our little officer has ordered refreshments. Do you think he might offer us some if we ask him nicely?"

Anna looked out into the audience. Lieutenant von Höllner was eagerly scooping food off a tray carried by a familiar figure. *Erzebet.* Anna felt her own face light up. At last, someone familiar! Anna caught the maid's eye, beaming—and Erzebet's face went blank. She ducked her head down, turned away, and walked stiffly out of the room.

"Well, dear?" Madame Zelinowsky asked. "Will you join me in charming a few refreshments out of that pretty boy in uniform?"

"No, thank you," Anna said, as the door closed behind Erzebet's rigid back. Tears prickled against her eyelids. She blinked hard to hold them back. Maidservant no longer, true enough . . . but where did she fit now? And what would she become?

"As you wish." Madame Zelinowsky shrugged gracefully and descended into the audience.

Anna looked away, toward the center of the stage, and caught Herr Pichler staring after the other woman with narrow, suspicious eyes. As soon as he realized Anna was watching him, his face cleared into bland uninterest.

They all have secrets, Anna thought wearily. She closed her eyes and focused on the music of the three songs she'd just learned, trying to push away the image of Erzebet's face and the expression it had worn as she'd looked at Anna sitting onstage in her new dress.

Chapter Ten

Charlotte was practicing one of Herr Haydn's keyboard sonatas when a knock sounded on the outer door of her chambers. An unfamiliar maid entered and curtseyed deeply.

"Her Serene Highness wishes me to ask, Baroness, if you would be so kind as to join her in her apartments for light refreshments."

"Her Serene—? *Oh.*" *The Princess.* Charlotte's hands stilled. "Now?"

"Yes, madam, if it pleases you."

How could it? Charlotte thought. To speak lightly with the wife of her sister's lover—to feel the weight of that pain and cold dignity . . .

She stood up. "I would be delighted, of course." What else could she say?

She followed the maid down the staircase to the first floor and along a long corridor to an ornately gilded door. The maid knocked as she opened it, to the sound of a Clementi keyboard sonata.

Sunlight filled the room, streaming in through large, arched windows to light up the deep gold of the seat cushions on the circle of chairs in the center of the room and the shining gold inlay that raced in flowering patterns across the white walls. A gilded gold-and-white clock sat on the marble mantelpiece of the fireplace across the room, inset with a reclining, melancholy muse. The light, gallant keyboard music came from behind Charlotte and to her left, but she sank into a deep curtsey without looking for its source.

"Baroness." Sitting in a high-backed chair in the center of the room, the Princess looked up from a sheaf of papers and smiled enigmatically. At her nod, the music cut off, and the little dog on her lap hopped off to crawl beneath her chair.

"Your Highness."

"Please do sit." The Princess set her sheaf of papers down on a little bureau inlaid in twining golden vines. She gestured toward the empty chair across from her. "My maids will bring refreshments."

"Thank you, Your Highness." Charlotte rose, and instinctively looked back to the source of the music. The clavichord itself was elegant but not unusual. But the sight of the clavichord's player stopped her breath for an instant of shock.

"Asa and Jean, you may join us." The Princess nodded at the clavichord, and a small woman slid down from the stool. She stood no higher than Charlotte's waist. "Baroness von Steinbeck, let me introduce you to Asa"—she nodded to the woman—"and to Monsieur Jean." A man the same size stepped out from behind the clavichord and bowed to Charlotte. "They are my companions here at Eszterháza, during the long summer months."

Charlotte nodded to them as she sat, sinking down into the deep golden cushion of her chair. They scrambled up onto their own chairs with agility, and Charlotte fought to keep her confusion from her face. They were the size of children, no more, yet they looked at her with measuring eyes from fully adult faces. She had never seen their like. And these were the Princess's sole companions in this palace full of elegant courtiers? The more Charlotte knew of the Princess, the less she understood her.

"I'm pleased to meet you both," Charlotte murmured.

A maid offered her a miniature cup of dark coffee, and she accepted it gratefully.

"Asa and Jean both sing, draw, and play the piano beautifully," the Princess said. "As, I understand, do you. I've heard excellent reports of your performance last night."

Charlotte's fingers tightened around her fragile cup. "The excellence resided all in Signor Morelli, Highness, rather than in any efforts of mine. I am a mere amateur."

"As are we all, of course. What else were any of us trained to be, from birth?" The Princess regarded her with piercing eyes. "Yet I would wager that your efforts were slightly more than amateur, Baroness. You do not strike me as one who would take any responsibility lightly."

Charlotte blinked. "Thank you, Your Highness."

"You need not thank me. I'm well aware of how uncomfortable that trait must prove for you, often enough. It would be far easier for you to follow your younger sister's path and not allow yourself the trouble of uncomfortable recollections or self-doubts."

Charlotte set down her cup. "I am very grateful to my sister, madam."

"Indeed. Without her invitation, you would still be—where?"

"In Saxony, Your Highness. At my late husband's country estate."

"Mm. Sequestered away among the relics. And what age were you when they married you off, Baroness?"

"Eighteen." Charlotte traced the gilded rim of the china cup with one finger. Looking at the pattern on the cup meant that she did not have to meet the Princess's eyes.

"I was nineteen, myself. I found the idea quite romantic at the time— naïve of me, I know, but then, I was young. I imagined myself most fortunate to have been chosen for a husband near my own age, with all the attractions of handsome looks, power, and brilliance to recommend him. You might not realize it now, Baroness, but in his youth my husband was a strikingly attractive man."

"He still is, Your Highness."

"Indeed. Gentlemen of a certain station often do retain all their attractions, even for much younger ladies, do they not? It is only we ladies who fade away and lose our charms . . . at least, in their eyes."

Charlotte met the Princess's cold gaze. The older woman must have shared something like Sophie's soft blonde beauty when she was younger, Charlotte thought. Now, though, the marks of character and intelligence had formed something deeper in her face—a gravity that went beyond mere beauty.

"I cannot see any loss of charms in you, Your Highness," Charlotte said sincerely.

Neither of the Princess's companions spoke, but Charlotte saw Asa shift in her seat, eyebrows rising skeptically. On the Princess's other side, Jean gave Charlotte a sunny smile that was not quite enough to hide the calculation in his gaze.

Notes, she was unhappily certain, were being taken by both of them for a careful dissection afterward.

The Princess herself only snorted. "Ha. And your husband? What did you think of him, when first married?"

It was an impertinent question. Yet Charlotte found herself answering it. "I was . . . frightened, at first. Saxony felt very far away from home, and the von Steinbeck estate is quite rural. Very far away from civilization."

The Princess's lips twisted. "That I can well understand. And your husband himself?"

Charlotte picked up the coffee cup. Its warmth felt reassuring against her fingers. "Ernst was five-and-sixty to my eighteen, Your Highness. But he was everything that was kind and good."

"And did he give you children, waiting for you now in Saxony?"

Charlotte stiffened. "His health was never good. By the second year of marriage, I was his nurse."

"I see." The Princess regarded her for a moment in silence. "Tell me, Baroness, do you purpose to marry again?"

Charlotte lifted the coffee to her lips to hide her expression. "I am but four months widowed, Your Highness. I hardly think—"

"Regardless. Do you long to reenter that happy state, once your year of mourning is over?"

Charlotte looked into the dark depths of the coffee. "My parents would certainly expect me to, to extend our family's connections."

"And you?"

"I cannot say." Charlotte smiled thinly at the Princess and shrugged. "I cannot tell you any plainer than that. I would not . . . seek out a second marriage, I think. Not of my own accord."

She tried to imagine, for a moment, the idea of a second wedding. The long walk down the aisle of the *Michaelerkirche* in Vienna, the pews filled with the cream of Austrian society, and at the altar . . .

Her stomach clenched. She emptied the rest of the coffee in one hot gulp.

No matter what lay in her future, *that* vision could never prove correct.

"In my first fifteen years of marriage, I would not have understood you," said the Princess. "Now, though . . ." She glanced down at the woman beside her, and Asa nodded in silent approval as she continued. "I would advise you, if possible, to avoid the wedded state entirely. Do not lightly surrender the power you hold within your own hands as a titled widow with an independent fortune. He did leave you a fortune, I assume?"

"Not a great fortune, Your Highness. His sons retained the estate and the majority of the revenues. But I am left with a comfortable annuity." Charlotte spoke quickly, hardly listening to her own words. Mad though it was, she found herself hoping that neither of the Princess's watchful companions could guess at the nature of her thoughts just now.

"Well, then." The Princess nodded gravely, recalling Charlotte to the conversation. "You are, what, thirty?—and with your life ahead of you. I would not anchor myself again, in your situation."

"I thank you for your advice." Charlotte took a sweet from the tray held out to her, and firmly dismissed the image of Signor Morelli's smooth, disconcertingly feminine face. She turned the sweet thoughtfully between her fingers. "May I ask . . ." She gathered her courage. "May I ask, Your Highness, why you invited me here today? In truth, I would not have expected a welcome here."

"What, only because your sister is my husband's whore? No, no, sit—sit *down*, Baroness! I am telling you the truth, as you asked for it."

Ice dripped off the Princess's voice, as her two companions' faces went studiously blank. Asa looked down at her hands discreetly, while Jean turned his gaze to the ceiling.

"We are both reasonable women, capable of recognizing an adult truth. I do not blame that foolish girl for her position here. Had it not been her, it would surely have been another. My husband has built himself a grand new Versailles, and he requires a beautiful young queen to reign by his side, as evidence to all of his continued virility. What are the demands of propriety beside such need?"

And is propriety all that ever held your marriage together? Charlotte wondered, looking at the bitter twist of the Princess's mouth. *Oh, Your High-*

ness, I do not believe that for a moment. She sank back into her own chair, swallowing hard.

"Good." The Princess nodded. "Now, then. I do not blame you for your sister's misdemeanors, much less for those of my husband. Particularly as I've heard reports that you show no great fondness for their situation, either."

"You must have . . . excellent information." Charlotte's throat felt dry. How many of the servants in this palace reported to the Princess? And how closely must they observe?

"Of course I do. I may be invisible to the majority of those resident here, but that does not render me blind. I know everything that happens in this palace." The Princess leaned forward, holding Charlotte's gaze. "It is out of friendship that I would issue you this warning, Baroness. There are more guests in this palace than you are aware."

"Pardon?" Charlotte blinked. "I don't understand."

"There is trouble brewing in this palace, far beyond any mere indiscretions of the body." The Princess's eyes were icy blue. On either side, her companions were studying Charlotte openly now, their own gazes intent. "If you have anywhere else to go, Baroness, I would strongly advise you to leave as soon as possible. Eszterháza may not long be safe."

Charlotte stared at her. "I've promised my sister a long visit," she said. "I could hardly leave in under a year. Not without an explicit reason."

"So be it." The Princess leaned back in her chair. "I'd expected as much, but I thought it only fair to warn you."

Asa looked primly satisfied; Jean's lips pursed in what looked like regret.

Charlotte lifted her empty cup to her mouth. The thin china felt cold against her skin, but it was her only protection from the three probing gazes fixed upon her. "Could . . . could you possibly explain a bit more to me, Your Highness? I should like to understand what you meant."

"That, I regret, I cannot do. But if you will insist on remaining here despite my warning, may I ask you to join me now and then for refreshments and conversation?" The Princess nodded at the grandly laid-out white and gold room around her and her two silent, watchful companions. "I've seen fit, as you may see, to allow my own ladies-in-waiting the freedom of my husband's court. It is no great act of mercy to rid oneself of mindless chatter. Intelligent company and conversation, however, would be most welcome."

"Thank you, Your Highness. I would be honored."

"Excellent." The Princess set down her own coffee cup and picked up the sheaf of papers from the bureau. "Let me show you what I have been studying. My husband chooses to indulge me in this one matter, as he will not allow me my true desire, to live away from Eszterháza while he resides here. These are my plans for a small menagerie . . ."

Charlotte stayed another half an hour, looking at the plans and chatting with the Princess about light topics that held no real interest for her—nor, she suspected, for her hostess. When she finally took her leave, the little dog jumped back up onto the Princess's lap, and the Princess's two companions nodded a grave farewell. As a maid closed the door behind her, Charlotte heard three voices finally mingle together in a calm murmur of discussion.

Undoubtedly, her judgment was being pronounced.

The door shut, and Charlotte stopped to collect herself in the silent corridor. She realized that her heartbeat was racing. There had been undercurrents to the Princess's every word. Of that, she was certain. Yet, what any of them had meant—or for what purpose she had just been measured by the Princess's two companions . . . *that*, now, she could hardly dare even to guess.

The sound of the clavichord began again behind the closed door. Charlotte took a deep breath and set off to find her way back to her own room, to gather her thoughts before she went down to dinner and to Sophie.

And this time, she wished for no observers.

No chanting sounded through the panels of the door. Within the room, the alchemist slept, head flat against his arms on the table piled with ancient books and papers. Inside a lantern on the table, dense gray smoke coiled and uncoiled itself. Strains of military music floated into the room through the cloth-covered window. A single stream of sunlight entered through a tear in the cloth and shot in a straight line to the corner of the table, setting the motes of dust aglow.

Quick footsteps sounded in the corridor outside. The smoke twitched within the lantern. A hard knock rapped against the door, and the alchemist jerked up, coughing. Within the lantern, two red eyes flashed open.

The alchemist staggered to his feet, still half-asleep. He smoothed down his dark hair as he crossed the room, and paused a moment at the door to clear his throat. His shoulders straightened as he turned the key in the door.

"At last!" Prince Nikolaus strode in, without sparing the alchemist a glance. His hungry gaze went straight to the table and to the lantern set atop it. "So here he is, eh?"

"Yes, Your Highness. At your service." The alchemist's voice rolled out, deep and compelling. "I trust you are satisfied with his work so far?"

The Prince snorted. "Satisfied? *Agape*, more like. Astonished and very, very pleased." He shook his head as he looked at the roiling mass within the lantern. "That such a creature can be contained within so small a space . . ."

"These elementals follow their own rules of matter, Your Highness."

"And *your* rules, eh, Radamowsky? At least, I trust so."

"Indeed." The alchemist smiled tightly. "You may trust wholeheartedly in that, Your Highness. After all, he fulfilled last night's experiment, did he not?"

"So Rahier told me. He said he watched the creature float straight past him, mild as a lamb."

"Quite." The alchemist pinched his lips together and shuttered his gaze.

The Prince's own gaze never wavered from the bright red eyes of the elemental. "Impressive indeed, my dear Count. And you're certain that it will be ready on time? We only have seven days, remember."

"Trust me, Your Highness." The alchemist bowed his head. "It shall succeed beyond your wildest expectations."

Chapter Eleven

Musket fire exploded across the stage. Smoke obscured the painted walls. Soldiers attacked and fell back, screaming.

A full mock-battle on the stage of the opera house . . . Carlo turned to look at the man who had ordered this. Prince Nikolaus sat still as he watched the battle, but his eyes darted back and forth, following every move. His mouth was set in a satisfied smile. *And why not?* Carlo thought. The seats in the audience around them were filled with noblemen shouting their partisanship for one side or another, while the ladies watched with a silent interest that was yet as fierce, clutching their fans in white-knuckled grips. How better, indeed, to distract a court from the threat of violence and death than by staging a true war? *Death as theater.*

Two soldiers crumpled and fell to the stage. Carlo blinked and glanced covertly at the Prince. He *hoped* that it was only theater . . .

The blue-coated army swept forward, overwhelming the red coats. The victorious commander leapt to the top of his enemy's cannon and raised his bayonet high.

"Esterházy triumphant!" he roared, and his soldiers roared it after him.

Cheers rocketed off the walls of the theater. They only died down when Prince Nikolaus finally rose, holding up his hands for silence.

"Let the commander accept the reward for his troops!"

The young commander saluted and jumped off the cannon. He ran nimbly between the rows of chairs, up the steps to the balcony, and into the royal box at its center. Then, with a flourish, he dropped down to kneel before his ruler. "Your Highness."

"Madam?" Prince Nikolaus stepped back and gestured for Frau von Höllner to take his place.

She did so, beaming, and held out a wreath. "The laurels of victory are yours, Commander." She laid the wreath atop his powdered head and stepped back, jewels sparkling and tall feathers bouncing in her ornately curled and piled, powdered hair.

"The laurels of victory are sweet indeed, but not so sweet as the fruits of loyalty." The young man took off the wreath and held it out to the Prince. "My rewards are yours, Your Highness, just as my life, loyalty, and service belong to your house forever."

Polite applause filled the opera house as the Prince accepted the wreath. *A pretty piece of theater*, Carlo thought, as he watched the Prince lift the young soldier to his feet. There was something about the way the two grinned at each other . . . *Aha*.

"A worthy answer indeed, Lieutenant Esterházy." The Prince slapped him on the shoulder and passed him a bulging velvet purse. Under cover of the applause, he added more softly, "Well done, Anton."

"I thank you, Cousin." The young man grinned and pocketed the purse.

He saluted smartly and ran back down to the stage to march out briskly with the rest of the soldiers, while servants hastened to clear the debris and prepare for the upcoming opera performance. Carlo was relieved to see the fallen soldiers picking themselves up and laughing as they marched out with their companions. So, not everything was subordinate to the Esterházy quest for glory . . .

"What thought you all of our little play?" The Prince turned to the seats around him.

Baroness von Steinbeck's cheeks were flushed and her light brown eyes glowing with pleasure. "Most impressive, Your Highness," she murmured.

Guernsey stared at her. The little man had been offered the rare honor of a seat in the Prince's royal box for this night's entertainment, and he looked near to expiration from sheer awe. "Impressive? It was astounding! Magnificent! I've seen nothing like it! I shall write of nothing else in my book, Your Highness. I am overwhelmed!"

Prince Nikolaus nodded graciously. "I shall look forward to reading your descriptions, Mr. Guernsey."

"Indeed," Carlo seconded blandly. "I can hardly wait to see them published." *Now that would be a wonder, indeed.* He turned to the Prince. "Did the soldiers require much rehearsal for tonight's performance, Your Highness?"

"None at all. They practice such maneuvers every day." The Prince chuckled. "I believe an opportunity such as tonight is their greatest pleasure, short of a true battle."

"I'm certain they would prove themselves anywhere!" Guernsey's eyes shone. "How many troops could you summon, if the Empress and the Emperor asked it of you?"

Giving away your game plan, eh, Guernsey? Carlo sighed and looked away as the little man drew the Prince into a discourse on troop numbers, strength, and deposition. No doubt the spy knew better than to take all of the Prince's boasts for literal truth, to be reported back to his master. When it came time to summon up troops for another Habsburg war, Carlo suspected there would be favors bought back and forth between Esterházy and his rulers, and a canny balancing of pride with economy.

He turned his gaze to Baroness von Steinbeck. Now that the pageant was over, her expression had turned inward and grave once more, her eyes downcast. Her powdered hair was dressed high and smooth, curled only at the back, with no ornamentation but a single black ribbon above the curls. Her fingers pleated and unpleated a fold of her black silk skirts.

She had barely spoken to him in the past two days, since their recital. He had intentionally refrained from speaking to her. Yet he had felt her gaze upon him often. His eyes seemed drawn to her with an irritatingly mesmeric force. Worse yet were the emotions that she inspired. Why should he feel concern when she looked abstracted and melancholy? What matter was that, to him?

He expelled a sigh and gave in. "Does something worry you, Baroness?" he asked softly, as the others conversed.

Her brown eyes flashed up to meet his. "Oh . . . no, I thank you. It's nothing." Her lips curved into a rueful half-smile. "I fear I grow nervous and maudlin, in my age."

"Really?" He arched an eyebrow. "I've felt that tendency in myself, of late. What were you musing over?"

"Those soldiers." She shook her head. "Nonsensical, I know. They play at war, and it is glorious to see . . . but for some of them, like those poor singers three nights ago, it will be nothing like a game. And I was warned . . . no." She laughed, although it sounded forced. "Never mind my wanderings! You see, signor, I am in truth unbearably morbid in my private thoughts."

"I would not describe you so." He took a breath. "I don't believe I ever thanked you for your accompaniment of my singing, madam. I was most grateful."

"To me?" She shook her head. "Signor, I was honored to be included in such a performance. It was truly heavenly."

Her light brown eyes looked straight into his. Carlo found himself unable to look away. Her cheeks colored as their gazes held.

"Heavenly," Carlo repeated softly.

Her chest rose and fell, but the laugh she gave sounded almost breathless. "So . . . you were not too misled by the effusions of my old music master, after all?"

Carlo raised a hand to discreetly wipe a bead of sweat from his neck. "On the contrary, madam. Should I ever have the pleasure of meeting him, I will compliment him on his acumen."

"Lotte!" Frau von Höllner turned from the others to summon her sister's attention. "We are making plans for Saturday night's ball!"

The moment was broken. Baroness von Steinbeck turned to listen to her sister, and Carlo leaned back in his seat, fighting to maintain a composed expression.

The court of Eszterháza proved far more dangerous than he'd expected. There were some dangers, though, that he knew better than to court. From this moment onward, he would avoid intimate conversations with Baroness von Steinbeck at all costs.

He'd reached six-and-thirty years on his last birthday. He might well be growing maudlin, but no one could accuse the foremost musico in Europe of being a fool.

Backstage, Anna was shaking as she leaned against the thin wooden wall. A jumble of music and phrases ran meaninglessly through her head. The singers around her paced up and down, whispering lines to themselves and gesturing sweepingly. Spirit lamps had been carefully placed at each wing of the stage to send hot beams through the air and illuminate the coming performance. Anna couldn't even make herself move. Would they have to carry her onstage?

An unfamiliar footman walked past her to carry a sealed note to Franz Pichler. The singer paused in his pacing to rip it open. Anna watched, caught by the fierce satisfaction that lit his face. A smaller, separately-sealed note sat inside the first; Herr Pichler slipped the enclosed note inside his waistcoat, unread, as his gaze ran across the larger, open message.

"Beginning positions!"

Monsieur Delacroix clapped for their attention. A sudden hush in the audience preceded a round of applause. Herr Haydn and his musicians must be filing into the orchestra's benches.

"Pichler and Kettner, ready yourselves!" Delacroix shot a look of pure loathing at the younger man as the orchestra struck up the overture's first chord.

Herr Pichler stepped up to Frau Kettner, his face turning pale and set as he straightened his injured back. With his movement, the unsealed piece of paper slipped out of his wide, ruffled sleeve and fell to the floor.

Delacroix turned, frowning. He leaned over to pick it up—but Anna darted forward and snatched it first. It had fallen partially open on the floor.

She folded it before whispering, "Herr Pichler? This is yours, I think."

His eyes flared open in shock as he turned and saw what she held out to him. He snatched it roughly from her hands and tucked it into a pocket. The music sounded his cue, and he strode onstage without a backward look.

Anna glared after him. Would it have injured his precious dignity to give her simple thanks?

"The man is a scoundrel," Delacroix hissed. He spared Anna a sour look. "Did you happen to see, Fräulein Dommayer, what that note said?"

"I would never read another's correspondence, monsieur," Anna said primly.

She wouldn't, truly. At least, not by intention. The first line of the message had meant nothing to her, anyway.

We are most pleased by your release. Your first instructions . . . The rest had been maddeningly hidden by the folds of the paper.

Anna lowered her gaze demurely and stepped away from the theatrical director, leaving him to simmer.

Who was sending Herr Pichler instructions? And for what purpose?

But the opening duet came to an end far too soon, and then it was her turn to walk past the hot spirit lamps, onto the stage.

Charlotte leaned forward in her seat to watch as Anna walked onstage.

The hero had left, swearing to return, and the heroine paced around the stage, while the rippling music showed the confusion of her thoughts. At Anna's entrance, she looked up and sang, "*Sorella!*" Sister.

Charlotte tightened her fingers around the arms of her chair. Only let Anna do well, let her not be embarrassed . . .

Anna's voice soared up, high and confident. Her blush was just right as she sang of the handsome stranger she'd just seen from her window. She'd sent a servant running after him to discover his name and invite him to dinner . . .

The audience groaned in sympathy for the shock and dismay on her older sister's face.

"Perhaps," Anna/Carolina sang, in heavily accented Italian, "Papa will let him marry me, as we have given up waiting to find you a husband!"

Charlotte bit back a laugh at the byplay of looks that passed between the two women.

She didn't have to fear for her erstwhile maid after all. Instead, Charlotte leaned back in her seat and abandoned herself to enjoyment. If, every so often, the Italian phrases blended an inch or so too far in Anna's German mouth—well, what matter was that, when compared to the ringing beauty of her voice?

And she arranged my hair every day of the last six years, Charlotte thought, during the applause. She hardly knew whether to feel shamed or proud.

At the intermission, Prince Nikolaus nodded gravely to her. "Our thanks, Baroness. Your Fräulein Dommayer is indeed an asset to our little company."

"Her voice is lovely, is it not?" Charlotte had rarely spoken directly with the Prince, but now she was overflowing with relief. "I believe it must be what she was born for."

"It is a great fortune for us that you brought her here and relinquished her from your service."

"How *is* your new maid, Lotte?" Sophie tapped the Prince's arm with her fan. "I told Niko he ought really to have given you two or three maids in exchange for the inconvenience to you. I vow, it took my maid three months just to learn how to arrange my hair properly."

"My new maid does very well," Charlotte said. "I do thank you, Your Highness. She seems admirably efficient and hard-working."

"But no singing voice?" Signor Morelli asked. There was an edge to his voice, but whether of amusement or irritation, Charlotte could not tell.

"Not that I've yet heard."

"And a good thing, too." Sophie sniffed. "It would be too absurd for Lotte to have to give up another maid! But really, how likely is it for that class of person to come up with such an astonishing voice?"

"Anna's voice is beautiful," Charlotte said.

"Yes, but that must have been a freak occurrence. Think of it! She didn't even come from a musician's family. Not that musicians are worth so very much themselves, but at least—"

"If you'll excuse me." Signor Morelli stood up, smiling, but with a dangerous glitter in his eyes. "Your Highness, might I take a breath of fresh air before the second act?"

"Of course, signor."

At the Prince's nod, Morelli strode outside.

"I'm afraid you've offended our guest, my dear," the Prince said mildly, once Morelli had disappeared.

"I? Oh, pooh. I said nothing except—"

"You said he was beneath us!" Charlotte's nails dug into her hands. "Sophie, how could you?"

"I was talking about ordinary musicians, obviously. And anyway—"

"Do we even know what his family was? Perhaps his parents were servants, too. Perhaps—"

"Don't be ridiculous! Lotte, your nerves must be shattered. Look at the signor! Of course he isn't at our level—you know that as well as I do!—but does he look to you like a servant?"

"Wouldn't we, if we wore their uniforms?"

There was a thundering silence. The Prince, his niece, and Sophie all stared at her, openmouthed in shock. Charlotte, trembling, was belatedly aware that she had gone too far. And made a scene, too—other faces had turned to look.

She stood up, smoothing down her skirts. "I'm—I'm afraid I don't feel very well, Your Highness," she said. "Please forgive me my intemperance."

The Prince nodded stiffly. Sophie was glaring at her, with red spots flaring high on her cheeks. Charlotte swept past them and past the eager whispers of the Prince's niece and her companions.

She hurried out of the royal box, down the two sets of stairs, down the long, ornately decorated corridor and through the main entrance into the blessedly cool darkness outside. As the night air met her face and she stepped onto the shell-lined path, she fought down a wave of dizziness and anger. Coming to a halt, she clenched both hands around the cool, wrought-iron railing of the steps that led up to the balcony and took a long, shuddering breath.

"Baroness?" Signor Morelli's tall figure emerged on the balcony above her in the darkness. His face looked pale and forbidding in the glow of the torches, but his high, pure voice rang with concern. "Are you unwell?"

"No. Not really." Charlotte straightened and gave him a weary smile. "But I won't be able to stay and enjoy the rest of the performance."

"Then you are unwell." He ran lightly down the steps to meet her, frowning. "Do you need—"

"No." She sighed. She should devise a polite fiction—a headache, perhaps. But she felt too weary and disgusted, with herself and everyone else, to lie to him. "I left because I'd lost my temper, I'm afraid. I said some foolish things."

"That sounds unlikely." He looked down at her from the first step, only a hand's-breadth away. She imagined that she could feel his breath, warm on her cheeks. "You are truly loyal to your dependents, madam."

"My—oh, you mean Anna?" His eyes were dark wells in the greater darkness. Her chest tightened as she looked into them. "We did not argue about Anna," she whispered.

His eyes widened. She bit her lip and looked down, suddenly conscious of her slip. She shouldn't have said anything, should have let him think what he would. She—

She realized that his gaze had lowered and fixed on her lower lip, still held lightly between her teeth.

She took a quick, shallow breath. Darkness wrapped like velvet around them. Under his gaze, her lips seemed to throb. She lifted her eyes to his.

A bell rang inside the building, signaling the end of the interval. Signor Morelli stepped back, shaking his head as if to clear it.

"Signor?" Charlotte's voice came out as a rasp.

He swallowed visibly. "It seems that I must thank you, madam."

Charlotte blinked. "For—?"

"For arguing . . . as it was not over *Anna*, after all." He smiled tightly and sketched a bow. "I must return to see the drama played out. I bid you goodnight, Baroness."

"Goodnight." Charlotte curtseyed and watched him disappear into the lights of the opera house.

As she set out along the path that led back to the palace, the darkness felt suddenly far too empty.

Chapter Twelve

I
t was all very well to order some poor fool to go sit for hours in tedious opera rehearsals, but it was quite another thing to have to do it yourself, without even being allowed to fall asleep.

Friedrich scowled as he pushed himself upright in his chair, fighting the pull of his leaden eyelids. This whole thing felt like a bloody practical joke. *"Attend the rehearsals. Become a familiar figure."* Well, this was the fourth day he'd attended rehearsals, and when he'd walked in that morning, that sultry, older lady singer had given him a coy little wave. Was that familiar enough for the bastards?

The music struck up again, and Friedrich stifled a groan. *Bloody hell.* It was the same song *again.* They'd gone through it three times already in the past hour!

Enough was enough. He crossed his arms, let his eyes fall closed, and sank back down into the chair. He was here, anyway, whether or not he was awake. That would have to be enough for them.

Franz watched the blond officer sink lower in his seat. Another minute, to be safe—yes, he was definitely asleep. As Madame Zelinowsky and Monsieur Delacroix began a third attempt at their patter-song duet, Franz slipped off the stage and walked casually down the aisle.

He'd preserved the note carefully since receiving it inside his own instructions last night, fighting down all temptations to steam it open and read it himself. Whoever had sent this note through his care could presumably have delivered it to the officer themselves . . . which marked this as a personal test. A test that he was determined to pass with flying colors. Franz would prove his trustworthiness to the Brotherhood in any way they chose, whether it was by keeping the secrecy of their messages or by following orders without question. Each task marked one step closer to freedom and a fortune.

He dropped the letter onto the floor just beside the officer's sprawled legs, finished walking the length of the aisle as if nothing had occurred, turned around—and saw Fräulein Dommayer watching him from the stage with brightly speculative eyes.

Blast. Franz walked back at the same meandering pace, but his heartbeat was racing. Trust her, of all people, to have seen him. Seen him and speculated about his actions—she was cleverer than he'd thought when he'd first met her. She might look like a pretty, vacant Bavarian milkmaid, but he'd wager she saw and understood nearly everything that went on around her.

Wait. He paused halfway down the aisle as an idea seized him. It was so unlikely—and yet . . . what other explanation was there? Why else would she watch him so intently? Why else with such a measuring look? She had even rescued their note to him from Delacroix the night before.

She must work for the Brotherhood, too. She was reporting back to them on his movements. *Perhaps* . . . She didn't look like a spy. But then, the whole story of her employment had sounded so bizarre and unlikely. From personal maid to singer in one great leap? It would make so much more sense, in the same wild and dreamlike manner of that original nighttime visit, if he assumed instead that her "discovery" had been engineered by the same great forces that had found him in his prison and had planned a great design.

What if his inclusion in their plans depended on her reports of his success in this and other tests?

Franz smiled brilliantly at her and walked back up to the stage as quickly as his injured back would let him. His pulse was still racing as he nodded to her.

"Fräulein Dommayer. You're looking lovely, as ever, this morning."

She blinked and stepped back. "I . . . thank you, Herr Pichler."

"You sang beautifully in last night's performance." Was he laying it on too thick?

Perhaps. Her eyes narrowed.

"What were you leaving for that officer, Herr Pichler?"

"Nothing much," he said. "Only going about my business. Following instructions."

She sighed and rolled her eyes. "Your *instructions*—"

Herr Haydn called out, "Herr Pichler! Frau Kettner!"

Franz grinned at Fräulein Dommayer and took the risk. "I'm sure you know all about those instructions, Fräulein. I only hope you may be pleased with the way I accomplished them."

He limped up the steps onto the stage with a lighter heart than he'd felt for days.

"I shouldn't even be speaking to you," Sophie hissed to Charlotte.

They had fallen behind the rest of the group strolling through the pathways of the Prince's gardens. Sunlight shone down on the colorful beds of flowers and soaked through the black cloth of Charlotte's gown and all her undergarments until she felt ready to sink beneath the heat. The water shooting out from the nearby fountains called to her with a dangerously seductive appeal.

She sighed and wrenched her gaze away from the streams of cool water jetting out from Neptune's copper trident, five feet away. "I am sorry, Sophie," she whispered back, "but I have apologized several times already. What more do you want me to say?"

"It was inexcusable for you to embarrass me in front of everyone." Sophie glared straight ahead, her pretty face shadowed by her wide, curving hat. Blue ribbons dangled down across her shoulders, matching her parasol. "How did you think such behavior must reflect on me, your sister? Your *hostess*? I had to apologize to Niko and his niece for you, and promise—"

"There was no need for you to do any of that, as I had already apologized to them myself." Charlotte bit off the ends of her words as renewed temper threatened to overwhelm her. "Oh, Sophie." She closed her eyes a moment against the too-bright sunlight and took a deep breath. "Perhaps I am causing you too much trouble, after all. If you are finding my visit too much of a trial, you really can cut it short without injuring my feelings, I promise you."

"What?"

"Only say the word, and I can be packed to leave within the day. Perhaps it has been unfair for me to linger here and take advantage of your hospitality. I can go to Vienna—"

"To Maman? Don't be absurd, Lotte! You'd go mad within a fortnight. She would have you remarried and sold off—"

"I can manage Maman," Charlotte said evenly. "I'm old enough to say no to her nowadays." *I hope*, she added silently. Hidden in her skirts, her fingers clenched at the memory of the last time she had tried. "If you'll let me have the loan of a carriage for the journey, I'll—"

"Lotte, *no*." Sophie came to a halt and grasped her arm. "Please don't leave. For my sake, not yours." Her face twitched, as though she fought back tears. "It's meant so much to me to have you here. Twelve years since we'd last seen each other. Twelve *years*, Lotte!"

"I know." Charlotte squeezed Sophie's gloved hand. "It was far too long."

"And who knows where Maman will marry you off to next? You might have to travel to the wilds of Poland, for all I know! Besides . . ." Sophie's smile was watery. She took her hand back to wipe her eyes. "I need you here, Lotte. I love Niko, of course I do, but there's no one else here for me, apart from him. No one who cares about *me*, Sophie, and doesn't just think of me as Niko's pet, or hope that he'll be rid of me soon, or—"

"Sophie!" Charlotte stared at her. "Dearest, I'm sure that isn't true."

"It is. Of course it is. They all give me lip-service as Niko's hostess, but I know what they really think. I'm a joke to them, or else a scandal. I hate it!"

"I never knew you felt that way."

"I try not to think about it." Sophie shrugged and patted her face, smoothing it back into order. "Oh, Lotte, please do say you'll stay and forget about my silliness. You will, won't you?"

"Of course I will."

Charlotte would have embraced her, if they hadn't stood in so public a place. They were already attracting curious glances from the others, now that they had fallen so far behind. Charlotte took Sophie's arm and walked forward in silence to catch up with the rest of the group. She hadn't felt so fiercely protective since they had been children and she'd had to comfort Sophie after some particularly scathing nursery visit from their mother.

They'd been each other's sole defense, back then, against their mother's mercurial moods and her venomous temper, which could strike so suddenly and unexpectedly. Charlotte could still remember the feel of her younger sister's consoling embrace—though Sophie had been only ten years old at the time—as eighteen-year-old Charlotte had wept, lashed by their mother's words after her first, humiliating debut into Viennese society. When the news of Charlotte's betrothal was announced three months later, to a man above sixty years of age, whom she had never met, it had been Sophie who had vowed resistance.

It was Sophie, too, who had given Charlotte the courage to stand against her mother then, for once in her life trying to refuse the course that her parents had set for her. The coldly calculated threats that she'd garnered from her father for that resistance had been nothing to the burn of her mother's tirade, scorching her for her disloyalty and for the dishonor that a broken engagement would bring to her entire family.

In the end, of course, there had been no choice. She would have lost both her home and her family if she had refused to fulfill her allotted path. But once Charlotte had given in . . .

Oh. She shut her eyes against the vivid memory. Sophie, weeping bitterly over her older sister's upcoming marriage, and Charlotte weeping, too, even as she promised frequent visits. Little had she known that, within a year, any visits would be out of the question. Within four years, she had relinquished even the faintest hope of them.

Charlotte had taken the place of a mother to Sophie from the moment that her younger sister had been born. Their love and loyalty to each other had been the only warmth that either of them ever knew in their family's cold household. Once married, though, and hundreds of miles away, Charlotte had become so absorbed in Ernst's worsening health, the endless demands of his wide-ranging correspondence, and the urgent needs of his estate and dependents, that her own correspondence had faltered and faded for lack of time and energy. Meanwhile, Sophie's letters from Vienna, once so frequent and full of news, had become shorter and rarer with every year, until they disappeared entirely. By the time of Ernst's death, Charlotte hadn't exchanged so much as a page-long note with her sister in years.

Had she been responsible for abandoning her younger sister? At the time, she had guiltily excused her lack of effort by telling herself that Sophie must surely have formed new friendships to replace their former closeness. But, clearly, not one of them had worked to protect Sophie from her own whimsical nature, or reinforce her own better judgment and sense of honor. If Charlotte had kept up the correspondence and maintained her former loving support, would Sophie still have made this foolish, hurtful bargain with her husband and the Prince?

Walking arm in arm, their faces turned to one another, Charlotte and Sophie nearly bumped into the tall, stooped gentleman who approached from an intersecting path, his hands locked behind his back and his own gaze fixed on the ground. At their near-collision, his eyes widened. He jerked around to look after the group of walkers in the distance.

"I do beg your pardon." With a hasty bow, he began to move away, but Sophie stepped forward to stop him.

"My goodness, I don't believe I've ever met you! How funny. I thought I knew everyone here."

Ahead, the rest of the group had come to a halt. Charlotte watched the Prince turn back to stride toward them, followed by the others.

Sophie shook the bright ribbons out of her face and smiled enchantingly, holding out her gloved hand. "I know we really ought to wait for a proper introduction, but just this once . . . I am Frau von Höllner, and this is my sister, the Baroness von Steinbeck. And who are you?"

The man shot a quick look at the approaching group, sighed, and removed his hat with a flourish. He bowed sweepingly. "It is an inestimable pleasure to meet both of you ladies. I am Count Radamowsky."

Friedrich woke with a start as percussion crashed in the orchestra. God, how long had he slept? All the actors were singing together now, while the full assembled orchestra played support for them. It made an utterly godawful racket.

He sighed and wriggled into a more comfortable position. No chance of sleeping any longer, but still . . .

His foot brushed against paper. He froze.

No. They couldn't be watching him all the time. This had to be something completely innocent. There was no reason to be worried at all. And since there wasn't . . .

He reached down to pick it up just as anyone would, quite naturally, out of simple curiosity . . . or, no, to *prove* exactly how safe it really was, so he wouldn't even be tempted to waste his time on absurd worries any longer.

There was no name on the note. But when he turned it over, the familiar seal sent a sinking sensation through his gut.

Goddammit.

So, they'd caught him sleeping on duty. So? He ripped open the note, cursing his trembling fingers.

Brother Friedrich. As an initiate into our sacred mysteries, you are invited and required to attend our ritual tonight inside the Eszterháza Bagatelle at the hour of eleven o'clock. The password will be "The Elements of Fire." Do not neglect . . .

Friedrich crumpled the note into a ball without bothering to read any of the rest of their bloody nagging. It was all too unbearably depressing for words.

Of course, there was no question about it.

He would go.

"Radamowsky." It wasn't the Prince who spoke first, but Ignaz von Born. The alchemist stepped forward, brandishing his walking stick like a weapon, and glared at the other man, ignoring Charlotte and Sophie just beside him. "What do you think you're doing here?"

"Why, the same as you must be, Herr von Born." Radamowsky smiled easily, but Charlotte had not missed his glance of appeal to the Prince. "Have you had a pleasant visit so far, my friend?"

Von Born tightened his lips and grasped the handle of his walking stick as if it were a throat that he was throttling. "Until now, I had."

"My dear Count." Prince Nikolaus walked forward, rubbing his hands together in what Charlotte might have taken as a nervous gesture, in another man. "When did you arrive?"

"But half an hour ago, Your Highness." Count Radamowsky turned to smile at the assembled company. "I was so enchanted by the beauty of the view from my window that I set off to enjoy your fine gardens immediately. Will you forgive my rudeness in not waiting inside to be greeted by you?"

Prince Nikolaus gave an unusually expansive wave of his hand, heartiness—and relief?—emanating through his voice. "Of course. There is nothing to forgive."

"But—oh!" Beside Charlotte, Sophie gasped. "Pardon me, sir, but are you *the* Count Radamowsky? The one I've been told of? Herr von Born said that you can conjure ghosts and—"

"Ahem. I didn't *quite* say—"

"I am," Count Radamowsky said, with a bow, "that very Count Radamowsky of whom you speak. Perhaps someday I may have the privilege of seeing you in one of my Viennese *salons*, madam, or—"

"Someday? But it must be soon—today! Oh, Niko!" Sophie flew to the Prince's side and gazed up at him adoringly. "You lovely, lovely man. You promised me I should see a ghost conjured, and then you invited Count Radamowsky to do it for me! You knew how much I longed to see him. You were wicked, to keep his visit such a surprise!"

"Well . . ." The Prince patted Sophie's hand. A long look passed between the two men. Charlotte fancied she caught the merest suggestion of a shrug in the Prince's shoulders. "Now that you are here, Radamowsky, would you be so kind as to oblige Frau von Höllner in her whim?"

Ignaz von Born snorted and spun around to glare into the closest flowerbeds. Behind him, Charlotte saw Signor Morelli watching in silence. Her breath sped up. She turned away. She had made a fool of herself last night. Now, he probably thought her doubly a fool for involving herself in this supernatural play.

"Sophie," she began, in an undertone.

"Of course I shall," Count Radamowsky said. "But we will need darkness for the proper ambience. May I have the use of a good-sized room, Your Highness, at—shall we say—eleven o'clock tonight?"

At five minutes to eleven, Friedrich neared the end of the long path to the Eszterháza Bagatelle. Half the torches had been extinguished, so he had to find his way through near-blackness. Only the sound of his boots crunching against the path served as proof that he hadn't lost his way.

He wasn't drunk this time. *To say the least.* He'd tried to drink beforehand, to bolster up his nerves, but he'd only gagged and had to spit the beer out when his stomach had rebelled against him.

Ridiculous to be so afraid. He was sober, not prey to nightmare fancies. He was a lieutenant, even if that was only an honorary title. More than that, he was a von Höllner, and that still meant something, didn't it?

Friedrich drew up his shoulders into a martial stance as he marched up the angled set of stairs to the central door. Perhaps it would be locked, he thought hopefully. Perhaps . . .

It cracked open before he could even touch it.

"Password?" a voice whispered, behind the door.

Oh, hell. "The elements of fire," Friedrich muttered.

"Pass, Brother." The door swung inward.

Blackness yawned through the open door. Friedrich could hear the far-off sound of male voices chanting deep within the building. He swallowed.

"Brother?" the voice prompted.

"Yes, all right." Friedrich scowled. "I know what I need to do."

He stepped into the darkness.

Chapter Thirteen

"Close your eyes," Count Radamowsky intoned. "Let your breathing slow. The aetheric veil is only just beyond our sight."

Carlo crossed his arms and watched from slitted eyes. In the darkness, lit only by flickering candles, Radamowsky's smile looked nearly demonic. Carlo wasn't surprised that Ignaz von Born had walked out with a snort of open disgust, only moments after entering the room. He couldn't entirely explain why he hadn't followed von Born's example.

The seats in the music room had been arranged into a circle surrounding the alchemist. Radamowsky carried no props save his own expressive gestures and the deep, reverberating timbre of his voice—which, Carlo thought, made this already a far better show than most of the attempts he'd been forced to witness in various other courts in his career.

His narrowed gaze fell on Baroness von Steinbeck beside him—the mark of her dark eyelashes against her cheek, the slow, even breathing that moved her chest—and jerked away.

Shadows flickered across Radamowsky's face.

"The aetheric veil draws closer now. Closer, closer—*ah*."

Friedrich felt his way through blackness with one hand pressed against the wall. The chanting grew louder and louder, until it nearly deafened him.

His outstretched foot hit a closed door that emanated heat through its wooden bulk. He took a breath. When he finally found the handle of the door, after a fumbling search, it nearly burned him.

He turned it anyway . . . and walked straight into Hell.

"I call upon the ancient masters to help me raise the aetheric veil between the worlds of the spirit and the flesh," Count Radamowsky declared. "I call upon them in the ancient tongues."

Thick syllables rolled out of his lips. Some of it was very nearly Italian, Carlo thought—or Latin, at least—but the rest he could not identify. Yet his first instinct—to dismiss it as invented gibberish—faded as the words continued. They rolled out in order—in *perfect* order. They filled his head and resonated within it. They almost made sense. They meant something . . . if he could only see it . . .

His head tipped forward as the strength flooded out of the muscles in his neck. He couldn't even find the will to be afraid.

Red flames shot up from the floor in all directions, filling the Bagatelle's dance hall. Heat licked Friedrich's face as he staggered back and stared, bewildered, into the inferno that had appeared in the middle of Prince Nikolaus's pride and glory. On the ceiling above him, the familiar black-lacquered paintings of Chinese life overlooked a scene from a nightmare. Before him, black-robed figures mingled in the fire. The mirrors on the walls reflected the flames and multiplied them in dizzying profusion, until the room seemed to stretch out forever in a sea of red and black.

"Brother Friedrich, how good to see you."

The familiar voice behind him was filled with devilish amusement. A firm hand on Friedrich's back propelled him into the room.

Friedrich stumbled forward, flinging his hands out to protect his face from the leaping flames. He stopped himself just at the edge of the fire.

The dark-robed figure behind him swept forward into the heart of the flames, clapping his hands for attention.

"Brothers! Welcome all. Whether you found your way here from Esz-terháza, Vienna, Salzburg, Pressburg, or somewhere very, very different . . ."

Friedrich blinked at the list and took a step too far.

Fire scalded his hands and raced up his neck. It covered his face, burning him, until he was weeping with the agony of it, crying out, begging incoherently—

A hand grabbed his collar and dragged him out of the flames. Ruthless hands beat at his clothing.

"Look, brothers! An initiate who did not follow our guidance. Brother Friedrich, did your invitation not clearly inform you where you would find a cloak of our order?"

Tears streamed down Friedrich's raw face. "I didn't—didn't—"

"Didn't want to? Didn't even want to admit you are one of us, perhaps?" The voice hardened. "Look at this man, brothers. Allowed access into our mysteries, inclusion in our sacred rites—and he flaunts the contempt in which he holds us. What should we do with such a case as this?"

"Please," Friedrich mumbled. "Please, I didn't know—didn't read—didn't—"

Shouts echoed through the room, overwhelming his protests.

"Throw him into the flames!"

"Burn him!"

"Roast him!"

"Now, brothers." The voice chuckled indulgently. "He is a sworn member of our order. We will show him the mercy of granting him one more chance. Brother Friedrich . . ." The hood swung toward him. Friedrich's eyes were too blurred by tears to make out any more than the keen eyes within its shadow. "Brother Friedrich, do you repent the choice you made?"

"Yes," Friedrich choked. "God, yes." He repented everything —everything . . .

"You have one more moment of choice, Brother Friedrich," the voice said. "It is your choice to make. I am certain—entirely certain—that we could find another cloak to shelter you. But only committed members of our Brotherhood may wear our cloaks. Are you committed to us, Brother Friedrich?"

"I—I—"

The hand around his collar shoved him back toward the leaping flames. "Are you a believing member of our Brotherhood or not?"

"I am!" Friedrich screamed.

"I am very glad to hear it." Still, the firm grip held him, struggling, barely an inch away from the flames. "Brothers? Shall we grant him mercy and accept him back within our hearts?"

Mutters rose up within the crowd.

"Please," Friedrich mumbled. "Please. Please!"

"Bring me a cloak," the voice commanded. "Brother Friedrich has seen the error of his ways."

A black-robed figure approached, holding a second cloak spread over his arms. But there was something terribly wrong in the way the figure walked—no, glided—through the flames.

It held out the spare cloak as it reached them.

Oh, God. Tears flooded Friedrich's face once again, burning as they touched his scalded skin.

The figure's feet did not touch the ground.

"You may open your eyes," Count Radamowsky murmured.

Charlotte forced her heavy eyelids open with an effort. She couldn't lift her head, but neither could she summon up the effort to worry about it.

Pale light shimmered around Count Radamowsky's body.

"The first of my spirit guides, Nemenel, has joined us," said Count Radamowsky. "Nemenel, my child, greet this audience."

The pale light withdrew from Radamowsky's body. It flattened into a long, streaming path of luminescence and floated across the open circle.

Gasps and sighs of appreciation sounded in the darkened room as Nemenel floated around the circle. Tears of wonder prickled at Charlotte's eyes as she watched the stream of incandescent light approach her. She had never expected this summoning to work. She would never have imagined that it could be so beautiful.

Nemenel floated past Charlotte, hovering a moment before her chair. If Charlotte could have lifted her arms, she would have reached out. Such shimmering radiance—she yearned to feel it. But her arms remained stubbornly leaden, and Nemenel floated onward.

As the spirit reached Sophie's chair, Count Radamowsky spoke. "Nemenel, that is Frau von Höllner, who asked for tonight's meeting. Will you greet her properly?"

Charlotte could only see the edges of Sophie's face, suffused with fear and excitement. As the glowing light neared her, Sophie gasped. The light wrapped around her.

Charlotte could not even turn her head to look closer. She sat frozen, tormented by curiosity . . . and shameful envy. If only it could have been her . . .

A soft giggle escaped Sophie's throat as the light pulled away. "She— she tickles!"

Radamowsky chuckled. "Bow to His Serene Highness, Nemenel."

The glowing light floated high in the air and then dipped down, in a perfect caricature of a bow. Delighted laughter filled the room.

"She is precious," Sophie said. "Oh, Niko . . ."

"Return to me, Nemenel," Count Radamowsky said. As the light streamed back toward him, he raised his hands. "I thank you, gracious gentlemen and ladies, for your attendance. Now, if you will be so kind as to close your eyes once more, I—"

"Wait." Prince Nikolaus's voice rapped out, though he sat as frozen as all the rest of the onlookers.

Count Radamowsky turned to him. "Your Highness? Is something—"

"Summon another one, Radamowsky." The Prince's voice seemed edged with other meanings as he added, "Let my court see your most impressive work."

"I don't—"

"You know exactly the one I mean," said Prince Nikolaus. "And I insist upon it."

"Your cloak, Brother Friedrich." The leader stepped back to make room for the black cloak to be tossed around Friedrich's shoulders.

Friedrich moaned and backed away from the figure who held out the cloak. *The specter.*

"What, too proud to accept help when it is offered to you?" The leader of the group pushed him forward. "Or would you prefer to return to the flames?"

"No," Friedrich mumbled.

He clamped his teeth together and stood quietly as the floating figure arranged the hooded cloak around him. Was it only his imagination that conjured up the sound of scraping bones?

The figure stepped back and flashed him a grin. Its shining white teeth were the only visible remnants of its face beneath the hood.

Before Friedrich could speak, the man behind him shoved him straight into the center of the flames.

"No!" Friedrich screamed and fought—then stopped.

Flames surrounded him, yet his skin remained cool beneath his cloak. Even his damaged face, protected within the billowing hood, felt only distant heat.

He laughed out loud in sheer relief, despite the pain. He wasn't dead. It was beyond miraculous.

"You see, now, the advantages of your membership." The leader of the Brotherhood raised his voice, speaking to the crowd at large. "We are men of reason here, untethered by the superstitious fears that hold back lesser beings. Unafraid to touch the deepest darkness in order to protect what belongs to us. Brothers, would any of you follow the weaklings' way of Prince Nikolaus Esterházy and his brethren, who lick the hand of our Habsburg overlords even as it turns into a fist? The Empress may yet believe in compromise, but she won't be able to rein in her hotheaded son forever. One day soon our young Emperor will take sole control—and what then? Will you bow your heads and wag your tails like obedient lapdogs while this so-called enlightened Emperor wrests away all the rights to property and pride that our ancestors won for us centuries ago? While he denies the very nobility of our blood and raises our own peasants above us?"

The answering, rage-filled cry shivered through Friedrich's bones.

Through the flames, he saw faces open in anger beneath dark hoods. In a few of them, he recognized the oldest aristocracy of the land. And in a few . . . He swallowed. Rotting, long-dead faces joined the living, here, on common ground.

The leader's voice swelled. "We in this room wear cloaks of protection. The darkness we step through cannot harm us, for we are the chosen among mankind." He stepped back, leaving Friedrich free to move. "Are you glad now to be wearing one of our cloaks, Brother Friedrich?"

"Yes," Friedrich mumbled. His cheeks hurt even more when he spoke.

"Excellent. Brother . . ." The leader gestured to another black-robed figure, who hurried forward, both feet reassuringly solid upon the ground. "Take Brother Friedrich away and find salve to repair his face. We cannot have him too injured to perform his duties."

"Duties?" Friedrich echoed faintly, as he turned to leave.

"Of course." The leader's smile echoed in his voice. "You are now one of the most highly valued members of our Brotherhood. And in only five days, you will be our shining star."

"Your Highness . . ." The pale light that was Nemenel rippled and wrapped around Count Radamowsky's straight figure as he spoke. "With great respect, I do not believe that would be a wise idea."

"It is my idea, Radamowsky. And my command."

Charlotte swallowed uneasily as she watched Nemenel's nervous ripples. It was as though the pale spirit reflected her master's disturbance.

"The other is not ready yet."

"It has been tested, has it not?"

The Count darted a quick look at the listening circle. "Perhaps we might discuss this later, in private, when—"

"I wish to see your other summoning, and I will be most seriously displeased if you refuse me. Is that discussion enough for you?"

Count Radamowsky stared at him a moment in rigid silence. Then, abruptly, he nodded. "As you wish."

His shoulders rose and fell in a sigh as he turned to speak to the circle as a whole. Charlotte could almost see the mantle of calm he assumed as he stretched his lips into an unconvincing smile.

"My noble audience! Might I beg you to prepare for an experience quite unlike any that you have ever felt before? In my latest researches, I have delved long and deep into the ancient texts of scientists and wise men. Clinging to the aetheric veil are many spirits like the gentle Nemenel. But they are not the only ones to migrate from the spirit world." His voice deepened. "In the darker regions of the spirit world exist elementals of a different order. Only by the most powerful mastery can such creatures be summoned through the veil. And then only . . ." He flicked a glance back at the Prince. "Only with the greatest care and for the highest causes."

Charlotte's head twinged, fighting against the soothing rhythms of his voice. She misliked the sound of this new elemental. She wanted to leave—but she could barely even feel her legs any more, much less move them. She was trapped.

She glanced at Signor Morelli, on her left, and saw his forehead tense with effort. He, too, must be trying to move. Trying, and failing. Their common effort gave her no comfort.

"Gentlemen and ladies, please close your eyes."

Radamowsky's voice tolled out, rich and compelling, and, despite herself, Charlotte found her eyelids falling shut.

"I call upon it with the words of power. I call upon it with the words of compulsion."

His voice changed, shaping words in Latin, Greek, and Hebrew. They tolled through Charlotte's head until they nearly deafened her. They started a nerve throbbing in her skull.

It seemed to go on for hours. The pain in Charlotte's head intensified until it felt overwhelming, a red haze. Finally, the chant ended.

"You may open your eyes," Count Radamowsky said.

The red pain in Charlotte's head had vanished with the cessation of his chant. She opened her eyes warily.

A thick, roiling, dark gray mass of smoke wrapped around the alchemist's waist. Count Radamowsky's face looked strained and pale. Nemenel had flown up to the high ceiling, where she hovered, rippling convulsively.

"Ladies and gentlemen, may I present before you an elemental from far across the veil?"

There was no giggling or sighed appreciation now. A taut silence gripped the circle of chairs. Charlotte felt her heart beat quickly against her chest.

Deep within the dark smoke, two red eyes flashed open.

"Let it move around the circle, too," Prince Nikolaus commanded.

No, Charlotte thought. If she could have moved, she would have run.

"Your Highness—"

"Niko?" Sophie's voice wavered. "Perhaps—"

"Can you control the thing or not, Radamowsky?"

"I can." The alchemist bit off the words.

"Then we have naught to fear. Let it loose."

Count Radamowsky raised one arm. He began to chant softly as the elemental unwrapped itself from his waist. Slowly, it began to float around the circle.

Hisses and grunts of effort sounded as people fought to lean backward. As the gray, twisting smoke floated closer and closer to her, Charlotte's chest stiffened into rigidity. She hardly dared even to breathe, for fear of attracting the thing's attention. Even in the dim candlelight, she could see the shining beads of perspiration that stood out on the alchemist's forehead as he chanted.

The gray fog floated slowly past Signor Morelli and paused before Charlotte. She held her breath, praying silently. *Move on, move on, move on . . .*

Its red eyes gazed straight into hers. She couldn't restrain the gasp that tore itself from her mouth. The elemental uncoiled itself, slid closer—

The alchemist's voice sharpened into urgency. The red eyes vanished. The smoky mass withdrew and floated on to the next seat.

Air flooded Charlotte's chest until she nearly choked. She blinked rapidly, and found Signor Morelli staring at her with wide, dark eyes. She tried to smile at him in reassurance. She failed.

As the gray smoke floated the rest of the way around the circle, Charlotte turned her eyes up to the ceiling where Nemenel floated, a safe distance from the roiling gray mass. Charlotte wished she could join the spirit there.

Even as she watched, though, Nemenel began to float downward, toward the chanting alchemist, whose gaze was fixed on his second summoning. The mass of gray smoke passed Sophie, who did not ask to touch it. It passed the Prince, who gazed at it with hard satisfaction. It passed his niece and her companion—both of whom, Charlotte noted, for once in their lives neither giggled nor whispered. As Nemenel floated down, closer and closer to the Count, the gray smoke drifted up to the English traveler, Edmund Guernsey.

With a nearly audible sigh, Nemenel finally dropped onto the Radamowsky's shoulder, wrapping lovingly around him. The alchemist jerked in surprise. His voice cut off in midchant.

Red eyes flashed open within the smoke as it shot forward, straight at Guernsey's face.

Chapter Fourteen

Guernsey's scream cut off in a gurgling hiss as the gray smoke enveloped his face. Other screams filled the room, but no one moved. That was the worst of the horror, Charlotte thought with numb clarity—that they couldn't even run or hide. Even Guernsey's own arms remained leadenly at his side. There should have been chairs crashing to the ground, people racing to save the poor man—

Count Radamowsky's shout silenced all the rest. His words rapped out as Nemenel slid down behind him.

The gray smoke rippled and condensed around Guernsey's face. Count Radamowsky snapped out a sharp string of words.

Slowly, the smoke pulled away from its victim. Radamowsky's voice deepened into a rolling chant, dragging the smoke back toward him. Finally, only long, thin tendrils of smoke still clung to Guernsey's face. They separated from it with a wet pop, and Charlotte gasped.

Blood streamed out of the dozen holes that the tendrils had left behind. As gasps and cries erupted around the circle, Guernsey's breath sobbed out. He tried to say something, but his eyes rolled up and his head tipped forward. Still, his body remained fixed to his chair.

"Ladies and gentlemen." Radamowsky held the gray smoke before him as he addressed the circle. "If you will aid me with your full attention, we may work together to dismiss both these spirits for the night. Then, all of your fears will be assuaged. Please, let your eyes fall closed."

The 'please' was no more than a formality, his compulsion blatant now, Charlotte thought, as her eyelids closed of their own accord. Still, the oblivion of the trance state came as a blessed relief this time. Radamowsky's words droned through her ears, and her racing heartbeat gradually slowed. By the time he spoke in German again, her breathing had almost returned to its normal rhythms.

"You may open your eyes."

Feeling flooded into Charlotte's arms and legs. She opened her eyes just in time to see Mr. Guernsey crumple and fall to the ground. Blood covered his face.

Sophie let out a piercing scream and covered her face with her hands. Charlotte paused a moment—but no, the Prince's niece and her companion were already bending over Sophie. Charlotte lifted her skirts and hurried across the circle to drop down beside the fallen man instead. Guernsey was still breathing, but only in short, shallow gasps. Beneath the mask of blood, his face was deathly pale. Charlotte snatched out her silk handkerchief and began to wipe at his skin, fighting down panic. There were too many wounds to even try to staunch them all.

She saw the buckled toes of elegant shoes before her and looked up to find Signor Morelli standing over her.

"I've summoned the Prince's physician." He glanced back at the sobbing women, muttering men, and various fainting fits taking place around the circle, and his lips twisted. He knelt down beside her. "Is there aught I can do until he arrives?"

"I'd be grateful for your handkerchief. The wounds are deep, and I fear he's lost too much blood already."

Signor Morelli's voice was soft as he passed her a creamy white handkerchief. "There are spots of blood on the floor above which the elemental floated."

"Horrible." Charlotte swallowed convulsively and pressed the new handkerchief against Guernsey's face. Red blood blossomed against the white cloth. Her own handkerchief was already soaked. How long would the physician take?

She looked toward the door and saw the Prince and the alchemist engaged in a heated, whispered argument. Their hands swept through the air in cutting gestures.

Signor Morelli followed her gaze. "Not quite the demonstration they'd planned."

"I should think not." Charlotte shuddered.

A round man carrying a medical bag, followed by two sturdy

footmen, hurried into the room, pausing only to listen to the Prince's commands. He bent over Guernsey's body and signaled to the footmen.

"We'll take him back to his quarters immediately, as His Highness wishes for him to be treated in privacy." He gave Charlotte a brief, dismissive smile and nod of the head. "Have no fear, madam, I shall attend upon him myself. I'm certain he will be recovered shortly."

"Did His Highness tell you how he was injured?" Signor Morelli's voice was bland, but his eyes were sharp and focused.

"No need, sir, no need. His Highness wishes me to treat him with the greatest care and not to concern myself about the causes."

"A loyal servant," Morelli murmured.

"Thank you, sir."

The footmen managed to haul Guernsey's body onto a chair, and they carried him out under the physician's clucking supervision. As soon as they passed through the door, Prince Nikolaus stepped into the center of the room, holding up his hands for the crowd's attention. As the Prince began to speak, Count Radamowsky walked out of the room, his back ramrod-straight.

"Well, it's been an instructive evening, no doubt. A great pity about our poor Mister . . . our poor English visitor, but still, my physician assures me that he will recover shortly. Every new weapon needs some testing out, eh? Like a skittish colt being broken in." The Prince laughed overheartily and turned to Sophie, who was red-eyed but quiet now. He murmured something to her, and she laughed prettily, fluttering her eyelashes.

Charlotte stared at them, her head whirling. When she turned away, she found Signor Morelli looking down at her. He held out his hand.

"May I help you to your feet?"

"Thank you." His long fingers felt reassuringly warm around hers. Exhaustion flooded her as she stood up. She swayed, and he caught her.

"Baroness?"

"Forgive me." She released his hand, stepping back. "I only—"

"It's been a tiring evening." He offered her his arm. "May I escort you back to your quarters? This is no night for walking alone."

She bit her lip. "I should go to Sophie—"

His voice was dry. "Frau von Höllner seems to have recovered admirably."

Sophie's laugh rang out across the room, and Charlotte sighed. "Well, then . . . I thank you, signor. I would be most grateful for your escort."

She wrapped her fingers lightly around his proffered arm and walked beside him out of the room.

After nearly five minutes, Baroness von Steinbeck still hadn't uttered a word, yet Carlo could feel her fingers trembling against his arm. He would have spoken himself if he could, but rage choked him. *An instructive evening*, indeed. And a fine game for the Prince to play on his guests.

Carlo remembered again the moment the elemental had paused before the Baroness and begun to float toward her. His muscles had refused to move. He would have been forced to sit and merely watch as it devoured her. Would the Prince have found that instructive, too?

"Signor?" She was looking up at him now, her light eyes wide. "Are you unwell?"

"Only in spirit," he said tightly, then clamped his lips together to hold back any worse.

"Pray, don't even mention the word 'spirit.'" She shuddered and gave a rueful laugh. "I have lost any fascination I ever felt for those beings."

"Have you? I confess, I'd never believed in them until tonight."

"Tonight was . . . convincing." He felt her shiver.

"Count Radamowsky is a fine mesmerist. Had his exploits ended with Nemenel, I might yet wonder whether it had all been a trick of our imaginations, guided by his will."

Her fingers tightened around his arm. "That was no trick of the imagination."

"More's the pity. Poor Guernsey's proof of that." Carlo glanced up and down the taper-lit corridor and dropped his voice. "But have you thought through the other implications of this evening's work?"

She stopped walking to frown up at him. "What do you mean?"

It was impolitic madness to speak of this. Yet the burning fuse inside Carlo's chest would be satisfied with nothing less. "I mean," Carlo said deliberately, "that the great mystery of what caused the singers' deaths may just have been solved."

"What—oh!" She sucked in her breath in a gasp. "No, that cannot be right."

"No? You saw Guernsey's face. The singers were drained of blood, were they not? And—"

"But Count Radamowsky did not even arrive until this morning. How could it have—"

"The Prince did not speak to him as to a new guest, did he? Prince Nikolaus asked most particularly for that elemental."

"Well . . ." She withdrew her hand from his arm and stepped back, her face filled with distress. "Perhaps they'd discussed it beforehand, in letters or—"

"Or perhaps he'd already seen and made use of it, only days ago." Carlo's arm felt cold, deprived of her touch. "You heard what he said to all of us, Baroness—'Every new weapon needs testing out.'"

"But he didn't mean—he couldn't mean—"

"Who better to test it out on than two disobedient servants? They'd broken their contracts and were thus—in his eyes—utterly disposable. Who would care that they had died? They were only singers!"

"Signor, it is simply inconceivable. No matter what—coincidences, or fantasies you have imagined—the Prince is a gentleman. As is Count Radamowsky!"

"And?" Carlo stared at her, conscious of a sharp pain in his chest. "What matter is that? Their birth is significant as it relates to their wealth, certainly—and, perhaps, to their thirst for power. But—"

"It is significant as it relates to honor." She took a deep breath. "The Prince is—as powerful men often are, I suppose. But that he would knowingly set that creature on any man or woman—and most particularly to ones he had employed and promised to care for—no. No! I cannot believe it."

"Then you are not the intelligent woman I took you for."

Her head jerked up, and spots of color appeared on her cheeks, but he carried on regardless.

"Not everyone of noble birth follows the code of honor you believe in, Baroness. You could have been that creature's victim tonight, and you know it. Does that not give you any pause?"

"If I were to be frightened off by warnings . . ." She stopped, biting her lip.

"Warnings? I'd call this more than—ah." Carlo paused, caught. "Who has been giving you warnings, Baroness?"

Voices sounded behind them as two noblewomen rounded the corner. They raised their eyebrows and giggled as they passed; Carlo stiffened. Baroness von Steinbeck drew back, lifting her chin. When the other women had passed, whispering to each other, the Baroness curtseyed stiffly to him.

"I thank you for your escort, signor. My rooms are here, and you have delivered me safely to them."

He bowed, cursing inwardly. "It was my privilege."

"Then I bid you goodnight."

She walked to her room and did not turn to look back even once. The door closed behind her, and Carlo fought down the urge to kick it.

She could not believe the obvious truth? *Hardly.* She chose to blind herself—and thus render him doubly a fool: for speaking the truth to her in a royal court and for caring how she responded to it. To him. *Damnation.*

Stupidity beyond anything, that he had somehow imagined she might look beyond his birth and believe him before a man of her own station.

He swiveled around to return to his own room—and stopped.

He was not alone.

The man who stood before him was barely three feet tall—less than half Carlo's height—and looked up at him with a face creased in open amusement. Before Carlo could speak, he bowed with a flourish.

"Signor Morelli? I've been sent to find you."

Charlotte stalked into her outer room and sank down onto a chair, burying her head in her hands. She kneaded her throbbing forehead with her fingertips.

Not possible. Everything about this evening. The beauty. The horror. Guernsey's screams . . . She shuddered convulsively. Signor Morelli was right. That could so easily have been her.

"Baroness?"

It was her new maid. Charlotte lifted her head from her hands to give the girl a reassuring smile.

"I beg your pardon, Marta. I am only tired." For the first time, her gaze took in the rest of the room. "Dear God! What has happened?"

Quill pens lay scattered across her writing desk. The sheets of music that had been set atop her clavichord lay strewn about the carpet. Charlotte leapt up and threw open the door to her bedroom. Gowns billowed across the bed. She turned to stare at her maid.

"I don't know, madam. I found it this way half an hour ago." Marta gestured helplessly. "I thought I should leave it for you to see. And perhaps the Prince—"

"No!" Charlotte put a hand to her throat, taken aback by her own vehemence. But—"No, certainly not. We won't disturb His Highness with this."

Of course, she did not, could not, *would* not believe Signor Morelli's wild theory. But every nerve in her body protested the idea of Prince Nikolaus walking through her private chambers tonight and surveying the intimate display.

She took a deep breath, forcing her voice into steadiness. "Thank you, Marta. You decided very rightly. You didn't happen to see anyone coming out of here, did you? Or anything suspicious?"

"No, madam. Shall I ask the other servants?"

"I don't know . . ."

Charlotte's head was whirling. The last thing she wanted was any gossip spread through the servants' hall—but could she possibly hope to prevent it? Marta must surely feel more loyalty to her fellows than to her new, foreign employer. Charlotte missed Anna, with a sudden sharp pang. Now that Anna was gone . . .

She looked around the wreckage of her rooms and sighed. Without Anna, Charlotte had no one in this great palace whom she could entirely trust.

Apart from Sophie, she told herself. And winced.

"Never mind, Marta," Charlotte said. "We'll clean this up together and worry no more about it."

"Yes, madam." The girl's eyes widened, but she moved forward obediently to begin the task.

Charlotte knelt to pick up the scattered pages of her music. Weariness so acute that it felt like pain dragged at her arms and her head. If she left for Vienna the next day, she would never have to worry about this or wonder who had done it. If she left, she would never need to fear the possibility of Signor Morelli's disturbing theory. If she left . . .

No. Now that Ernst was dead, Sophie was the only true family Charlotte had. She had abandoned her sister once already, with disastrous consequences. She would not do it again.

"Sent to find me? By whom?" Carlo frowned down at the man before him, fighting to keep his discomfort off his face.

It wasn't the man's size that disconcerted him. Carlo had met several such men and women at other courts, playing much the same role as himself—set on display for the aristocrats' amusement. But the man in front of him, in turn, showed none of the shock or discomfort that most men displayed when meeting a castrato for the first time. Instead, his expression showed a subversive, lurking amusement that discomfited Carlo far more than any outright horror could have done.

"The Princess Esterházy, Princess Marie Elisabeth von Weissenwolf Esterházy. My mistress." The man bowed again, even more deeply. "I am Monsieur Jean, her page."

"And what does the Princess want of me at this hour?"

"Why, nothing," Monsieur Jean said blandly, "but to send you her compliments, signor, and pray that you will wait upon her in the next few days."

"She chooses a peculiar hour to issue her invitations."

"The hour is of my own choosing, I confess." He smiled engagingly. "I'd hoped to intercept you in time to invite you for a drink. There's a charming little tavern in the village nearby. A bit of fresh air? An evening's respite from the palace?"

Carlo stared at him. Whether this was the Princess's plot, or one of Monsieur Jean's own devising, undercurrents of scheming rippled almost tangibly through the air. The last thing Carlo needed, after this disastrous evening, was another round of courtly maneuvers.

Yet, for the sake of an escape from the palace . . .

"Very well," said Carlo. "Lead on, Monsieur Jean."

Chapter Fifteen

Heavy wooden doors closed behind Carlo and Monsieur Jean, and the entire tavern fell silent. Coarse-looking men, huddled over the bar, looked up gape-mouthed at the pair's appearance. Soldiers halted in their rounds of billiards and drinking games to blink at them. Only the relentless drip of a leaking tap broke the silence.

Carlo turned to look down at his companion. *"A charming little tavern?"* he repeated in a faint whisper, barely moving his lips.

Monsieur Jean shrugged, still beaming, and strode forward. "Two beers for the gentleman and myself, barmaid," he called out. "The Prince's most honored guest deserves your finest."

The tavern slowly settled back into a normal low-level roar, and Carlo walked across the sanded floor, conscious of the still-staring eyes fixed on him.

"Is that a woman or a man?" someone whispered, piercingly, from the soldiers' billiard table.

Another soldier whispered back knowingly: "Neither one. It's a castrato. Heard one of them in Vienna, once."

"What does it do?"

Carlo swung around, fixing a determined smile on his lips. He let his voice rise until it filled the tavern. "It sings," he declared, in his purest and most ringing tones. "For kings and empresses, and for your prince. And it also has ears to hear what's being said about it."

"What the devil—!" The first soldier stepped away from the billiards table, reaching down for the hilt of his sword. "I didn't ask you to listen in on my private conversation. *Freak.*"

"I didn't ask to hear it, either. And yet . . ." Carlo raised his eyebrows, holding the rest of his face rigidly still. "We appear to be at an impasse."

Monsieur Jean was back at his side in a heartbeat, smiling dazzlingly.

"What are such small misunderstandings between friends?" He bowed sweepingly to the angry soldier. "My esteemed employer, the Princess Esterházy, would like to buy the entire house a round of drinks."

The sizzling tension dissipated into a roar of huzzahs as the soldiers surged forward. Monsieur Jean led Carlo to a secluded table in a back corner, stepping carefully between the larger men. The soldier who'd spoken earlier nodded stiffly to Carlo. Carlo nodded, infinitesimally, in return, conscious of the burn of frustration in his chest. It would have felt shockingly good to fight, just then, and release the night's simmering store of outrage.

Truly, he was losing all his wits.

"Now, then . . ." Monsieur Jean set the two beers on the table and sat down across from Carlo, smiling intently. "Tell me, Signor Morelli, all about yourself."

A new group of soldiers burst into the tavern just as Carlo began his fourth beer. It had been some time since he'd drunk beer instead of wine, he realized. It was a plain drink, for plain men, not the refined nectar of the aristocrats. He'd forgotten just how much he liked it. His head felt pleasantly dizzy as he glanced across at the incoming group, led by the Esterházy scion who'd so dramatically won the battle games on the opera stage the night before.

As the Esterházy lieutenant—*Anton* Esterházy, that was it—strode inside, his eyes swept across the room and passed over Carlo without interest.

"Anyone seen von Höllner?" he called out. "We've been searching all over the palace for him."

"Off with his wench in Vienna," one man called out, waving his beer stein.

"Or with his wife," someone muttered, sniggering, close by Carlo.

Stifled laughter sounded. It was cut off hastily, though, as Anton Esterházy turned to that corner of the room, his face taking on a chill that made the resemblance to his cousin suddenly inescapable.

"I didn't hear that piece of idiocy," Anton said. "And I trust that no one else did either."

A dead silence greeted his words. He raised his eyebrows, waiting, then shrugged. "Good enough. I'm giving up on him for the night. Who's for a game of billiards?"

Carlo turned back to Monsieur Jean as the byplay ended. The expression he saw on his companion's face made him blink. It cleared away instantly, and Monsieur Jean smiled winningly, his face open and trustworthy. Carlo hadn't merely imagined that look of narrow-eyed calculation . . . had he? He set down his beer, keeping his own expression bland. Perhaps he'd drunk enough for one evening.

"A pretty performance, that, was it not?" Monsieur Jean said. "I always enjoy visiting the soldiers' tavern to watch the drama, particularly as the night goes on. Much like stags fighting over dominance in the wild, I think. Fascinating for any student of human nature and philosophy."

"If you find such conflicts fascinating, perhaps you should spend more of your time in Prince Nikolaus's court." Carlo narrowed his own eyes, searching the other man's face. "There is surely more primitive jostling for precedence and domination in a royal court than anywhere else on earth."

"And if you do not share my fascination for the subject, signor, perhaps you should spend less of your own time in royal courts."

"A veritable point, monsieur." Carlo gave a half-laugh. "But not the key to a brilliant career for a musico. For that, one must play the nobles' game."

But never be accepted as one of them.

He bit his tongue at the memory of Baroness von Steinbeck's horrified expression. *"The Prince is a gentleman."* And Carlo was not. He lifted the beer stein to his lips and took a long, burning draught that emptied the stein.

Monsieur Jean signaled to a barmaid, and replacement beer steins arrived at the table.

"Tell me," Monsieur Jean said, "what brought you to accept the Prince's invitation to Eszterháza? Surely, there were other invitations. Other courts, other kingdoms . . ."

Carlo shrugged. "I'd never been to Eszterháza. And the Prince's musical establishment is famous throughout Europe. The chance to meet Herr Haydn in person was not to be brushed aside."

"And others in the court?"

"Pardon?" Carlo met the other man's gaze. His fingers tightened around the handle of his beer stein. "I'm afraid I don't take your meaning, monsieur." The Baroness's light brown eyes looking up at him through the darkness outside the opera house . . .

"Surely you'd met one or two of the gentlemen at this court before your arrival," Monsieur Jean said easily. "Was this not an opportunity to renew any old friendships? Or, at any rate, acquaintances?"

"Not at all." Carlo's shoulders relaxed. "No, I'd never met any of Prince Nikolaus's courtiers before."

"Or his other guests?"

Carlo frowned. "You seem remarkably interested in my acquaintances, Monsieur Jean. Are you compiling a list?"

"You are too quick for me, signor." Monsieur Jean's face broke into a grin. "Indeed, I'm certain I could sell off such a list for hundreds of ducats to connoisseurs. The private acquaintances of Europe's most celebrated musico . . . Alas, you've found me out in my dastardly plan."

He leaned forward, his eyes sparkling. "Tell me, though, man-to-man. In strictest confidence: with whom would you wish to become more intimately acquainted, here at Eszterháza? For the palace is filled with a multitude of beauties at the moment. His Highness's own niece is a fine figure of a woman, as are a number of the singers in his opera troupe." He lowered his voice. "With all due respect to our fiery young lieutenant across the room, I wouldn't mind spending an hour or two alone with the lovely Sophie von Höllner, myself."

Carlo sat back in his seat, shaking his head. "You are asking the wrong person to share in your game of what-if, monsieur," he said dryly. "Did not you hear the soldier who greeted us? An 'it' can hardly even fantasize of such things."

"Perhaps an 'it' may not, indeed. But we are men of the world, you and I. And I know a fair bit more than our charming guardsmen about the astonishing reputation of the musici across the courts of Europe, and of how well a few of them have deserved it." Monsieur Jean added, smirking, "I heard, as well, that the noblewomen of this court were fairly swarming around you after your performance a few nights ago."

"Not all of them," Carlo said. He looked into the murky depths of the beer, but did not see it. "Even men of the world must accept their own limits, one day, and give up on impossible dreams." His fingers tightened around his beer stein, and he bit off his words with careful precision. "Eventually, no matter what our preferences might be, we must all learn to play the roles in life that were assigned to us."

"Perhaps you are right," Monsieur Jean murmured. But the tone of his voice contradicted his words. Rich satisfaction rippled through it.

Carlo glanced up quickly, searching the other man's face. Monsieur Jean smiled back sunnily and lifted his own beer stein.

"To the theater of life, signor!"

"To the theater," Carlo echoed, warily, and drank.

Alone in her grand salon, the Princess Esterházy sat by the window. Darkness filled the room, unlit by a single candle. Her pet dog snored on her lap, and she stroked his white fur absently with her bejeweled fingers as she gazed through the arched window into the darkened gardens outside.

The still water in the fountains gleamed in the darkness, reflecting pale moonlight. No figures moved across the manicured lawns that lay between the palace and the tall hedges beyond.

But the Princess's searching gaze moved restlessly across the view for hours yet, before the night was done.

Chapter Sixteen

"Ny God, man, what's happened to your face?"

Friedrich woke to find Anton Esterházy bending over his bed and peering down at him.

"Wha—ow!" Friedrich cupped his hands to his stinging cheeks.

"Look at yourself!" Anton scooped up Friedrich's small shaving mirror and tilted it toward him.

Friedrich blinked into it. His cheeks, chin, and forehead were bright scarlet. Every prickle of morning's beard burned against his sore skin. And yet—

He touched his face wonderingly. It had healed. That godawful smelly cream had worked. No yellow blisters, no oozing pustules—

"Amazing," he breathed.

"What the devil did you do to yourself last night?"

"Ah . . ." Friedrich pulled himself up into a sitting position and rubbed the back of his neck. "It's a long story."

"Ha." Anton set down the mirror and flung himself down onto the chair next to Friedrich's bed. "I've told your valet to bring us both food, so you have all the time you need. Start talking."

"Well . . ."

"You've turned into a bloody mystery, you know that? Where were you last night, anyway? A whole group of us went looking for you."

"Here and there?" Friedrich offered. He glanced past Anton, searching for escape. "What time is it, anyway?"

"Ten."

"Oh, God, I've overslept!" Friedrich leapt up and searched for clothing. "You'll have to eat by yourself, Esterházy. I'll see you—"

"*Overslept*? At ten o'clock?" Anton stared at him. "What appointments could *you* have?"

Halfway into his uniform, Friedrich tried to look suave. "I've been attending the opera rehearsals."

"You listen to opera now?"

"I'm learning."

"I'll wager you are." Anton stood up and crossed his arms.

Friedrich eyed him warily. "I really do have to go. Sorry about the trouble, but—"

"Nothing to be sorry about, my friend." Anton smiled beatifically. "I'm coming with you."

Half an hour later, Friedrich slumped down into a seat at the back of the opera house, while Anton looked around with bright curiosity. Twenty minutes of desperate persuasion had only made him more devilishly determined.

"Don't you have any real duties to attend to?" Friedrich muttered now.

Anton gave a muffled shout of laughter. "Is that Friedrich von Höllner speaking? Herr Honorary-Lieutenancy-sleep-till-noon—"

"Not lately." Friedrich snorted. "I've been waking up early all *week*." *Damn it.*

"Have you?" Anton raised his eyebrows. "Now that is interesting. I can hardly wait for you to explain it to me."

Friedrich sank lower in his seat. Onstage, the kapellmeister was having a long debate with one of the singers, an old man. The old man stomped off, making a rude gesture at one of the younger men. The dark-haired older lady smirked, and the kapellmeister shook his head.

"Next piece," he called out. "Dommayer! Pichler!"

Anton leaned forward in his seat, enlightenment dawning on his features. "*Now* I see why you've been going to rehearsals!"

"Sorry?" Friedrich blinked and sat up.

"She's adorable," Anton breathed. "That hair—that figure!"

"Eh?" Friedrich scanned the stage. At least four women stood at various points.

The director sat down at the harpsichord and began to play, and the blonde girl stepped forward. She opened her mouth and began to sing; the dark-haired man behind her joined in a moment later.

"I've heard this one before." Friedrich sat back, sighing. "Don't worry about trying to pay attention, anyway. All the songs sound the same."

"She's an angel. And that voice—!" Anton turned and fixed Friedrich with a glittering gaze. "You have to introduce me."

"To her? I don't know her."

"You don't—?!"

"I know that dark-haired lady." Friedrich pointed. "Madame Zel-something-or-other. Very charming. If we order any refreshments, you'll get to know her, too."

"Von Höllner, you're a Philistine."

The music broke off, and the director shook his head. He made the blonde sing again on her own, again and then again—the words sounded slightly different each time, but it had been too long since Friedrich had studied or spoken Italian for him to understand many of them.

"What's he doing?" Anton stared at the stage. "Look, she's flushed!"

"I think he's making her fix the pronunciation. He does that a lot with her. Ungodly boring." Friedrich sighed. "Speaking of which, Ester-házy, what would you say to some refreshments? I could—"

"He's a monster. Who cares how she pronounces the words?"

"We could—"

"I couldn't eat. Not until I've met her." Anton turned back to grin fiercely. "Come on, man! I know you've got your secrets. For the moment, I won't press you on them—but you're the one who comes here every day. You have to help me meet her."

"Well . . ." Friedrich sighed and thought wistfully of pastries and wine. "All right. But *then* we'll order refreshments."

Anna's legs nearly gave out underneath her as she stepped away from the harpsichord. When would it grow any easier? She'd spent the last day

and a half memorizing and practicing every single incomprehensible syllable for the opera they would perform tonight. How could they still all
be wrong?

"Fräulein Dommayer." Herr Pichler took her arm, smiling charm-
ingly. "Your Italian improves by the day."

"It does not." She pulled her arm back and glared at him. His face
fell, and she relented. "I'm sorry, but I cannot believe you. It—" She
lowered her voice, conscious of the other singers' eyes on them. "It is a
nightmare."

"Nonsense." He retrieved her arm and steered her off the stage to
a corner at the front of the audience. "Everyone but you can hear the
improvement. If you desired it . . ." He leaned closer, and his warm breath
brushed against her cheek. "I could assist you with private lessons."

Anna swallowed. Her heartbeat was fluttering uncomfortably—he
was terribly handsome, even though he did know it—but his words still
made no sense. "As I recall, sir, our last tutorial was a disaster."

He shrugged. "I was overset by grief. I can only apologize for my bad
manners." He rested his palm on the wall by her cheek, closing her into
the corner, and fixed his warm gaze on her. "Won't you let me make up
for them now?"

"Why, Herr Pichler," Madame Zelinowsky purred behind him, "you
grow quite heated. Whatever can you be speaking of?" He jerked back,
and her smile deepened. "I'm afraid you must surrender our little Anna
for the moment, as these two gentlemen are most desirous of making her
acquaintance." She took his arm and drew him firmly to one side. "Anna,
my dear, this is Lieutenant von Höllner, a delightful new friend of mine."

Freed, Anna stepped out of the corner and dropped a curtsey, holding
her head up high as the great ladies did. Of course, Lieutenant von
Höllner was Frau von Höllner's husband, the blond officer who always
slept in the back row of the audience. Today his face was reddened from
some injury, and he barely looked at her as he made his bow. His friend,
on the other hand—

"May I introduce Lieutenant Anton Esterházy?" Lieutenant von
Höllner stepped aside. "He is—"

"—Enchanted." Lieutenant Esterházy grinned and took Anna's hand in a strong, warm grip. His hair was smoothly powdered, but energy seemed to burn from his tanned skin. His lips brushed softly against the back of her hand while his blue eyes devoured her face.

Anna fought down a shiver. She'd never had her hand kissed in her life. Was this some sort of joke?

No, she told herself. She was a professional singer now, and an actress. She must learn to take this as her due.

"I'm pleased to meet you, lieutenant."

He released her hand slowly, as if he were reluctant to let it go. "I had to pay my compliments, Fräulein. Your voice is heavenly—angelic! I was overwhelmed."

Herr Pichler let out a muffled snort. Lieutenant Esterházy shifted position so that his broad shoulders were between Anna and the actor. He smiled down at her dazzlingly from a foot's advantage in height. "How long have you been a singer, Fräulein?"

"Ah . . . five days?"

He let out a shout of laughter. "No, really."

"Oh, but she is telling the truth, lieutenant," Madame Zelinowsky purred. "It's a charming story. Our little Anna was a noblewoman's maid until her discovery, only a few days ago."

"Amazing." Lieutenant Esterházy shook his head. "Such a jewel, to be hidden until now." Lifting her hand once more, he pressed it between his palms. "Fräulein Dommayer, may I ask—may I beg—the honor and the privilege of being allowed to speak with you after your performance tonight?"

"Well, I—I don't see why not," Anna faltered.

"Your servant, Fräulein." He turned her hand over and pressed a lingering kiss on the inside of her wrist. Then he bowed deeply before walking away, his friend following behind.

Anna raised her tingling wrist to her chest. She rubbed it lightly with her other hand, trying to reorder her senses.

"My, my," Madame Zelinowsky murmured. "You must be careful to wear your sweetest perfume tonight, my dear."

"Why should I?" Anna lifted her chin. "It will only be a few moments' conversation."

"As you say." The older woman glided away, chuckling.

Anna finally allowed herself to look at Herr Pichler. His arms were crossed. She could not read the expression on his face.

"I trust your plans are proceeding well, Fräulein?" he asked evenly.

"Plans?" She frowned. "I don't—"

"Of course. You're not allowed to share them with me." He bowed stiffly, his face tightening with the movement of his back. "I can only apologize for so clumsily intruding upon them."

"Herr Pichler—"

But he was already walking away from her.

Anna gritted her teeth and fought down the urge to throw something after him.

"Dommayer and Kettner!" the kapellmeister called.

Anna took a deep breath. Music and meaningless Italian words swirled through her head.

She walked onstage.

"Did you see how he was annoying her?" Anton glared across the audience. "What a cad."

"Mm." Friedrich leaned over the cart of pastries and drinks that the maidservant had brought. "Strudel or torte, Esterházy?"

"Have you ever seen such perfect beauty? Such innocence?" Anton shook his head. "I'm telling you, I felt her shiver when I kissed her hand! What kind of actress would do that?"

"One who used to be a maid?" Friedrich pointed at the tray. "I asked—"

His hand hovered over the top shelf of pastries, and stilled. Beneath the plate of strudel slices, a sliver of ivory paper stuck out.

Not again. He looked up at the maidservant's face for the first time. She looked back blandly.

"Sir?"

"Never mind." He yanked out the sliver of paper—and went limp with relief.

It was only a napkin. A fine, smooth, linen napkin that had looked like paper from the wrong angle. Friedrich laughed in sheer relief. There was a blur of noise in the background—Anton saying something he didn't catch—but he couldn't stop laughing once he'd started. It was too absurd. His face was burned, and he was watching godawful Italian opera, but he hadn't been sent a missive from the Brotherhood after all. It was too wonderful for words. He finally hiccupped to a halt, with the napkin in his hands.

"Von Höllner?" Anton was looking at him oddly. "Are you all right?"

"Fine, fine." Friedrich scooped up a slice of strudel for himself, grinning widely. He bit into the sweet, juicy apples and felt a ripple of sheer pleasure run through him.

"I just said, I need your help," Anton repeated. "Keep an eye on that Pichler fellow while I'm at maneuvers. See if he tries to pester her again."

"And?" Friedrich raised his eyebrows. "What do you want me to do about it? Shout for help?"

Anton narrowed his eyes. "Just tell me later, and I'll deal with it. Meantime, I'm going to see what I can find out about him. I'll ask my cousin if there have been any problems with him in the past." He turned back toward the stage, one finger tapping impatiently on his leg. "Keep your eyes open, von Höllner. You can do that?"

"Why not?" Friedrich licked pastry off his fingers and shrugged. Keep his eyes open? Spy without understanding or agreement? *Why not*, indeed. It was become almost second nature by now.

Chapter Seventeen

Carlo closed his eyes against waves of nausea as his valet dressed him, to the accompaniment of a pounding headache.

What in the name of God had he been thinking, to match the Princess's lackey drink for drink last night? Bad enough that they'd so clearly been on show in that rural tavern—Eszterháza's two prize freaks, out on display. Worse yet that he'd been out-drunk by a man less than half his own size, all the while being none-too-subtly interrogated.

Carlo groaned, and his valet's hands stilled on his neckcloth.

"Signor?"

"It's nothing." Carlo set his teeth together.

It was clear enough that he'd been thoroughly examined. But why? He still had no idea.

He did, however, have a morning appointment.

"Signor Morelli."

For all the Princess Esterházy's glaring absence from her husband's court, her own rooms were those of a reigning monarch—and, Carlo noted, as far removed from the befrilled and befeathered style of her replacement as any mode of decorations could reasonably be. The barely ornamented, gold-and-white pattern of the room was a model of restrained elegance, and the sunlight through the windows made the bright gilding along the white walls and mantelpiece blaze with regal authority.

The Princess herself sat in a chair like a throne, with her lavender skirts spread around her and a tiny dog asleep on her lap. Three maids hovered in the far corner of the room, watching their mistress's every move. Another woman, perhaps a lady-in-waiting, sat directly across from her in a smaller, high-backed chair that faced the Princess but revealed only the back of her powdered hair to Carlo. Still, Carlo found himself grateful for the unknown company as he stepped into the spacious, light-filled room and met the Princess Esterházy's sharp, intelligent gaze. He was almost certainly not up to making courtly conversation on his own this morning.

The Princess nodded at him, her eyes cool and assessing. "I thank you for attending me, signor."

"I was honored by the invitation, Your Highness." Carlo bowed as minimally as courtesy would allow, for the sake of his throbbing head. From the twitch of her lips, he wondered if she knew his reason.

As he bowed, the occupant of the chair across from the Princess turned to look at him. Carlo's jaw clenched. "Baroness von Steinbeck."

"Signor." Her eyes were wide with surprise.

Carlo straightened, cursing inwardly as waves of nausea rolled through him. How soon could he make his excuses?

"You look in need of sustenance, signor," the Princess said. "My page thought that you might be." She nodded at one of the hovering maids, then turned back to Carlo. Diamonds flashed on her fingers, catching the light as she pointed to the chair beside the Baroness. "Do sit down."

"I thank you, Your Highness."

As the maid hurried away—in search of some dainty, ladylike confection, no doubt—Carlo sank down onto the appointed chair, keeping a pleasant smile fixed to his face. His foot brushed against the edge of the Baroness's black silk skirts. She twitched them away, and he jerked back. The Princess watched with palpable amusement.

The rest of the magnificent chamber was empty, apart from the two remaining maids who waited in the background, watching the Princess intently.

"I trust Monsieur Jean is well?" Carlo asked.

"Oh, yes. His system is remarkably resilient, I find. He and Asa are out riding now, while the Baroness keeps me company."

"Ah." Carlo slid a discreet glance at the Baroness, whose face was composed, giving nothing away. How long had she been on visiting terms with the wife of her sister's lover?

"And here is your sustenance." The Princess smiled faintly as the first maid returned, bearing a tray with dry crackers and a tall glass of fizzing liquid. At Carlo's involuntary start, she let out a dry laugh. "Never fear, signor. This remedy is a specialty of Monsieur Jean's. I think you'll find it quite appropriate."

Carlo took a wary sip. It burned, nearly choking him—but in the next moment, his head cleared. He blinked and drained the glass. When the burning sensation subsided in his throat, the nausea vanished with it. He straightened his shoulders and took a deep breath.

Both women were watching him—the Princess with amused interest and the Baroness with a mixture of confusion and—was it distaste? *Probably.* She had dismissed his theory about the singers' death as a wild and ungentlemanly fantasy . . . a verdict that must label him, in her eyes, as either a mischief-maker or a coward. Was she now adding "drunkard" to her list?

He shrugged and lifted his empty glass in a salute to the Princess.

"My compliments to your page. An excellent remedy, Your Highness."

"I am glad. Particularly as it allows me now to ask you both for a favor." She stroked the short white fur of her sleeping lapdog as she watched them. "I was exceedingly distressed to have missed your joint recital, a few nights ago. As you are both here now, won't you indulge me with one song?" Her gaze rested on Carlo. "It would be a pity indeed to say that the greatest musico in Europe had spent the entire summer at Eszterháza and I had never heard him sing."

"Your pardon, Highness," Baroness von Steinbeck murmured. "I have not practiced the accompaniments, so—"

"You played them marvelously well four nights ago," Carlo said coolly. "I'm certain you could play them again."

She bit her full lower lip. He wished he hadn't noted it. She was not for him and had made that clear enough.

"It's settled, then," the Princess said. "Signor—"

"I'm afraid I have not memorized the parts," the Baroness said quietly. "The music is in my apartments."

"Then we'll send a maid to fetch it." The Princess's nod sent another maid scurrying out the door. "You have had the rooms cleaned, have you not?"

The Baroness's head jerked up. "The rooms——?"

"After last night's disarray." The Princess shook her head. "Shocking, that it could happen here. Was anything taken?"

"I . . . no. Nothing was taken. But . . ." The Baroness took a breath. "I didn't know that the news had spread."

"Nonsense, my dear. News always spreads. And news of a burglary—even if it was really only a search . . ."

Carlo watched the interaction like a theatrical play. The Baroness's face was taut with distress.

"I did warn you," the Princess murmured softly. "But I am sorry for your discomfort, Baroness." She turned her razor-sharp smile to Carlo. "And you, signor? I trust you've suffered no such inconveniences in your stay here?"

"Not that I'm aware of, Your Highness." Carlo kept his voice even. "But then, I'm sure Monsieur Jean could have told you that already, after last night's conversation."

She raised her eyebrows. "No doubt. But you must indulge me, signor, in telling me yourself of your last stopping points, before Eszterháza. I may live in seclusion, but I am prodigiously fond of imaginary travels. Tell me of the wonders of Constantinople and Saint Petersburg, pray, and how those courts compare to my husband's palace here."

And do you desire compliments or insults on your husband's behalf? Carlo wondered. But he knew better than to ask. He obliged her instead, filling the minutes with polished tales of the two different courts, while the Princess stroked the dog on her lap and listened with every appearance of enjoyment, and the Baroness stared down at her own knotted fingers and failed entirely to look anything but worried and unhappy.

At last, a soft knock sounded on the door.

"Aha!" The Princess looked up as her maid returned. "Here is your music now, Baroness. I am all attention."

Carlo stood and gestured for the Baroness to walk before him. Her back was straight, her face tense. He felt a momentary pang of sympathy.

She was no fool, even if she did choose to blind herself to the natures of those around her. What could she hope to gain by such willful ignorance?

"Which piece, signor?"

He looked down into her clear brown eyes and named a different piece than he had planned.

"The serenade."

He hadn't warmed up his voice with exercises yet, and he would pay for that later with strain. But for now he only closed his eyes, summoning up the mood of the song. When he drew in his preparatory breath, her fingers brushed against the keyboard. He began to sing.

The song was aimed at the Princess, his audience, who sat listening with her eyes half-closed. But with every breath, Carlo was conscious of the Baroness beside him, watching him, playing below his voice and against it, supporting his song with grace and strength.

The serenade was familiar, one he had sung for years. It showed off the top range of his voice; it was pretty and sentimental; today, it felt like more. He found real tenderness infusing his voice, instead of theatrical emotion. The second time through, instead of adding the usual carnival of showy ornamentations to the notes, he only bent them in sweet, rippling inflections.

He never looked away from the Princess, but he felt the Baroness's every breath.

At the end of the piece, the Princess clapped slowly. "Bravo, signor. I see the reports have understated the truth, for once. And *brava*, Baroness."

The outer door opened, and Monsieur Jean walked in with a lady his own size. They made their courtesies to the Princess.

"Asa, this is the famous Signor Morelli. He and the Baroness have been delighting me with a recital."

"Hmm," said Asa, and took her seat with the air of one restraining herself from comment.

Her companion, though, showed no such restraint. "Delightful indeed!" Monsieur Jean grinned up at Carlo as he pulled up his own chair. He looked healthy and windswept, his cheeks still red from exertion. "And how are you feeling this morning, signor?"

Carlo smiled thinly. "Tolerably well, I thank you, sir. Your Highness." He bowed. "I am distraught to have to take my leave of you, but I cannot be late for dinner."

"Of course. And neither can the Baroness. We wouldn't want to risk the two of you being missed together, would we?" Laughter rippled through the Princess's cool voice. "Signor, you will escort the Baroness, won't you?"

Carlo set his teeth together at the smirk on Monsieur Jean's face. The Princess had an efficient network of spies. How far did it go? Could they report to her not only the content of his actions, but also of his thoughts? His most secret desires?

"It would be an honor," he said, and offered the Baroness his arm.

If there was anything worse than walking through Eszterháza's endless corridors with a man who had taken her into contempt, Charlotte thought, then it was being seated at dinner beside the man who had nearly caused a murder the night before.

Count Radamowsky did not appear discomposed in the slightest by the looks and whispers of the other guests at Prince Nikolaus's high table, nor by the looks of sheer hatred that were directed at him by Herr Ignaz von Born, across the table. He gestured for a footman to refill his wine as he smiled at Charlotte.

"I hear that your late husband was interested in the alchemical arts, Baroness?"

Not in your sort of alchemy. She bit back the words, as Ernst's kind face, drawn with pain, appeared in her mind's eye. No matter how great his sufferings, Ernst had rarely complained, nor had he ever been discourteous, even to his oldest son's grasping wife as she'd pushed past Charlotte to count the silver, china, and family jewels, visibly impatient for Ernst's demise. He would not have been rude now, either.

"He took a keen interest in the quest for the Philosopher's Stone," Charlotte said quietly.

Radamowsky laughed. "And why should he not? The transmutation of lead into gold, the kiss of immortality, the search for ultimate power— but von Born knows more of such things than I."

"I beg your pardon?" Herr von Born jerked as if stung.

"You've spent hours messing about with noxious liquids and stones, have you not, my friend? Have you yet discovered the infamous Philosopher's Stone that you're all looking for?"

"I am a seeker of knowledge." Herr von Born enunciated his words clearly. "Whereas you trick people into believing in illusions."

"What we saw last night was no illusion," Charlotte said. Her fingers clenched beneath the table. "Has anyone heard news of Mr. Guernsey's health?"

Herr von Born stared at her as if she had spoken Turkish. Count Radamowsky dropped his gaze and toyed with his wine glass.

"A sad case. Most regrettable. But the Prince's physician is excellent—or so I hear."

"Mm."

Despite herself, Charlotte found her gaze slipping up the table to where Signor Morelli sat. His face was as pale and beautiful as ever, in that disturbingly feminine way, and his mouth was set in a polite smile as he tilted his head to listen to the Prince.

Charlotte remembered his words from the night before and swallowed. Madness, truly.

Yet she couldn't stop herself from picking at the dilemma, like a scab she was hopeless to ignore.

"I wonder if you could tell me, Count Radamowsky," she said. "How did His Highness know to ask for your elemental last night?"

Radamowsky blinked. "I beg your pardon?"

Across the table, Herr von Born's eyes narrowed with sudden interest.

Charlotte fought to keep her tone pleasantly cool, as though she were discussing only the weather, or her sister's favorite fashions. "I only wondered, sir, how Prince Nikolaus knew of your elemental." She paused, then dropped in the last words like pebbles into deep water. "As you had only arrived yesterday morning."

"Well . . ." Radamowsky took a sip of wine and shrugged. "My projects are not entirely secret, Baroness. I'd imagine—"

"I'd certainly never heard of your so-called 'elemental,'" von Born said, with relish.

"My friend." Radamowsky smiled at him. "We do not, as you know, always see eye-to-eye. Do you really expect me to share all of my experiments with you?" He leaned forward, still smiling. "Do you tell me all that you do in private? I've heard tell of strange doings, darker offshoots gathered from the Viennese houses of Freemasonry—"

"That's enough!" Von Born drew himself up, eyes flashing. "You slander me and my work."

"And you disparage mine to all and sundry. I—"

"Gentlemen!" the Prince called, from the head of the long table. Everyone was craning their necks to look at them now, drawn by the increasing volume of the men's voices. The Prince's stare was glacial. "Is aught amiss with your food?"

Herr von Born only shook his head tightly.

Count Radamowsky said, "Not at all, Your Highness. It is superb beyond description."

"Then I hope you may both save your breath for your meal."

The Prince turned back to his companions, but Signor Morelli's gaze lingered a moment longer. It burned against Charlotte's skin.

He thought her a fool for disbelieving his wild theories. Charlotte stabbed her knife into her meal with the force of her frustration.

The two men beside and across from her ate in fuming silence, and she did not attempt to draw either of them out.

She had found their conversation to be anything but reassuring.

Chapter Eighteen

F ranz held his smile through the interminable rounds of bowing to their noble audience. He kept it pinned to his face through the endless applause and while Herr Haydn was summoned up to the balcony to receive a velvet pouch full of gold, a mark of His Highness's great appreciation. He kept his smile clamped to his face even when he spotted Lieutenant Anton Esterházy sitting three feet away from Prince Nikolaus in the royal box. Not the usual seat for a mere military officer, surely, but for one with the right last name . . .

When a footman ran up to the stage to present Fräulein Dommayer with a great bouquet of red roses, Franz lost his smile entirely.

Bloody Esterházy name. Bloody Esterházy fortune.

Fräulein Dommayer blushed and held the flowers close to her as she curtseyed, breathing in the scent, oblivious to the venomous looks shot at her by the other ladies in the cast. And if Prince Nikolaus's cousin did make his way into Fräulein Dommayer's bed, Franz thought viciously as he bowed again, there'd be no royal outcries of immorality *then*, oh, no. "Immorality" only transpired when two servants fell in love, like poor Antonicek and Madame Delacroix, and never when another wealthy, indulged aristocrat bought his own way into an actress's arms.

Not that Franz was in any danger of falling in love himself. He turned on his heel and stalked offstage as the applause finally, finally faded. He'd been playacting his heart out this morning, as he'd learned to years before. But to be so ignominiously shoved aside, and for a petty aristocrat with that cursed last name . . .

He changed out of his costume, seething. His back flamed with renewed agony every time he leaned over. The other men around him chatted, trading jokes and making plans for the rest of the evening. Delacroix pointedly ignored him, as usual. Franz didn't care. He'd show them all, soon enough. Especially the Esterházys.

He stepped out of the men's changing room just in time to see Lieutenant Esterházy stride backstage as confidently as if he owned it. Franz bowed, biting down rage. The lieutenant gazed evenly at him and nodded infinitesimally. Then his face lit up.

"Fräulein Dommayer!" He crossed the wide floor in a few quick steps to bow over her hand.

Franz hesitated—then crossed his arms and leaned back against the wall, bracing his muscles against the pain. Why shouldn't he stay and watch, after all? If it afforded Esterházy the slightest hint of embarrassment, then Franz would be richly rewarded indeed.

"Lieutenant Esterházy." Anna curtseyed awkwardly, one hand in his and her other arm occupied with her bouquet. "You are very kind, sir. The roses are beautiful."

At first, she'd thought they might have come from the Baroness, who had sent her a small bouquet and a kind note the day after her first performance. But a card had been buried deep in their midst, and she'd found it while changing out of her costume.

Anton Esterházy. In admiration.

It was a terribly strange feeling. It was nearly intoxicating, like the scent of the dozen roses in her arms. She felt her breathing quicken as she looked up at the intensity of his gaze.

Anna swallowed and withdrew her hand. "Where . . . wherever did you find such beautiful flowers, sir?"

"I begged them from my cousin's gardens." His face opened into laughter. "I hope you'll not think the less of me for it! I would have ordered them from Vienna or Paris for you, if I could. But as such beauties were blossoming here already, only waiting to be picked . . ."

Anna flushed. "They are perfect." She buried her face in them for a moment to escape the meaning in his eyes. As she lifted her head, she saw Herr Pichler glaring at her from across the room. She sighed.

"Are you tired?" Lieutenant Esterházy leaned closer. "You gave a marvelous performance. My cousin was most impressed, and I—I was bewitched." He smiled crookedly. "I think my heart may never recover from it."

A maid curtseyed before Herr Pichler and handed him a note. His eyes widened as he read it.

"Fräulein?" The lieutenant frowned.

"Forgive me, sir. I am only tired. As you said." Anna smiled up at him, but half her attention remained on Herr Pichler, who had folded up the note and slipped it inside the inner pocket of his frock coat. His gaze slipped from side to side, as though he were calculating an escape route. He began to saunter, ever-so-casually, toward the back door.

There were so many mysteries in this palace . . . but perhaps Anna might solve this one tonight.

Lieutenant Esterházy had been speaking words she hadn't heard. Anna curtseyed again and held out her hand to him.

"Please forgive me," she said, "but I must go to sleep. I've been rehearsing so much for tonight's performance. And . . . and, of course, I must find water for my roses."

"We could find a maid to do that," he said quickly, "and then perhaps a short walk outside in the evening air—"

"Not tonight."

She backed away, smiling apologetically. Herr Pichler had already disappeared out the back door. She'd have to find somewhere to deposit the roses, then circle around the building and try to find him in the miles of parkland. Difficult, but not impossible—if she hurried. She fought down images of ghouls and demons out in the darkness.

"Perhaps tomorrow, sir?" she offered, and fled.

Franz turned past the first tall hedge, as the message had directed—and a hand reached out to seize him by the throat.

"You've disappointed us, Herr Pichler."

The gloved hand was too strong to fight. If he squirmed, his breath would be cut off entirely. Franz went limp, breathing shallowly through his nose. He couldn't see his captor in the shadows of the hedge, but he recognized the voice.

"How?" he gasped. "I haven't—"

"I told you to be discreet. I ordered you not to make yourself unpleasant to the Esterházys or draw their notice."

"And?" Franz swallowed against the iron grip around his throat.

"Anton Esterházy complained to the Prince of your impertinence today. His Highness has asked Rahier to keep a sharp eye on you and report your every doing." The hand tightened around Franz's throat. "Now do you understand how you've failed me?"

Franz closed his eyes, lanced by horror. "I didn't—I only meant—"

"Yes?" The hand loosened infinitesimally. "Do explain yourself."

Franz paused, licking his lips. What could he say? That he'd been too jealous and discomfited to even consider the consequences of irritating Anton Esterházy? That he'd been foiled in his own plan to insinuate himself deeper into the Brotherhood's secrets by making up to Fräulein Dommayer? That—

No. He opened his eyes and took a rasping breath. "It won't happen again."

"It won't have the chance to happen, ever again. You should know that already, Herr Pichler. We do not tolerate failure."

"I haven't—" His captor's hand pressed hard against Franz's Adam's apple and he choked. When he recovered, he gasped out the words. "I haven't failed. Yet."

"You think not?"

"Rahier is a suspicious bastard. But he delegates the work, he doesn't do it himself. He trusts Haydn and Delacroix to report back to him." Franz took another shallow breath. "Herr Haydn detests Rahier. He'll only speak to me himself, give me a warning, and then turn a blind eye. That's his way."

The hand remained firmly wrapped around his throat. "And Monsieur Delacroix?"

"He hated me already. This will make no difference to him.

Anyway . . ." Franz swallowed, fighting dizziness. Too little breath . . .
how much longer could he last like this? "The man's a fool."

"Then how did he find you out the first time, for aiding his wife?"

"He didn't. It was someone else. They sent him a letter."

"Mm."

"It must have been a stableboy. Someone who saw me take the horses.
Or—I don't know! Not Delacroix. He couldn't sniff out a conspiracy if
his life depended on it."

"Which it may." The hand tightened. "Yours certainly does."

Franz's vision blurred. Stars formed in front of his eyes. He couldn't
breathe—couldn't—

Abruptly, the hand released him. "You're a fortunate man, Herr
Pichler. I've decided to give you one more chance to redeem yourself."

Franz stumbled back, rubbing his throat. "How? When?"

"You'll find out after tomorrow night's masked ball. Once the royal visitors arrive." The voice hardened. "In the meantime, stay away from Esterházys. Irritate no one. Be a paragon of public virtue. Do you understand?"

Franz's throat throbbed with pain when he spoke. "I understand."

"Good."

The hedge rustled. A moment later, Franz was alone in the beautifully laid-out garden.

He stood for a long moment staring at the peaceful Greek sculptures
in the fountain six feet away. The water was still and smooth as glass, and
lit by moonlight.

He'd never thought to come so close to death on this adventure.

A cool night breeze blew against the nape of his neck. He shook his
head and turned to leave.

When he turned the corner of the hedge, he walked straight into
Fräulein Dommayer.

Anna stumbled back. At first, Herr Pichler didn't even seem to recognize
her. Then he laughed, in a tone that frightened her.

"You're too late, Fräulein. He's already gone. You shouldn't have let your officer delay you so long."

Anna stepped forward, frowning. "I was looking for you."

"Me?" He backed away, into a patch of grass illuminated by the moonlight that glanced off the water of the fountain. His face looked pale as death. "Why look for me? It hardly fits with your plans to play at romance with another singer. Not when you have an Esterházy to reel in."

"What?" Anna's cheeks flooded with heat. "I have no plans, Herr Pichler. Nor *instructions*, either, unlike you. And I—I would never—!" She shook her head, too angry to speak. She'd crept all the way across the gardens in the darkness, terrified by every noise—for this? "How dare you say such things?"

He blinked. "Then—"

"I have no intention of reeling in anybody, no matter what their name might be! I'm not so—so—I just wouldn't. And I am not playing at romance with you, either!" She lifted her chin. "You may think yourself very wonderful, sir, but I am not so easily taken in by playacting."

He stared at her. "Then what in the name of God are you doing here, Fräulein?"

"I followed you, of course." Her cheeks burned, but she lifted her chin defiantly. "I'm not in love with you, but I do have eyes. You're in some kind of trouble, aren't you?"

He rubbed his throat and looked away. "Are you seriously telling me that you don't know?"

"Well . . ."

"And you aren't involved in it at all?"

"I have no idea what you mean," Anna said.

He dropped his hand from his throat and began to laugh. "Oh, sweet Christ and all the saints . . ."

"Sir?" She stepped forward, but he put his hand out to stop her.

"It's nothing. I'm only a fool beyond compare." He shook his head and glanced at the thick hedges that rose up beside her. "If he is still here watching us . . ."

Anna jumped back—then moved forward, neck prickling, to peer into the black depths of the hedges. *Nothing.* Only the night breeze rustled through the thick branches. She let out her held breath.

"We're alone," she said.

"Thank God." He slumped down onto the low stone wall of the fountain and put his head in his hands.

Anna felt her chest tighten as she looked at his crumpled figure.

She'd spent half her time, as she crept after him—when she wasn't imagining demons out of the shadows that surrounded her—berating herself for her own foolishness in falling prey to a handsome face and romantically injured figure, when she'd known full well he wasn't interested in her in that way. Now, though, as she looked down at the lead singer she'd been so struck by, all that she could feel was compassion.

"You were trying to charm me this morning," she said. "Why?"

He shrugged. "Does it matter? It's naught to do with you. Not anymore."

"Herr Pichler . . ." Anna felt the whispering night breeze on her neck and shoulders. She fought down the urge to glance behind her in search of watching eyes. "You've been drawn into some dangerous endeavor," she said softly. "Can't you take yourself out of it? I would help you, if you'd let me. I would like to be your friend."

His lips twisted. "You're very kind, Fräulein. But it's far too late for me to escape it now."

Chapter Nineteen

"I can't," Charlotte said. "Sophie, see reason! I'm a widow."

"Of nearly five months. And this is a masked ball, Lotte! No one will even know who you are." Sophie's eyes were alight with mischief. "It's too late for you to find another costume, anyway."

Charlotte glanced at the windows and sighed. The sky outside was already shaded with twilight. "All I wanted was a plain domino. Black. Nothing too—"

"No more black!" Sophie's ankle bracelets and necklaces jangled as she pounced on Charlotte and dragged her back toward the bed, where Sophie's maid had laid out the bright blue officer's uniform. "You'll make a charming captain of the guard. The gloves might not fit, but everything else should work perfectly."

Charlotte groaned. "You're impossible!"

"And you're provincial. Haven't you ever dressed up as a man before? I must have done it a dozen times at least."

"I didn't attend many masked balls in Saxony."

Sophie rolled her eyes. "Am I surprised? Now, put it on!"

"No. I can't—"

"Lotte, it's perfectly proper here. I promise! Everyone dresses *en travesti* sometimes. Niko did, at our last ball. He made a magnificent old lady. I giggled for weeks over it!"

"I'm sure. But that's not—"

"I'd wager Signor Morelli has dressed as a woman often enough. Can't you just see it?"

Charlotte blinked. "I . . . yes, I can." Almost too easily, actually.

Sophie echoed her thoughts. "A well-cut gown, a bit of padding around the chest . . . Niko and the other gentlemen have to plaster on cosmetics and flirt and preen to carry it off, and even then, it's all a great joke. But I don't think I'd be able to tell that it was a masquerade, with Signor Morelli. Could you?"

Charlotte sank down onto her bed. "I don't think so." Sickening discomfort crawled through her stomach. "Sophie, I don't—"

Sophie sat down next to her, her forehead scrunched in thought. "What do you think a castrato really is, anyway? I mean, I know we call him 'signor,' to be polite, but maybe it should really be 'signora.' Or—how else could you say it? If someone isn't a real man or a woman, then—him? Her? *It?*"

"Sophie!" Charlotte leapt up, staring at her sister. "How could you be so cruel? Of course Signor Morelli is a man. How can you say such things?"

Sophie shrugged. "It's an interesting question, is it not? He started life as a boy, truly. But the operation came before his voice could change, and after that—I mean, without the, ah, *entire* parts that make you a man or a woman—"

"He is a man, and one of the most admirable ones I've ever met!"

Charlotte would have given anything to swallow back her words the moment they escaped her mouth. Her younger sister's eyes widened in surprise—and then, horribly, in mischievous comprehension.

"Lotte! I am shocked. Why didn't you tell me before?"

"There is nothing to tell." Charlotte was hideously conscious of both her own maid and Sophie's maid watching them from the corners of the room. This would certainly provide fodder for gossip in the servants' hall, and probably in the Princess's chambers, as well.

"I never even imagined it. My prim and proper older sister falling under the spell of an Italian castrato—"

"I haven't done any such thing. I only meant—"

"He's very experienced, you know. He's probably slept with hundreds of lovers." Sophie's eyes narrowed. "Women *and* men. That's what they all do, you know."

"And what of it?" Charlotte swung around, turning her back to her sister. "If everything you say is true, then you need hardly worry that he would take any interest in me, would he? As you've pointed out many times, I'm far too unsophisticated for courtly life." Tears stung behind her eyes, but she made her voice cool. "Now, if you don't have anything better to discuss, I think you'd better leave."

Sophie's small hand tugged at her shoulder. "Oh, Lotte, don't be such a prude! I was only teasing you."

Charlotte gritted her teeth. "It isn't amusing."

Sophie sighed. "Don't you ever get tired of being so dull and serious all the time? Don't you ever just want to enjoy yourself?"

Charlotte pressed her lips together to hold back the stream of words that pushed against them.

Not the sort of fun you have. Not the sort that dishonors your family and your marriage. The sort that doesn't care whom it hurts.

"Of course I know you aren't truly attracted to Signor Morelli, silly. I'm not a total fool! I was only mocking you a little. You do set yourself so high, Lotte. It's a bit intimidating." Sophie's laugh held an edge. "Can't you ever be just a little bit wicked, for my sake?"

You wouldn't care for it, if I did.

Charlotte took a deep breath, quashing her anger. What good would it do to spew venom at her own sister?

She turned and met Sophie's pouting look. "I'm sorry," she said quietly. "I'm not made that way."

"Well, pretend that you are, for tonight. For the ball!" Sophie grabbed her hand. "This is your chance to be someone else for one night. Someone daring and wild. Do it, Lotte! For me."

The gardens of Eszterháza had been transformed into a fairyland. Chinese lanterns glittered in the hedges and trees and found a thousand sparkling reflections in the curving, mirrored walls of the Bagatelle. Orchestral musicians, dressed in rustic peasants' outfits, played jangling Turkish music in a nearby clearing, under Herr Haydn's direction. Servants mingled in the colorful crowd, carrying tall glasses of imported French wine and trays filled with exotic fruits.

Carlo swept back his short velvet cape and moved through the crowd of sultans, gods and goddesses, peasants, priests, magicians, and mysteries.

The masquerade had begun.

Charlotte hesitated at the edge of the clearing, wiping her bare hands on the white uniform breeches that encased her thighs. They felt extraordinary against her skin, tight and indecent above the knee-high boots. Without the usual wide padding around her hips, the weight of layers of skirts and petticoats or the tightness of a whalebone corset, she felt half-naked—and amazingly light. If she took but one step, it might carry her all the way across the clearing.

"Swagger," Sophie had ordered her. *"That's how they all walk! You need to throw your whole body into it."*

Swagger, Charlotte told herself. She swaggered forward experimentally—and came to a dead halt, fighting down helpless laughter. It was too ludicrous! She couldn't do it. She shook her head and switched back to her normal pace. Hopelessly ladylike, no doubt. Ladylike and *dull,* just as Sophie had said.

Charlotte stepped forward into the light, grateful for the thin, shaped leather half-mask that covered her forehead, nose and cheeks. She took a glass of wine from a hovering servant and faded into the sidelines of the crowd.

A tall, imposing figure mounted the steps of the Bagatelle—Prince Nikolaus, clearly, although his face was fully covered by an ivory mask, and he was dressed in the robes, turban, and glittering jewelry of an imaginary pasha. Sophie wiggled beside him in Ottoman rose-pink, her blonde hair free of powder but lushly feathered and piled high above layers of jewelry. Her tiny mask, covering only a thin band around her eyes, could not conceal her open delight.

Prince Nikolaus's voice boomed out behind the ivory cherub's mask. "Let the dancing begin!"

The finest part of any masquerade, Carlo thought, was the high-handed freedom it gave to ignore the rules of polite society. At any ordinary ball, one had to play a finely measured game of hierarchy and social expectations in choosing whom to partner. Without masks, he'd have been forced to play the dutiful guest by approaching first Frau von Höllner and then the Prince's giggling, gossiping niece, and so spend his evening being supremely bored as he partnered them around the ballroom floor. Masked, he could pretend not to recognize them, and was thus set free to seek out his own diversions.

He sipped his wine, walked the pathways of the fairy-lit gardens, and told himself, as he searched through the glittering throng of dancers, that he wasn't looking for any one woman in particular.

The jangling, exotic music shot tingles straight through Charlotte's fingers. Cymbals and triangles added an infectious edge to the sound, while a shrill piccolo piped a warning of danger—or was it only adventure? She moved closer to the orchestra, drawn inexorably by the sound.

The night sky was cloudless, filled with stars. It was a night for reckless adventure and romance, for anyone exotic and brave enough to snatch it . . . anyone utterly unlike the Baroness von Steinbeck, Ernst's dutiful young wife, her parents' dutiful oldest daughter, Sophie von Höllner's proper, prudish older sister.

Within the stiff, unfamiliar military boot, her foot was tapping to the music. She wanted to spin into it, to dance, to find her own partner instead of waiting to be asked.

It had to be this strange music that gave her such wild ideas, inchoate, impossible longings for adventures she'd never have, a daring that she'd never feel. This music, this night, the masks and costumes whirling past her in the steps of a frantic dance . . .

She sighed, spun around to walk away—
—And found Signor Morelli watching her.

She would be wearing a domino, he'd decided. Not that it was his concern, but still, it was always diverting to construct costumes in his mind. It would be a plain domino—black, of course. Some masquers wore great enveloping, soft hats over Venetian beaked masks to complete an all-encompassing disguise when wearing simple dominoes, but not the Baroness. That would strike too hard and close against the grain for her, that frightening ambiguity—of sex and of rank—that total anonymity gave. No, she would wear a plain black domino over her usual black gown, a black half-mask on her face, and her hair would be powdered and piled atop her head, as usual. And no doubt, if she danced, it would only be with the most suitable Hungarian or visiting Austrian nobles.

He turned away from the dancers. What did he care whom she chose to partner? He would look at the orchestra instead and enjoy the fine music.

He wasn't the only one to do so. Ahead of him, a slim officer stood watching the orchestra intently, his back to Carlo. One knee-high boot tapped to the Janissary rhythms. Something about the man's posture looked disconcertingly familiar. That intense concentration of attention . . .

The officer swung around, and Carlo blinked. *Not* a man after all, despite the uniform and the thick brown hair pulled back into a military queue. No man could have that chest, bound down though it appeared to be. And that mouth . . .

Recognition tingled through him, mixed with a jolt of sheer erotic awareness.

All day, he'd cherished the anger that had lingered from their words the night before. He'd held the memory of his injury like a shield, to protect himself from any rash actions too tempting to resist. But now, as he looked at her transformed . . .

The Baroness's eyes widened behind her leather half-mask. She took a breath, and her chest moved underneath her military uniform.

Run, Carlo ordered himself. *Turn around. Now!*

Instead, he walked straight toward her.

She would have recognized Signor Morelli in any costume, Charlotte thought, for his height and his build, if nothing else. But in the toga of a Roman emperor, he looked startlingly natural. A wreath of laurels balanced on his shining black curls. Below his half-mask, his smooth, hairless cheeks looked, for once, only appropriate—like the dazzling neutrality of a god in a Greek statue.

Tingling, percussive music surrounded them as he walked toward her.

She'd ordered herself to avoid him tonight, after his behavior during the day. But her feet wouldn't move to carry her away.

"Baroness." He bowed, flipping back his short cape. "Would you care to dance?"

Charlotte had to stifle the automatic impulse to curtsey—absurd in her tight breeches.

"I . . . don't know if I can. In this outfit, I mean."

His lips curved. "Would it be easier if I let you take the lead?"

"No!" She flushed. "That's not what I meant."

"Did you never take the man's role, when you and your sister had dancing lessons?"

"That was many years ago," she said. But she could imagine—couldn't stop herself from imagining—doing it now. Leading him through the steps of the dance, crossing the square with the other men to greet him in the women's line—

No. She swallowed hard, fighting down the vivid images. The wine and the music must have gone to her head.

He was watching her as if he knew the madness in her thoughts.

She should excuse herself, apologize, turn and run away before she lost her wits entirely—

But the music shifted into a new and wilder dance, and Charlotte didn't leave.

"I think I can manage, even without my skirts," she said, and then flushed deeper at her own words.

He nodded gravely. "Shall we try?"

He took her bare, gloveless hand. Warmth ran up her arm, beneath her uniform jacket.

"Your hair," he said. "It's brown."

"I'm sorry?" She blinked at him, half-dizzy from the heat that rose from his skin.

"It's nothing," he said. He shook his head. "Forgive me. It's only . . . I'd always wondered what the true color was."

"Oh." Charlotte took a quick, almost airless, breath, fighting the impulse to step even closer. "Are you . . . surprised?"

He closed his eyes briefly. She saw a muscle work in his jaw. "You always surprise me, Baroness," he said, and swept her into the dance.

Chapter Twenty

Friedrich hurried through the side door of the Bagatelle and closed it behind him, shutting out the music and the lights. He felt his way up the stairs in darkness, his own breath loud in his ears.

If Sophie saw him sneaking around the edges of her ball, she'd throw a fit. But he couldn't help it.

He had to know. He had to see for himself what had been left in the dance hall, after the flames and the pits of darkness. He stretched his face tentatively, and the burned skin stung, proof that he hadn't just gone mad or dreamed the whole thing in a drunken haze.

He came to a halt in front of the dance hall door, breathing hard. The door handle was cool against his sweaty palm. He twisted it and pushed the door open.

Whispered voices cut off abruptly. Two dark figures spun around to face him, backlit by a single lantern.

Bloody hell. Friedrich's mouth went dry. They had no faces!

No. They were only wearing masks—dark masks that covered their faces entirely. His shoulders sagged in relief. He waved cheerily and let the door fall closed behind him.

"Sorry to intrude," he said. "Only wanted to take a look around—didn't realize anyone else would be here right now."

One of the figures turned and strode to the unlit far corner of the room, slipping quickly into the all-encompassing darkness. The other stepped forward, his vast cloak flinging rippling shadows onto the smooth, unmarked floor.

"Only wanted to look around, Brother Friedrich?" he purred. "And what exactly were you looking for?"

Friedrich stumbled backward. His mind gibbered frantically: *Oh God oh God oh God* . . . It offered him no help.

"My—my—my handkerchief?" he finally offered. "Couldn't find it anywhere, so I thought—I thought I might've dropped it here the other night?"

"Your *handkerchief?*" The figure advanced on him inexorably. "And the honorary Lieutenant von Höllner, living off the generosity of his wife's princely lover, couldn't afford to replace a single handkerchief?"

"Well . . ." Friedrich glanced desperately around the great, shadowed room. No scorch marks, no pits—it didn't even look the same size anymore!—and no scraps of cloth for him to snatch.

The figure held out his cloaked arm in a gesture of generosity. "Look your fill, Brother Friedrich. In fact, I'll aid you in your search. What color was this famous handkerchief?"

"Ah . . . it doesn't matter. Truly." Friedrich fumbled behind his back, hunting for the door handle. "It's probably just fallen under my bed."

"No doubt."

"So I'll be off then," Friedrich said. His fingers closed around the door handle. "Sorry to disturb you. Have a good eve—aah!"

He leapt backward, flattening himself against the door. "What the hell is that?"

Red eyes glared out at him from a cloud of smoke in the corner of the hall. It drifted closer, watching him, until a low voice rapped out from the darkness at the far end of the room, and it came to a halt. Friedrich shuddered at the look in its eyes as it pulled back.

The masked figure turned to follow Friedrich's trembling finger.

"That?" He shrugged. "I wouldn't worry about that . . . not anymore. Think of it as a mere illusion, set to trap the unwary."

Without any wide, billowing skirts to act as a shield between them, Carlo found himself tinglingly close to the Baroness each time the steps of the dance brought them together.

Around them, priests danced with Greek goddesses and Harlequins with sorceresses. Dancers filled the wide lawn before the Bagatelle and filtered off through the pathways of the formal gardens that spiraled out around it, separated by tall hedges.

The Baroness laughed softly.

"What is it?"

Carlo breathed the words into her ear as they met between the lines of dancers. She lifted her hand and pressed her palm against his in burning symmetry.

"It's only odd," she said, "that we met scarcely a week ago. I feel . . ." She cut herself off.

"I know," Carlo said. Pressure built behind his chest. He fought to recover his hard-learned courtier's detachment. *Remember who she is. Who you are.* But she did not look the unapproachable, noble lady now, as her breech-clad legs moved close to his. The masks lent too much freedom. Freedom to fantasize the impossible . . .

Carlo breathed in the scent of her rich brown hair and let it dizzy him.

Behind him, he heard a half-familiar voice. But when the steps of the dance turned him away from her to look in that direction, all he saw were masks and shadows.

"Don't worry," Lieutenant Esterházy whispered. "No one will recognize you." He grinned beneath his half-mask, flashing strong teeth. "Even if they did, what then? My cousin doesn't dictate whom I bring as partner to his masquerades."

Anna hesitated a moment longer at the edge of the crowded lawn, smoothing down the folds of the black domino he'd brought her. Through the eye slits of her mask, shapes and colors seemed oddly thrown out of proportion, and even the sounds seemed more intense than usual. The glittering jewelry of the ladies and the gentlemen alike, the bewildering array of masks, the laughter, the music . . .

"Come, Fräulein!" He took her hand and led her into the mad whirl.

Anna had never danced in such exalted company. She found herself stumbling with excitement and fear. She shouldn't be here, would never be allowed to be here, pretending to be one of them—but Lieutenant Esterházy swept her through the ball, grinning and confident, and it became an exhilarating game.

After a panicked moment at the beginning, Anna recognized the steps of the country dances, though they were set to strange, exotic music, a world away from the tunes she'd heard in the servants' hall back in Saxony. She stumbled once against Lieutenant Esterházy, thrown by a sudden, unexpected shift in the rhythm, but it didn't matter. Everything she said made him laugh. His eyes never left her face. She felt herself to be different and strange—exalted beneath the intensity of his gaze.

Between each dance, he clicked his fingers for more wine, more, more!—until she was dizzy and reeling half-against him with laughter and confusion in the shadows of a tall hedge.

"I think . . ." She took a breath and looked up at his eager face, scant inches from her own. "I think I ought to sit down, lieutenant. Or perhaps . . ." She blinked and put one hand out to steady herself against his shoulder. "Perhaps I ought to go to bed?"

"Not yet." He leaned over her, holding her shoulders with strong, warm hands, his gaze intent. "Hasn't this evening been wonderful for you, Fräulein? As it has been for me?"

Anna blinked up at him. The dizziness was starting to blend into nausea. "Wonderful," she said weakly. "Very wonderful. But I ought—"

"To come back with me. To my bed."

"What?" She frowned, trying to make sense of his words through her fogged brain.

He kissed her. His warm tongue eased open her lips and swept inside. She staggered. When he pulled back, he was grinning.

"It will all be wonderful," he said. "I promise. My cousin is very generous to me. I can be generous to you, too. Jewels, money—anything you want. I'll take good care of you, Fräulein. Anna." He kissed her again, more thoroughly.

Anna's head whirled. *Generous* . . . She remembered Madame Zelinowsky's gentle, leading words during the rehearsal, days ago. *"It's never a bad idea to have supplementary plans for your career . . ."*

Then Herr Pichler's bitter words sounded again in her ears: *"You have an Esterházy to reel in."* And his pale, ravaged face as he said it—

"No!"

She jerked backward, pushing Lieutenant Esterházy away.

He stumbled. "Is something wrong?"

"I can't," Anna said. "I'm sorry—I'm so sorry . . ."

She backed away. Tears clogged her throat as she glanced back at the glittering company of aristocrats and princes. She should never have put on that mask.

"What are you talking about?" Lieutenant Esterházy caught her hand. "Anna, please—"

She pulled away. "I can't be your mistress," she said. "I just can't!"

Heads turned at her raised voice. High, tinkling laughter sounded behind her.

Anna spun around and plunged down the pathways of the garden, back toward the musicians' quarters and reality.

Friedrich found Anton sitting slumped outside the Bagatelle, his mask discarded on the grass by his feet.

"Bad luck?" Friedrich asked. He'd been wandering through the gardens himself for almost two hours, trying to dismiss the memory of those hateful red eyes.

Anton snorted. Friedrich sat down next to him, stretching his legs out on the grass.

"Want to go to the tavern and talk it over?" Friedrich paused. "It is *her*, isn't it? That singer, the little blonde one—"

"Yes, damn it!" Anton slammed his fist onto the grass. "I don't understand it. She was all ready, and then . . ."

"Changed her mind? Well, fickle women, eh?" Friedrich sighed. He'd had to duck behind three different hedges tonight to avoid Sophie. "There'll be another. There's always the leading lady—"

"She's a cow. Von Höllner, I'm serious about this one. I offered her everything. Jewels, money . . ."

Friedrich frowned, trying to concentrate his memory. "Well . . . She's a little young, isn't she? She looks young, anyway. Maybe she's not interested yet in—"

"She's a singer, for God's sake! An *actress*. That's their whole career, finding men to take care of them. And I was ready to do it, too." Anton shook his head. "It's that actor. Pichler. The one who's always watching her. He's the reason she said no. I'm certain of it."

In the distance, Friedrich saw Sophie and the Prince approaching. On their way to order the fireworks to be set off, no doubt. It was always the climax of these outdoor evenings.

Friedrich scrambled to his feet. "I have to go," he said. "Are you coming? We'll go out to the tavern and find you a pretty serving wench to flirt with. You'll feel much better."

Anton shrugged and stood up. "Fine. I'll come." His look darkened. "But I'm not giving up."

Somehow, they had spun further and further away from the central lawn, down well-lit garden pathways, into shadows. They had been dancing for hours. Charlotte never wanted to stop. If they stopped—when they stopped—she would have to take off her mask and transform back into the dreary Baroness von Steinbeck, proper and decorous and *dull*. She couldn't bear it.

Recklessness shot through her as she looked up into Signor Morelli's dark eyes. She felt every shift of his gaze, every breath he took. They'd left the safe, protected lines of the group dance long ago, abandoning it for a private version, newly invented, shockingly free and unorthodox in its intimacy. If anyone saw them, they would cause a scandal. But Charlotte didn't care.

Her legs moved swiftly through the turns of their improvised dance, free and lithe in her close-fitting breeches. She stepped closer to him with every turn. Her fingers brushed against his, sparking warmth down Charlotte's hand. *And his.* She could swear it. If she were truly as wild as she wished she were, tonight . . .

She took a breath, and watched his eyes follow the rise and fall of her chest beneath her military jacket. *Just for tonight.* For one masked night, she could experiment with being wicked, just as Sophie had suggested. People were expected to misbehave at masquerades, weren't they?

They came together in the steps of the dance . . . and this time, instead of laying her palm flat against his hand, she dared to twine her bare fingers around his.

He sucked in a breath that sounded hoarse. "Baroness . . ."

They were dancing in the darkness now, the music and the laughter growing faint behind them. Only a few lonely Chinese lanterns were laid out this far from the Bagatelle to light their way. The rich, verdant smells of the garden and the greenery filled her senses.

"Signor?" she murmured.

He stopped dancing. Slowly, cautiously, he set his right hand against her waist. The heat of his fingers, both shocking and enticing, warmed her skin through the cloth of her military jacket. He gazed down at her searchingly, as if trying to read her mind.

Charlotte's quick breath pushed against her chest. Cool night air played against her hair and her cheek, beneath the mask.

The music ended, far away. Applause filtered through the distance. Regret lanced Charlotte. She loosed her fingers from his.

"Forgive me," she whispered. "I only—"

Her voice dried up as he caught her withdrawing hand in his. He shook his head.

"I believe I could forgive you anything, madam."

Her heartbeat had become a thrumming motion, pushing her forward, toward his warmth. She moistened her lips.

"And I you. Signor."

He released her hand to slide both arms around her waist, as cautiously as if she were made of glass. She set both hands against his shoulders, devoid of shame, and pressed herself forward, wanton, craving—

Noise exploded overhead, and Charlotte leapt back.

Fireworks rained through the darkness above them, exploding riotously in glorious purple, green, and red, and Charlotte began to laugh helplessly, in amazement and rue. Signor Morelli laughed too, his face open in pure happiness for the first time since she'd met him.

His back was warm and strong against her hands, his hands against her own back as he pressed her close against him. His mouth felt like heaven. Like his voice. Warm and searching and exactly *right*. Charlotte wanted to devour it.

He loosened her laboriously tied cravat. She tossed it aside, impatient to be rid of the constriction, and his warm mouth moved away from her lips, tracing a path down her naked throat. Charlotte gasped and grabbed hold of his shoulders to keep her legs from melting beneath her. She closed her eyes, savoring the blissful chaos, the unfamiliar, ecstatic whirl—then opened her eyes again, as more fireworks exploded overhead, to let the color and the marvel of it take a part in her pleasure, too.

His long fingers stroked underneath her coat, down the side of her bound breast. Charlotte bit back a moan.

"Lotte!" Sophie's voice was nearly a scream.

Charlotte jerked around, gasping, holding onto Morelli's arm for balance. Sophie stood at the turn in the path, staring at them, her mouth a wide open "O" of shock.

Sophie closed her mouth and opened it again. "Lotte, what do you think you're *doing?*"

Charlotte staggered back. The night air suddenly felt cold, like ice water against her sweat-streaked skin. "I was—I only—"

Signor Morelli let out a choke of laughter. "Surely you don't truly need to ask, Frau von Höllner?"

"You—!" Sophie dismissed him with a glare and turned back to Charlotte. "I've been looking for you everywhere! We are to lead the last dance, Niko and I. I thought—I assumed—Lotte, you ought to want to see it!" Her face screwed up in rage and hurt.

Charlotte took a deep breath and straightened her jacket. Her cravat was lost to her, hopelessly tangled in the branches of the hedge. She felt sick at the look in her sister's eyes.

"Forgive me, Sophie. I was—"

"Look at you! Look at the state of you! What were you thinking?" Tears glimmered in Sophie's eyes. "Lotte, how could you!"

How could you? It was the echo of her mother's words, all those years ago . . . the last time she'd ever dared try to step off her path, risking shame for her family and ruination for herself.

Signor Morelli stepped forward, angling himself between Charlotte and her sister. She put a hand on his arm to turn him back.

"Baroness—"

"It's all right," she whispered. "I should have—I cannot . . ." She shrugged helplessly, miserably.

His arm was warm beneath her hand. She remembered, all-too-vividly, how it had felt pressed against her back, holding her so urgently close as they'd kissed—

"Please," he whispered. The word sounded raw, as if he weren't used to saying it.

But it had been a different woman kissing him. A woman in a mask, disguised, set free of responsibilities and cares. A woman without a family to consider.

Charlotte stepped away from him, swallowing down bitter pain. The masquerade was truly over.

"I'm coming now, Sophie," she said. "See?"

She followed her younger sister out of the garden, leaving Signor Morelli standing alone.

ACT THREE

Chapter Twenty-One

T he four royal carriages rolled up to Eszterháza at noon the next day. Carlo watched them from the window of his bedroom.

Dinner had been put off until five o'clock, for the sake of the court's late night at the ball. And early-morning Mass . . . Carlo's lips twisted. Sunday or no, he doubted that it had been well-attended, even by the most pious of His Serene Highness's court and family. Dancing and drinking until the early hours of the morning left little energy for prayer for even the most determined. Or the most virtuous . . . Carlo's smile dimmed.

Had the Baroness bestirred herself for Mass that morning? Praying to wash away the memory of her mistake?

Carlo's nails bit into his palms.

He should have known better. He had known better. And yet, still, he'd let himself believe . . .

Too late. He couldn't change the past, or unmake the memory of his own idiocy. All he could do now was vow never to repeat it.

He unclenched his fists and forced himself to focus on the view outside as the ornately gilded royal carriages swept to a halt and footmen ran up to open the doors. The Prince advanced toward the front carriage, his arms held wide in welcome and his powdered wig spotless in the sunshine.

The door opened at the hands of one footman, while a second lowered the steps. A young man in dazzling colors leapt to the ground, ignoring the steps. He grinned and waved at the Prince, then turned back to the carriage. A second, older man walked down the steps after him, wearing the uniform of a field marshal. Spare and lean, he walked with quick precision, his gaze sweeping hawk-like around the wide courtyard.

"My God," Carlo breathed, straightening.

The Emperor. How had Prince Nikolaus managed to keep this news such a secret? And why? Carlo would have expected the Prince to have swaggered for weeks ahead of time at the honor of receiving the second-most-powerful figure in the realm as a guest in his summer palace.

Emperor Joseph II nodded, smiling, at his host, but made no move to step forward. Instead, he and his nephew turned back together to the carriage door to assist the last figure down the steps, a massive, billowing woman with a prow-like bosom.

Prince Nikolaus fell to his knees on the ground. It did not, even to Carlo's jaded eye, look a well-rehearsed gesture. It looked painful. The Prince, too, had apparently been taken by surprise.

Empress Maria Theresia, supreme ruler of all Austria, Hungary, and half of Italy, and mother of several of Europe's other monarchs, allowed her son and great-nephew to assist her down the stairs before she nodded for Prince Nikolaus to rise to his feet.

Deep within the palace, Carlo imagined bells being frantically rung. His lips twitched. How quickly could a suite of rooms fit for an empress— not to mention her co-regent son—be prepared on demand, even in this efficient palace? And how long could the Prince delay his imperial guests, while his servants panicked? It was amusing enough to merit a close viewing. Carlo turned aside and rang the bell for his own valet.

The nobility of Eszterháza would assemble with haste to greet their true rulers, and Carlo would not be absent from the performance.

"I just can't understand how you could have done it." Sophie sprawled across Charlotte's bed, pouting as she picked at the covers. "He's a freak, Lotte! Hadn't you even noticed that?"

Sitting at her dressing table, Charlotte gritted her teeth to hold back a scream. Marta was arranging and powdering her hair. Hopeless to think she wasn't also listening in.

"Could we please not discuss this any more, Sophie? It's done! It's over."

Over. The word echoed through her head, magnifying her throbbing headache. Her face in the mirror looked pale and tense, her eyes deeply shadowed. She had barely slept. And when she had . . .

Hopeless madness, to dream back all of those sensations, when she would never have the chance to feel them again.

"It's just not like you!" Sophie said. "What were you thinking?"

"Nothing," Charlotte said crisply. "Obviously."

She met her own eyes in the mirror and winced.

Last night had been madness. Sophie was right. Charlotte had abandoned propriety, honor, and her responsibilities to Sophie herself, as Charlotte's hostess.

But she still wanted to throttle her younger sister.

"It's so embarrassing for me. Hadn't you even considered that much? Imagine if Niko had been with me when I came! What if he had seen—"

"Seen what?" Charlotte swung around, driven past endurance. "A widow and an unmarried gentleman, kissing? And on your direct orders, I might add?"

"I would *never*—!"

"Don't you recall your own words? 'Be wicked,' you told me. And—"

"It was only a jest!"

"It didn't amuse me."

"Well, I didn't mean it seriously!" Sophie's cheeks flushed bright pink. "I only meant to tease you a little. You're so prudish, it's irresistible. I thought you'd be shocked. You should have been shocked! How could I know you'd be mad enough to actually throw yourself at him?"

"Sophie—"

"And you can hardly call him a gentleman! You're the one who said, days ago, that we don't know who his family was."

"I didn't mean—"

"Not to mention his freakishness. Doesn't any of that matter to you anymore? It would be one thing if it were only a game, to amuse yourself for a week or two. I wouldn't even care—I'd be relieved you were acting like a normal woman, for once, not such a boring patterncard of virtue. But I know you, Lotte! You wouldn't have let him touch you unless you meant something more by it."

I meant everything! The retort rang in Charlotte's aching head as if she'd shouted it, hurting even more for its truth.

But that was the hopeless fantasy of a girl, not the common sense of a grown woman. Charlotte drew a long breath through her teeth. "Sophie—"

"It isn't even legal for him to marry, you know. And you're a baroness—and the daughter of a count! He wouldn't be an eligible match even if it hadn't been for the operation. Think of your honor! Our family's honor! Mine!"

"Yours? You think, by kissing Signor Morelli, I could have damaged *your* honor?" Something inside Charlotte snapped. A broken laugh pushed its way up her throat, like jagged glass. She stood up, waving Marta aside. "Don't you think that's a trifle rich, Sophie?"

Sophie's eyes widened. She drew herself up on Charlotte's bed. "I don't know what you can mean by that, Lotte. I think your mind has been disordered. And it was that castrato—"

"*Musico,*" Charlotte said.

"That *castrato* who did it, too! When I tell Niko—"

"Sophie! You—"

The outer door opened, without a knock. A maid curtseyed hastily to both of them and hurried straight to Sophie.

"A message from His Highness, madam. He said it was urgent."

Sophie blinked. "Thank you." She took the folded note off the silver tray. "It must be about the Archduke. Perhaps he's already here! Perhaps . . ." Her voice trailed off as she read the note.

"Any reply, madam?"

Sophie crushed the paper in her hand. "No," she whispered. "I understand."

The maid curtseyed again and left at a near-run. Charlotte stared at Sophie's white, sick face, torn between anger and concern. Concern won out.

"Sophie, what is it?" She sat down beside her sister and took Sophie's free hand in both of hers. "What's the matter?"

Sophie opened her clenched fist. A ball of crumpled paper rolled out and fell onto the bedcovers.

"It's my *congé*," she whispered. "Niko doesn't want me here."

"What?" Charlotte scooped up the note. "He's sending you away? How—why—?" She stopped, gathering her breath. "It will be all right. I promise. Dearest, perhaps it's better this way. We'll go back to Vienna, and—"

"No! Don't be a fool. He's not sending me away. Just read it!"

Charlotte bit back a sharp retort as tears welled up in Sophie's blue eyes. Taking a steadying breath, she opened the note. Prince Nikolaus's scrawl covered the page, for all that he'd written only a few lines.

Sweetheart, there's been a surprise to all of us. I've been honored by the arrival of the Emperor and the Empress herself, come with the Archduke. You'll see that we have to change our plans. Marie will be my hostess these few weeks. I will attend upon you as often as I can. Yrs, N.E., Rex.

"It's the Empress." Sophie's voice was low. "That bloody *cow*. The Emperor wouldn't care. He has affairs of his own. And the Archduke means nothing. It's the Empress's fault."

"Sophie . . ." Charlotte set the note back on the bed.

"She can't stand anyone to enjoy themselves. That's why Schönbrunn and the Hofburg are so deadly dull. She noses into everyone's morals, stomps out any bit of fun . . . just because she had sixteen children by her husband doesn't mean we all have to follow her example! And anyway, from what I've heard, the old Emperor had plenty of flings she didn't know about, or couldn't stop! Well, who could blame him?" Sophie's voice broke into a nerve-jangling wail.

"Sophie, please! You're overset. It won't be so bad. It's only—"

"It's going to be terrible!" Sophie collapsed into Charlotte's arms, weeping. Tears leaked through Charlotte's sleeves, onto her skin. "Oh, Lotte, I'm so miserable."

Charlotte stroked her sister's powdered hair through its layers of jewels and feathers. She closed her eyes, trying to think.

"Can you still attend the meals?"

"What would be the point? I'd have to sit at the bottom of the table and watch Niko pretend not to know me. And listen to the whole court laugh at me for it!"

Charlotte sighed. "Well, this visit isn't set to last so long, is it? Only a week, two weeks at the most—"

"It's practically forever! And it's just what that old witch always wanted."

"Old—?"

"His *wife*," Sophie gritted. "The bloody Princess Esterházy. Can't you see? This is going to be her revenge. She's going to show herself off with Niko to everyone. As though it were her place—her *right*! While I have to hide here in my rooms, forgotten, invisible . . ."

Just like the Princess, Charlotte thought bleakly.

"Oh, Lotte, what if he forgets me?" Sophie wailed. Her soft body quivered in Charlotte's arms. "She'll be speaking against me, I know it—making horrid comments—"

"I . . ." Charlotte shook her head. What could she say? "I'm so sorry, darling. I'll stay here with you. I'll keep you company and—"

"No!" Sophie jerked up, staring at her with tear-drenched intensity. "You must go, Lotte. You have to watch them for me. Watch everything! I need to know what's happening." Her lips quivered. "It's so unfair! I'm the one who helped Niko prepare for this visit. And now I won't see any of it."

"Well . . ."

"Watch the Princess," Sophie ordered. "Tell me exactly what Niko says to her. How he acts. How everyone else acts, too." She bit her lip. She looked more sixteen than twenty-two, as helpless and vulnerable as a child. "Please, Lotte. I need you. I'm sorry—I know I said horrible, unjust things to you, earlier, but I truly didn't mean to hurt your feelings. I was only so afraid for you! Afraid that you'd forget who you are, forget what you deserve—"

Afraid I'd forget you, Charlotte finished silently. But the cynical small voice inside her didn't matter. Couldn't be allowed to matter, next to the pain in her younger sister's voice.

Sophie had been right. She couldn't let herself give in to such irrational feelings, no matter how powerful they might be. And without them . . . without them, Sophie was all that she had left.

"You could have lost everything." Sophie clung to the sleeve of Charlotte's wrapper, blinking away more tears. "You do understand, don't you, Lotte? And you forgive me?"

"Of course." Charlotte's lungs felt half-choked. She was suffocating. But she forced herself to smile back at her sister. "I would always forgive you. You know that."

"I do." Sophie leaned into her shoulder and let out a small sigh, like a kitten. "You'll always take care of me, Lotte, won't you?"

"Of course," Charlotte repeated. "Of course."

Franz found the note in his closet-like room when he returned from the morning's rehearsal. He hadn't been able to face dinner with the rest of the company.

The event we've been awaiting has arrived. Meet me tonight at the same spot for your instructions.

The distinctive seal was stamped at the bottom.

Franz took his candle stub and lit it, ignoring the twinge of guilt he felt at its expense. It was the only candle he was allowed for the month from the Eszterháza storerooms.

He watched the note char and burn away. The final, blackened fragments dropped from his fingers.

At last, he thought. It was exactly what he'd been waiting for, ever since that first meeting in the darkness of his prison cell.

All he felt now, though, was dread.

Chapter Twenty-Two

The *Sala Terrena* had never seemed so full, nor the crowd of courtiers so intimidating. Dinner would not be served for another four hours, but Prince Nikolaus's entire court had already assembled to greet the imperial visitors. Without Sophie to pull her in and sweep straight through them . . . Charlotte set her jaw and stepped inside, breathing in the overpowering smells of lavender water, powder, and sweat that emanated from the mass of bodies around her. She was out of place indeed now, and every person in the room certainly knew it—but she would not let that stop her. She would remain on the sidelines, quiet and unobserved, and fulfil her promises to her sister.

"Ah, Baroness!" The Princess's cool voice hailed her. She stood, resplendent in ice-blue silk, her gloved hand resting lightly on her husband's arm, before two familiar, imposing figures. Her smile glittered with satisfaction. "Won't you come and be introduced to our guests, my dear?"

The Prince gave a visible start of surprise and looked askance at his wife, whose smile only deepened. The Princess stepped back to make room for Charlotte, and courtiers cleared a path between them. In the distance, Charlotte thought she caught a glimpse of a small, upright figure, the Princess's female attendant, looking as martial as any soldier as she kept a watchful gaze on the shifting crowd around her mistress . . . but Charlotte's own gaze was caught only a moment later by someone much closer.

Signor Morelli stood just behind the Prince, included in the small circle of conversation. His dark eyes met Charlotte's. Her breath caught in her throat.

She had thought of nothing but him all through the long walk from her apartments to the drawing room. His kiss, his warmth, his skin beneath her fingers, the look on his face as she'd turned away . . . and what she would do when she had to meet him again, in public.

The best tactic, of course, would be to avoid him entirely. Any voluntary encounter would be too difficult, too awkward . . . too tempting. She'd told herself she didn't even wish to risk it.

Every one of her resolutions fell away as she saw him. She stepped forward, holding her breath.

His eyes narrowed, and he turned pointedly away . . . just as she had, last night. Pain stabbed through Charlotte's chest.

Just as well, she told herself. Yet the pain did not subside.

She walked to the Princess's side. Prince Nikolaus's smile looked forced. *And no wonder*, Charlotte thought grimly. No doubt the last thing he wanted was to be reminded of his mistress in this company.

"My dear Baroness, let me introduce you to the Empress and the Emperor," the Princess murmured. "Your Majesties, the Baroness von Steinbeck."

"Your Majesties." Charlotte curtseyed deeply, quashing down her emotions. "I am honored."

"You look familiar, Baroness." The Empress's plump hands raised Charlotte from her curtsey. She smiled warmly as she studied Charlotte's face. "I've seen you before, haven't I? Who are your parents, child?"

Charlotte had not been called a child for over twelve years, but she bowed her head submissively. "The Count and Countess von Hinterberg, Majesty."

"Ah, yes. I spoke to your mother at our last ball, a few weeks ago. She mentioned that you had been widowed." The Empress sighed. Her own billowing, old-fashioned gown was the unremitting black of first mourning, though her husband had been dead these past fourteen years. "I am sorry for your loss, dear."

"I thank you, Majesty."

"And . . ." The Empress glanced at her son as if for support, but the Emperor was gazing off into the distance, looking bored. "You have a sister, do you not? She was presented to me at court before her marriage. I think your mother said she was here as well?" The Empress turned to the Princess. "Marie, isn't the Baroness's sister one of your ladies-in-waiting?"

The Princess smiled faintly as her husband's face tightened. "In a manner of speaking, but the title is purely honorary."

The Prince cleared his throat. "The Baroness is a fine musician, Your Majesty. She accompanied Signor Morelli in his recital and even supplied us with an addition to our opera troupe. Our new second soprano, Fräulein Dommayer, was previously in service to the Baroness."

"Really?" Emperor Joseph blinked and came to attention. "I look forward to hearing her. My own new opera troupe, in Vienna—"

"Ah, but what do we care about Vienna? The operas are always so much finer here at Eszterháza." His mother turned her smile to the Prince. "I could not resist accompanying Ferdinand and Joseph to hear your fine performances, Nikolaus. I've been longing for some really good music."

"They are fine here because Esterházy gives them proper support and attention," the Emperor said sharply. "They will be just as fine in Vienna, soon enough, once we've found more truly outstanding singers for my own national opera troupe. And their all-German performances—"

"German is far too dull a language for opera," said the Empress. "Italian may be well enough, but you know your father always preferred the French performances best."

"As my father, madam, was French himself, he would hardly—!" The Emperor cut himself off with a snap and turned back to the Prince and Princess, his shoulders stiffening. "You are wise in your patronage here. There is no finer medium than opera for moral education and the development of a national character."

"Joseph, I beg you will not seize the opportunity for one of your tedious rants!"

Charlotte sucked in a breath and looked discreetly away from the glares of the co-rulers.

"Ah! Von Born."

The Emperor, still flushed, stepped away from his mother to hail the alchemist, who had eased close to the central group. His mother only sniffed and looked away.

Ignaz von Born stepped up, smiling, and tucked his walking stick beneath his arm to bow to the Emperor.

"Your Majesty. A delightful surprise to see you here."

"We kept it a secret these past weeks to surprise Esterházy and to escape the heat in the capital. Ferdinand is here, too—somewhere." The Emperor grinned. "Chatting with some fine young lady of the court, no doubt. How go your experiments? You must give me a tour of your traveling laboratory."

The Empress coughed pointedly. "I hope your scientific experiments are taking up all of your time nowadays, Herr von Born?"

"Majesty?" He smiled questioningly, leaning on the head of his walking stick.

Her plump face hardened. "When we invited you to arrange our Imperial Museum, we did so on the basis of your scientific work, not your political theories. But we hear odd rumors about the goings-on in some of the Lodges of Freemasonry these days. False rumors, we hope. And rumors . . ." She paused, exchanging a look with her son. "Rumors that there may be a new lodge, not properly registered with the authorities."

"I am shocked indeed." Von Born half-bowed. "But I would be honored to look more deeply into the matter, if it would please Your Majesties. I can swear to you I know of no new order of Freemasonry."

"Good Lord, there's Radamowsky in the corner." The Emperor let out a crack of laughter. "The French ambassador may quiz us over Vienna being the center of alchemy, but it seems Eszterháza holds that title, now! You've gathered quite a nest of alchemists here, Esterházy."

The Empress's voice was sour. "I hope we may have an evening Mass tonight, Nikolaus. We were forced to have a very truncated morning Mass in the course of our travels, and I feel . . ." Her pale gaze settled on Count Radamowsky's tall figure in the corner. "I am greatly in need of that comfort."

"Of course, Your Majesty," Prince Nikolaus said smoothly. "We shall all attend."

Oh, yes. Charlotte let out a sigh of sheer relief. She had missed services that morning, too exhausted and troubled to pull herself out of bed in time. If ever there had been a moment that she needed the comfort and reassurance of a Mass, today was surely that day.

She felt Signor Morelli watching her. She did not meet his gaze.

"I am glad." The Empress's face softened again as she turned away from the two alchemists. "And perhaps I may soon have the pleasure of hearing the famous Signor Morelli sing?"

"I would be honored, Your Majesty." Signor Morelli bowed.

"Signor Morelli and the Baroness perform beautifully," the Princess murmured. "I look forward to hearing them together again."

Charlotte swallowed and opened her mouth to speak. Signor Morelli replied first.

"Your pardon, Highness, but I should not like to trouble the Baroness again. I have already taken far too much advantage of her good will."

Charlotte dropped her gaze. Her bare fingers looked pale against the black of her dress. She forced them not to clench into fists.

Signor Morelli's voice was smooth. "I know, however, that Herr Haydn would be pleased to oblige me as accompanist before Your Majesties."

"Ah, now that would be a rare pleasure." The Empress beamed. "May we hope for a new opera from him on this visit?"

"You may," the Prince said. "Tomorrow night, in fact." He smiled and shifted a few more inches away from his wife. "I hope that it may prove a great triumph."

The lock on Radamowsky's study door was proving difficult. The Prussian spy cursed softly to himself as his sweat-slick fingers slipped on the tiny iron tool he used. It fell to the ground with a clatter that made him jerk, but he quickly steadied himself.

The long corridor was still. Everyone would be occupied with the imperial guests for hours yet.

Guernsey leaned over to retrieve the tool. Blood flooded into his face with the exertion. Sweat streamed down his cheeks and neck, and dizziness nearly overcame him. He swore underneath his breath.

After all the futile searches, all the false leads and time wasted, he had finally discovered the source of Eszterháza's secrets. Only forty minutes more, at most, and he'd be back in bed recovering and writing his report to the Prussian king. The physician wasn't due to check in on him until an hour after that. Plenty of time, if only his cursed injuries didn't render him completely useless.

The iron clicked softly in the lock. Guernsey took one last look down the empty corridor and slipped inside. He left the door open by a fraction of an inch, so that he could hear any approach.

The room was dark and filled with dust. Most of the light from the windows had been blocked off. Guernsey moved cautiously through the room, careful not to tread on the scattered books. In the center of the room, atop a table covered with yet more books and papers, dirty gray smoke filled up a lantern case. Guernsey took a quick step back, then forced himself onward. He leaned over the table to peer into the lantern.

Red eyes snapped open inside the smoke. Guernsey glared back at them, forcing himself to ignore the churning in his stomach.

"Not this time," he whispered.

He searched through the books and papers on the table, committing the titles to memory. When he found one written in fresh ink, in obvious code, he took out a blank sheet of paper from the inner pocket of his frock coat and copied the symbols down, using the alchemist's own feather pen. The gray smoke roiled but could not escape its prison.

In the far distance, footsteps sounded. Guernsey stiffened and thrust the paper back into his coat. No one but Radamowsky stayed in this corridor, nor did the servants ever visit it. The alchemist must have abandoned his social duties early.

He glanced quickly around the room. No closets in which to hide.

The footsteps were still some distance away. He would have to brazen it out.

He dropped the pen back into its holder and darted out of the room, closing the door behind him. No sign of anyone in the corridor yet. He leaned over to re-lock the door from outside.

"Mister—Guernsey, was it?" Count Radamowsky paused a moment at the end of the corridor and then strode toward him. "Were you looking for me, sir?"

"I was indeed." Guernsey straightened hastily, forcing a smile. He'd have to hope the Count hadn't seen the quick flow of motion as he'd slipped the lock-picking tool from his hand into the wide sleeve of his coat. "I was afraid I'd missed you."

"You nearly did." The Count smiled, but his eyes focused intently on Guernsey as he walked toward him. "I hope you didn't have to wait long?"

"Only a moment, no longer." Guernsey didn't have to feign the sudden spell of dizziness that made him stumble. "Forgive me. I came to thank you, sir, for rescuing me the other night. I fear, though, I may have overestimated my recovery."

"A natural error."

The Count put his hand on the door handle and pressed it lightly. It held firm. *Locked*. Guernsey held his gaze, smiling inanely.

The Count's eyes narrowed. "You must hurry back to your sickbed, Mister Guernsey. I hope we may speak again soon."

Guernsey felt the alchemist's gaze on his back, all the way down the long corridor.

Too close. It was time to leave Eszterháza. He would send his apologies and compliments to the Prince this afternoon and arrange to leave the next morning for Vienna. Vienna and then Dresden . . . where King Frederick's appreciation would more than outweigh the wounds that he had suffered.

He slipped back into his bed gratefully and rested his head on his pillow with a sigh of relief. Before memory could fail, he would record the names of all the books that he had seen, all the clues that might help King Frederick's own pet alchemists follow Count Radamowsky's example.

He was halfway through the list when a knock sounded at the door. The physician was half an hour early. Guernsey shoved the letter under his pillow with a grunt of frustration.

"Come in!"

The door opened. Guernsey blinked.

"Herr von Born! I was not expecting you."

"No?" Ignaz von Born closed the door behind him and crossed the room, his walking stick tapping lightly against the floor. "I thought the very least I could do was pay a condolence call, as your former traveling companion. How goes your recovery, sir?"

"Very well, sir. Well indeed." Guernsey beamed up at the older man, mind racing. He had theories about von Born, theories already passed on to King Frederick in his earlier letters. The man had political ambitions and connections to spare, and a mind that had already switched loyalties once, from the quest for scientific knowledge to the quest for material power. He was a figure to be reckoned with in the game of espionage and bought loyalties. "I am honored by your visit."

"That pleases me." Von Born smiled thinly. He leaned over to touch a drop of spilled ink on the sheet. "Writing letters in bed, Mister Guernsey? A dangerous habit."

"I've been working on my book." Guernsey began to push himself up onto his elbows. "Let me—"

Before he had moved more than an inch, the heavy walking stick pressed against his chest, forcing him back down.

"Ah, the book," said von Born. "How could I have forgotten?"

The older man held down the stick with only one hand, but all Guernsey's struggles came to nothing. It was like a rod of iron against his chest. If he moved too sharply, he'd break his own ribs.

"Herr von Born," Guernsey gasped. "I must protest—I don't understand—"

"Do you not?" Von Born raised one eyebrow. With a quick flick, he scooped the pillow from beneath Guernsey's head. The hidden letter fell off the mattress, onto the floor. Von Born shook his head. "As I said, Mister Guernsey. A dangerous habit indeed."

Guernsey opened his mouth to scream. But the pillow was on top of his face, suffocating him, before he could make a sound.

Chapter Twenty-Three

Gossip flew along the musicians' dining table all through dinner, but Anna didn't know what to believe—nor, in her miserably hungover state, could she force herself to care much, either way. She dragged herself back to rehearsal at one o'clock and found the kapellmeister nearly rabid with impatience.

"Hurry, hurry! Ladies and gentlemen, we are honored—beyond all of my hopes are we honored!" He gathered them around him on the stage, his back to the audience where Lieutenant von Höllner was snoring in his accustomed seat. "The Archduke has arrived indeed—and has brought with him the Emperor and the Empress herself!"

Whispers rippled through the company. The wildest rumor of the day had been confirmed. Anna rubbed her aching forehead and tried to summon up excitement.

"Tonight we perform Traetta's comedy, as rehearsed. Tomorrow, though . . ." Herr Haydn swelled with pride. "Tomorrow, as the climax to a day and night of royal celebrations, the Prince wishes us to premiere my new opera for his great visitors. And everything, my friends, must be *perfect*." He clapped his hands together. "We rehearse them both today!"

Wonderful, Anna thought drearily. Her head already hurt. Now she would have to try to recall two sets of Italian at once.

Herr Pichler, too, looked pale and wan. He caught her gazing at him and smiled briefly at her.

The door to the audience opened and he jerked his gaze away.

For one terrible moment, Anna expected to see Lieutenant Esterházy step into the theater. She couldn't bear it. Not now, not after last night's humiliating encounter. She stiffened, turned away—

But it was an unfamiliar voice that spoke. "Herr Haydn? Is that you?"

The kapellmeister spun around. His face lit up, and he bowed deeply.

"Your Highness!"

The young man grinned, openly appraising the group of singers on the stage. His face was plain but good-natured beneath his powdered hair. "I hope you don't mind my intrusion, sir. My uncle couldn't escape the formalities this afternoon, so he sent me in his place to hear your rehearsal."

"I am delighted, Your Highness, and deeply honored. Won't you take a seat? I'll call for refreshments."

"I won't turn them down, sir. It was a long ride from Vienna." The Archduke's eyes rested briefly on Anna and on Frau Kettner, the leading lady. His smile broadened. "I'm delighted to finally be here."

As the Archduke turned to find a seat, Herr Haydn hurried offstage to find a footman. Madame Zelinowsky drifted close to Anna.

"I hope you remember our little discussion, my dear. Lieutenant Esterházy is all very well in his way, but the Archduke is a very fine figure of a man. And he certainly noted *you*."

Anna was horribly conscious of Herr Pichler, listening in. "Lieutenant Esterházy and I are . . . not a concern, madam."

"No? Last night—"

"Ended. Last night." Anna's cheeks burned. "I thank you for your kind advice, madam, but I am not interested in advancing my career in that fashion."

The older woman tsk'd. "No need to be self-righteous, little Anna. A fine voice can only carry you so far. If you ever wish to rise higher—"

"I've risen quite high enough. Thank you."

"If you say so. Once a maidservant, always . . ." Madame Zelinowsky's voice drifted off meaningfully. She walked away, skirts rustling.

Anna let out her held breath. She couldn't stop herself from looking to Herr Pichler for his reaction.

He was frowning. "Is it—Fräulein Dommayer, were you telling her the truth?"

It was the end of enough. Anna's temper snapped. "Unlike some people, I don't make a habit of lying, Herr Pichler! Even to malicious, gossiping cats like her." She cut herself off belatedly and spun around to look for eavesdroppers. "Oh, I shouldn't have . . ."

But he was laughing. "I thank you, Fräulein. It is good to hear truth spoken on this stage, for once."

Anna lifted her chin. "I always tell the truth."

"I know." His eyes were warm. "It's one of the things I most admire about you."

"Oh." Her eyes widened.

He took a breath. "Fräulein, I am not permitted to speak to you. To spend time with you, or show admiration for you." He grimaced. "Or, in other words, to offend Anton Esterházy in any way."

"What?" She stared at him. "Anton Esterházy is *not*—! I mean to say, I refused him." She flushed anew, but forced herself to continue in a low voice. "Last night I told him I would not—could not—be what he wanted me to be."

"I'm glad of it," Herr Pichler said. "But it's the worse for me, if he blames me for it."

The audience door opened and he jerked away, but it was only Herr Haydn, joining the Archduke for one last moment of conversation. In the back of the audience, Lieutenant von Höllner stirred in his sleep.

Herr Pichler finished in a hasty undertone. "I only wanted to tell you, because you have been kind. I don't avoid you out of dislike or . . . any other cause. I would do otherwise if I could."

"But why can you not? I don't understand!"

Herr Haydn leapt up onto the stage and brushed his hands against his breeches. "Places, everyone! We shall begin with the Traetta. Kettner! Pichler!"

Anna gritted her teeth as Herr Pichler walked away from her without a backward look.

When she looked up and out into the audience, she found the Archduke watching her with bright attention.

Anna stifled a groan.

Franz waited until Monsieur Delacroix was deep in rehearsal of his *buffo* aria before he went in search of Madame Zelinowsky. He found her standing in a corner backstage, writing quickly.

"An important letter, madam?"

She straightened hastily, slipping the paper into the folds of her skirt. "Why, Herr Pichler, you startled me. You ought to be more careful—if you keep creeping around this way, people will start to take you for a spy." He smiled and propped himself against the wall beside her, carefully angling his still-healing back. "A spy, madam? What would make you think of that?"

Madame Zelinowsky tsk'd irritably, even as her color rose. "I am no young ingénue to be intrigued by your riddles, Herr Pichler. And, if I recall correctly, we both have a rehearsal to think of." She paused, widening her dark eyes in mock-horror. "Unless you've been tossed out?"

"Your wit is remarkable, madam. As is your persistence." He leaned closer, watching her hands in her skirts. In just one move, he could—*no*. Not yet. "Tell me," he said smoothly, "why did you send Monsieur Delacroix the letter that incriminated me?"

"What?"

She stumbled back, her hands slipping for a moment from their hiding place. He leapt forward and snatched the half-written note.

"Give that back!"

"I think not." He whipped it behind his back. The painful stretch of muscles along his scabs only intensified his resolve. "Now tell me the truth, madam. Why did you inform on me?"

She dropped her gaze. "I don't know what you mean, but—"

"You knew I'd helped them. That much I could see even at the time. But what possible reason could you have had for telling Delacroix? You'd heard Marianna Delacroix—we all did!—when he beat her. You *knew* . . ." He drew in a shuddering breath, fighting to retrieve his self-control. But it was a lost cause, just like his poor doomed attempt at heroism had been, when he'd sought to help his friends. "Poor Antonicek sincerely loved her. Now they are both dead and buried, for their pains! How could you?"

"I didn't," she hissed. "Antonicek and Marianna would have died regardless. The Prince had no information from me on where they fled. I didn't even know which direction they would take."

"And I? How had I fallen into your bad graces? Enlighten me, I beg you."

"You—idiot—boy!"

She darted for his hand and the letter, but he jumped back too quickly for her.

"Now, now, madam. You'll have to wait before you inform on someone else. Would it be Fräulein Dommayer, by any chance? Do you write to Lieutenant Esterházy to accuse her of some imagined infidelity?" He shook his head. "By God, you are a cat."

"You have no idea what you're talking about." She glared at him, nearly spitting. "I *didn't* write to Delacroix, you fool."

"No?" He raised the letter before him, still unread, and set his hands atop it to rip it in half.

"I wrote to someone else! Just as I pass on all interesting gossip. It means nothing, it's perfectly harmless—"

"And then the anonymous letter was sent to Monsieur Delacroix, using the information you'd given." Franz lowered the letter, staring at her. "You kept sending more information after that?"

She shrugged. "I could hardly take back the strokes of the bastinado from your back, merely by giving up a perfectly good source of income, could I?"

"But . . ." Franz glanced at the heading of the letter in his hand. *My dear sir*, it began, without a name. "Why harass Fräulein Dommayer? I heard you working to persuade her."

"She's young and ignorant. I only tried to help her a little, as a kindness." Madame Zelinowsky stepped forward. "Now give me my letter."

Franz backed away. "You've no interest in helping out beautiful new, young singers. Someone told you to do it. Someone who wants her to attract the Archduke. Why?"

"I am not writing about Fräulein Dommayer and the *Archduke*, you fool! She's of no interest to him. At least . . ." Her eyes slitted. "Not directly."

"Then—"

"I am weary of your importunities, Herr Pichler, and of your wild imagination. If you'd please—"

Herr Haydn's voice sounded through the closed stage door. "Zelinowsky! Pichler!"

"There." She snatched the letter back from him and flashed a triumphant smile. "Now, if we can finally return to work . . ."

Paper whispered against cloth and then against the floor—a different, folded letter, fallen from her sleeve when she had reached for the first note.

They both dove for it. Franz's hand reached it first, and he snatched it. "Yet another secret letter," he purred. "How intriguing."

Voices called their names from the stage. Still kneeling, he raised one arm to block her reaching hands. He turned the letter over to open it—and froze.

The seal was black and only too familiar.

Franz's mouth opened, but no sound came out. He looked up and met Madame Zelinowsky's petrified stare.

The stage door burst open.

"There you are!" The kapellmeister glared at both of them. Other actors peered over his shoulder. "If the two of you would be so kind as to indulge us in a moment or two of dull rehearsal . . ."

Madame Zelinowsky twitched the letter from Franz's frozen hand. She stood up, smoothing down her skirts.

"Of course, Herr Kapellmeister. I am so sorry for the delay, but to be fair, I can hardly accept any blame for it."

She sailed out, past Herr Haydn's waiting figure. After a long, paralyzed moment, Franz managed to pull himself up from the ground to follow her.

Every inch of abraded flesh on his back ached with the movements.

Fräulein Dommayer was among the group of singers watching him. Her eyes were wide and worried. He winced away from them.

Sweet Christ. He passed through the door, past Herr Haydn, and stepped onstage. All he could see, though, was that familiar seal.

How could he have been such a fool?

Kettledrums crashed, and Friedrich woke with a start. He'd been dreaming confused, whirling dreams of fire and darkness, cloaks and skeletons, and a deep voice saying, *"In just five days . . ."*

Five days, Friedrich thought sleepily. It sounded familiar. He blinked and yawned and took it in. It was what the leader had told him, four nights ago, at that nightmare ritual. *"In just five days, you will be our shining star."* More bloody riddles. Riddles and . . .

Tomorrow.

Friedrich shot up in his seat, heart pumping. Five days from that ritual meant *tomorrow*, damn it. All their plans would be coming true, and they wanted him to be their "star"?

He bloody well thought *not*.

If he ran . . .

"There you are. Might've known it, hmm?" Anton slid into the seat beside him, shadowed eyes already fixed on the stage. "Surprised you're not asleep yet."

"I was."

Those actors had tried to run, hadn't they? Tried, and been devoured for their plans. And the leader of the Brotherhood had laughed about it.

Anton frowned into the audience. "Isn't that the Archduke?"

"Mmm . . ." Friedrich blinked. "Suppose so."

"I haven't seen Ferdinand in years. We'll have to go greet him properly in a moment. But not yet." Anton leaned closer. "Listen. My cousin had his administrator look into that Pichler fellow, but they haven't found anything yet. So I'm taking the matter into my own hands. After tonight's performance, I'm going to follow him. See where he goes, what he does . . . who he sees." Anton grinned fiercely. "Are you with me?"

Friedrich sighed. "No."

"No?" Anton stared at him. "What are you talking about?"

"I want to go drinking tonight. Relax. Have a bit of fun." *It might be my last.* Where would he be, two nights from now? Dead? Strapped against the rack, being tortured in one of the Empress's prisons? Or, worse yet, trapped in that private room in Hell where the Brotherhood had met the other night? Friedrich shivered. "Trust me. Tonight is not the night for me to go creeping around bushes in the dark."

"Come on, man. I have to do this!"

"Then you'll have to do it on your own."

"Von Höllner . . ."

"I mean it."

"Who says it won't be fun? Creep around a bush or two, pretend we're spies in enemy territory . . ."

Friedrich snorted. Anton beamed.

"You see? I knew you'd get into the spirit of it. It'll be as if we were boys again, skipping our lessons, playing at soldiers. And if we haven't seen anything interesting in an hour, then I promise we'll go straight back to the tavern and drink till we fall over. Eh?"

"Until you fall over, you mean," Friedrich said.

"Ha! Western weakling."

"Barbarian."

They grinned at each other.

What the hell, Friedrich thought.

He still had one more day.

Half an hour after Edmund Guernsey had left it for the first and last time, the door to Count Radamowsky's room opened. Inside, the Count started up from the table, his face pale. Beside him, the elemental roiled within its lantern, constantly seeking escape.

Ignaz von Born closed the door behind him and snorted at the look on Radamowsky's face.

"What? My dear Count, don't tell me you were actually concerned for me? Our Mister Guernsey was hardly a fearsome challenge to confront."

"And if you had been caught?" Radamowsky subsided back into his seat, scowling. "That door might next have opened to a squadron of Prince Nikolaus's guards."

"Surely not," von Born said. He dropped into the chair across from

Radamowsky, fingering the head of his walking stick. "I'm certain only three or four of the Prince's guards would have been sent for your arrest."

"Your jest's ill-timed. As are you, I might add." Radamowsky regarded him sourly. "You were gone too long for my liking."

"Not more than half an hour, surely. Your nerves are running away with you. Have you never entered into a simple scheme before?" Von Born's eyes narrowed. "The little spy's been taken care of, as I promised, and there's nothing left for you to fidget about. You know exactly what we need from you tomorrow, and what prizes you'll win from it, now that we know how useful you can be. Only be prepared, do what's required, and—"

"Don't talk to me like a lackwitted servant, or one of the serfs from those miserable shacks outside the palace!" Radamowsky's lips curled into a snarl. "I'm your equal, by birth and abilities. And if I choose to walk away—"

"Then you'll never have access to the funds and space that you require." Von Born's voice softened to a hiss. "Not to mention official support and sanction for the . . . less savory experiments you've been dreaming of for years. Do you think our prudish Empress would ever condone them? Or her son? No matter what you may like to think, you've exhausted the limits of Prince Nikolaus's generosity, and you know it. All he wanted from you was his chance to impress the world, and you've handed it to him on a platter."

Von Born snorted, leaning back in his chair and crossing his legs. "You must have been desperate indeed, my friend, to agree to hand over all those years of hard-won knowledge in exchange for mere room and board and the repayment of your debts. Once the Prince presents his fabulous new weapon to the Empress and her co-regent, what then? Do you plan to spend the next ten years tromping around imperial battlefields like a common soldier in its wake?"

Radamowsky bit out his words. "I am no commoner."

"No, indeed," von Born agreed smoothly. "So I can only imagine that you must have agreed to teach Prince Nikolaus's own officers how to control your creature themselves . . . thus leaving yourself with nothing more of value to offer the Prince afterward. Eh?" He raised his eyebrows, his lips curving in contemptuous amusement. "Have I guessed aright?"

Radamowsky did not answer. But his hands clenched around his desk.

"Ah, my poor, unworldly friend." Von Born sighed, laying his walking stick across his legs. "Your mind may be keen enough in the quest for alchemical power, but you should have learned what I did, years ago—that power over men is so much more important. Once our petty Prince has his imperial honors, and your elemental in his keeping, he'll toss you out of Eszterháza without a second thought. And then where will you turn for your support?" Von Born shook his head slowly. "No, Radamowsky, you may bluster all you like, but I don't think you'll be walking away from what I offer."

Radamowsky took a deep, shuddering breath, but his voice remained even. "And if you choose to rescind that fine offer, when the moment finally comes? Once the Emperor and the Empress are dead and you've had what *you* wanted—your new Emperor calling a halt to his older brother's reforms, his new government filling up with all of your cronies, your precious Brotherhood running it all behind the curtains . . . What then? Why in God's name should I trust you to deliver on any promises?"

"Come now, Count. Have a little respect for both of our intellects, please." Ignaz von Born gave him an indulgent smile. "We all know what an impressive mesmerist you were even before your recent alchemical advances. But really, are you fooling even yourself with these maunderings now? Because we have may have been opposed for most of our lives, but at the moment, we both know I'm the only patron you have left. So the truth is . . ." He cocked his head. "Like it or not, you have no option but to trust me. What a novel experience for both of us!"

Radamowsky regarded him in seething silence. Von Born stood up, tucking the walking stick beneath his arm.

"I can't linger to calm any more of your fears, my friend. If anyone sees me coming out of your room, there'll be questions enough for me to answer. But don't forget, when we see each other at dinner . . ." Von Born's lips stretched into a thin smile. "Do, please, remember to act as if we are still bitter enemies."

He closed the door softly behind him. A moment later, Radamowsky heard the walking stick rapping down the corridor into the distance. Within the lantern, the elemental pressed against the glass, compressing itself into a quivering ball of rage.

"Shh, little one," Radamowsky murmured. He reached out to stroke his hand soothingly down the lantern's side. "Shh . . ."

But as he gazed at the closed door, his eyes burned as fiercely as the elemental's own.

Chapter Twenty-Four

Prince Nikolaus's enormous touring carriage rolled to a stop behind the palace at four o'clock. Charlotte had to force herself to wait her turn to step decorously out of the coach after the Empress, the Princess, and the Prince's niece and her companion, instead of shoving her way directly out and gasping for fresh air. That or simply running away . . .

"Delightful," the Empress pronounced, once she'd been helped out of the carriage to stand in the sunlight. "Nikolaus, Marie, you've done wonders with the grounds. I am most impressed."

"It was nothing," the Princess murmured, as she stepped out after the Empress. She flashed a barbed smile back at her husband. "Truly nothing."

An upper servant ran out of the palace to greet the carriage, but waited, hovering, until all the ladies had stepped out, followed by the six gentlemen in their ranked procession. As soon as the Prince appeared, the man hurried to his side, whispering frantically. The Prince stepped away from the rest to listen, frowning.

Charlotte took deep breaths of the warm air and tried to feel grateful. Hundreds of women in the Empire would have fought tooth and nail for the privilege of spending the afternoon in intimate quarters with such exalted company.

Signor Morelli stepped out of the carriage last and glanced casually around the courtyard. Despite the breadth of his survey, his glance never touched upon Charlotte. He had not looked at her once in the entire afternoon.

She'd been right to walk away from him, the night before. She knew she had. She couldn't have imagined, though, just how painful the effects would feel.

"Ah, signor." The Princess turned to him gracefully. "When can we hope for your recital?"

"At your own convenience, Your Highness." He bowed. "I sent a note to Herr Haydn early this afternoon, and he assured me that he was only waiting upon your summons for the performance."

The Princess turned to her guests. "Majesties?"

"By all means," said the Emperor, "let's have it now. I could do with some good music to settle my stomach before dinner."

His mother nodded smiling assent.

"We'll summon Herr Haydn, then, and meet in the music room." The Princess glanced at her husband, who was still locked in conversation with the agitated servant. Her eyebrows drew together. "As soon as Nikolaus is ready . . ."

Charlotte stifled a sigh. She hadn't been in the music room since the disastrous summoning, four nights ago. She had no desire to return.

"If Your Majesties and Your Highness will forgive me . . ." She curtseyed deeply.

"My dear Baroness, don't say that you're leaving now. What, and miss the recital?" The Princess turned her cool gaze onto Charlotte. "I couldn't possibly brook such an insult to Signor Morelli's talents."

Under the combined gaze of three royals, Charlotte surrendered. There would be no hour of escape, after all. "Of course not, Your Highness," she murmured. "I only need to . . . refresh myself. I would be honored to join you in the music room."

"I am glad. We'll expect you there in half an hour, then."

As Charlotte backed away, the Prince finally disengaged himself from the whispered conversation and returned to his wife and guests with a nod and a smile. "What have you decided upon, my dear?"

"We are to enjoy a recital," she said. She placed one hand on his arm and frowned at him. "What were you discussing for so long, Nikolaus? Is aught amiss?"

He shook his head and covered her hand with his own. "Only a small mishap," he said. "Nothing of any significance."

"Dead?" Charlotte repeated.

She stared at her sister. Sophie was sprawled across her bed, surrounded by scattered fashion journals and five of the costumed dolls that were sent to her from Paris every season to show off the latest designs and hairstyles. She looked utterly undisturbed by the news she'd just related.

"What do you mean, *dead*? How did Mr. Guernsey die?"

"Well, he was attacked by a horrible smoke creature, wasn't he? Honestly, Lotte! How do you think he died?"

"But the physician said that he was recovering."

"Oh, physicians will say anything." Sophie shrugged. "Anyway, the physician himself was the one who found Mr. Guernsey this afternoon, just after dinner. So, obviously, he was wrong."

Charlotte sank down onto the bed. "That poor man!"

"Mm." Sophie sighed. "What do you think?" She pulled together two of the dolls. "I was thinking I might order this underskirt"—she held up the first doll—"but matched with the overdress *á la reine*, from this one." She gestured with the second doll. "Do you think they would match?"

"I don't know. Probably." Charlotte shook her head. "How can you worry about such a thing? Poor Mr. Guernsey was perfectly healthy only a few days ago, and now . . ."

"I know, I know. It's terrible." Sophie sat up, pushing the dolls aside. "But please, spare me any self-righteous lectures. I was horrified when I first heard of it, I really was. But that was hours ago, while you were off enjoying yourself with Niko's guests."

"I was not enjoying myself."

"Of course you were. And I was trapped here, bored out of my mind. I'm going crazy in this room, Lotte!" Sophie grabbed Charlotte's hand. "Tell me everything. What did they talk about? What did they do?" She scowled. "Did *she* smirk and cling to Niko the whole time?"

"The Princess?" Charlotte sighed. "No, she didn't smirk. Or cling. She was very . . . dignified."

"Cow."

Charlotte bit her lip. She couldn't remove the image of the little

Englishman from her head. He'd always been so pathetically eager to please. So excited about his visit.

"It was a monstrous poor entertainment that the Prince insisted upon, with Count Radamowsky."

Sophie grimaced. "You needn't tell me that. I vow, my heart nearly stopped when that thing floated past me. Those horrid red eyes—oof. It gave me nightmares!"

Charlotte leaned forward. "How did the Prince know to request—no, *insist* upon the elemental?"

"What do you mean?"

"Count Radamowsky had only just arrived. How did the Prince—"

"How would I know? Niko doesn't talk about that sort of thing with me. I'm not interested in all his tedious correspondence."

"I wouldn't call the elemental tedious."

"I told Niko I didn't want to see that thing ever again. But he said he would protect me from it." A secretive smile played around Sophie's lips. "He was very—impressive, in his apology."

"Not to Mr. Guernsey."

"Don't be disgusting!" Sophie stared at her. "I don't know what's wrong with you lately. Is it that freakish castrato turning your head? I am very sorry that Mr. Guernsey died, of course I am. But aren't you at all relieved that it wasn't anyone more important?"

"I'm sure he was important enough to his own family."

"But they aren't our concern. And regardless, it was an *accident*. Or had you forgotten that part?"

"Sophie . . ." Charlotte took a breath. "Haven't you considered—the singers? The ones who ran away?"

"Yes?"

"They were killed by having their blood drained out of them. Just as that elemental started to do—did!—with Mr. Guernsey."

Sophie blinked, drawing back. "What a perfectly horrid thought."

"But what if it's more than just a coincidence? Is it possible? What if—"

"What if—*what*?" Sophie shook her head. "You're overwrought, Lotte. It's a mere coincidence. They were killed miles and miles from

Eszterháza, in completely different circumstances. Besides, Count Rad-amowsky was in Vienna at the time, and I hardly think two common run-aways were holding séances to summon up elementals, do you?"

"I didn't say that. I'm asking you . . ." Charlotte paused. "Do you truly believe, in your heart, that the Prince was entirely innocent in that first death?"

"You think Niko—that *Niko*—?" Sophie let out a breath of disbe-lieving laughter. "Have you gone mad?"

"I'm not saying that he must have been involved. I'm only asking—"

"It was a horrible, nasty little coincidence, but that is all. And no matter how many coincidences there ever were, there would never be enough for you to speak against Niko. Not ever! And especially never to me." Her blue eyes steeled. "Do you understand?"

Charlotte looked at her younger sister, surrounded by dolls and jour-nals, and all of her planned words dried up in her mouth. "Yes," she said quietly. "I suppose I do."

"Good." Sophie looked back at the exquisitely dressed doll in her hands. "I won't mention your foolishness to anyone."

"Thank you."

"It's getting late, you know. You should hurry to be at the recital." She laughed shortly, still looking down at the doll. "Just don't let yourself forget that you're a true part of the audience, this time. Not on the same level as hired entertainment."

Charlotte shook her head wearily as she rose to her feet. "I don't know why the Princess insists on inviting me to these functions. I can't even imagine—"

"I can," said Sophie. "She's using you to gloat over me. It makes perfect sense." Her lips twisted. "It's exactly what I would do, in her place."

"Well." Charlotte sighed and straightened her shoulders. "I'd better go back for more gloating, then."

After the recital finished, after the customary gifts of appreciation from the Prince and the Emperor had been received, and after all the kind words from the Princess and the Empress, Carlo saw Baroness von Steinbeck waiting to approach him. He hadn't looked at her once during the performance; he'd trained his gaze away from her that entire day. But in that single involuntary flash of vision, he saw her face, pale and troubled, and his resolve weakened.

The royal patrons had already moved on to Herr Haydn. Carlo detached himself from the Prince's giggling niece and walked toward the Baroness. Her eyes flicked up to meet his, then looked down again. He watched her long fingers plait themselves nervously together.

"The music was marvelous, signor." She smiled faintly. "As usual."

"I thank you, Baroness." He half-bowed, keeping his voice cool. "I'm pleased you decided to attend, after all."

"Signor . . ." She paused, then looked him directly in the eye. "I must apologize to you."

He stiffened. "No apologies are necessary. I clearly misjudged your feelings last night. Rest assured, madam. I won't offend you in that way again."

"I wasn't talking about that!"

"You weren't?"

"No!" She stared at him, her light brown eyes wide. "I meant . . ." She hesitated, glancing around the crowded room, then lowered her voice to a whisper. "I—Signor—I wasn't apologizing for last night."

"Really?" He lowered his voice to match hers. "I thought you'd made it abundantly clear that you regretted it."

Color flushed her cheeks. "Not because—that is, you didn't misjudge what I wanted last night. As you must know."

A woman laughed, close by. Carlo made his voice the barest whisper. "Then why did you walk away without a word?"

She looked down. "I couldn't—I mustn't follow my own desires. I can't! Sophie was right. I owe her a duty, and my family . . ."

". . . Not to involve yourself with a common musician, you mean." His mouth twisted on the words.

She let out a puff of air, not quite a laugh. "You are anything but common, signor."

"No? You mean to say, I'm a freak."

Her face jerked up. "You are deliberately misunderstanding me."

"And you are insulting me."

"Only because you insist upon—"

"My dears." The Princess's amused voice cut across the Baroness's angry whisper. She patted the Baroness's arm and smiled at both of them serenely. "We are moving on to dinner. Do please join us."

"Yes, Your Highness," the Baroness said softly.

She curtseyed, Carlo bowed, and the Princess glided away. The room emptied rapidly, as the rest of the court swirled behind the royal leaders, including Monsieur Jean, who lingered near the back and sent Carlo an impudent wink on his way out. Carlo gave him a withering look in return, but the man only grinned.

As the last few groups left the room, Carlo turned back to the Baroness, dismissing all the rest.

"Well, madam?"

She shook her head, her face tight. "I don't know what to say."

"No? I thought you were telling me how I had overstepped myself." They were alone now.

"You did nothing wrong. It was I who—"

"Baroness, you cannot avoid insulting me by telling me that you were wrong to accept my advances. That is anything but flattering."

"As I recall, they were my advances," she said crisply.

A tight knot of tension in Carlo's chest released itself. He began to laugh helplessly. "Madam . . ."

"And I don't know what you find amusing." She raised one hand to her head. "I don't even know what I'm doing here! I promised Sophie I wouldn't talk to you, and now I'm arguing with you in private."

Carlo shook his head. He couldn't stop himself from reaching out to take her hand. It was cool and firm in his grasp. Her fingers closed around his palm.

He raised her hand to his lips and saw her eyes half-close with pleasure.

"My poor Baroness," he murmured. "I could happily throttle your sister, you know."

She bit her lip but did not release his hand. "It isn't Sophie's fault. She only repeats what we were taught all our lives. What anyone would say." She closed her eyes briefly. "I'm sure—I mean, it must be true. I know it is. It's only . . ."

"Quite." He slowly untangled his fingers from hers, regretting every lost touch. "Your family would never understand a misstep."

"They've made that very clear, in the past." She took a deep breath. "I've always done my duty. I always will."

"I understand." He sighed. "I wish I didn't."

"So do I," she whispered. Her eyes were wide and lost. "So do I."

"Well, then." Carlo offered her his arm. "May I escort you in to dinner, at least, Baroness?"

"Yes, please."

She took his arm. The top of her powdered hair brushed against his cheek. He fought down the urge to pull her away in some different direction. To his bedroom, to a carriage, to somewhere, anywhere, far away . . .

They stepped out into the corridor. Attentive footmen closed the doors behind them, faces carefully expressionless. Carlo cleared his throat.

"What were you apologizing for?" he asked.

"Oh." Her fingers tightened around his arm. "I've just found out from Sophie that Mr. Guernsey—the Englishman—died this afternoon."

"Died?" Carlo blinked, jolted out of his reverie. *Not an Englishman*, he added silently. Aloud, he asked, "How did it happen?"

"He was found by the Prince's physician. I think—I believe they assume he must have died from his wounds."

"But he had been recovering."

"Yes." She looked up at him, her face drawn. "And I wanted to apologize for doubting you, before. The night of Mr. Guernsey's attack. You were right—the coincidences are too great to ignore. And the Princess warned me, when I first visited her . . ." Her voice dropped to the merest thread of a whisper. "She told me there were more guests at Eszterháza than I knew of."

"Aha," said Carlo. "So the Count was here already, after all."

"Perhaps." She hesitated. "The Princess also warned me there was trouble brewing in the palace. She told me that Eszterháza would soon become a place of danger."

"How very intriguing." They turned the corner. At the end of the corridor, wide doors stood open, exposing the Chinese Drawing Room, crowded with people mingling before dinner. Carlo slowed his steps. "She warned you . . . but you chose not to leave?"

"And abandon Sophie? I couldn't." She looked up at him. "But . . . you could. Still."

"No," he said softly. "I couldn't."

"But—"

"Something holds me here just as strongly as your love for your sister binds you, Baroness."

She blinked. "And that is—?"

"Call it curiosity," Carlo said, and drew her into the salon.

But in his head he named it for what it was.

Call it love.

Chapter Twenty-Five

Franz changed back into his own clothes and slipped out of the opera house while applause still sounded in the audience. Delacroix would rant at him later for missing half of the requisite bows, but he couldn't—wouldn't—take the chance of letting Fräulein Dommayer follow him again. He'd made a stupid, deadly mistake in letting the Brotherhood trick and use him. The least he could do was to keep anyone else from paying for it.

Franz set out across the darkened lawn, though tension spiraled through his gut. Whether they gave him the promised reward or not, whether he was a fool or not, he was well and truly committed to their service. All he could do now was follow their wishes to the letter and pray that he'd survive them.

He stepped into the shadows of the hedge-lined paths, holding his breath.

"Ouch!" Friedrich hissed. "Your damned sword just caught my shin!"

"Sorry." Anton leaned over his shoulder, peering into the darkness. He adjusted the sword that hung at his waist. "Which way did he go?"

"I don't know. There are too many paths. Aren't you in charge of this expedition, anyway?"

"Don't be a grouch, von Höllner."

"Thanks." Friedrich gritted his teeth. He couldn't stop the panic crawling through his stomach. It was only because they were walking in the direction of the Bagatelle. It was ridiculous. Unmanly. But every inch of his body was screaming for him to turn and run. He cleared his throat. "I think he's gone. Can we go back to the tavern now?"

"Don't be so fainthearted!" Something moved in the distance, and Anton whispered, "There! Let's go."

Friedrich followed, sighing. His own sword—insisted upon by Anton—slapped against his legs as he walked. He must've fastened it improperly, after so long without wearing it.

As they moved farther and farther into the maze of gardens, reluctant curiosity began to mingle with his nerves. What was the actor doing this far from the palace, anyway? Meeting some wench from the village? No need to walk this far only to meet with Anton's little actress.

The actor stopped in a flower-lined clearing. He tilted his head to one side—waiting? Anton led Friedrich into the hedges ten feet away. They crouched down to watch. Sharp branches tickled Friedrich's nose and ears. He twitched, and Anton put one hand on his shoulder to still him. Friedrich didn't need to see his friend's face to know that Anton would be grinning, filled with delight at the whole escapade.

And why not? Friedrich sighed and gave up, peering through the hedges as if he cared, too. Half an hour was already past, after all, and only half an hour left until the agreed-upon hour was up and he could drag Anton back to the tavern. As long as his legs didn't go entirely numb in the meantime, he might as well enjoy it.

Then a deep, familiar voice spoke in the clearing ahead, and Friedrich realized just how great a mistake he had made.

"Herr Pichler. I'm pleased to see you." This time, the leader's face was obscured by a wide, drooping hat. He carried a walking stick, but he swung it freely in the air as he walked toward Franz. "I trust your performance tonight went well?"

Franz had to clear his throat before he could speak. "Tolerably well, sir. Thank you."

"Excellent. A fine preparation for tomorrow's duties." He stopped next to Franz and rested his walking stick on the ground. "Listen carefully, now. This is what we need you to do . . ."

Friedrich couldn't move. He had to run, had to get way—but as the hideously familiar voice rolled through the air, it seemed to turn his bones to glass. If he moved, they might shatter entirely.

It took him a moment to see through his haze of terror and realize that Anton was inching forward, toward the voice.

"What are you doing?" Friedrich whispered. "Get back, man! It's not—"

"Aren't you listening to him?" Anton whispered back. "It's a plot! They're scheming against my cousin and the Empress and Emperor themselves!" He inched further forward, reaching into the brambles of the hedge to clear a spyhole. "If I can just get a good look at his face . . ."

"You'll be waiting for one of our Brotherhood at the back door during the chorus at the end of the first act. He will reveal himself to you with our mark. When he comes, take him—"

A crack sounded in the hedges, and the leader's voice cut off. His head snapped around.

Franz swallowed. "I don't—I still don't quite understand why—"

"Shh!"

In three quick steps, the leader crossed the garden and pulled the branches aside.

Moonlight broke through the hedges and was blocked by the leader's dark silhouette. Friedrich squeezed his eyes shut.

"Oh, God . . ."

"Why, Brother Friedrich. How good of you to join us." The leader's gaze followed Anton as he stood up. "And you've brought company. What a delightful surprise."

"It's not my fault!" Friedrich said. "I didn't realize—how was I supposed to know that—"

"Do shut up, von Höllner." Anton didn't spare him a glance. "Sir—whomever you may be—I am Lieutenant Anton Esterházy, my friend is a lieutenant in the Esterházy Grenadier Guards, and you have been well and truly caught out." His hand rested on the hilt of his sword. "Will you do me the honor of showing me your face before I arrest you?"

There was a moment of taut silence. Then the leader chuckled.

"Yes, why not?"

He took off his hat and dropped it to the ground, then wrapped both hands around the head of his walking stick. Dark, compelling eyes stood out in a pale, thin face made entirely of hard angles.

"Well?" he said. "Are you satisfied, lieutenant?"

From the corner of his eye, Friedrich saw the man's hands fiddling with the narrow head of his walking stick.

Anton leaned forward, frowning. "I know you," he said. "I met you in my cousin's company, in the opera house. You're Herr von . . . von Born?"

"Very good," said the man, and gave one sharp jerk to the head of his walking stick. A long, thin blade shot out in his hand, and the bottom of the stick, a hollow case, fell to the ground.

"You wish to fight?" Anton pulled out his own sword, grinning fiercely. "All right, then!" He glanced back. "Come on, von Höllner!"

"I . . ." Friedrich hesitated, still half-crouching, looking back and forth between them.

"Yes, Brother Friedrich. Do join in, by all means." Von Born's teeth flashed in a thin smile. "What an interesting dilemma for you. Whose side are you on?"

Anton shook his head irritably. "What are you talking about?"

He lunged forward. Von Born's sword deflected the blow. The singer, Pichler, hovered far in the background. Panic thundered through Friedrich's brain.

"Are you going to help me or not, von Höllner?" Anton panted, as he fought.

"In case you're curious, Brother," von Born added, circling the younger man, "that letter of yours is still stored with our brethren in Vienna. And if anything should happen to me . . ."

Anton glanced around, eyes widening. "Letter?"

He'd only looked away a moment, but his feet slipped. He stumbled.

Von Born's sword flashed out. Blood blossomed on Anton's hand. The sword fell from his hands. He jumped back.

"Von Höllner!"

"I can't," Friedrich whispered. "I wish—"

Anton leapt forward, toward his fallen sword. Von Born's sword halted him, sweeping out to press lightly against his chest.

Anton backed away, eyes wide. "Friedrich?"

"Yes, Brother Friedrich, now is definitely the moment for action." Von Born smiled thinly as he advanced, holding the tip of the blade lightly pressed against Anton's chest. "Take the lieutenant's hands, please."

Friedrich stood up slowly. His whole body was shivering. "I can't do that!"

"No? Then you will be tortured in the Empress's prisons. First they'll whip you, then they'll stretch you on the rack, press burning coals against your balls, break your fingers one by one—"

"No!" Tears formed in Friedrich's eyes. "I'm no commoner! They can't—"

"In matters of treason, the torturer makes no distinction."

Anton stared at Friedrich. "What the devil is he talking about?"

"Take his hands, Brother Friedrich. Now!"

Friedrich stumbled forward. He couldn't bring himself to look at Anton's face.

"I made a mistake," he mumbled.

"A very useful mistake," said von Born. "Now hold his hands behind his back."

Anton's fingers clenched around Friedrich's. Nausea boiled up Friedrich's throat.

"Friedrich—?" Anton's voice spiraled toward panic. "Friedrich, damn it, don't let him—"

"It's all right," Friedrich said hastily. "We'll just hide you some-where, so you can't tell anyone. I'm sure it'll only be for a day or two; it won't be so bad, it's just—"

Von Born's sword stabbed straight through Anton's chest.

Anton's body convulsed.

Screams—so much screaming—Friedrich couldn't stop screaming. Blood—Anton's hands clutching his, and then—his voice, choking on his own blood, bubbling, frothing—

Friedrich fell to the ground and retched violently, over and over again.

Everything was red fog around him. He couldn't see Anton's body on the ground nearby. He couldn't see anything. Could barely hear anything.

Only one voice briefly pierced the fog.

"Hide him somewhere?" von Born said pityingly. "Oh, Brother Friedrich. You have so much to learn."

Chapter Twenty-Six

They dragged the body together, under von Born's direction. Von Höllner was sobbing, tears streaming down his face as he stumbled along, holding Lieutenant Esterházy's feet. Could he see the dead man's eyes staring back at him through the darkness? Franz didn't ask. Esterházy's hands were still warm in his as he dragged the body backward. The smell of blood was overpowering. His feet moved, following von Born's orders. His mind floated high above him, where it wouldn't have to think about what he was doing.

"Stop," von Born's voice rapped out. "Set him down."

Franz lowered the lieutenant's heavy body to the ground, wincing with the effort. They stood in the clearing before the Bagatelle. The tall building loomed over them in the darkness. Atop its curving roof, the seated Chinese figure gazed down at them impassively.

This couldn't be real, Franz thought desperately. This was only like acting in an opera. It should have been an opera, really. In tragic operas, people were stabbed and fell over all the time, only to sing their dying arias and rise up again afterward to take a bow. If there was blood, it was only stage blood. Nothing like this finality. This . . .

"Hurry up," von Born snapped. "Help me draw in the symbol!"

Franz turned and followed him mechanically.

"You'll need Brother Friedrich's sword, Herr Pichler. Take it."

Lieutenant von Höllner was still standing at his friend's booted feet, staring down. Streaks of his own vomit clung to his shirt front. Franz approached him hesitantly.

"Ah—the sword?"

Von Höllner fiddled with his sword belt, and it fell to the ground. He didn't look away from Esterházy's limp body even when Franz knelt before him to detach the blade from its sheath.

Franz had never held a real sword before. It felt strange and unwieldy in his hands as he stood up.

"What do you want me to do?" he asked von Born.

"We need to carve one side of a pyramid in the grass around him. Come, we'll make this the peak." Von Born drew his own blade and beckoned Franz to join him by Esterházy's head.

Franz's borrowed sword dug through the dirt, between shoots of grass. He couldn't even see the lines he drew, but von Born grunted approval.

Von Höllner spoke abruptly. "What are we going to tell everyone?"

"Tell? We shan't tell anyone anything, of course." Von Born's blade turned a sharp angle around the lieutenant's feet. "Make haste, Herr Pichler."

"Not tell anyone?" Von Höllner shook his head. "But . . . the Prince's own cousin! He'll look everywhere! Interrogate everyone!"

"Only once he realizes that Lieutenant Esterházy is truly missing— which certainly won't be for at least two more days. Plenty of time for us."

"And then?"

"Then, Brother Friedrich, you will say, *if* questioned, that he told you he was thinking of making a short trip to Kismarton."

"Why?"

"Say he was planning some surprise for his cousin, if you must. Say anything—or, better yet, say nothing at all. You don't know why he left or what he meant to do there. He kept it a secret from you, as well."

"Oh." Von Höllner nodded and seemed to lose interest. He turned his gaze back to Lieutenant Esterházy's body.

Franz swallowed. Perhaps von Höllner was too shocked, still, to see the implications of this plan—but Franz was not. Von Born's plan would immediately render Lieutenant von Höllner everyone's first suspect, as soon as any questions were asked.

". . . And close the side of the pyramid here, Herr Pichler. Yes. Very good."

The two blades touched at the center of the pyramid's base, closing the three points into a triangle. A jolt of tingling energy ran up Franz's arm. He looked up. Von Born smiled at him.

"And now we begin. One at each point. Brother Friedrich!"

Von Höllner jerked. "What?"

"Step outside the pyramid now, please, and stand just *there*. Yes." Von Born pointed to the spot just outside the peak of the pyramid's side and waited for the lieutenant to step into it. "Raise your arms, both of you."

Franz raised his arms. A hot wind swept against his face, emanating from the center of the triangle. He flinched.

"I don't—"

"Repeat after me: 'We summon you through our bond of fellowship.'"

"We summon you . . ." Franz mumbled the words, trying not to listen to the voice of warning that was screaming in the back of his head: *Get out, get out, get out!*

"We summon you through the rites of atonement."

"We summon you . . ."

Franz watched von Höllner's mouth shape the words. Was the man even aware of what he said?

"We summon you to our company. Now!"

Sheets of flame shot up along the borders of the pyramid. Franz staggered back. The roar and crackle of fire filled his ears.

"You're perfectly safe, Herr Pichler," von Born called to him, over the noise. "The lines of the pyramid cannot be broken while at least two guardians stand at its points." He smiled. "And now, the final invocation: 'We invite the flames to fill us!'"

"We invite the flames to fill us," Franz whispered.

Fire swept from the lines of the pyramid into its center—and sizzled as it enveloped Esterházy's body. Heat bathed Franz's face. It smelled of burning meat.

Oh, God . . . Franz's gorge rose in his throat.

Von Höllner was screaming again, but this time, the sound was cracked and helpless. He fell to his knees. Reflected flames lit his face, a rictus of horror.

No more, Franz thought. *Please, God, no more. Let me wake up* . . .

The living lieutenant lunged forward, toward the fire. He fell back as if he'd hit a wall.

"You cannot step inside, Brother Friedrich," von Born called. "It's too late. In a moment we will dismiss these flames back to their proper sphere, and the remains of Lieutenant Esterházy's body will be taken back with them."

Franz found his voice. "And you don't think anyone will wonder why there's a great triangle burned into the ground out here?"

Von Born turned his hard gaze onto him. "They may well wonder, but they will not *know*—and the Prince will be anything but anxious to parade domestic worries in front of his imperial guests. *Particularly* tomorrow, the day of their gala celebrations. And, for us, nothing after tomorrow matters." His mouth curved in a tight smile. "So, gentlemen, let us finish this now, and free the two of you to sleep and prepare yourselves. You both have important parts to play in tomorrow night's performance." His voice sharpened. "Raise your arms!"

Franz raised his arms. Even Lieutenant von Höllner, still moaning, raised his shaking arms. Franz looked into the fire, at the burning husk trapped at its center, and his voice came out as a croak.

"Where . . ." He stopped and licked his dry lips. "Where are we sending it all back to, exactly?"

"Where?" Von Born's eyes burned with reflected flames. "Why, to Hell, Herr Pichler," he said. "Where else?"

Chapter Twenty-Seven

"It's all wrong!" Herr Haydn paced up and down the stage. "The balance is wrong. The timing is wrong. I'm even hearing wrong notes!" He wheeled around to glare at the collected singers, his normally mild face bright red. "Ladies—gentlemen—have you forgotten for whom we are performing tonight?"

Not likely, Anna thought, as she stifled a yawn. Rehearsal had begun a full two hours earlier than usual this morning. When had six o'clock become so *early*?

"We perform for the Empress and the Emperor of the Holy Roman Empire: the Queen herself and her co-regent of all the Habsburg lands. They come to hear us tonight with an Archduke and our own Prince and Princess. Reviews of tonight's performance will be published across the Empire. And *everything must be perfect!*" He clutched the wide lapels of his jacket and stared at them entreatingly. "Don't you understand?"

Anna nodded limply, swallowing her yawns, as his wild gaze passed over her. *Perfect*, she thought, and stiffened her shoulders. *Be perfect!*

Herr Haydn sighed. "We'll begin again at the Act One Finale. Chorus first!"

Anna took her place, waiting in the wings to one side of the stage as the orchestra and chorus struck up and Herr Pichler paced dramatically up and down along the front of the stage, belaboring the crisis which had overtaken his character. Technicians labored behind the scene to operate the bright blue waves that appeared to rise and fall behind the singers and the white-and-silver clouds that drifted through the painted sky. Tropical plants were set at intervals around the stage, and the wooden platform had been dusted with gold paint to look like sand.

Anna took a deep breath and let the music wash over her. She tried to imagine herself into her role, as the kapellmeister had explained it to her.

She was in a mysterious, hidden kingdom by the sea . . . she was a Count's beautiful and spoilt young daughter . . . It would have been easier if she knew what all the words she was singing actually meant. It would have been easier yet if the leading lady weren't casting her a glare fit to kill.

Anna sighed. Last night, after the performance, she had been summoned up to the royal box in the center of the balcony, along with Herr Haydn, to be presented to the Emperor and Empress themselves. She hadn't asked for the honor; she'd been so nervous and tongue-tied before them, she would have much preferred to give up her place to Frau Kettner. Without the Baroness's quiet support, Anna wouldn't have been able to answer even the simplest question she was asked.

But from the moment the summons had arrived, Frau Kettner had treated her like a rat caught in a housekeeper's tidy kitchen.

The cue chord sounded. Anna and Frau Kettner linked arms and, singing in sweet harmony, ran onstage into the gold-dusted, tropical paradise that had been created beneath the frescoed, Italianate ceiling of the opera house. Singing, Anna forgot about everything except the music and the endless, unforgiving stream of Italian words. Their voices mingled with the chorus and with Herr Pichler's. The second tenor joined them a moment later, and the bass singer sang below them in a threatening undertone, plotting certain disaster. She lost herself in the music, in a blur of concentrated effort—until Herr Pichler's voice cracked and disappeared entirely, and the rehearsal was called to a halt.

Herr Pichler's shoulders hunched in the sudden silence, as the rest of the cast stared at him. "I—forgive me." His voice came out as a hoarse rasp.

Herr Haydn took a deep breath. He ran a hand over his wig. "Are you unwell, Herr Pichler?"

"I'm fine," he rasped. "Fine. I just—I need . . ." He put one hand to his throat.

"We'll take a rest. Twenty minutes. And I'll call for tea with honey for your throat." The kapellmeister nodded decisively and hopped off the stage in search of a footman.

Frau Kettner released Anna's arm with a poisonous flourish, raking her long fingernails straight across Anna's bare flesh.

"Ouch!" Anna clapped her hand to her arm. A trickle of blood emerged from the deepest scratch.

"*So* sorry," Frau Kettner murmured. She smirked and faded back to her giggling admirers among the chorus.

Anna gritted her teeth. The rest of the singers were forming whispering groups. Herr Hofner, the second tenor, threw back his shoulders and strutted before his friends with anticipated glory. Herr Pichler stood alone, pale and ill-looking.

Anna hurried straight to him, holding her chin raised high against the swirling gossip.

"What's wrong?" she asked in an urgent whisper. "Herr Pichler— what's happened?"

He blinked and recalled himself from his daze. "I—don't know. My voice just wouldn't come out for a moment." He cleared his throat, and some of the rich timbre returned. "It's getting better now, though—do you hear?"

"It's more than just your voice, though. Isn't it?" Anna stepped closer, lowering her whisper. "You've looked terrible all morning. Sick, but—not just sick." She shook her head, impatient with herself. "I can't say it right! Herr Pichler, what is wrong? Really?"

His eyes widened. He licked his lips and glanced around the stage, then back at her. "I don't think I can—"

"I only want to help you," she said. "Please. You can trust me."

He smiled weakly. "I know that. I do know." His voice lowered to the faintest of whispers. "Fräulein Dommayer, last night I saw—"

The sound of quick, heavy footsteps in the corridor outside roused Count Radamowsky from his writing. He glanced at his pocket watch. Only half past eight. Most of the nobility in Eszterháza wouldn't be awake for hours.

He set his quilled pen back in its holder, covered the sheet of paper he'd been writing on, and rose to open the door just as the first knock sounded.

"Radamowsky!" Prince Nikolaus was caught with his hand still raised in the air. "Good, you're awake."

"Of course, Your Highness." He stepped back, gesturing for the Prince to step past him into the cluttered study. "I am merely preparing for tonight . . . and, of course, writing out my notes for the officers who will take charge of our friend here tomorrow."

"Good, good. Glad to hear it." The Prince rapped his knuckles nervously across the stacks of books as he walked past them. His gaze crisscrossed the room.

"Are you well, Highness?"

"What? Oh, yes, perfectly well." The Prince rapped his knuckles against the wooden table, then started backward as the elemental's red eyes flashed open within its lamp. "By God, that thing is always impressive!"

"Thank you, Your Highness." Radamowsky leaned against an overflowing bookcase, watching the Prince through shuttered eyes. "I trust everything is going well for your visitors?"

"Splendidly, splendidly." The Prince was still staring into the elemental's red gaze. "I only . . ." He shook himself and swung around to face Radamowsky. "You are certain, are you not, that this will work?"

"Work?" Radamowsky raised his eyebrows. "How do you mean?"

"That it will be safe, tonight. With our guests." The Prince coughed. "I . . . had been very confident, as you know, but—well, that Englishman died yesterday from his injuries."

"Yes?" Radamowsky frowned. "With respect, Your Highness, we've already discussed this in some detail. You said you were satisfied with it as a learning experience."

"I was. Am." The Prince grimaced. "It's only—ah, damn it, Radamowsky, you know exactly what bothers me. I designed this plan for the Archduke. Now that it's also the Emperor and the Empress herself—"

"The glory of your success will be increased a thousandfold."

"I hope so. We may both hope so. But if it fails—if there were to be another accident like the last one—if, God forbid, the Empress or—"

"It will not fail." Radamowsky straightened away from the bookcase and looked directly into the Prince's eyes. "You need have no fear, Your Highness. You will amaze and astound your imperial guests, and the name of Esterházy will be written across history for a hundred years to come."

"Yes?" The Prince blinked, then threw back his shoulders with a short, hard laugh. "Yes. Of course. How could it not?"

"Quite." Radamowsky glanced pointedly at the pile of papers on his desk. "But if you will excuse me . . ."

"Of course. Your preparations. Excellent. Good man." The Prince clapped him on the shoulder. "Quite the challenge for you, I'm afraid, now that our little ruse has been undone—having to playact being a guest, and work as a scholar, both at once."

"Difficult, but not impossible." Radamowsky paused, considering, then let his lips curve into a full smile as he met the red eyes of the elemental in the lamp . . . the discovery he would not be giving up to anyone else, after all. "Especially when the rewards will be so great."

Half past eight o'clock. Voices and footsteps moved in the corridor outside. Friedrich shaved in front of his mirror. He had thrown his valet out of the room. Out of the barracks. The razor moved up and down. He saw it from a distance, without interest.

"Are you going to help me or not, von Höllner?"

The lather from his soap had been used up. The razor scraped across bare and reddened skin.

"What the devil is he talking about?"

The razor moved in a stinging path. A spark of pain flickered against Friedrich's cheek.

"Friedrich, don't let him——!"

"I couldn't help it!" Friedrich screamed.

The voices in the corridor cut off. Friedrich stared into his mirror, panting. Blood trickled down his face from three different cuts.

A tentative knock sounded on the door.

"Von Höllner? Are you all right?"

"Fine," Friedrich called. His voice cracked. "I'm fine."

He put on his uniform quickly, haphazardly, not bothering to straighten his jacket or comb out his hair. He waited until the corridor was silent, then hurried out of his room, out of the building, and across the grass. Toward his next task. The opera rehearsal.

"It wasn't my fault," he whispered as he walked. His feet thudded against soft grass. "I couldn't help it. I couldn't—"

"Von Höllner!" Lautzner intercepted him, just five feet from the opera house. "Have you seen Esterházy?"

"Anton?" Friedrich's mouth went dry.

"He's late for maneuvers. How late were you two out last night, anyway?"

"Ah . . ." Friedrich shrugged. His heartbeat thrummed behind his chest. "I haven't seen him."

"Well, I'm off to check his room, but Forgàcs said he never heard Esterházy come back in last night. Didn't he say anything to you, then?"

Bile rose up Friedrich's throat and nearly choked him.

"I haven't seen him," he repeated, and broke into a run.

She was so earnest. And he needed so badly to talk and lift some of the madness. "Fräulein Dommayer," Franz began softly, "last night I saw—"

The door to the audience burst open. Lieutenant von Höllner stumbled across the floor and fell into his usual seat.

"My God," Franz whispered.

The man looked like walking death. Yet he was still here—on assignment? It could only be that. He, of all men, was wholly under the Brotherhood's thrall. He raised his head and looked straight up at Franz. His face twisted.

"What were you starting to say, Herr Pichler?" Fräulein Dommayer asked.

Franz wrenched his gaze away from the lieutenant's tortured face. Fräulein Dommayer's blue eyes were wide and worried.

"I want to help you," she whispered. "I'm sure, if you tell me what's happening, we can think of something to do about it. The Baroness—my former employer—her sister is very close to the Prince. And the Baroness promised she would always help me. If she goes to the Prince and lays your problem before him—"

"The Prince?" Madame Zelinowsky purred. She'd slipped up beside them, her gaze avid. "What on earth can the two of you be speaking of now?"

"Nothing worth writing about," Franz said crisply. He stepped back and forced a contemptuous glare. "You have an overactive imagination, Fräulein Dommayer."

"But—"

"My voice will be perfectly recovered by tonight. And even if it weren't, I certainly wouldn't have any desire to consult the Prince about it."

"Did you really imagine that His Highness would be interested?" Madame Zelinowsky stared at Fräulein Dommayer and began to laugh. "Oh, Anna, my dear little Anna, what sort of education do you maidservants receive, nowadays?" She stepped back, opening up the joke to the other singers standing nearby. "You have so much still to learn."

Fräulein Dommayer flushed bright red. "Apparently I do." She stared at Franz accusingly.

Forgive me, Franz thought, as he turned away. His gaze passed over Lieutenant von Höllner, and he repressed a shudder.

For a moment, he'd felt so tempted to share his terror with someone who seemed to care. But it would only have put her in danger, too.

It's for the best, he thought bleakly, as he walked away from her.

Chapter Twenty-Eight

"*Something holds me here just as strongly as your love for your sister binds you,*" he had told her. Charlotte had memorized his words. Easy enough, as they sounded anew in her ears at every moment. Uttered in his high, pure voice, they had resonated through her entire body. The look in his eyes, as he had said them . . .

Had she understood him? Or had she been hopelessly naïve? Surely she couldn't have been mistaken. The surge of joy that had suffused her at his words had felt so right. She had looked up at him with—with pleasure, yes, with admiration, with

With adoration, she thought. Helpless adoration. And he had looked back at her, and she had felt—

"Lotte, are you even listening to me?"

Charlotte blinked, and snapped back into the present. She was sitting on her younger sister's bed, and Sophie was holding up two different gowns for her inspection.

"I like the blue," Charlotte said. *It doesn't matter what I like.* She drew a deep, restraining breath, fighting to calm her racing heartbeat. Trying to stop counting the hours, and the minutes, until she would see Signor Morelli again. She was as pathetic as a girl of fifteen—and as hopeless. As a responsible, adult woman, she should not even wish him to admire her. *To desire her.* The thought that he might find even half the appeal in her that she found in him—it should be a pity. A shame, to be quietly and kindly discouraged. It shouldn't bring this host of fantasies into her head. Impossible fantasies. Improbable, immoral . . .

She had never felt anything like this. It was completely inappropriate. Utterly mad.

But she couldn't seem to make herself stop.

She glanced at the clock that stood in the corner. Only two more hours until dinner.

"Well, let's hope that Niko likes this one." Sophie turned to the mirror and held the blue gown up before her, frowning speculatively. "He's going to see me in it tonight."

"When?" Charlotte asked—then bit her tongue. It was one thing to fantasize madly about herself. It was another thing to have to consider her little sister's fantasies. "I mean—you don't have to answer that."

"Why not?" Sophie spun around, grinning. "I'm sneaking into the opera tonight!"

"What? How?" Charlotte stared at her. "Why?"

"'How' is easy enough. I am one of the Princess's ladies-in-waiting, remember?"

"Yes, but . . ." Charlotte's heart sank. "Sophie, think how awkward it would be for you. To sit in the same box as the Princess, to see—"

"Why shouldn't I?"

"You said the Prince . . . Oh, never mind."

Charlotte looked down at her fingers, spread across the ruffled cover of Sophie's bed. *Bought by the Prince.* She winced. When she looked back up, Sophie had lost her mischievous grin.

"I know," Sophie said, "Niko doesn't want to sit between me and Her High-and-Frozenness in public. That's all right. He explained it to me. He doesn't want me to have to pretend to be anything less than what I really am."

Then why has he kept you in hiding? Charlotte thought. But she did not ask the question. There were too many layers of pain and complication in this palace. She had no right to probe at the open sores.

Instead, she stood up and laid a hand on her younger sister's shoulder.

"I'll stay in with you tonight," she said. "I'll plead a headache."

"And miss Herr Haydn's new opera? Lotte, you've been talking of it for the past week."

"It wouldn't be the greatest loss I could imagine," Charlotte said lightly.

The greatest loss would be the hours missed. How many hours did she have left before Signor Morelli left Eszterháza for another grand tour, another noble visit or operatic engagement? How many chances did she have left to listen to music at his side, absorbed in the beauty and sharing it with him? How many chances to look up and find his dark eyes fixed on her—perhaps, accidentally, to brush hands, or . . .

Charlotte let out her held breath. "Don't concern yourself, Sophie. I won't mind it at all."

"You won't have to. I wouldn't miss tonight's performance for the world!" Sophie turned her head and rested her pointed chin on Charlotte's hand. "I'll have to miss all the rest of the visit, but I can't miss this. Niko's been planning it for ages. Months! It's not just the opera. There's some secret—it's a great mystery, very exciting—"

"A secret?" Charlotte felt a twinge of shadow—the Princess's warning whispering through her. "What sort of secret?"

"That's just it! He won't tell me, no matter how much I tease him. All he'll say is that it's a great surprise for his guests. Of course, he thought he would only have one guest, the Archduke, but now that they're all here . . ." Sophie sighed. "He says it's going to make his name in history. How can I not be there to share it with him?"

"It must be a great event indeed," Charlotte said slowly. "Sophie—"

"Don't even try to talk me out of this, Lotte! I'm determined to see it myself."

"But—"

"Don't worry, silly. I won't sit in the royal box. I'm not entirely lacking in sense, you know! I'm going to sit with the officers, instead."

Charlotte frowned. "How?"

"With my husband, of course. Remember him?" Sophie stepped away and clapped for her maid. "Friedrich has done nothing but gamble and drink and ogle actresses from the first day we arrived at Eszterháza. It's about time he finally does something worthwhile."

"So you'll go to the opera with him as your escort," Charlotte said. "Has he really agreed to this?"

Sophie shrugged. "I've sent him a note, telling him he had to do it. I told him it was Niko's express desire." Her cheeks flushed; she wouldn't meet Charlotte's eyes. "Well, it should be his desire, even if it isn't."

"And the Prince—have you told *him*?"

Sophie turned to look at her, her eyes bright. "I think it will do Niko a great deal of good to catch sight of me unawares," she said. "Watch him for me, Lotte. Tell me exactly how he reacts."

Sophie's maid hurried in from the outer chamber, carrying combs and pins. Charlotte phrased her next words carefully, watching her sister's glittering excitement.

"Sophie—dearest—I don't think this is a good idea."

"Of course it's a good idea! I've been plotting it ever since last night, while you were probably off flirting with that freak."

"Sophie!" Charlotte's cheeks burned.

"Ha. I knew it. And after you promised me not to." Sophie shook her head.

"It's not—it's only—"

"Don't tell me, Lotte. I promise you, I don't want to hear, or to know anything about it. Just as long as you don't do anything stupid in public to embarrass me . . ." Sophie took a breath and turned around to let her maid reach the buttons behind her neck. "Remember, Lotte, for once in our lives you truly have no moral superiority over me."

Charlotte sighed and stepped back. "I never thought I did," she said softly.

Sophie's high, chattering voice followed her out of the room, issuing instructions to the maid. Charlotte closed the door behind her and leaned against it for a moment, taking a deep breath.

She wasn't looking forward to the evening, after all.

Carlo paced up and down the corridor outside his room. One more hour left before dinner. This was his first free moment in a day full of rigorously scheduled entertainments for the imperial guests, but he was too irritated and weary to settle into anything useful.

The worst had come in the midafternoon. Alternately bored and horrified, he'd had to sit with the rest of the court through an hour-long display of folk dancing by ferociously smiling local peasants so thin they'd looked to topple in the next strong wind. Two had been called up at the end for an interrogation on their health and happiness; at the conclusion of their set speeches of gratitude and contentment, Prince Nikolaus had smiled with rich satisfaction and tossed the leader a jingling velvet sack. The gesture might have meant more, Carlo thought, if the money hadn't been worked off their frail backs in the first place.

Still, it had spurred his first truly kind thoughts about the Empress and Emperor when he had seen their exchange of speaking looks. Empress Maria Theresia had been struggling against her magnates for nearly forty years to abolish the miserable state of serfdom in the Hungarian lands. From all appearances, her co-regent shared in her disgust—and the tactless, single-minded Emperor, by all accounts, was far less willing to accept political compromises than his mother. Prince Nikolaus and his fellows would have a hard battle to fight against imperial reforms in these coming years. The Empress might still be the most powerful figure in the land, but she was also an aging woman; it would not be long before her son inherited sole control and the whole empire shook beneath his plans.

For now, though, Carlo shook his head impatiently and swung around at the end of the corridor. He had one hour of freedom. He would not waste any more of it in thoughts of tiresome aristocrats. He should exercise his voice; catch up on his vast correspondence; even take a nap. He should pin down his next destination after Eszterháza. He should stop pining after the one particular aristocrat who never tired him—the one he could surely never have.

He glanced at his pocket watch and sighed. Fifty-eight minutes left to wait.

Princess Marie Elisabeth Esterházy frowned at her two companions, as the pale light of early evening spilled through the windows into her spacious sitting room.

"No details at all?" she asked. "You have no idea what will happen tonight?"

Monsieur Jean shrugged. "Your Highness, we've told you all we know. *Something*—the culmination of all this frantic plotting—will take place during the celebrations at the opera house."

"But you still don't know any of the details?"

"Signor Morelli is not involved," Jean said easily. "I'm certain enough of that. And as for the Baroness . . ." He glanced at Asa.

"There were no letters hidden in her room," Asa said, without looking up from her embroidery. She snapped one end of her thread off with her teeth, and sighed. "Nothing with that seal. Nothing suspicious."

"And she would never put her sister in danger." The Princess tapped her bejeweled fingers on her knee. "What a pity. I really thought they might have been the ones. It would have made so much sense! Perhaps our Herr von Born is not so subtle as I'd thought."

Jean coughed. "Shall I go to the Prince now, Your Highness? Summon him to you, to hear all that we've learned?"

"No." The Princess's face tightened. "I don't think that would do the slightest bit of good. In fact, it would be entirely counterproductive."

"But—"

"If we had tangible evidence to present, I might tell him. Possibly." She pressed her lips together. Her gaze turned inward a moment . . . and then she sighed. "No. Herr von Born may be masquerading around the palace grounds and plotting his political heart out, but the opera house tonight will be full of officers and surrounded by Her Majesty's own Hungarian Bodyguard. There will be a guard even at the royal box. There is no more protection that we could possibly put into place." She snorted. "And at any rate, Nikolaus would never call off such a grand performance merely on the suspicions of his wife and her servants. He wouldn't even think twice about it." She drew a sudden breath. "And yet, perhaps . . ."

"Your Highness?"

"*Yes*," the Princess breathed. "I shall write a note, now, begging him to call off the performance on my bidding, to assuage my sensible fears. I'll tell him I'm certain of disaster for our imperial guests, if the performance does take place . . . and I'll keep a copy for myself. It will be a note that will shame him afterward when he recalls it, if anything does go wrong. Then he shall be forced to account to the Empress for his decision to ignore my warning and thus put her in danger . . . as he most certainly will ignore my warning. Oh, how perfect!"

"Your Highness," Asa murmured, as she began a new thread, "perhaps, still, it would be better for you not to attend the opera tonight yourself, for your own safety. If you say you have been taken ill, or—"

"No." The Princess's eyes hardened. "I am Nikolaus's consort, whether that stupid little girl realizes it or not. This is my place, and the risk that I must take. And if it succeeds, and I can look him in the face afterward, before the Emperor and Empress, to confront him with how little account he has taken of me . . ." She drew a deep breath. "If it succeeds, then perhaps I may finally be free of this palace after all. Forever."

Chapter Twenty-Nine

Hundreds of wax lights filled the opera house. Set in mirrored sconces, they shot sparkling reflections off the glittering array of diamonds, emeralds, and rubies worn by the courtiers throughout the audience. For a moment, as she stepped into the royal box, the brilliant light blinded Charlotte. She paused and put a hand out to the gilded rail.

Far below, the orchestral musicians warmed up with a myriad of different melodies and scales competing in strings, warm brass, and high, fluting woodwinds. Ahead of her, the Empress and Emperor had already taken their seats in the first row of the box, overlooking the crowded auditorium of nobles, officers, and local gentry. The Prince helped the Princess to her seat at the end of the first row with charming gallantry, while the Archduke seated the Prince's niece in the row behind. The rounded, frescoed ceiling soared high above them.

"Baroness?" Signor Morelli held her seat for her, the second to the last in the order of precedence, directly behind the Prince's own seat. He smiled as he caught her eyes. "Are you ready?"

She met his eyes and her vision cleared. She stepped forward to take his hand. "Oh, yes," she said. "I'm ready."

Friedrich let his wife's chatter float straight past him as he followed her into the officers' row of seats. Once upon a time, he had enjoyed the way she could burble on endlessly without ever really saying much; when they'd first married, and life had looked very different, he'd found it rather sweet. Endearing. He'd thought he would cherish it, and her, forever. Odd, that. It seemed like far more than only a few years since he had felt that way. He felt like a different person.

He was a different person, since last night.

He tried to sit down in the last seat of the row, but Sophie tugged him onward.

"No! I want to sit in the center." Her glance flicked up toward the balcony. "Hardly anyone can see us here."

"Good." Friedrich dug in his feet, fighting against her pull on his arm. "I need to leave in the middle of the act, Sophie. I'm not going any further."

"What are you talking about? You can't just leave in the middle of a performance! How do you think it would look for me to be left sitting here alone? You can't—"

"I told you I didn't have time for this tonight. I have an appointment."

"Don't be ridiculous! What sort of appointment could you possibly have? You never do anything!"

Friedrich stared at her pretty, petulant face, and felt pressure pound behind his temples. "I never do anything?" he repeated. "Never? Are you sure?"

She blinked and stepped back. "Friedrich, what is the matter with you tonight? You're behaving very oddly."

I just helped murder my best friend, he thought. *Isn't that enough?* His fingers twitched in his clenched fists. *Do you want to be next?*

"Oh, for heaven's sake. If you're going to be stupid about it, then I suppose we can sit here." She swept out her skirts and sat with a sniff. "But I don't know what could possibly be so important that you'd need to leave the opera for it."

"No," Friedrich agreed. He unclenched his fingers and sat down at the end of the row, where he could slip out before the finale of the first act. *Following more orders.* His fingers were trembling.

"Friedrich, don't let him—"

What else could he do? What could anyone possibly expect him to do differently?

"No," he repeated grimly. "You have no idea."

"Baroness von Steinbeck." The Empress pointed a plump, black-gloved finger at the auditorium below the balcony. "Isn't that your sister, there, in the officers' row?"

Charlotte stiffened. She'd been arranging her full, black silk skirts around her seat; now, keeping her expression mild, she half-stood to look down into the auditorium.

Sophie stood at the end of the third row, next to her husband; from the set of his shoulders and the look on her face, they were in the midst of a heated argument. Charlotte stifled a sigh.

"Yes, Your Majesty, that is my sister."

"Is that so?" The Princess raised her eyebrows and leaned over the wide balustrade to look.

Her husband stayed rigidly upright, his face suffusing with red color. Behind the Emperor and Empress, the Archduke leaned over the Prince's niece in flirtatious conversation, ignoring the rest of the party.

"Why, it is indeed Frau von Höllner," said the Princess. "With her husband. What a rare sight indeed."

The Empress frowned. "What do you mean?"

"Herr von Höllner is a lieutenant in my private bodyguard," the Prince said curtly. "His duties keep him much occupied."

The Emperor snorted. "Well, they don't seem terribly well pleased with each other now that they are together."

"Who knows?" said the Princess. "Any marriage can be improved by close companionship. Perhaps their hearts will grow fonder by the end of the piece."

"Indeed. I have always thought modern couples ought to spend a great deal more time together. My own dear Franz and I shared many of the happiest hours of my life." The Empress sighed. "I only wish that Joseph would find himself a new wife to keep me company in my old age and give me more grandchildren to coddle."

The Emperor's lips twitched. "One might think, with all your many children, your lust for grandchildren might finally be sated."

"Joseph, your vile sense of humor—"

"Never fear, madam. I am perfectly well aware of your wishes."

"Good." The Empress nodded firmly. "Marie, Frau von Höllner ought to be presented before me, so that I can give news of her to her mother in Vienna. Summon her up to us after the first act."

"As you wish, Your Majesty." The Princess smiled serenely. "That will, of course, be a great pleasure."

Charlotte wrapped her fingers tightly in the silken folds of her skirt. The look on the Prince's face filled her with foreboding.

Oh, Sophie, she thought. *What have you done?*

Signor Morelli's hand brushed lightly against hers. She looked up and found him watching her, his eyes concerned. She smiled at him and let her fingers relax their death grip on her skirt.

The door to the box swung open behind her. The tap of a walking stick sounded before the first footstep.

"Majesties." Herr von Born bowed before them. "I only wished to present my duty to you before the opera began, as I wasn't able to attend dinner tonight."

The Empress nodded stiffly; the Emperor smiled.

"Why, Herr von Born," said the Princess. "I did not think you were a lover of opera."

He deepened his bow. "In truth, Your Highness, I am not. But to watch a premiere in such a company . . ." He straightened, crossing his hands over the head of his walking stick, and smiled. "How could I resist?"

Backstage, Anna practiced walking in her great billowing skirts. They swung so far around her padded hips, she nearly tripped each time she turned around, even after all the dress rehearsals and performances so far. How could noble ladies bear to wear such costumes every day?

"Anna." Herr Haydn had been walking up and down the floor, stopping by each singer for a moment of conversation. Now, he smiled at her as kindly as if he hadn't had to spend over half an hour of last-minute rehearsal time in correcting her pronunciation. "How are you holding up, child? Do you feel ready?"

"Yes, sir. Thank you."

The noise of the orchestra warming up outside had been joined by the muted roar of conversation. Anna hoped her smile hid the churning of her stomach. Her stage fright never seemed to grow less, no matter how many performances she gave.

As if he'd heard the turn of her thoughts, the kapellmeister frowned. "This is your last performance without a contract, you know. I had forgotten that myself in the confusion of these past days."

"Oh." Anna swallowed. "*Oh*. I forgot that, too."

She'd been working so hard, she had completely lost sight of the most basic of truths: all of this was only a test. No matter how hard she tried, tomorrow she might well become once again a maid, waking at dawn, scrubbing clothing, and singing only when she could steal a spare moment of privacy.

How could she ever bear it?

"Forgive me, Kapellmeister." The words tumbled out of her. "I know my Italian is still terrible, but I am trying, I really—"

"Shh, shh. My dear child, do you think I said it to frighten you? You have been doing an excellent job."

Anna steeled herself. "I still can't read music well. And my Italian—"

"Is better than it was a week and a half ago, when you first joined us. It takes time to learn a new language." He patted her shoulder. "Don't worry. The Prince is pleased with your performance so far—you saw that last night. The Emperor himself was most impressed. And if you do well tonight . . ."

"Yes, sir?"

He lowered his voice. "I think, if tonight's performance pleases the Prince, you may look forward to a very pleasing contract indeed. At a salary you will truly enjoy."

Relief flooded through her in such a rush, her legs turned weak. "So you won't be dismissing me?"

He snorted. "Trust me, my dear. Unless something goes horrendously wrong tonight, I wouldn't dream of it."

Anna hadn't made the sign against evil for over six years, since she

was ten years old and first admitted into the service of Baron von Steinbeck. She made that sign now.

"Nothing will go wrong, then," she said. "I promise!"

Madame Zelinowsky passed Franz a sealed note just as Herr Haydn
walked out into the theater. Silence fell in the audience; the singers froze
backstage, listening. The Prince must have given his nod of approval: the
overture began with a flourish. Franz looked down at the note in his hand
and half laughed.

"It lacked only that," he whispered.

She narrowed her eyes at him. "You don't seem honored."

"Have you read it already?" The seal looked unbroken, certainly, but
with steam, curiosity and persistence . . .

"It was only passed on to me fifteen minutes ago." She paused. "He
said you should know that these were your final orders."

Franz's lips twisted. "How charming." He slipped it into the inner
pocket of his costume jacket.

"Aren't you even going to read it?"

Franz stepped away, toward the stage door. In a moment, his cue
would come. In the meantime, he would cherish the illusion of being a
free man.

"Not yet," he said. "I have time, madam. Still."

Minutes, probably.

Anna didn't want to watch the exchange, but she couldn't look away. The
sounds of the storm in the overture intensified as Herr Pichler slipped the
note into his pocket.

Stupid. She'd offered him her help in every way she could, and all he'd
done was humiliate her in public. Well, she had learned her lesson at last.
She wouldn't feel sorry for him anymore, and she wouldn't try to save him

from his problems. She needed all her energy now for herself, to give the best possible performance tonight. To win herself a future.

Still, when Herr Pichler came to stand beside her, waiting to step onstage, she hesitated.

By all rights, she ought to ignore him—or say something as horrid as what he had said to her earlier, to repay him. But when she looked at the shadows beneath his eyes and the hunched, defensive set of his shoulders, she couldn't do it.

Instead, she whispered, "Be careful."

His eyes widened. "I will," he whispered back, without looking at her.

The overture drew to a close. Flutes and strings signaled the morning, and Herr Pichler's cue.

He gave her the fraction of a nod and stepped onstage.

Chapter Thirty

Astorm broke through the orchestra. Shuddering strings and percussion charted its progress. From his seat at the harpsichord, Herr Haydn nodded firmly to the horns. They entered, building tension, building—

Carlo frowned, shaken out of the music of the overture. From his seat by the closed door of the royal box, he'd heard unexpected movement outside. Footsteps—and the unmistakable tap of a walking stick.

After making his bows to their Majesties, Herr von Born had excused himself to find a seat in the auditorium below. What was he thinking now, to be pacing around the royal box in midperformance?

The storm in the music peaked and faded. Whispering flutes and oboes replaced the chaos, mimicking the calls of birds. Carlo shook off the irritating mystery and returned his attention to the stage as the curtains drew apart to reveal an island scene.

Even as the lead tenor stepped out and began to sing, though, Carlo could not rid himself of the sensation of lingering unease.

The first scene went well, Franz thought. He sang his opening recitative loudly and clearly, aiming it straight at the royal box. Illuminated by the hot beams of the spirit lamps in the wings, he knew he made a striking figure. He sang of his character's bewilderment at the strange island the storm had washed him onto. As mechanical waves swayed behind him, he launched into his aria, commending himself to the love and trust of his long-missing beloved. He made the tune as soulful and as heartfelt as he possibly could. After all, it might well be his last performance.

The applause of the audience rewarded him at the end of the aria. He bowed deeply and strode offstage, ears ringing.

The ladies swept onstage as he left it, followed by Delacroix and the chorus. Franz collapsed against the wall, sweating, and glanced around. The few remaining men backstage stood in a small cluster at the far corner, throwing dice.

It was time.

As women's voices soared up in greeting to the new day, Franz reached into his pocket and withdrew the sealed note. It felt limp in his hand. He handled it as carefully as he would a viper.

He stared at it for a long moment. If he never opened it, he would never have to know . . .

But then he would not survive the night.

Franz broke open the seal.

As the ladies of the chorus finished their paean to the new day, the rest of the islanders ran in and swept into a festive dance, and Charlotte half-closed her eyes to appreciate the sheer beauty of the music. Bright colors swept across her narrowed vision. Then the lead soprano entered with a high, thrilling note, from the right of the stage, and the chorus silenced to give her full pride of place.

She was, of course, the tenor's long-lost beloved, first kidnapped by pirates and then washed up from a shipwreck onto this shore. Now, she had been taken in by the local count and was living as his ward, oppressed both by the pain of her lost love, and by the count's determined and unwelcome courtship. As her melancholy aria ended, she was swept unwillingly into the village's celebrations—and the lead tenor entered, from the other side of the stage, too far away to see her. He raised his voice in appeal. It should have soared across the orchestra and chorus. Instead, Charlotte could barely hear it. She blinked, and fully opened her eyes.

Something was terribly wrong with the lead tenor. Even through the haze of beauty that the music had spun around her, Charlotte could see it. As he continued to sing, Herr Pichler's voice was a pale shadow of its normal self. His actions were slow and sluggish; his face, a sickly white. Was he ill?

Charlotte glanced around the royal box. Signor Morelli frowned at the stage; *he* had noticed the change, certainly. The Emperor and Empress, in the row ahead of them, watched with every appearance of enjoyment. The Prince glared down at the audience below him . . . at Sophie. Charlotte looked past him, at the Princess—and stilled.

The Princess's face was rigid with tension. Her bejeweled hands had clenched into fists around the balcony's rail. She looked a veritable statue. Only her eyes moved, sweeping the audience—for what? Unease crawled up Charlotte's neck. Suddenly, the opera seemed far less compelling.

A flicker of motion in the audience caught Charlotte's attention. She leaned forward and saw her brother-in-law standing and slipping out through the auditorium doors.

Clearly, the opera wasn't holding his attention, either.

"It's time," Friedrich whispered as he stood.

Sophie pouted, but she didn't move to stop him. The interminable music droned on and on as he slipped out of his seat and out of the auditorium. The corridor outside was dim, with only a single brace of candles burning. The servants hadn't arrived yet for the break between acts.

He walked up the corridor quickly, listening to the echoes of his boot-heels against the marble floor and clenching his jaw to hold back the voices. All the damned voices. The voices that would send him to Hell—*where he'd sent Anton.*

I had no choice.

He pushed open the door to the backstage waiting area. Five or six singers looked up at the sound, then recognized him and looked away again, focused on their card game. For a moment, Friedrich was tempted to join them.

Then the singing onstage finished, amidst loud applause, and Friedrich leaned back against the wall to wait for the singer he'd met before, Franz Pichler, and the beginning of his final orders.

Anna hurried backstage as the chorus took over. She arrived just in time to catch Herr Pichler as he tripped.

"Careful!"

"Sorry," he muttered. "Sorry . . ."

He was heavy in her arms for a moment, before he straightened and stepped away. Anna gasped when she saw his face.

"You're ill!" she whispered.

"No. I'm fine."

He tried to move away, but she caught his arm.

"You look like death! What's happened to you?" She narrowed her eyes. "Was it—that letter?"

He let out a puff of air, not quite a laugh. "I . . . yes. The letter. But not just that." He shook his head. "I've been a fool."

"Tell me what's wrong."

"It's too late."

He glanced over her head. Lieutenant von Höllner stood propped against the back wall, watching them with grim intensity. Anna's stomach twisted.

"Is—is he involved as well?"

Herr Pichler's lips twisted. "You could say that."

Monsieur Delacroix had been moving around the groups of singers, whispering orders. Now he stepped up beside Anna, pointedly ignoring Herr Pichler. "Orders from the Prince," he hissed. "He has a surprise planned for his guests, and he wants the stage cleared immediately after the finale. No second round of bows. Singers and musicians are all to leave the building until summoned. All except for you, Pichler." His lips curled. "No flowers for you yet, I'm afraid, Fräulein."

Anna lifted her chin. "I don't desire them, monsieur."

He snorted and walked away. Anna turned back to Herr Pichler. He'd looked ill before Delacroix's visit; now, he looked as though he might collapse.

"Tell me!" she whispered. "What's going on?"

Franz licked his lips. They were so dry, they cracked. Everything was cracking around him.

He couldn't stop making the calculations in his head. Two people, perhaps, he could have understood. Four people even. But there were four hundred people in the audience tonight. The two-pointed base of the pyramid's triangular side would be bounded by each end of the stage, and the figure would peak high above the royal box, where the Brotherhood's leader had stood, gazing down at him, through nearly all of the act so far. The pyramid would angle in from its base, leaving some innocents untouched, but still including . . . what? Two hundred and fifty people? Three hundred? As well as all the occupants of the royal box itself? It was beyond comprehension. Three hundred people to die because Franz had been angry and hurt and stupid, that night in his prison cell, and he had let himself be tricked.

The stench last night, as the lieutenant's body had burned . . .

Oh, God. He was going to be sick.

Fräulein Dommayer was speaking to him. "Look at me!" she said. "You're too ill to go back on. Just sit down! I'll tell Monsieur Delacroix you can't continue, and—"

"No!" He blinked through the gray haze. "I have to go back on. If I don't . . ." He looked over her head at Lieutenant von Höllner, who stood watching him evenly. Just as the letter had promised. "I'll be killed if I try to run," he whispered.

Von Höllner had held his closest friend's hands behind his back while the man was stabbed, for the Brotherhood's sake. No chance he would feel any more compunction for the death of a singer he didn't know.

"Killed?" Fräulein Dommayer stared at him. "Why would they care so much that you sing tonight?"

"It's not the singing," he said. "It's after. It's . . ."

Aristos, he told himself. Only stupid, arrogant aristocrats sat in the audience and filled up the royal box . . . aristocrats, their hired soldiers, and the invited local gentry who fawned all over them. Why should he even care? They wouldn't give so much as a shrug for news of his death. Prince Nikolaus had ordered his beating. He was no more than a trained monkey, in their eyes. Why should he care what became of any of them?

Fräulein Dommayer stepped closer, until she was breathing in his ear. "What have you been ordered to do?"

"Kill every one of them," Franz whispered. "In the flames of Hell." *And listen to their screams forever.*

She fell back. "What—?"

"It's an attack on the Empress and Emperor," he said numbly. *"They* knew the Emperor and the Empress herself were coming, somehow—but they're going to kill everyone else with them. Not just the royal box, almost all the audience—it's going to—"

"The Baroness," she whispered. "Oh, sweet heaven!"

The chorus finished. Drums sounded. Nearly time, now, for the finale to begin.

"When?" Fräulein Dommayer whispered. "How?"

"Just after the end of this act's finale," he whispered. "But there's nothing we can do. I can't leave—they're watching me—I can't!"

She stared at him, her face working, for a long moment. Then she said, "But I can."

She picked up her wide skirts, whirled around, and ran out through the door before he could stop her.

Chapter Thirty-One

Anna raced down the long corridor, heart pounding. Her high-heeled shoes pinched her toes and sent agony shooting up her calves; her arms ached with the effort of holding up her heavy skirts as she ran.

Through the doors, she heard the music of the finale begin.

"Where the devil is she?" Delacroix's whisper neared hysteria. "How could she have left? At a time like this?!"

"She took a sudden whim, I suppose." Franz shrugged, fighting panic. "I couldn't stop her."

"She probably took offence at something you said." Madame Zelinowsky sighed. "Really, Herr Pichler, why do you bother with her? You know these servant girls. So temperamental."

The cue for Fräulein Dommayer and Frau Kettner sounded for a third time in the orchestra pit. Franz heard rustlings in the audience as the music repeated itself yet again. Herr Haydn would be frantic by now at the delay.

"We'll have to stop the performance," Franz said. "Someone should go out there and announce—"

"Don't be ridiculous!" Frau Kettner hissed. "We don't need a bloody maidservant to perform before the Emperor. We'll be fine."

Franz raised his eyebrows. "The plot won't make much sense without her character."

Frau Kettner snorted. "It's not as if she ever really acted, anyway."

"She never will again, after tonight," Delacroix muttered. The cue sounded a fourth time, even louder, and he vented an explosive sigh. "Kettner—go! Just sing your part. Let the kapellmeister and his musicians decide how to handle the missing lines. Everyone else . . ." He scowled at Franz as Frau Kettner lunged at the stage door. "This performance is proceeding as planned. Understood?"

Franz nodded jerkily. He didn't trust himself to speak.

They're all going to die, he thought.

As he turned back to the stage door, he saw Lieutenant von Höllner's hand drop away from the hilt of his sword. Franz released a sigh.

They would die, but he would live . . . at least for another hour or two.

Anna turned the final corner and skidded to a halt. Guards surrounded the foot of the grand staircase that led up to the balcony and the royal box. They faced away from her, chatting. She fell back behind the corner before they could see her.

Without an explicit summons, they would never let a mere singer up into the royal box, not even at the break between acts. And she didn't have time to argue with them. Frau Kettner's voice soared through the closed doors. Anna gritted her teeth, listening to the gaps in the music that her voice should have filled.

She would not give up now. Not when she'd already sacrificed her future for this.

Her wrists ached. She let her heavy skirts fall to touch the ground—and realization struck. She was dressed as a grand lady. Her hair was powdered and piled on top of her head. The character she'd played was the daughter of a count. Would three of the Empress's bodyguards from Vienna be able to tell the difference?

She raised her chin. *Be a grand lady*, she told herself.

How many ladies had she watched in her years as a maid? She closed her eyes, summoning up the elegant, gliding carriage, the tilt of the head—the air of absolute confidence, which no mere soldier would dare to gainsay.

Inside the theater, the chorus joined Frau Kettner. Her voice and

Herr Pichler's twined together in harmony. Only five more minutes until the end of the act.

Anna turned the corner again and walked straight toward the guards.

The music was *wrong*. It was filled with empty spaces and harmonies left gapingly hollow. Charlotte couldn't fathom it. Where was Anna? How could the finale of the act not include one of the major characters?

Signor Morelli touched her elbow. When she turned to him, he nodded slightly, tipping his head toward the corner of the stage. On the floor just beneath the stage, a dark figure stood, nearly hidden by the shadows.

Count Radamowsky.

Alarm squeezed Charlotte's breath tight in her chest. Signor Morelli's face set in lines of rigid anger; his eyes widened. She followed his gaze to the front row of the royal box and saw Prince Nikolaus nodding across the theater at the Count, his own expression smug.

What madness is approaching? Charlotte thought.

But it was too late to escape.

Anna forced herself to look past the guards with cool hauteur as she reached the grand staircase. She had one foot already on the first marbled step when one of them spoke.

"My lady." He bowed curtly. "They're in midperformance. I don't think—"

She stared him down. "They are expecting me." She walked past him up the stairs, head held high.

Her hands were quivering so badly she nearly dropped her skirts. But no one had stopped her.

She opened the door at the head of the stairs and emerged onto a carpeted dais in the center of the balcony, between two sets of stairs, one leading up to the top of the balcony and one down to the auditorium below. Before her was the closed inner door to the royal box itself. Two more guards stood between her and the inner door as the final chorus began.

Hurry, Franz thought. *Hurry, damn it!*

He was singing as slowly as he could, forcing the other singers and orchestra to adapt to his pace against all musical sense and dramatic logic. Franz forced himself to ignore the kapellmeister's anguished glare from the harpsichord. Instead, he peered up into the balcony. The leader of the Brotherhood smiled down at him from his post behind and above the royal box. Still, no sign of Fräulein Dommayer.

Ten more lines of music—less than three minutes—

Herr Haydn took advantage of Franz's abstraction to push the music faster. The others joined in loudly, forcing the tempo forward; helplessly, Franz followed.

It was madness to have even hoped. Foolish, naïve—

The outer door to the royal box opened. A lady emerged and spoke to the two soldiers stationed at the inner door. Franz's pulse leapt. It must be—it was—

The leader of the Brotherhood moved as quickly as a pouncing snake.

Anna knew as soon as she saw the guards in front of the royal box that mere arrogance would not serve to carry her past them.

"No admittance during the performance," the first guard whispered. "I beg your pardon, madam, but the Empress gave explicit instructions that they not be disturbed."

"I am here on a matter of the greatest urgency." Anna tried to step past them. "They would wish to see me. I have—"

The second guard stepped in front of her, holding out a bulky arm. "I'm sorry, madam, but that's simply not possible."

The chorus was beginning their final verse. Anna could have screamed with impatience. "I'm here to warn the Empress. There—"

An unfamiliar voice rapped out from the steps to the gallery above them.

"Shame on you, Fräulein Dommayer."

Anna jerked around. A tall man in a richly embroidered black coat and satin breeches was running down the carpeted stairs toward them. He covered the last two steps in a bound, despite the walking stick he carried. His eyes glittered feverishly.

"Masquerading as a lady?" he asked. "Surely you couldn't have expected it to work. The fact that you're Lieutenant Esterházy's whore won't save you from his cousin's wrath."

"I—what?" She stared at him, rendered momentarily speechless.

The first guard blinked. "Sir?"

"This is Lieutenant Esterházy's actress," the man said. "Publicly cast off by him only a few days ago—and here, no doubt, to make a scene before both his cousin and the Empress."

"I am not!" Anna regained her breath. "I wouldn't—I wasn't!" She raised her voice. She was a professional singer, at least for this one last evening. Surely she could project her voice through the thin walls of the royal box. "I am here to save their Majesties' lives!"

"A sweet attempt." The man smiled thinly. "But not, I'm afraid, quite good enough." He nodded at the second guard. "Take her away."

Raised voices filtered into Charlotte's consciousness, through the music and the air thick with tension. Voices, arguing, familiar—

"I am here to save their Majesties' lives!"

"Anna," Charlotte breathed. "What's happening?"

The Empress scowled. "I can barely hear the music. Nikolaus, do take care of it."

The Prince gave an irritated jerk of the head, and a footman jumped to open the door. He peered out, whispering to one of the guards; through the narrow opening, Charlotte glimpsed her former maid struggling against the second guard.

The door closed. The footman bowed.

"One of the singers, sir, trying to intrude and make a scene."

"Anna wouldn't do that!" Charlotte said. "She isn't like that."

The footman coughed. "The lieutenant says she is . . . ah . . . *was* acquainted with Lieutenant Esterházy. Until he, ah, dismissed her a few days ago."

"Ah." The Prince grimaced. "Tell them to get rid of her and let us enjoy the rest of the performance in peace."

The Empress nodded firmly.

Charlotte spoke in a fierce whisper. "She said she was trying to save their Majesties' lives. Won't you even listen to what she has to say?"

The Prince snorted. "She was trying to frighten the guards into letting her in."

"With respect, Your Highness, the Baroness may have a point," Signor Morelli murmured. "Fräulein Dommayer doesn't seem to be—"

"May we please stop discussing this and listen to the rest of the act?" the Empress said. "For heaven's sake, Nikolaus, have the guards question her somewhere else, if you must, but let us—oh. It's over!"

The theater hung in silence. The audience and the singers onstage all peered up at the balcony, waiting for the Prince to signal the beginning of the applause. Only the sound of Anna arguing with the guards filtered in through the walls of the box. Charlotte watched the Prince glance covertly down to where Count Radamowsky waited in the shadows beside the stage.

"Please," Charlotte said urgently. "I truly believe—"

The Prince cut one hand through the air. "Enough." He nodded at the footman. "Tell them to take her somewhere quiet. I'll question her myself, tomorrow."

"Nikolaus," the Princess began, mildly.

"No!" Charlotte said, at the same moment. "Your Highness, I beg you—"

The footman opened the door, interrupting the argument outside.

"Your Highness, please!" Anna lunged at the opening—

—And Herr von Born stepped into view, his walking stick flying up in his hand. He hit her hard on the head with the knob of the stick. Anna crumpled to the ground. Charlotte cried out, jumping to her feet.

"How dare you?"

Herr von Born bowed at the royals through the open door. "She won't intrude upon Your Majesties now."

The Prince nodded back, breathing heavily. "Our thanks, von Born."

Charlotte gripped her hands together, shaking. "Your Highness, I must protest! This is an intolerable abuse of—"

"You may protest later, Baroness, but not now."

The Princess's gaze flicked to von Born and back. "Nikolaus, perhaps we really ought—"

"*Enough*, madam." He dropped his voice, but Charlotte still heard his piercing whisper: "I have heard more than enough of your fretting already tonight."

With his jaw set hard, the Prince signaled to the stage, and the four hundred audience members burst into loud applause. The guards closed the door to the royal box, shutting out the view of Anna's crumpled form. The singers onstage leapt into action, sweeping deep bows and curtseys, and then clearing off the stage with unusual haste. Anger and fear simmered through Charlotte's chest as she slowly sank back down into her seat. There was nothing more she could do now, with the Prince in this mood. All she could do was wait and hope that, in his pleasure at the end of the operatic performance, he would be more open to her persuasion.

But helpless rage nearly strangled her. If Anna had been seriously hurt . . .

The Prince's smile looked strained as he turned to his guests, rubbing his hands together.

"I have a surprise planned for Your Majesties," he said, "to erase even the memory of all such unpleasantness. A surprise . . . and a gift."

The Emperor and Empress turned together to their host.

"What sort of gift?" the Empress asked.

The Prince took a visible breath. "One more powerful than any cannon. One before which even Turkish or Prussian soldiers would have no strength, nor courage to stand and fight."

What? Charlotte thought. And then, as perception pierced through rage: *Oh.* She sucked in a gasp. He wouldn't. Would he? Not after what had happened to the poor Englishman. Not . . .

The Emperor leaned forward, his face hardening. "Explain."

Prince Nikolaus's smile relaxed. "You'll see for yourself, Your Majesty, in only a minute's time."

At the Prince's nod, Count Radamowsky stepped up onto the stage.

Chapter Thirty-Two

"Ladies and gentlemen. Your Majesties. Your Highnesses." Radamowsky strode to the center of the stage and bowed deeply.

The lighting had not changed, yet Charlotte could have sworn that darkness gathered behind him. The shadows seemed to thicken and bunch together.

Nonsense, she told herself. Yet she couldn't rid herself of the illusion.

His voice rolled out, projecting easily through the theater. "His Highness Prince Nikolaus Esterházy has entrusted me with the great honor of studying a source of power and strength previously unknown to any monarch on earth. Allied to this elemental force and its kin from beyond the aetheric veil, any army would prove irresistible. This, Your Majesties, is His Highness's royal gift to the House of Habsburg."

The Empress's plump face tightened into hard focus. Beside her, her son's figure was a pure line of intensity, aimed at the stage. Charlotte fought to stay decorously seated instead of running for her life. Had no one told the imperial guests what had happened the last time this elemental had been summoned?

It had to have been tamed by now, she told herself. Prince Nikolaus would never countenance any danger to his honored guests.

A week ago, that reassurance might have comforted her. But now . . .

"Ladies and gentlemen, distinguished guests and hosts, if you will only grant me your attention, we may prepare for the presentation of this royal gift. If you will but close your eyes and focus on my voice . . ."

No, Charlotte thought. *Not this time!*

She saw Signor Morelli's hands clench into fists as Radamowsky's voice turned into a drone. Beads of sweat stood out on Morelli's forehead. Dizziness spun through Charlotte as she fought to resist the pull of the Count's voice. His words pushed at her head, tugging at her, pulling her down into the trance and filling all her limbs with torpor. She wouldn't give in this time—she wouldn't let herself—

Something clicked in the back of her head. *Enough.*

She had done what was expected of her every year and minute of her life. She had never offended a host or disobeyed her parents, husband, or superiors in rank. She had paid scrupulous attention to the laws of polite society. She had followed every one of those laws . . . until tonight. Tonight, she could finally see with cold clarity that none of them truly mattered—not enough to risk her life. She *would* escape this!

She threw herself forward. She would jump from her chair, run out of the theater, run as far as she needed to escape this bloated travesty of power—

But she couldn't move. Her arms and legs had turned to lead. She struggled desperately, trying to scream. No sound came out. She saw her arms lying quietly on her lap. Her mind floated high above the rest of her body, shrieking silently.

Charlotte's eyes closed. Her head tipped forward.

Franz waited until he saw Radamowsky's signal before he took the wads of cloth out of his ears. Lieutenant von Höllner, at the other end of the stage, did the same. They walked out to join the Count in the center of the stage.

Radamowsky bowed. "The field is yours, gentlemen." He did not bother to lower his voice.

Franz looked out into the audience and shivered. Four hundred people sat before them, eyes closed, entranced. Insensible. Waiting for their deaths.

He'd thought his own voice had power. He'd had no idea.

This had to be more than mere mesmerism. There was dark, frightening magic mixed in with this man's skills as a performer . . . and he had chosen to use it all for *this*?

Franz shouldn't have said anything, he knew that. Now that he was committed, he should have been able to ignore the self-loathing that gnawed at his stomach. But his voice came out in a cracked whisper, far beyond his control.

"Why are you doing this?"

Radamowsky raised his eyebrows, looking amused rather than offended. "For much the same reasons as you, I'd imagine. What fool wouldn't desire the patronage of powerful men?" He smiled. "In my case, the new government in Vienna will be infinitely supportive of my researches and of my, ah, personal requirements for them."

Franz blinked. "New government? But there's an heir—the Emperor's brother—"

"Ah, but who do you think will step in to rule the new Emperor, in this crisis?" Radamowsky shook his head gently. "Especially once Austria's relations with the Hungarian magnates are thrown into chaos by tonight's massacre? And—"

"Enough!" von Höllner snapped. The lieutenant was visibly trembling. "Let's get it over with, damn it!"

"An excellent notion." Von Born called the words down through the theater as he stepped up above the royal box, setting his walking stick down on the floor. "Radamowsky, I thank you for your help. It will be well-rewarded, as we've discussed. Von Höllner, Pichler, take your positions. It is finally time."

Anna swam up out of unconsciousness, head pounding, with a tight constriction clamped around her arm and waist. The ground rolled up and down beneath her.

She cracked open her eyes and gasped with pain. Nausea whirled through her body. The shell-lined path outside the opera house crunched beneath her dragging feet. The pressure at her arm and waist was the tight grip of an imperial soldier, dragging her away from the opera house. Toward . . . She swallowed, and pain crashed through her head. *Toward the prison.*

It was too late. The finale had ended. The Prince hadn't believed her.

Hundreds of people would die. She had given up her newfound career and missed her chance for a shining new life. All for nothing?

No!

She'd remained slumped, her eyes still mostly closed, as the thoughts had played through her head. The soldier had no way of knowing that she had woken. He wouldn't expect any trouble.

How much worse could her own trouble become?

She counted down in her head, preparing herself. *Three . . . two . . . one!*

She spun around with all her weight, throwing herself against him. Her captor's grip loosened. She kicked out her leg from within her great mass of skirts, slamming her foot behind his knee. He stumbled and fell, cursing, onto the path. Murderous rage darkened his face as he rolled onto his back, preparing to jump to his feet.

"You little—!"

Anna stomped the sharp heel of her elegant shoe straight onto his diaphragm, and ran.

Friedrich strode across the stage without a moment's hesitation, taking his place on the mark von Born had set for him. Not something he'd ever thought to do, stepping onto a stage—not something his parents would ever have imagined for him, either—but then, it was the least of the madness taking place tonight. If he'd been in his right mind, he probably would have been bloody terrified.

He should have felt frightened even now, shouldn't he? When he looked at his hands, he could see them shaking. But his head felt cool, safe and far removed from what he was doing . . . at least as long as the bloody singer shut up about it. What was the point in talking about it? Anton was already dead, and Friedrich had killed him. It was too late to pretend that anything could be made right, after that.

He'd always thought it was enough to mean well, to be liked, to be a good fellow. Well, it wasn't enough. It hadn't saved him, had it? All that was left now was to give in, because it was too late to care anymore.

He looked out at the audience, at the sea of empty faces waiting for their deaths. What he realized, then, surprised him into a near-laugh, for the first time in nearly twenty-four hours.

Sophie was safely outside the pyramid, at the far edge of the third row of seats. If they'd sat in the center, as she'd wanted, she would have been in the middle of the pyramid, sucked down to Hell with the rest of them.

"Ha!" he breathed. "You see?" She couldn't hear him, but he said it anyway, in a moment of fierce elation. "You don't know everything, after all. I'm the one who was right this time!"

For a moment, that was nearly enough.

Anna ran along the side of the opera house, kicking off her shoes for speed. She only had a minute or less of grace from the gasping, wheezing soldier behind her. She sped through the side entrance, ignoring the pain that filled her head. *She couldn't be too late.*

She threw herself up the stairs to the auditorium. The sharp corners of the marble stairs scraped at her stockinged feet. She slipped.

She grabbed the wrought-iron railing and caught herself just in time. The soldier's footsteps sounded at the bottom of the stairs just as she launched herself through the door, into the audience.

"Raise your arms," von Born called.

Franz raised his arms. What was the point of resisting? All this time, everything he'd done, everything he'd hoped—futile, all of it. All of it had led inexorably to this moment.

They're only aristocrats, he told himself. *They wouldn't lift a finger for me, either.*

"Repeat after me," the leader called. "*We summon you through our bond of fellowship.*"

"We summon you . . ." As Franz droned through the words, something moved in the corner of his vision. He blinked.

It was a woman, hurrying through the back rows of the auditorium. A woman in a familiar blue gown.

What in the name of God?

Franz snapped his gaze back to von Born. The man's gaze was focused and intense as he stared down at the stage. He hadn't seen Fräulein Dommayer yet. Franz could swear to it.

What the hell was he to do?

"*We summon you through the rites of atonement,*" the leader intoned.

"We summon you . . ."

Franz breathed all the words, hardly aware of what he said. All his attention focused on Fräulein Dommayer as she raced up the stairs to the balcony and neared the royal box. She pushed past the entranced guard, whose head nodded against his chest. She threw the door open and hurtled inside.

Von Born's head snapped around . . . and then he shrugged. Even from the stage, Franz could see his fierce grin.

"*We summon you to our company. Now!*"

Flames shot up along the lines of the triangle and closed Fräulein Dommayer within it.

Chapter Thirty-Three

Fräulein Dommayer's screams ripped through the theater, filling Franz's ears. They were the only sound of protest from the rows and rows of people who sat, blank-faced, within the great triangle formed by crackling flames.

Von Born didn't even blink at the sound as he raised his arms. "Call the flames into the pyramid with me, gentlemen! *We invite you to—*"

"Wake up!" Fräulein Dommayer screamed, throwing herself at one of the women in the royal box.

"No," Franz breathed.

The lines of the pyramid cannot be broken while at least two guardians stand at its points.

Franz leapt back from his post and launched himself across the stage, straight at Lieutenant von Höllner.

"Wake up!" Anna screamed. "Wake up, wake up, wake up!"

Heat blazed against her skin, and the scent of burning wood filled the air. A sheet of fire outside the box blocked the open doorway, while two lines of flame crossed through the top corners of the royal box, setting the thin wooden walls alight. She didn't understand why the fire wasn't spreading to the rest of the box. She was too desperate to care.

How could they all sleep through this? It could only be magic, witchcraft, to hold them all unconscious while strange, still lines of flame rose around them. She would have taken them for dead already, had she not seen the steady rise and fall of their chests.

She was trapped in a sea of ghosts.

Heat licked at Charlotte's face. Something was burning, somewhere close. A voice rose in entreaty, calling her name. Hands touched her shoulders and shook them urgently. The voice broke into sobs.

Anna? Charlotte thought. But she couldn't open her eyes to look.

Franz slammed into von Höllner and fell with him to the gold-dusted wooden floorboards of the stage, letting out a muffled groan as his back hit the ground and the half-healed scabs split open. He hadn't fought since he was a boy; he barely even knew how to fight. All he could do was clamp his arms around von Höllner's, pinning them down, and commit all his strength to trying to roll the other man away from his point at the pyramid's base. The leader of the Brotherhood screamed orders and imprecations from the top of the balcony above them. Franz ignored him.

"Have you gone mad?" von Höllner grunted, as he struggled against Franz, fighting to free his arms.

"We can't do this," Franz panted. "You have to see that. It's—"

"It's too late!" Von Höllner pushed him back, holding them still at the pyramid's base. "Do you want to be arrested? Tortured? Executed?"

"There are hundreds of people here! We can't—"

"Are you just too stupid to see the truth? It doesn't matter anymore! *Nothing matters!*"

Fräulein Dommayer's screams filled Franz's ears, rising above the roar of the flames and von Born's shouted threats. Franz looked into the other man's bloodshot eyes, a bare inch from his own. Their arms were locked; their weights, equal.

"Some things still matter," Franz said. "Even now."

"Oh, God, please wake up!"

Anna sobbed as she shook the Baroness's shoulders. The flames rose high around the royal box. How long until this strange spell broke and they swept inside?

"Her Majesty!"

The soldier behind her had finally reached the open door. He threw himself at the line of flames—and rebounded as though he'd hit a wall. He landed, stumbling, two feet back from the line of fire. His clothing wasn't even singed.

"What the hell?" He stared at Anna, panting, eyes wild.

"Help us!" she screamed. "Go get help. They're all sleeping. I can't—"

Through the open door, she saw him turn away, his hand falling to the hilt of his sword. Above them, hidden by the back wall of the royal box, she could hear Herr von Born still shouting threats at the men who fought onstage. The soldier set his jaw and started up the steps.

"No!" Anna yelled. "Get help! Go—"

But it was too late.

The thin sword hissed free of its casing. The bottom of von Born's walking stick clattered to the ground. He raised his sword and smiled down at the approaching guardsman.

"Yes? You had something you wished to say to me?"

The soldier pulled out his own sword, his face pale. "Sir, I hereby arrest you in the name of Her Imperial Majesty and her co-regent the Emperor." He swallowed. "And I order you to dismiss this black magic."

Von Born's gaze flicked to the stage and back. He shrugged. "If you want to arrest me, you'll have to come and take my sword."

The soldier took the last four steps in a run.

Swords met and sparked.

Metal clattered to the ground.

The soldier's sword had fallen from his hand. He lunged forward to retrieve it—

—But the tip of von Born's sword darted forward to rest against his throat. The soldier froze, panting.

"I'm terribly sorry," von Born said. "But I really can't leave this spot."

He thrust the sword straight through the other man's neck.

Anna fought against every instinct that had been trained into her.

"I'm sorry," she whispered.

She slammed the flat of her hand against the Baroness's smooth face. A red mark blossomed on the Baroness's powdered cheek. The Baroness's eyelids twitched—and opened. She blinked. Her lips moved.

"Anna?" she croaked. "What—what's happening?"

"It's not too late," the leader called. "Pichler, think what you're giving up, you fool! Don't you even want a future? A *life*?"

Franz didn't bother to shout out a response. All his effort was concentrated on the grim, silent struggle he fought. If he could only move von Höllner by an inch . . .

"Very well, then. You've made your choice." Von Born's voice filled with venom. "Von Höllner—just kill him and get him out of our way."

Sensation tingled back into Charlotte's arms and legs. She took a deep breath, turned—and screamed.

"Fire!"

Flames crossed through the top corners of the royal box and swept in diagonal lines down across the auditorium below. Why did the flames not move? Why hadn't they spread?

"You were so sound asleep—you all were. I didn't know what to do! Herr von Born led it all. I couldn't stop it, I was too late . . ."

Anna broke off, but Charlotte barely heard her. Next to her, Signor Morelli sat barely a foot and a half away from the line of flames that blocked the open door, yet his smooth, curving face was set in peaceful repose. His eyes were closed. The moment the flames moved toward them, he would die.

"Signor!" Charlotte flung herself at his chair and seized his hands. "Signor, please—Signor Morelli—Carlo!"

Anna spoke behind her. "Madam, it won't work. With you, I had to—well . . ." She paused and cleared her throat. "I'm sorry, but I had to slap you."

"Anna, you're an angel. You did exactly right. I'm so grateful—if we escape this, I'll prove it to you, I swear." Charlotte took a deep breath. "Now if I can only be as strong as you . . ."

She slapped Signor Morelli's cheek, as if to wake him from a faint. His eyes moved beneath his closed eyelids, but his expression didn't change.

"It didn't work." Panic sucked away Charlotte's breath, leaving her reeling. It wasn't too late for him. It couldn't be. Not now, not when she'd wasted so much time already.

Hadn't she decided to fight for what she wanted, after all, earlier tonight?

Steeling herself, she drew back her arm . . . and this time, she hit him with all her might.

His face jerked back, and she cringed with sympathetic pain . . . but a moment later, his eyes flickered open, pupils dilated. He blinked, and focused on her face with a visible effort. "Baroness? What—"

"Move!" Charlotte said. "I beg you. We are in desperate danger."

But it already seemed to be too late.

None of the others would wake, despite all of their attempts. Von Born's shouted instructions carried on throughout, growing angrier and more desperate. His own subordinates seemed not to be responding to him, either. It was the only source of satisfaction that Carlo could find in the whole nightmare.

"It's useless," the Baroness said, at last.

She stood over the Empress of the Holy Roman Empire, whose face was red from slaps. Next to them, the Baroness's former maid shook the shoulders of the Emperor, whose head rocked limply back and forth. The girl's face was streaked with tears. She'd shown remarkable bravery, Carlo thought, but she wasn't stupid; she must know by now how useless that, too, had been. Were these tears of fear, or of regret?

"The others must not have fought so hard against Radamowsky's mesmerism," Carlo said.

"The Princess, surely—"

"The Princess had not experienced it once already, as we had. She must have been less prepared for it." Carlo shrugged, swallowing bitterness. "I swore I wouldn't give in this time, and yet . . ."

"I did the same." The Baroness sighed. "At least it was enough that we could be woken."

"So that we may stand and watch the fire overtake us? At least the others are saved that fate!" Carlo spun around. Rage coursed through him but found no outlet. The Prince, the idiot who had allowed and abetted this, was unconscious; Radamowsky . . .

"Radamowsky could wake them," he said.

"But he's gone."

"Then I'll find him." Carlo looked at the line of flames, nearly eight feet high, that filled the open door. He set his teeth and looked back at the two women. "I swear we will not die in this box!"

"You're . . . going . . . to . . . *die*." The muscles in von Höllner's forehead stood out with the intensity of his effort as he pressed Franz's bleeding back against the hard wooden floor. "When I get my sword free . . ."

"You can't follow orders forever." Franz tightened his grip on the other man's arms, ignoring the agony in his back. "You let yourself be frightened into killing your friend. Wasn't that enough?"

"Don't talk about Anton!" Von Höllner glared at him. "You have no right to talk about him!"

"And you do?"

"You stupid bloody actor. Anton was following you! That's why we were out there! It was all because you stole that little actress he wanted." Von Höllner's face suffused with red. "It's your fault that Anton's dead!"

Franz opened his mouth—then stopped himself. Perhaps it was too late, after all.

He slammed his head forward, into von Höllner's forehead. Pain bloomed, filling his vision, but he'd already started the motion of throwing his weight forward. Von Höllner went limp, for a fraction of a moment. It was long enough.

They rolled backward, away from the pyramid's point.

Flames hissed and snaked across the stage.

Chapter Thirty-Four

Flames, suddenly alive with movement, crackled along the wooden frame of the royal box and caught on the velvet hangings within it.

Charlotte gasped as she lunged forward, nearly tripping on her skirts. She pulled the Princess out of her seat by the wall and dragged her limp, heavy body to the center of the aisle. The smell of burning wood and velvet filled Charlotte's senses as the fire abruptly shifted from a supernatural, distant horror to an all-too-real calamity.

One of the velvet hangings sagged and fell, still flaming, over the open doorway.

She scrambled forward, fighting to squeeze between the chairs to reach the Prince's niece. A hand closed around her arm.

"There's no time!"

Charlotte turned. Reflected flames lit Signor Morelli's pale face as the fire spread along the wooden sides of the box.

"We can't leave them!" Charlotte said.

"But we can't carry them out. Not all of them. Not even most of them."

"But—"

"Do you want to waste our time choosing two or three people to save? If we summon all the soldiers outside, we'll give everyone a chance. They can bring buckets, water . . ."

Charlotte nodded. Taking a deep breath, she hiked up her overskirt. She wouldn't let propriety hold her back. Not anymore. She grabbed the top layer of her petticoats and ripped. In the corner of her vision, she saw Anna doing the same. They both emerged with long, wide strips of white cotton cloth.

If she was going to die, then let it be while running for her life, not passively waiting for the flames to overcome her.

Signor Morelli pulled off his jacket and lifted it over his head. "Go!"

Charlotte wadded the cloth into a thick pad, wrapped it around her mouth and nose, and ran after him, straight into the flames that blocked the door.

The heat was overwhelming. For a moment, she saw blackness as flaming sparks dropped from the doorway above her and landed in her hair, sizzling. Fire licked at her bare arms. She smelled burning powder . . .

And then she was through. Hands caught her, in the sudden absence of heat, and beat against her. Cloth swept around her piled, powdered, burning hair.

She dropped the cotton from her face and took a deep, painful breath. Coughing wracked her body. At last, she could open her eyes again.

She stood in the stairwell, protected, for the moment, from the fire. Signor Morelli bent over Anna, beating the flames from her hair and gown just as he had for Charlotte. His clothes were blackened but his face unharmed. Charlotte took a deep breath and flexed her burned arms. The soft hairs on her forearms had been completely burned off; small patches of blisters, excruciatingly painful, marked her reddened skin where the burning drops had landed.

She was alive.

Signor Morelli straightened. His eyes met Charlotte's for a brief, searing moment. She nodded, unable to speak. Shivers wracked her body, despite the blazing heat. She felt raw and strange, marked by the fire.

She had come to Eszterháza to find herself. Somehow, despite everything, she thought she had finally succeeded.

His shoulders relaxed.

"Go," he said. "Both of you, quickly! Summon help."

Anna started down the steps, her face grim and set. Charlotte hesitated.

"What about you? What—" She stopped, blinking, as he pulled off his cravat and ripped it into strips. "What are you doing?"

"Providing myself with a shield." Face grim, Signor Morelli wadded up two of the pieces of cloth and tucked them into his ears. "I'm going to find Radamowsky," he said. "And this time, I won't be mesmerized into obedience."

The sight of the flames crackling into life among the audience made Pichler freeze for a moment. It was enough.

Friedrich tore his arms free of the singer's hold. He lunged to his feet and kicked out hard, catching the bastard on his face. Blood streamed out of Pichler's nose. Friedrich looked down, panting, with fierce satisfaction. In the edges of his vision, flames leapt high, catching on wooden chairs . . . and people.

"You see?" Friedrich said. "Look! They're all going to die, because of you! You let it free."

Pichler's voice was muffled behind the hand he'd lifted to his face. "But they can escape, now. The lines of the pyramid are broken."

"Escape?" Friedrich stared at him. "*Escape?*"

Suddenly, tears were burning against his eyes. He'd raised his foot to kick the actor again, but he let it fall back to the ground. What was the point? He looked up. The leader of the Brotherhood had disappeared from his post above the royal box. *Of course.* On his way to wreak vengeance, no doubt. Friedrich's shoulders sagged.

"You still don't see it, do you?" he said. "It's too late for us. We'll never escape."

They were halfway down the steps, running, when Charlotte realized the truth. She froze for a moment in pure horror. Then she began to run faster than she'd known she could.

"Madam?" Anna called, as Charlotte overtook her. "What is it? What—"

"Sophie," Charlotte gasped. "Sophie!"

Sophie, who shouldn't have even been here tonight. Sophie, so willful and impossible to check. Sophie, whom Charlotte had nearly abandoned—*again.*

She threw the heavy door open and barreled through the group of soldiers.

"Fire!" she screamed. "Fire!"

But she kept running, running around the turn in the front hall, down the corridor to the ground floor entrance.

She prayed as she ran, hurtling through the words of the rosary with every moment that brought her closer to the flames.

She prayed that she hadn't failed her younger sister again.

Carlo had snatched a sword from the entranced soldier who stood outside the royal box. Now he fought his way down through the Esterházys' opera house with the weapon bumping awkwardly against his side.

The supernatural fire had cut across the auditorium in twin lines of unmoving flame. Now flames caught and spread onto neighboring wooden chairs and the clothing of the people within. Carlo felt his way along the side of the auditorium as the fire spread inexorably outward from its original central triangle. Above him, the fire had already spread from the corners of the royal box down to the balcony. It spread along the roof above the auditorium, dripping flame onto the paralyzed guests below and catching on the velvet hangings that hung from the edges of the balcony. The smell of burning wood, paint and velvet mixed with smoke and the hellish stench of burning meat.

The deaths had already begun.

Nausea threatened to overwhelm him. He fought it down. He couldn't drag each one of the still-breathing, helpless bodies out of the theater, but he could at least do his best to wake them all up and let them save themselves.

Behind and above him, the sounds muffled by the wadded-up cloth in his ears, Carlo could faintly hear men's raised voices, shouting orders. Help had arrived—and gone directly to the royal box, of course. He didn't bother to look back to see if the soldiers had been in time to save the royal families.

If Radamowsky had left after his betrayal, then all of Carlo's hopes were for nothing and he would be proven useless indeed. But if the alchemist had stayed to witness the progress of his plan, as a prudent man might, he would have waited in concealment, either backstage or in the Chinese ballroom connected to the opera house.

Gripping his borrowed sword, Carlo plunged through the door beside the stage, into darkness.

"Of course we can escape," the singer said. He blinked up at Friedrich from a blood-covered face. "There's a door backstage that leads out to the grass. We—"

"And then what? The bloody Brotherhood hunts us both down, or the Emperor tortures and executes us and they read our stupid letter, and they find out about everything, and—and . . ." Friedrich's words dried up in his throat as he took in the other man's expression.

"What letter?"

"It doesn't matter," Friedrich said. "Nothing matters. I just . . ." He sighed and pulled out his sword. "If I kill you, I'll have followed all their orders, so at least they can't blame me. And after that . . ." He shrugged. "It doesn't matter."

The actor's voice was bizarrely calm, almost curious. "Doesn't anything matter to you anymore, lieutenant?"

Friedrich stared at him. The fire was approaching across the stage, crackling along the dusted floor, creeping up the palm trees and painted wooden sets, and catching on the bottom of the curtains, but he couldn't make himself care about any of it. His mind was occupied, turning the man's question over and over. *Doesn't anything matter?*

His honor had mattered, when he was younger. His parents had raised him to be proud that he was a von Höllner, proud of what that name meant. But he had lost that consolation a week ago.

No. He tasted acid. He had lost his honor nearly two years ago, when he had accepted the Prince's offer.

Friendship had mattered, even yesterday, but that was over now, too. Anton was dead. Friedrich's friendship had killed him.

A burning stage set toppled forward off the stage, setting the closest wooden pillar alight, but still Friedrich didn't move.

Sophie had mattered, for a time—a very short time, really, looking back on it. Only the first year or so of their marriage. But Sophie . . .

"Sophie!"

A woman's scream sent him jerking around to face the audience.

Sophie's sister stood at the edge of the audience. A great velvet hanging had fallen, burning, from the roof of the auditorium and set half a dozen seats and people alight directly in front of her. Horror made a mockery of her features as she screamed, staring beyond the impassable inferno—

—To where Sophie sat only ten feet away, eyes closed, while flames spread toward her from the fiery triangle on her right.

Flames caught on her skirt and sleeve, and spread.

"No," Friedrich whispered.

He barely felt himself move. One moment, he stood high up on the stage, holding the sword poised above Franz Pichler. The next, he was in the middle of the flames.

Someone had blown out all the candles backstage. Carlo peered through the darkness, searching for his prey. He held the hilt of the sword clamped in his right hand, slick with his own sweat. With the wadded-up cloth filling his ears, all that he could hear was his own labored breathing as he shuffled softly along the wooden floor.

He was the most famous *castrato* in Europe, at the peak of his career, and he might well be about to die in the dark with the real, nontheatrical sword of an imperial soldier. It wasn't how he had planned to end his days. He could have let the soldiers do their own work, while he retired to safety. He could have comfortably raged against the idiocy of the Prince while he sat safely in the palace, sipping a restorative glass of fine, imported wine. He could imagine that scenario even now as he crept through the darkness, his ears muffled against the screams and the roar of the fire outside.

He had spent too long on the sidelines, swallowing his fury, playing the role of a noble guest and pretending not to notice the injustices that surrounded him.

It was finally time to act.

Carlo felt his way along the back wall, running his left hand against the wood. But the pressure of the darkness behind him was too much—with a grimace, he paused to pull out one wad of cloth, freeing his left ear to listen out for any telltale creaks or whispers. He tried to breathe as quietly as possible, all of his senses attuned to the darkness around him. At last, he found the edges of the door that led out of the building.

If Count Radamowsky were indeed hiding backstage, he would have to come this way to escape and abandon his victims to the flames.

But he'll have to pass me first.

Behind him, Carlo heard a footstep. He spun around.

Chapter Thirty-Five

"Sophie!" Charlotte screamed. She fought down useless, blinding tears. She couldn't even see her sister any longer, past the leaping flames that blocked her way. "Sophie!"

The uniformed man on the stage turned around, as if in reaction, and she recognized him at last.

It was too much to take in. She staggered.

"Friedrich?" she whispered.

He dropped his sword and leapt into the flames.

Above the stage, the rod that held the burning curtains creaked and split. Burning red velvet fell across the front of the stage, barely missing the lead singer where he lay.

"Signor . . . Morelli, is it not?" A dark figure loomed before Carlo as he blocked the backstage door. Rich amusement threaded through the familiar, resonant voice. "Now, let me think. Why exactly would you be waiting for me? One last performance, perhaps?"

Carlo raised the sword before him, squinting in the darkness. His left hand clenched around the second strip of cloth, ready to stop his hearing at the very first hint of those too-familiar, rolling, mesmeric cadences. "You've failed," he said plainly. "Von Born's run away, and the royals have all been saved."

"What a pity." Radamowsky shrugged his shoulders. "I must confess, though, I had guessed as much from the noises outside. And?"

"Save the rest of them." Carlo had spent years learning perfect control of his voice. It was his instrument and his vocation. He would not let it fail him now. "You have no reason not to let them wake and save themselves. If you help now, the Empress may be merciful and—"

"You clearly do not know the Habsburgs." The shadowy figure let out a breath of laughter. "For all her famous piety, our great Empress is no more familiar with mercy than her hardheaded son. Have you never read the torture code devised by the Emperor himself?" A gleam of teeth showed in a smile. "It is enlightening, to say the least. I thank you for your news and your advice, but I think—"

"What of threats, then?" Carlo lunged forward, breathing hard, until his heavy sword hovered only an inch away from the man's chest. "If you don't wake the audience, I'll murder you here and now."

"Ah. Now that is, admittedly, somewhat more persuasive." The Count raised his hands slowly. "And yet, I'm afraid you still haven't quite convinced me. So, if you'll just let me pass . . ."

Carlo firmed his grip on the slippery handle of the sword, lifting his left hand until the cloth hovered just outside his ear, ready to save him from any mesmeric attack. He was doing exactly as he'd planned—but his breath hurt his chest, escaping all of his vaunted control. "I'm not bluffing," he said hoarsely. "I've never injured a man in my life, but I will kill you now if you refuse."

"I'm certain you would. After all, you've had so much practice onstage, haven't you?" Radamowsky's voice filled with amusement. "What you don't realize, signor, is that, in this case, you are outnumbered."

"I beg your pardon?" Carlo blinked, and tried to focus his gaze. Something about the darkness just behind the alchemist . . .

Red eyes flicked open above Radamowsky's shoulder.

Carlo stumbled back against the closed door, his left hand loosening around the useless strip of cloth as his breath caught in his throat.

Fool, he thought. He'd only prepared himself for the least of the alchemist's weapons.

Gray smoke floated forward. Red eyes watched him with greedy anticipation.

Radamowsky's voice turned into a purr of satisfaction.

"You see," he said, "I haven't been waiting here alone. And all that you've managed, with this heroic display, is to delay me by a moment."

Friedrich barely felt the burning heat. All his focus was on Sophie, sitting still and entranced as the flames leapt up her sleeve.

Sophie, whom he had promised to love and protect, on his word as a von Höllner, before God and the gathered society in the *Michaelerkirche*. He would not let the flames take her, too.

He lunged past the orchestral benches and the long wooden music stands. The ashes of sheet music flaked against his clothes. He pushed past the corpses and the still-living bodies. He fell against Sophie and bore her to the ground, rolling over and over, beating out the flames. Fire surrounded them. He covered her body with his own.

Tears streamed from his eyes. Smoke scoured his nose with every breath. Flames burned his hair and skin until every inch of it seemed to scream at once, as Anton had screamed, as Sophie's sister had screamed.

He stood within the flames and scooped up his wife with strength he hadn't known he possessed. He bore her through the flames, her face pressed against his shirt, her arms protected between their bodies as the sleeves and the back of his own coat burned.

He lifted her to the height of his shoulders, above the mass of blazing seats and bodies, and he threw her body over it to fall at her sister's feet. Through the fire, he saw the older woman drop to her knees to beat the flames from Sophie's clothes. If she hurried, she could still drag Sophie out of the building to safety.

Friedrich turned before she could look up again.

The door that led from the audience to the back of the stage was blocked by the burning, toppled stage set; the fallen curtain on the stage itself blazed with fire, more effective than any wall.

There was no way out. But then, he had known that even before he had leapt off the stage.

He thought, at first, that he saw Anton's face within the flames. Then, in the final moments before blackness devoured him, he realized that the man he truly looked at was himself.

Friedrich watched himself burning and melting within the fire, and for the first time in years, he was not ashamed of what he saw.

Franz staggered to his feet and stumbled across the stage, away from the blazing fallen curtain. His head hurt blindingly, and his back had stiffened into a warped, unnatural angle. His nose throbbed with pain as it dripped warm blood down his lips and chin. His ribs, his arms, his knees—everything was in agony.

But he was alive. It was incredible. It was more than he had dreamed possible.

His crashed through the thin door in the set that led backstage, away from the flames and the stink of death. As soon as he was free, in the fresh night air, he would run and keep on running until—

The door from the opposite end of the stage opened, letting in a narrow stream of light and heat that cut across the backstage floor. A familiar voice spoke behind him in the semi-darkness.

"I've been looking for you, Herr Pichler."

Franz turned around, feeling a heavy weight settle in his stomach. Lieutenant von Höllner had been right after all.

"You've failed," he said to the leader of the Brotherhood. "Why haven't you run?"

"I told you you would never escape if you betrayed us." Von Born stepped forward and circled him slowly, smoothly, in the near-darkness. The tip of his blade hovered barely an inch from Franz's skin. "Do you have any idea how long I planned tonight's performance, only to see it ruined by your cowardice?"

"I'm sorry." Franz licked his dry lips, watching the blade circle around him. "I couldn't do it. I couldn't be a party to mass murder."

"No? I can." The leader leaned in closer. "The Brotherhood does not suffer its enemies to live. Particularly when they are the only witnesses left."

"I'm hardly the only witness to what happened! There's Lieutenant von Höllner, Fräulein Dom- . . ." Franz stumbled to a halt, as his mind made belated connections.

"Von Höllner is already dead. Fräulein Dommayer will be taken care of as soon as I finish with you here. And after that, only two of the Prince's guests remain to be accounted for. By the time any questions come to be asked, all that anyone will remember is the dangerous Count Radamowsky putting us all to sleep. I, of course, will be as horrified as everyone else." He pressed the tip of the sword lightly against Franz's neck. "You see? You've accomplished nothing. You've gambled your life for nothing. And in betraying me, you've lost your future. Do you begin to regret your actions yet, Herr Pichler?"

Franz closed his eyes. He took a breath, feeling his throat move against the cold steel, as clarity filled him for the first time in weeks. "No," he said. "I don't."

A deep voice spoke behind him, from the depths of the shadows by the back door that led outside to safety. The alchemist who had entranced the entire audience stepped out of the shadows, his eyes blazing, followed by the most famous castrato in Europe.

"Well, well," Count Radamowsky said to his companion. "Signor Morelli, your little delay may have persuaded me after all."

Carlo had held still, at Radamowsky's signal, ever since the other two men had come backstage. Now he stepped forward, following Radamowsky. The hilt of his borrowed sword felt warm in his hand; his heart beat quickly against his chest. He pulled out the cloth that muffled his right ear, willing all of his senses onto high alert. The elemental hung somewhere behind them in the darkness, hidden from him. He tried not to imagine its hot breath on his neck.

The two alchemists faced each other in the darkness, lit only by the thin stream of light from the open stage door.

"Radamowsky." Von Born lowered his sword, frowning. "I told you to wait for me outside Eszterháza."

"And yet I didn't choose to trust you after all. Astonishing, is it not?" Radamowsky glided forward. "All your promises, von Born. All of your tricks. I should have known better than to have ever believed a single word you said."

Von Born's eyes narrowed as he shifted, turning the sword in his hand. "I had a glorious vision," he said softly. "I had hoped to include you."

"Only as your scapegoat. Do you take me for deaf as well as gullible?" Radamowsky raised his own hand. "Do you know, unworldly or not, I think I'd rather not allow everyone to hold me solely to blame, after all. What do you say to that, *friend?*"

Von Born's sword hissed through the air, poised and ready. "I'd say you're a fool, as you ever were." His sword flashed forward.

Radamowsky's voice rapped out. His arm fell.

The elemental dropped straight onto von Born's head from above.

Von Born's screams seemed to last forever.

His sword dropped to the wooden floor. He reached up, desperately trying to claw away the mass of smoke that surrounded his face. His body wove in the air. His hands wavered and dropped to his sides. His screams slowly died to a gurgling moan.

Finally, only the hissing sound of the elemental's feeding mingled with the sound of the flames and breaking furniture through the open stage door.

The actor, Pichler, dropped to his own knees, vomiting. Carlo only watched, held frozen by numb horror.

The other alchemist stood, unmoving, through it all, as von Born's body gradually crumpled and fell to the ground. Only when the elemental finally rose into the air, bloated and dripping blood above the empty corpse, did Count Radamowsky move.

"Come," he said, and crossed the floor in three rapid steps to stand within the open stage door. The elemental floated after him.

Carlo followed from a safe distance. He felt amazed—in a distant, unreal way—that his legs chose to support him after all. There would be a price to pay later, he knew, for this temporary gift of numbness. For now, he only concentrated on remembering to breathe . . . and on trying to forget.

Radamowsky's voice rolled out, chanting a mix of archaic languages through the roar of the flames that filled the stage and spread back toward the alchemist himself. Driven by horrified fascination, Carlo finally dared to step closer, to look over Radamowsky's shoulder at the chaos without. Fire blazed from the fallen curtain at the front of the stage, and painted blue waves had turned into points of flame, crackling toward the back of the stage. High up in the burning balcony, soldiers on duty labored to rescue the highest nobility, while the entranced or dying bodies of their military comrades and the local gentry filled the auditorium.

At last Radamowsky's chant cut off. Through the flames, Carlo glimpsed sudden movement among those who were still alive, throughout the theater. Eyes opening, adjusting. The paralysis of total shock and then panic, as people woke to find themselves aflame.

Radamowsky's voice called out, impossibly loud, speaking German once more. At the unexpected sound, even the soldiers in the balcony turned to listen.

"You will all remember that it was I, Count Radamowsky, who chose to save you tonight from the traitorous machinations of Ignaz von Born."

There was another moment—perhaps only a fraction of a second—of paralyzed silence. Then the screaming began, along with the thud of a hundred chairs being turned over, as the survivors fought to escape, scrambling over the corpses of their neighbors.

Radamowsky turned to face Carlo, ignoring the carnage and the approaching flames. The elemental hovered above his shoulder, staring at Carlo with hungry, blood-red eyes.

"You will not, I trust, try to hinder my escape any longer?"

There was a time for heroism . . . and a time for sanity. Carlo dropped the sword.

It clattered to the floor as he spoke, forcing his voice into an attempt at coolness. "I don't imagine that I could stop you."

"You are a wise man, signor." Count Radamowsky smiled faintly. "Let us both hope that we shan't meet again . . . entertaining though such a performance might be."

He walked across the backstage floor at a deliberate pace, brushing past the huddled form of Franz Pichler and stepping over the remains of Ignaz von Born. The elemental followed after, at shoulder height, still dripping.

The door to the gardens opened and closed. Carlo gave a long, shuddering sigh.

"It's over, isn't it?" Franz Pichler pushed himself up from the floor. He looked astonishingly young in that moment, his face open in wonder. "It's actually finished."

"No," Carlo said heavily. He felt every one of his years as he turned back toward the stage. "Not quite yet."

Taking a deep breath, he stepped forward, to return to the flames and join the rescue attempts.

Chapter Thirty-Six

Many hours later, Carlo found Herr Haydn outside, standing near the wreckage of the opera house. Flames still shot high into the night sky above the crumbling building, though hundreds of workers fought with buckets of water to stem the blaze. Smoke veiled the stars over Eszterháza.

The shells in the path crunched under Carlo's feet as he walked forward to join the composer.

Haydn spoke without turning around. "Every copy of tonight's opera. All of the orchestral and vocal parts. My score." He choked on the words, raising one hand to his face. A moment later, he added, "And all of my other operas, nearly. I kept all of my music in the theater. For safe-keeping!"

Carlo shook his head silently. What was there to say? He stood next to the older man, looking into the fire. It had been one of the grandest opera houses of any noble estate in Europe.

Almost two hundred people had been rescued from the flames, in total. He hoped that most of them would survive. It was more of a blessing than he could have dreamed of before Radamowsky's change of heart.

It was still not nearly enough.

"I am sorry," Carlo said softly, as he looked into the blazing ruin of Nikolaus Esterházy's pride.

"Well." The kapellmeister straightened his shoulders. "I had one or two of the older opera scores in my room, for revisions. The marionette operas are all gone, with no hope of restoration . . . but I remember tonight's opera well enough. I ought to, after all the blood I've sweated over it." He sighed. "I'll start work on its recreation tonight, before I even go to bed. Before I can forget any more of the details. And I'll write to my publishers—"

"You will do no such thing," a harsh voice said, behind them.

Prince Nikolaus stood two feet away, trailed by guards. His face was ravaged beneath his clean white wig; deep, raw burns ran all the way up his cheeks. He gripped a blanket around his shoulders with thickly bandaged hands, but his voice was as commanding and inflexible as ever.

"Tonight's performance, Herr Kapellmeister, never took place."

Carlo's eyebrows rose. "Never, Your Highness? With so many witnesses?"

"Signor Morelli." The Prince's face tightened. "Her Imperial Majesty Maria Theresia, Emperor Joseph, and I have all discussed the matter, and we have come to the conclusion that tonight's . . . incidents . . . are best forgotten by everyone involved."

Carlo took a breath to loosen the tight constriction in his chest. "Over two hundred people have died already, Your Highness. Is that to be forgotten, as well?"

"They died," the Prince said curtly, "in a most regrettable fire, caused by the combustion of three of the stoves in the Chinese ballroom. As the newspapers will report, all over the Empire, in a few months' time . . . and as, I am sure, you will confirm to any who ask. It was a most deplorable accident." He looked past Carlo to the blazing remains of his opera theater, and his voice flattened. "Their Majesties and I agree that no blame accrues to anyone here for the event."

And how much did you pay the Habsburgs to bribe them into that decision? Carlo watched the flickering shadows cross the Prince's burned face. Had it been money? Esterházy gold? More soldiers to be sent out to the next Habsburg war? Or—could it have taken the form of the political concessions Maria Theresia had fought for since her accession to the throne, nearly forty years ago?

Perhaps the state of the Esterházy serfs would see improvement, after all, to fall in line with the Habsburgs' reforming laws for the rest of the Empire. Carlo could only hope as much.

"It will all be rebuilt, of course." Flames found reflection in Prince Nikolaus's eyes. "It will be larger and grander than ever before. It will be the amazement of the Empire."

"And my opera will be performed again, too," Haydn said quickly. "I was just telling Signor Morelli, Your Highness, that I still remember the full score, and I can certainly order another copy of the libretto. If I start rewriting it tonight—"

"No," the Prince snapped. "Never again."

"Your Highness?"

The Prince scowled. "I want no reminders of tonight."

"But . . ." The kapellmeister cut himself off, biting his lip. A moment later, in a muffled tone, he said, "Of course, Your Highness. I understand and obey. I'll only write it out for myself, and—"

"Re-read your contract, Herr Haydn. You write only with my permission and only those pieces that I wish to hear. And I never want anyone to hear of this opera or its conception, ever again."

"But—"

"*Enough.*" The Prince turned and strode away.

The guards fell into step behind him. Carlo glanced at Herr Haydn . . . then had to look away. Such naked anguish was not meant to be seen. He felt the twist of it in his own chest.

He put out his hand. The older man took it and squeezed it briefly.

"Do you know, Signor Morelli," the kapellmeister said, "sometimes . . . sometimes I could almost wonder if you and young Mozart are in the right of it after all."

Carlo sighed and shook his head. He stepped back, away from the wreckage. His head ached with smoke, exhaustion, and grief. If he didn't go to bed soon, he would collapse straight onto Eszterháza's well-manicured grass.

In the distance, he saw the Princess approach the Prince, flanked by the Empress herself. He couldn't hear the words that followed, but he could see the lines of confrontation in the Princess's cutting gestures.

"Ah, well. It's probably for the best." Haydn turned and gave Carlo an unconvincing smile. "Why cling to old ideas, eh? Always best to move forward. In the next few weeks, my friend, we must take the opportunity to work together at last. Perhaps a new opera, if you would lend your voice—"

"No," said Carlo. "Forgive me, sir, but . . ." His weary gaze passed over the flaming remains of the opera house and settled on Herr Haydn's face. "I cannot play this part any longer," he said quietly. "I leave Eszterháza tomorrow."

Charlotte left her sister's room at five-thirty in the morning, half an hour after Sophie had finally fallen asleep again, after her first awakening, hysterics, and medical treatment. Deep burns covered Sophie's skin, turning it from peach to deep red and oozing yellow. Prince Nikolaus had come and gone, and promised to return later. The doctor, too, had promised to return, but he also swore that the only permanent damage was to Sophie's right arm, which would never again be perfectly smooth and unmarked. Gloves and long sleeves would hide that, Charlotte supposed . . . but still, the news of the small disfigurement had struck Sophie with even more outward horror than the news of her husband's death.

Three maids hovered near Sophie's bed, ready and waiting to fill any of her needs. Even with her damaged skin, Sophie looked like a beautiful doll, tucked up beneath soft covers with her burned hands hidden beneath silk sheets. As dawn broke through the window, Charlotte finally stood, stretched her aching arms and legs, and walked out of the darkened room.

Exhaustion had transformed itself, hours ago, into a numb and hollow wakefulness. She knew she ought to go to bed, but the horrors of the night still felt too close. Instead, she walked, forcing energy into her tingling legs, down the long corridor, down the grand stairway, out of the palace, and into the coolness of the early-morning air. Her arms throbbed steadily despite the soothing creams that the doctor had applied to her own burns.

Smoke tinged the breeze that swept against her face. Across the wide lawn, she saw a line of dark smoke rising from the ruins of the opera theater.

She couldn't bring herself to think, yet, about all that she had witnessed there. She turned around—and sucked in a breath.

Signor Morelli stood framed in the doorway, scarcely a foot away. His face was pale, his eyes shadowed; he leaned against the golden wall for balance.

"Signor." Charlotte stepped back, lifting a hand to her hair. It was a mangled mess, she knew; nearly half of its curled and piled mass had burned off, leaving the remains sticking out in wildly different lengths, unbrushed and horribly disordered. She would have taken the time to have it fixed, or to put on a wig, had she imagined that she would see anyone outside at this hour.

"Baroness." He nodded, but did not smile. "I followed you outside. I hope you don't mind."

"Mind? No, of course not. But . . ." Charlotte bit her lip. He had changed his outfit, at least, since the fire—but his expression . . . "Should you not be in bed, signor?"

"I couldn't sleep." His dark eyes fixed on hers. "How does your sister fare?"

"She is sleeping, and safe, and she should recover soon."

"Thanks to you."

"No." Charlotte swallowed. "I was too late. It was her husband who saved her."

"Her—? Oh, yes." Signor Morelli's eyebrows lifted. "The young lieutenant."

"He lost his life in saving hers." Charlotte closed her eyes, but she couldn't escape the memory. "I watched him disappear into the flames."

"I'm so sorry."

"As am I. He was very brave. Heroic." She paused, fighting down the impulse to tears. "I was so certain, all the way down to the auditorium—I thought it had to be me, to save her. And then I was too late."

"Yet she was still rescued, after all. Perhaps . . ." His voice trailed off; she saw him draw a breath. "Will you walk with me, Baroness?"

"I'd like that."

His arm felt strong and warm beneath Charlotte's fingers. She walked beside him across the wide lawn, into the first of the Eszterháza gardens.

Birds chattered in the tall hedges that lined the garden paths. Charlotte matched her steps to Signor Morelli's as they walked in silence past clusters of bright flowers just beginning to open to the sun, roses and lilies and bowing tulips. Bees hummed through the unfurling blossoms, droning softly. Rising sunlight warmed Charlotte's skin.

She found herself lapsing into a near-daze, lulled by the tranquility. She had to struggle to restrain herself from letting her head drop to rest on Signor Morelli's strong shoulder. It was situated at such a perfect height for her . . . Impossible to believe, now, how alien he had seemed to her, when they'd first met.

His high, pure voice broke the peaceful silence. "I couldn't sleep," he said. "I tried, but every time I closed my eyes . . ."

"I understand." Charlotte winced.

"Do you?" He stopped walking and turned to look down at her. "I leave Eszterháza today. I've already made the arrangements."

"You—today?" She stared at him, almost too numb to absorb the shock. "But . . . where will you go?"

"I have standing invitations from half the royal families in Europe," he said. "Frederick of Prussia, Gustavus of Sweden, George of England . . ."

Charlotte couldn't meet his eyes. She had to force herself to breathe, against the tightening in her chest. "Which one shall you accept?"

"None of them." His mouth twisted. "I find I can no longer stomach the role of courtly guest. The dance of belonging . . . has finally lost its attractions for me."

"Oh." She looked down. Perhaps she ought to withdraw her hand from his arm—but her fingers clung stubbornly to the fabric of his jacket. They would feel so cold, bereft of his heat. "Where will you go, then?"

"Back to Naples," he said. "I have a house there. A palace, nearly." He gave a muffled laugh. "My voice has made my fortune, at least, if not my . . . I can still sing there, if I choose; there's a fine opera house in the city that's sent me invitations every year. And my brothers live in Naples, too. I thought . . . I wondered . . ."

He paused so long, she looked back up to see what was wrong. When she met his gaze, it made her breath catch in her throat.

"I could not sleep," he said softly, "for wondering if I had any chance at all of persuading you to come with me."

Charlotte stared at him. His smooth, feminine face was open and vulnerable. His high voice rang in her ears.

In the distance, she heard the hum of other voices: gardeners, beginning their day's work. Warmth spread through the early morning air. All around her, thousands of flowers opened to the rising sun.

"Will you?" Signor Morelli asked. "Will you come?"

Chapter Thirty-Seven

Anna parted from Franz Pichler in bright sunlight, the day after Eszterháza's opera house had burned down and her life had changed forever.

"Well." He shook his head and laughed. They stood outside the servants' hall, but the carriage that waited for Anna was as gilded and ornate as any princess's conveyance. "The Emperor must be in a great hurry for you to start rehearsals."

"He said his German-language troupe has needed a new soprano for months." Anna had to hold herself back from reaching out to run her hand along the gilding in wonder. "When he summoned me this morning and asked whether I had a firm contract with the Prince, I—oh, I had no idea what he was leading to!"

"Why not? You are the heroine of the hour." Herr Pichler's face softened into a genuine smile. "And a wonderful singer. And I owe you my life."

"Herr Pichler—"

"No." He reached out and took her hand. "Let me thank you. You were the only witness to what I did—*all* I did. If you hadn't sworn to the Prince that I was innocent—"

"You were innocent. At the end, when it mattered." He really was the most handsome man that she had ever known; she felt a shiver run through her at the admiration in his gaze. "You saved all of our lives last night."

"I don't think it's that simple. But . . . I'm glad it wasn't any worse." He raised her hand to his lips. "I hope everything is perfect for you in Vienna." His kiss brushed warmth against her skin; he lowered her hand without letting it go. "It's odd. I thought, at first, that I'd be the one going to Vienna at the end of the masquerade."

Anna bit her lip. "I'm sorry."

"Don't be," he said. "I'm not. I couldn't make the bargain that von Born demanded. I'm grateful to you for helping me see that." His smile twisted. "Who knows? Perhaps I will find myself in Vienna one day. Then we'll see each other again."

"Perhaps," Anna echoed.

Tears rose behind her eyes; she blinked them back. She didn't know what she was crying for, exactly—but the mass of conflicting emotions rose within her chest so strongly that she had to brush her free hand across her eyes and turn away before he could see her tears.

"I hope I will see you again," she whispered.

"I hope so, too." He released her hand.

A footman stepped up to help her into the carriage. The incongruity of it helped to distract her a bit. She had jumped out of her mistress's carriage by herself less than a month before, hurrying to see to the Baroness's comfort. But when she arrived in Vienna as the new soprano in the Emperor's national opera company, a maid of her own would be waiting for her. It beggared belief.

She settled in the cushioned seat of the carriage and waited while the footman closed the door. The driver called out a command from above, and the carriage rolled smoothly forward.

She watched Franz Pichler's still figure until it disappeared from view behind the turns of the palace drive. The carriage rolled through Eszterháza's great wrought-iron gate. Anna pressed her face into the glass of the window and watched the golden palace recede behind her.

The tears she'd fought flowed freely down her cheeks. In her hand, she clutched the note the Baroness had sent her like a talisman. The note had been accompanied by a banker's draft so generous it would ensure her financial security if anything ever went wrong—but the note itself, of course, said nothing of money.

I wish you all the great good fortune and delight that you deserve, the Baroness had written, in the same flowing hand that had taught Anna her letters all those years ago. *Know that you can always call upon me, no matter where I am—and I hope you may find everything you've dreamed of in Vienna.*

"Vienna," Anna whispered.

The national opera company performed in the Burgtheater, Emperor Joseph had told her. The most beautiful, most elegant royal theater in the Empire—and she, Anna Dommayer, at sixteen years old, was to be fêted as its newest star.

Anna turned around in her seat to look west, toward Vienna. Her voice bubbled up inside her chest. *Why not?* she thought. Alone in the carriage, she set it free.

She sang for hours as she crossed the Hungarian plains, leaving Eszterháza behind forever.

"You can't leave!" Sophie stared at Charlotte from her great bed. Designs for mourning dress spilled across her lap, momentarily forgotten; her eyes were red with tears in her burnt face. "Lotte, you must be mad. You know you can't marry him, so—"

"What other course would you approve for me?" Charlotte reached out to stroke a patch of unblemished skin on Sophie's forehead. "You know you don't want to let Maman marry me off again, either."

"But why can't you just stay here with me?" Sophie leaned into Charlotte's hand. "You're welcome to stay as long as you like—forever! Niko says—"

"I couldn't stay. Not after what's happened here."

"But that's all over now. We're safe. We're—"

"I meant, after the actions that the Prince countenanced. The murder of the singers. His plans with Count Radamowsky. His . . ." Charlotte gave up as she took in the utter incomprehension on her sister's face. She sighed. "I would not feel comfortable remaining as his guest."

"But what about me?" Sophie's pretty face screwed up, as fresh tears appeared. "Don't you even care about me anymore?"

"I do. Of course I do! But Sophie, you could leave, as well. You could begin again."

"What on earth are you talking about?" Sophie blinked. "Lotte, you really have gone mad! Why would I ever want to leave?"

"Because—no. Never mind." Charlotte gently drew her fingers away. "I'll write to you, I promise. Will you write back?"

"When you're abandoning me?" Sophie's voice broke. "I can't believe you would do this to me. How can you? How can you leave me again?"

Charlotte stood up, drawing a steadying breath. "I do love you, Sophie. You know that. But I can't spend my life looking after you."

Sophie pushed herself up in the bed, shoving the fashion plates aside. "What about Maman? And Father? How do you think they'll feel, when they hear what you've chosen? What do you think Maman will say? And your stepsons! They'll be humiliated! Not to mention—"

"I'm sorry," Charlotte said. "But I've spent my entire life doing what would make everyone else happy. Now I need to find my own happiness."

Sophie's eyes narrowed into slits. "No one will even lower themselves to speak to you! Have you considered that? You'll be an outcast from good society. You'll—"

"Forgive me, Sophie," Charlotte whispered. She nodded for the maid to open the bedroom door. "Goodbye."

Carlo was waiting for her in the corridor outside. As the door closed behind her, Charlotte stumbled and nearly collapsed, trembling. He caught her and wrapped his arms around her, holding her up.

"You amaze me," he whispered into her ear.

Charlotte couldn't stop weeping. Sobs shook her, even as she clung to his shoulders.

Her mother's venomous words, all those years ago . . . Sophie's, now . . .

"She's so unhappy," Charlotte whispered, "because of me. Because I'm abandoning her. Again. And this time, it really is by my own choice."

Carlo's shoulders rose and fell with his sigh, but his embrace did not weaken. "She has made her own choices," he said. "And she will grow accustomed to yours, my love, I'm certain of it. Just give her time. She'll be writing to you within the month . . . if only to tell you of all the pleasures here you're missing."

"Perhaps," Charlotte whispered. She pressed her face into his coat, absorbing his warmth, as her sobs slowed and she found her breath again.

"Perhaps," she repeated. Her voice shook. "Oh, my love. I do hope you're right."

They left Eszterháza two hours later, in one of the Prince's carriages. Sophie hadn't come out to see them off, but the Princess had, along with her two companions. Monsieur Jean beamed up at them like a fond uncle, while even Asa looked quietly—and surprisingly—approving.

"You're choosing a brave path, Baroness," said the Princess. She was a picture of elegance even in her bandages, her wide, stiff skirts embedded with glittering threads of gold and silver. "I am most impressed."

"Thank you, Your Highness." Charlotte curtseyed, holding the older woman's gaze. "And you?"

"I?" The Princess smiled. "Why, I will be leaving soon, as well. My husband has finally agreed to let me spend my summers at the palace in Kismarton, far from here. My . . . negotiation techniques have succeeded at last. I only need travel with him to Vienna in the winters, to stand by his side before the Emperor and Empress."

"Congratulations," Charlotte said sincerely. "I wish you great happiness, Your Highness."

The Princess nodded her dismissal, and Charlotte turned to the carriage. Carlo already stood by the door, waiting for her. His fingers felt warm and sure against hers as he helped her up. By the time she had finished arranging her great silk skirts around her in her seat, the door had closed, and the carriage had rolled into motion.

Charlotte took a deep breath as they rode out through Eszterháza's great gate, leaving the golden palace behind them.

She rode with the most famous castrato in Europe, leaving family, honor, and prudence behind.

It felt absolutely marvelous.

Charlotte laughed out loud in sheer delight as she looked across at her lover. He smiled back at her, his face smooth and rounded, feminine and masculine, alien and beautiful all at once, and he raised her hand to his lips.

They rode away from Eszterháza, into their future.

HISTORICAL NOTE

The original opera house at Eszterháza really did burn down in 1779, destroying many priceless Haydn scores, but as far as I know, no alchemy was involved. And that's pretty much how this book goes, historically; I took lots of real historical figures and issues and then worked alchemy around them.

Prince Nikolaus was, of course, a real person; so was his wife, who fought exactly the battle described in this novel to win her freedom and independence, once Prince Nikolaus started living with a public mistress at Eszterháza. In the end, the Princess won the same concessions in real life that she did in my book, although I assume she used different methods along the way. Her two closest companions at Eszterháza were Asa and Monsieur Jean in real life, too, although the historical record only notes their short statures and their names, leaving me to imagine their personalities for myself.

Prince Nikolaus's real-life mistress was an even more enigmatic historical figure. She was only referred to in code in Haydn's letters, which described her prominence at court but left even her name a mystery. I've taken that mystery as an opportunity to create her personality out of thin air and to give her a sister of my own inventing. Charlotte is entirely fictional, as is Carlo.

Count Radamowsky is also invented, although I was inspired in his creation by reading about some of the exploits of the real-life Count von Thun. Ignaz von Born was a real and fascinating person, an alchemist, a Freemason, and a political intriguer, and his death in my book—years before his death in real life—represents my one really huge leap from the historical record.

If you'd like to find out more about Eszterháza itself in the time of this book, Mátyás Horányi's *The Magnificence of Eszterháza* is definitely the best place to start, and it's available in both the US and UK in affordable secondhand editions. H. C. Robbins Landon's *Haydn: His Life and Work* is a great introduction to Haydn himself and his working life at Eszterháza, and for a more in-depth approach, check out Robbins Landon's *Haydn at Eszterháza, 1766–90*, which was a major resource for me as I wrote this book.

There are several great books about the castrati singers of the eighteenth century, including Patricia Howard's *The Modern Castrato: Gaetano Guadagni and the Coming of a New Operatic Age*, Helen Berry's *The Castrato and His Wife*, and Patrick Barbier's *The World of the Castrati: The History of an Extraordinary Operatic Phenomenon*. I wouldn't personally recommend the movie *Farinelli*, but I would recommend its soundtrack. Not only is the music gorgeous, but the way that the voice of the singer was mixed gives us the closest hint we can get nowadays to what a castrato at the height of his powers might have sounded like.

ACKNOWLEDGMENTS

Thank you so much to everyone who critiqued this novel along the way: Patrick Samphire, Sarah Prineas, Justina Robson, Beth Bernobich, Marcy Bauman, Ben Burgis, David Burgis, Shawna McCarthy, and Delia Sherman. I appreciate your help so much!

Thank you to my historical performance professor at the Oberlin College Conservatory of Music, David Breitman, who was so helpful and generous when I emailed him out of the blue, many years after my graduation, to ask detailed questions about period-appropriate instruments. And thank you to Laurence Libin, who gave such thoughtful answers to my questions about the instruments that Charlotte would have played.

Thank you to all of my music history professors along the way, who inspired me with passion for the subject. Thank you to Des Harmon for first sparking my interest in the castrati singers of the eighteenth century through a fantastic talk given while we were grad students together. And thank you so much, especially, to Julian Rushton, my wonderful PhD supervisor at the University of Leeds, who helped me explore all the fascinating, intricate pathways of opera and politics in eighteenth-century Vienna and Eszterháza, and then supported me even when I decided to change careers completely. This is not exactly the book-length manuscript that you expected to result from my years of study . . . but I hope you enjoy it anyway!

Thank you so much to Jenn Reese for sending me such perfect feedback just when I needed it most, and to Justina Robson for baking me an amazing Esterházy torte in celebration when I finished the first draft of this book. Thank you to Rosalyn Eves for sending me photos of Eszterháza at just the right moment. And thank you to Tricia Sullivan for telling me to "Go for it!" so many times over the years.

Thank you so much to my husband, Patrick Samphire, for your love, support, insightful critiques, and great company on so many research trips to various palaces and historic sites across the years. Oh, do I know how lucky I am!

Thank you to Barry Goldblatt, Heather Baror-Shapiro, and Tricia Ready for so much hard work on my behalf, and thank you to my wonderful editor, Rene Sears, for bringing this book into the world and editing it so beautifully. Thank you to Sheila Stewart for thoughtful copyediting, to Peter Lukasiewicz for finding just the right blurbs, and to Lisa Michalski for publicizing *Masks and Shadows* so enthusiastically.

And finally, thank you so much to my readers—both the ones who are coming fresh to my work with this book and the ones who made the leap with me when I jumped between genres. I really appreciate it!

ABOUT THE AUTHOR

Stephanie Burgis grew up in East Lansing, Michigan, and was a Ful-
bright scholar in Vienna, Austria, where she studied music history,
attended the opera as often as possible, and ate far too much apple
strudel. After spending three years as a PhD student studying the opera
and politics of eighteenth-century Vienna and Eszterháza, she moved into
the more practical side of opera studies by going to work for an opera
company in the north of England. Nowadays, she lives in a small town in
Wales, surrounded by castles and coffee shops, with her husband, fellow
writer Patrick Samphire, and their two sons. She's published three historical fantasy novels for children and over thirty short stories for adults.
You can find out more at her website: www.stephanieburgis.com.